like arrows

Cedar Tree series #6

FREYA BARKER

LIKE ARROWS
(Cedar Tree, Book SIX)

Copyright © 2015 Margreet Asselbergs as Freya Barker

All rights reserved.

Editing: **Vanessa L. Bridges - PREMA**

Cover Image: **Dollarphotoclub: Tomalu**

Cover Image: **Margreet Asselbergs**

Cover Design: **RE&D - Margreet Asselbergs**

DEDICATION

To Kim and Kerry-Ann.

Two amazing women and bloggers whose unwavering support has been immeasurable. Not to mention their undying devotion to Malachi, since his character joined the Cedar Tree gang.

It's people like you who make this book world a better place!

Love you...

TABLE OF CONTENT

*"Thoughts are like arrows: once released,
they strike their mark.*

*Guard them well or one day you may be
your own victim."*

~ Navajo

PROLOGUE

Twelve years earlier

Kim

"Why don't I take you out for a coffee and some birthday cake?"

Mia is leaning over the divider between our tables and looks at me with pity. I hate that. I clean up my table and hand the keys and the tray over to the pit boss when my replacement takes my spot behind the table, and follow Mia to the locker room.

Both Mia and I started working at the Bellagio four years ago. Did our training as croupier at the same time and became friends. Strange really, because judging by outward appearances, we clash. Mia is a bombshell blonde with legs all the way up to her chin and a body to die for. I, on the other hand, am a Teletubby; a short, stumpy, brown-haired plain Jane. Mia never seemed put off by my reluctance to socialize though. She latched herself to me right off the bat and wouldn't let go.

By now, it's probably fair to say she knows me better than anyone and despite my hesitance at first, I share just about everything with her. She really is a good friend—my only friend—which is why when we came in for our shift earlier, I told her all about Peter.

Today's my birthday, and Peter didn't even call before my shift started so I᾽m bummed. Not that he's ever really shown himself to be the most attentive person, but I figured...I don't know what the hell I figured. I just know that birthdays suck. A card from my mom, some generic card with only "Happy Birthday, Mom" on it. Nothing from Britta, my sister, not that I'd expected anything from her. I'm used to them ignoring me. But it's Peter's lack of interest that hit home. Something that makes me question our relationship. Again. There is little I can do to please him these days, and he seems to be critical of anything I do or wear, or even eat. Thinking back, he's always been a bit critical, but I didn't question it at first. Was too thrilled he'd even paid me any attention. He'd been a regular at Mia's table until one day he came and sat at mine. Asked me out for dinner after I was done, and I was too stunned to say anything. Peter took that as me agreeing and was waiting by the table at the end of my shift. Despite his push for more right from the start, I held off sleeping with him for almost a month. I didn't have much experience other than a somewhat unfortunate misunderstanding at a graduation party. At least that's what my mother called it when I tried to tell her what happened. We were all still in shock with my father's unexpected death from a heart attack right before my finals. So I let it go.

Anyway, I made Peter work hard for it. Waited until I thought he felt the same for me as I felt for him, but once I gave myself to him, he changed. And not in a good way.

Mia never did like him, so when I told her he hadn't even taken the time to phone, she wasn't surprised at all, which is probably why she's offering to take me out.

"I don't know, Mia. I have an appointment at the clinic at five with the Naturopath and then I think I'll just go home and sleep. I'm wiped."

"Another doctor?" she asks.

"I have to try. No one else has been able to help much."

I can see the doubtful look in her eyes and it hurts. She's the only one I've told about my constant fatigue and listlessness. Something my family always dismissed as 'being lazy,' but I'm not. Never was. They also blame my excess weight on laziness, yet I hardly eat at all. With Mom and Britta being stickpins, I always stood out. Only Dad was a bit portly, although not much. He always said it was genetics since his mother had been short and plump. I never knew her. She died before I was born, so I only had old pictures to go by. Dad was young himself when he died, only forty-seven. It's one of the reasons I started looking for answers as soon as I had medical insurance. My first job as a nanny for a wealthy family here in Vegas didn't come with benefits, but as soon as I was through my trial period at the Bellagio, and got my coverage, I started my quest.

Mia doesn't say anything more, just shrugs. "Your loss, Kim."

"Can we do it this weekend maybe? We're both off on Sunday?" I try to compromise.

"Sure thing, honey," she says, grabbing her purse. "I'll call you." With that she is out the door.

An hour and a half I wait before I get to see this Naturopath who's supposed to have all the answers. Five minutes into the appointment, though, he tells me I need to lose weight and start exercising—exactly what every other doctor has told me for the past four years. It doesn't matter when I show him the journal where I meticulously keep track of my daily food intake. He doesn't buy it, I can tell. Dead end. Again.

I'm pissed and more than a little hurt and discouraged when I get to my car. Slipping behind the wheel, I blink furiously to get rid of the tears that threaten to fall. It's my damn birthday and I won't spend it crying by myself in the now abandoned parking lot of a clinic. Determined to perk myself up, I turn the car in the opposite direction from my apartment.

The smells inside the bakery are mouth watering. The sweet scent of sugar and cinnamon combined with the hint of yeasty fresh baked breads fight with my ingrained resistance to all things food. It's my goddamn birthday and I'm going to have something—anything—from the cornucopia of tarts and pastries spread out in the display case before me. I zoom in on a small round cake, topped with luscious curls of white chocolate. Too big for one but I order it anyway, thinking I might just initiate my own birthday celebration with Peter. Maybe he simply forgot.

"I'll take that one, please," I tell the girl behind the counter and watch her slip it into a pretty lilac box.

I feel better, walking to my car with the twine wrapped box in my hands. No more self-pity or morose woe-is-me thoughts. I have a good job, a girl that has my back, a boyfriend and a birthday to celebrate.

Empowering myself with those positive thoughts, I pull in to the parking lot of Peter's apartment building. I'm relieved to see his car already parked in its assigned spot, confirming he's home. Filled with happy anticipation, I make my way up to his apartment, holding the cake box in one hand, while searching my purse with the other for my key. The one he'd given me about a month ago, when he was out of town for a few days on business and asked if I could water his plants. He never asked for it back, and silly me, I hung onto it like the promise of a future.

It turns in the lock smoothly and the door opens almost soundlessly. I plaster a smile on my face despite my nerves and intend to walk straight through to the kitchen, where, given the dinner hour, I'm positive I'll find him.

I don't get any further than the doorway to the living room, because there on the couch I see Peter's naked backside pumping furiously between two long, slim legs that are wrapped around his thighs. Distantly I register the cake box slipping from my hands, but the writhing couple on the couch hears it clearly. Peter's head snaps around—first shock, then anger marking his face.

"What the fuck? How did you get in here?" he hisses and I stare at him slack-mouthed, not quite believing his hips are still moving inside whomever is underneath him as he glares at me. I want to turn and run, but find myself frozen in some kind of sick nightmare, unable to rip myself away. The urge to hurl so overwhelming, I slap both hands over my mouth in an effort to hold back the bile surging up my throat.

"Get the fuck out!" he yells at me. At *me*.

"I...what..." I can't even form a coherent sentence, too shocked for words. A fleeting thought shoots through my head that this is what I get when I indulge in flights of fancy. Mere seconds pass, yet I feel like I've stood rooted in the spot, watching this sickening display for hours.

"Fucking hell!" he spits, finally stilling his bucking hips, pulling away and standing up from the couch. I can't quite compute how it is that he's angry when I should be the one yelling at him. The words are stuck in my throat, right behind the remainder of my lunch, so the only thing that comes out is, "but it's my birthday." Ridiculous.

Stalking toward me with his cock still erect and glistening with some other woman's wetness, he holds out his hand, totally unashamed. "Give me my key," he demands, looking at me with distaste plain on his face. "Should've remembered I gave that to you," he mumbles. Then his eyes slide down my body and eventually hit the crushed cake box lying at my feet before they snap back to mine. "Cake, Kim? You wanna pack on more pounds? Christ, I was barely able to get it up for you to begin with. You were a means to an end, and only that."

I can feel the insult like a punch in my gut, and bend over from the impact. That does not stop him from driving his message home. "It was always her I was after from the very beginning. Banging you finally got her attention."

Finally, my eyes move over to the couch where a very naked Mia is looking at me with pity and maybe a hint of guilt in her eyes. This is where I finally lose control and I spew up all over my shoes, the crushed cake box and Peter's naked body. Then I run, finally, leaving the sounds of Peter's angry cursing behind me.

CHAPTER ONE

Mal

"I'll have a chicken salad and a glass of water, please."

Her voice is as timid as her appearance. Like a little mouse, she slipped in behind me and sat down at the furthest booth. Shocked, I tried my best not to display any reaction to her showing up here. I never expected to have one of the people I've been keeping an eye on show up at Arlene's Diner. Sure, it's popular around these parts, but given that I live in the apartment above and take most my meals here, it feels like more than a coincidence. This is why I'm keeping my back turned and my ears perked.

Arlene tags her the minute she comes out of the kitchen and is taking her order. Fucking chicken salad and water, who lives on that? I've had reason to keep her in my sights since taking on this assignment, and the woman rarely eats more than that from what I've seen. Seems to feel comfortable in the real estate office she works in, but the moment she steps out, she seems to want to disappear in the shadows. Head always low, never making eye contact and wrapping herself up in that godawful blanket thing—some kind of poncho.

It's her boss I'm really keeping track of. Gus got a call from the Ute Reservation a few weeks ago. The council had concerns about two farms backing onto reservation lands. The chief mentioned that both had sold within a month of the other through Martin Vedica, the little mouse's boss, and they had moved out within days. A third farm, owned by an older couple, was being targeted as well. The couple, Ezhno and Tiva Walker, had moved off the reservation some thirty years earlier to raise their family. They didn't go far, since their property backs right onto McElmo Creek near Finley Canyon, which is on reservation lands. In fact, it is wedged between reservation boundaries and the southern border of Canyons of the Ancients National Park.

Gus asked me to keep an eye out and I have, but with Vedica out of town since yesterday, I'd been using the time to do some online digging. So far, I have come up with little to nothing.

Keeping my eye on the stainless steel backsplash behind the counter, I can see in the reflection that her face is turned my way. It isn't busy in the diner right now, being lunchtime, but there are still a few booths occupied. Still I know they are her eyes burning in my back, and I wonder if she could possibly have spotted me before.

Kimeo Lowe. A rather exotic name for the pretty, but unassuming little thing hidden under layers of dark clothing. Soft voice, soft brown eyes, and from what I've been able to distinguish, a soft rounded body. Hardly the description for anyone associated with some kind of nefarious real estate deal, but you never know. Looks can be deceiving.

"Your burger," Arlene says, plopping a plate loaded with sweet potato fries and Seb's juicy signature burger on the counter in front of me. Seb is married to Arlene and is the cook and part owner of the diner. They're also my landlords.

"Thanks." I lift my eyes to smile at her.

I don't hesitate to dig in, starving, which pretty much is a constant state for me. Wicked fast metabolism or something, because I've always been able to eat whatever I want and none of it seems to stick. A healthy appetite. Maybe that's why seeing the woman listlessly pick at a bowl of salad just seems wrong to me. My eyes are back on her reflection where I can see her playing with her food, but not putting much of it in her mouth. She seems a little skittish, and when the door to the diner opens, her head whips around to see who's entered. I resist the urge to turn my head and keep my focus trained on her.

"Hey stranger, how's it going?" The familiar voice catches my attention. Kendra, the pretty physical therapist who joined Doc Waters the end of last year in the new clinic, is smiling at me. I smile back easily. She's a nice woman and since coming to town has fitted into our circle of friends easily. At some point I thought there might be something there, and we'd actually gone out a couple of times. After a movie in Cortez on our third date, I took our earlier friendly kisses a step further when I dropped her off. That kiss fell flat. Where I thought there might have been sparks before, they fizzled out the moment my mouth hit hers. No heat, and fucking awkward as hell. Almost felt like kissing your sister. The kiss ended very quickly and Kendra could barely keep a straight face. We both burst out laughing, and the memory puts a smile on my face.

"Hey yourself. You in for lunch?"

"Just picking something up for Naomi and me. We've got solid appointments well into the evening. Ugh."

Doctor Naomi Waters is the new town doctor and also the wife of the former sheriff, now my colleague, Joe Morris. He and I are the latest additions to GFI, an investigations and security company owned and run by Gus Flemming.

"You guys have really hit the ground running with the clinic, haven't you?" Arlene pipes up, having heard Kendra's comment.

"Sure have. Makes you wonder where the population of Cedar Tree went before Naomi decided to open up shop here," Kendra responds.

"Most of us would go to Cortez, but it's mighty convenient having you around the corner." Arlene smiles. "What can I get you?"

While Kendra places her order, I suddenly remember the focus of my earlier attention and lift my eyes to the backsplash. Nothing, the table she was sitting at is empty. I turn on my stool to look to the parking lot where the little blue Honda I've seen her drive was parked. My eyes hit two soft brown ones staring at me through the diner window, before they turn away and I see her head duck down as she slips into her car. I'm up and off my stool by the time she backs out of the parking spot and have my eyes peeled when I see her turning west.

"Be back. Add it to my tab," I tell Arlene as I pass by her followed by a "Later, Kendra." With a final chin lift to Seb I'm through the kitchen and out the back door where my truck is parked.

Kim

"Did you drop off that envelope with the Walkers yesterday?"

The phone was ringing the moment I walked into the office this morning. Martin Vedica, my boss, was in San Antonio for a few days to meet with some important clients coming up from Mexico. I wasn't privy to the nature of the business. Martin had said it was only a preliminary meeting, but he was nervous before he left yesterday and handed me the envelope. He insisted I drop it off on my way home, which is kind of strange, since I live just on the outskirts of Cortez, and the Walkers are in the opposite direction, about half an hour out of town. But whatever. I fully intended to drop it off last night, but when Kerry showed up after closing her bookstore next door, and insisted on taking me out for a celebratory drink for my birthday, I totally forgot about the envelope in my purse. Until now.

"Uh, yes." Dammit, I hate lying but I really don't want to piss him off any more than he's been these last two months. He's been irritable and I've had to walk on eggshells when approaching him. It started with the 'big deal' he mentioned to me before Christmas. One that would put his name on the map, in his words. That's when he started aggressively pursuing these properties down past Kelly's Place - Bed & Breakfast out on County Road G. He had me do title searches on all three farms, but other than that has kept me out of the loop. A couple of 'new clients' have come through the door in the past two months, none of whom he wanted me to have anything to do with. Other than bringing them coffee. But I've picked up words and snippets of conversation here and there and it's had my hair on end. Enough so that I don't really want to make a wrong move and piss him off. So I lie and he buys it.

"Excellent. I'll be back after the weekend. Probably Monday if I can get things rounded up here." By the time he hangs up after I reassured him, he sounds to be in a much better mood. I spend the next hour replying to phone messages and emails. By the time I'm done, it's almost noon. I grab my keys, my poncho and my purse and lock up. I'll use my lunch hour to quickly grab something on the way to the Walker farm.

Kerry has mentioned the diner in Cedar Tree before. Her husband Greg has taken her there a few times. He works for a contractor out of Cedar Tree, Mason Brothers. Said the food there was exceptional compared to what you'd expect from regular diner grub. So when I drive past the sign that says 'Arlene's Diner,' I make the split second decision to have a quick lunch first.

The place is pretty quiet, but it's still early on a Friday. Only a few occupied booths and a single man with long black hair tied back in a ponytail sitting at the counter with his back to me. A nice back from what I can see; wide shoulders tapering down to a narrow waist, all barely contained in the long-sleeved shirt he's wearing. A thick parka is draped over the stool beside his. The moment his head turns toward the door, I avert my eyes and duck down in the shawl of my poncho. I pick a booth by the window so that I have my back to the door and can observe the man at the counter. For some reason he makes me feel uncomfortable. Shaking off the feeling, I grab the menu which is tucked between the bottles of condiments on the table and start leafing through. Everything looks really good, but when the waitress walks up to my table I order a plain chicken salad and water, by rote. Dammit. I can't seem to get the sound of disparaging voices out of my head when I even think to order something off the menu. I've heard them my whole life and even yesterday, on my birthday, when Kerry brought over the pretty cupcake along with the 'Life starts at 40' birthday card, I had a hard time eating it. The encouraging and almost hopeful smile on Kerry's face made it impossible to refuse, so I took a bite. It tasted like sawdust and I had to battle my gag reflex. When she dragged me out to the Lounging Lizard afterwards, I managed to sneak away to the bathroom, to purge the contents of my stomach and immediately felt ten times better. Good enough to order a small chicken salad and a glass of wine. The first didn't make Kerry happy but the second did and we ended up having a good time, mostly filled with Kerry's excited chatter about a shipment of new books which had arrived earlier in the week. That's how we met, Kerry and I. My Kindle is attached to me. In fact I have a spare one at home, in case this one craps out. Occasionally though, I love the feel of a real book in my hands and the first time I ventured into Kerry's Korner, the smell of printed paper in the bookstore made me feel right at home. As did Kerry herself. And even though I am still hesitant to share too much of myself, I've come to trust her. Kind of.

The arrival of my salad at the table interrupts the inconspicuous looks I'm directing toward the counter. More specifically, toward the tall, built and gorgeous man at the counter. I catch him in profile only once, the rest of the time his back stays turned, but that one glimpse is enough to give me butterflies. He's beautiful. With his long hair pulled back from his face, a prominent brow, prominent nose with a bit of a bump, strong square jaws covered in stubble and the most luscious mouth I've ever seen on a man. It's obvious he's at least part Native American, which shouldn't surprise me in this area that is rich with indigenous cultures and a few of the larger reservations.

"Can I get you anything else?" The tall blonde waitress asks, one eyebrow raised. I shake my head and drop my eyes to my bowl of salad, feeling chastised for looking.

"No thank you. Just the bill please."

"Be right back," she says, turning around.

From the corner of my eye, I see her deliver a plate piled high with what I'm sure are sweet potato fries and I immediately look at my own lunch with some regret. Looks good enough, with a few interesting additions of beans, corn and cheese, but still, I shove most of that to the side and eat a few tentative bites of lettuce and chicken. When the tang of a chipotle dressing hits my taste buds I wish I could eat more.

The waitress comes back with the bill. "You can pay at the counter," she says. But with one look at the cash register right beside the man, I know I want to avoid it.

"Can I just pay you now?" I ask, looking at the receipt and fully prepared to hand over my twenty dollar bill even though the total doesn't even come to ten. It's worth not having to be embarrassed when I sidle up to the counter. A man like that would never even look twice at the likes of me.

The woman stands by my table, a weird expression on her face. I can't quite put my finger on it, but I scramble to dig my wallet from my purse. "Here," I say, handing over the twenty. "No need for change."

She shrugs and mumbles, "thanks," before turning away.

Just then the door opens and another statuesque blonde walks in and right up to the man with the ponytail. This one seems younger and is very curvaceous. Not only that, she smiles huge when she talks to him. Figures. I'm even more grateful now that I don't have to walk over there to pay.

I force down a few more bites and take a sip of my water, but whatever appetite I had is gone. I manage to pull on my poncho, tuck my purse under my arm, and slip out the door while the two blondes and the dark ponytail chat it up.

Once outside, I dig for my keys in my purse when I feel a tingle at the base of my neck. Lifting my head, my eyes zoom in on the man who is now looking straight at me through the window. Deep black eyes hold me hostage long enough to fumble with my keys and the lock. The moment I open the door, I see him begin to move and tear my eyes away, ducking into the car.

The drive is actually very pretty along County Road G. Some snow remains on the landscape, even though it's late March. I push thoughts of those dark eyes as far away as I can. Instead I look around me to see if the sights are able to give me any clues as to why Martin is almost rabid to purchase these properties. I have control of the filing system, except for the one cabinet in his office which houses his 'personal stuff,' or so he says. I've seen some of his recent visitors walk in with rolls of drawings and folders of papers which didn't make it out of the office with them. I assume they're still there. Somewhere. Maybe I'll use the time he's away to get a closer look. In the meantime I'll keep my eyes open. Nothing stands out other than that it's beautiful country.

The moment I pass the B&B, I start slowing down. I know the Walker's driveway is coming up on my left. The only other time I've been here was before the other two farms were sold through Martin. He'd sent me out to drop off an offer on the property, one that wasn't well received by the Walkers. In fact, I'd had a shotgun shoved in my face when they discovered why I was there. My boss is a manipulative bastard and had sent me, knowing they would be less than receptive, but had hoped a woman would soften them up a little. Not so much with the Walkers. The moment I identified myself, Ezhno Walker slipped inside the door and came out, his shotgun already cocked. I didn't hesitate and backed away when he yelled at me to leave. When I got back to the office I took Martin to task, but he waved it all off and said Ezhno Walker was no longer functioning at full capacity. That's why, when he asked me to drop off an envelope, I'd questioned him but he assured me they were expecting it.

I recognize their mailbox coming up and prepare to make my turn when a dark colored SUV comes barreling out of the driveway and turns left, speeding off toward the Utah border. Huh. I'm still wondering what kind of idiot would come blowing out of a driveway that fast, when I pull up to the old log farmhouse. The front door is open and just outside it, Mrs. Walker is on her knees, leaning over her husband. I get out of the car and at the sound of my door closing her head whips around. I can see blood coming from her nose. What the hell is going on?

"Mrs. Walker, are you okay?" I hurry over and upon getting closer, I can see Ezhno's face is bloodied too. I rush up the steps, but Tiva, Mrs. Walker, scrambles to her feet and rushes inside. Dropping down on my knees beside Ezhno, I immediately feel for a pulse, and it's there. Faint but there. A sound I've heard once before has me lift my eyes to the doorway where Tiva stands, this time it's her holding that same damn shotgun.

"Get off our property," she hisses.

"But Mrs. Walker, Tiva, your husband needs help. You're both hurt."

"You here to see if your goons did their job?"

I'm shocked at her words. "My goons? I don't know what you mean? Who are you talking about?"

The blast from the shotgun hits the dirt behind me, but the sound deafens me instantly and has me rearing back on my ass. She cocks the gun again and aims it at me.

"Get off our property!"

Not about to argue with an unmistakably irate woman toting a gun, I crab walk backward on hands and feet until my body hits the car. I scramble around it to the driver side and slip in, trying furiously to get it started. The moment it catches I floor it and skid around the barnyard, my tires spinning before they find traction. Just as I come up to the end of the driveway, a silver pick up truck pulls in. I manage to slip past it and I'm already turning back in the direction of Cedar Tree, planning to stop at the first opportunity so I can call the sheriff's office, when it hits me.

The man from the diner was behind the wheel.

CHAPTER TWO

Mal

I can't have been that far behind, but by the time I hit the road the little blue Honda was gone. I know she turned left, in a westerly direction, so that's where I'm heading. I'm going at a good clip when I pass Kelly's Place and suddenly I know where she's gone. The Walker place is up ahead and I'm just turning into the driveway when her blue compact comes streaking at me, barely avoiding my front left fender. Kimeo is at the wheel and other than a quick flick of her panicked eyes my way, she is focused on getting away. Fast. I intend to turn and follow her back toward town, where she's headed as if the devil is on her heels, when I spot the Walkers on their porch.

"She already called it in," Drew Carmel, our sheriff's voice comes over the line.

The moment I spotted the state of the poor elderly couple, I had my phone out and was calling for an ambulance. Two things occurred to me right away; Tiva had her shotgun propped beside the door and there was no way in hell that small woman had time to do this kind of damage. I left barely minutes behind her.

"Have a description of two vehicles from her; one a dark-colored, large SUV and the other one sounds a lot like yours. I'm thinking she has no clue who you are, right?"

"Pretty sure that's accurate. Tiva tells me when she heard her husband yell from the front of the house, she stepped out onto the porch. There were two guys working him over, one holding him and the other beating on him. Apparently she ran to them without thinking, and was rewarded with a few hits. One of the guys told her they should "take the offer" or they'd be back. They took off and not a minute later, according to her, that girl from Vedica's office drove up. Scared—and I'm guessing a bit confused—she pulled the shotgun on her."

"Christ. What would drive someone to beat up on a couple of seniors?" Drew sounds disgusted.

"Money," I offer as an explanation for most of the world's evil.

"Right," Drew says matter-of-factly. "I'm going to pay Ms. Lowe a visit. Also I'll have a word with her boss, see whether he can shine some light on the sudden interest in those properties."

"He's out of town," I volunteer. "Left yesterday."

"I have a feeling you and I need to sit down as well. You can enlighten me on what your involvement is in this."

"Got no problem with that, but don't be surprised if Gus shows up with me."

"GFI business?" Drew guesses.

"You got it."

"Fuck me. Right. Check with your boss and call me to set up a meet."

At that moment, the sound of sirens can be heard from the road and a sheriff's patrol car, followed by an ambulance, appear between the trees lining the Walkers' drive.

"Troops are here," I tell Drew.

"I can hear. I'll let you go and give my deputy a head's up before he gives you a hard time. Call me as soon as you can." With that he hangs up.

It's almost three in the afternoon before I get to Gus's house. The GFI offices are housed in an addition Gus and his wife Emma built a couple of years ago. Emma is a doll, a phenomenal cook and takes good care of anyone who walks through her door. That's why, despite the fact I downed lunch only a couple of hours ago, my mouth waters the moment I open the door to her "Come in!" and am assaulted with the smell of fresh baking. How Gus doesn't have a gut on him, I can't figure.

"Hey Mal." Emma beams her smile at me from the kitchen, her domain.

"Emma." I bend down and give her a kiss on the cheek. "What've you got cookin'?"

"Baking actually. The weekend order for the diner." She indicates the counter filled with a variety of pies and pastries. Seb at the diner is a fantastic cook, but Emma is the baking queen. She's baked all the sweets for the diner since she moved to Cedar Tree. Helps that she's Arlene's best friend.

"Smells great."

"I have muffins in the oven. Five more minutes and I can take them out. I'll come bring you guys some warm ones."

"You're the best." I give her a hug, noticing how soft and comfortable she is in my arms, when I hear a growl behind me and Emma starts to chuckle.

"Unhand my wife, will ya?" Gus is standing in the doorway with his arms crossed over his chest and a scowl on his face.

"Oh, keep your socks on, Gus," Emma says as she slips out of my arms and heads straight for her husband's. His face softens instantly with a look I see all too often these days from my brother as well. Caleb, just like most of the others in our little community, is happily in love. The last vestiges standing are Neil and I. The rest of the hard-assed males seem to have succumbed.

"Have an update on the farms," I prompt and Gus's eyes snap to mine.

"Heard something over the scanner. Neil's in the conference room. I'll be right in," he says with a tilt of his head down the hallway. I take that as an invitation to go ahead. By the time I open the right door, Gus is already behind me.

"Hey Neil."

The dark blond head bent over a keyboard snaps up. "Mal."

Not sure what's up but since the open house when Naomi's clinic opened, Neil's had a burr up his ass the size of a fist. Quite a change for someone who is generally fun loving and friendly. I asked him once what the fuck was up and he assured me nothing. Still the burr hasn't dislodged. I can feel the negative energy flowing around me.

Saying nothing, I pull out a chair and sit, while Gus does the same on the other side.

"What've you got?"

For the next half hour or so I give them an update on my findings, ending with a detailed description of today's events. Gus makes notes and Neil taps away on his keyboard, seemingly uninterested but I know he's dutifully doing his job.

Whatever issue he has with me, he's a great investigator and a man I trust to have my back when it comes down to it.

"Drew wants me to come in. He knows I'm working on something and with the assault on the Walkers, he wants to know what."

"Do it as soon as possible and see if you can catch him before he heads over to the Lowe woman. Be good if you could listen in. I'll be calling Chief Nakai to let him know what's going on." Gus leans back in his chair and looks over to where the youngest GFI employee has dropped all pretence of working and is instead following our conversation keenly.

"Neil? You start digging. Look for anything on the three farms in question and the surrounding areas. I mean anything; history, previous owners, who is listed as current owner, survey permits—anything that pops up, I want a report on. Also find me the owners of the two farms already sold. I know they were gone before anyone got wind of what was going on." Gus pushes up from the table and I do the same across from him, just as Emma walks in, a tray balancing on her walker. Emma is disabled, but that doesn't seem to slow her down one bit, and Gus doesn't even see it.

"Are you leaving?" she directs at me, when she sees me stand. "I was just bringing you guys fresh coffee and a warm muffin."

"I gotta run, but if you don't mind, I'll take some of that coffee and a muffin on the run."

"Yeah sure, I'll get you a travel mug."

With a two finger wave for Gus and a chin lift to a still scowling Neil, I follow Emma to the kitchen where she hands me a travel mug and a paper bag with two muffins. I bend down to kiss her cheek, and have to chuckle when I hear Gus growl behind me again.

"Oh for Christ's sake, Gus!" Is the last thing I hear before heading out to my truck.

Kim

"Come here, Boo. Momma's gonna take you for a walk."

As always, my babe is at the door when I come in and inevitably jumps up, backing me into the front door by way of greeting. He then runs to the backdoor, waiting to be let out after what usually is a long day without relief for him. Just because I'm home earlier than normal, doesn't seem to change the routine for him. Except where usually I'd have something to eat first, let him out for a quick piddle, feed him and take him for his walk, today I want to get his walk out of the way before I take my shoes off.

A little confused—my dog is a huge, goofy Great Dane—he saunters back to me and sits down, an expectant expression on his face. I clip the leash on his collar and grab a poop-bag.

My house sits toward the end of Canyon Drive on the northwest side of Cortez. It's a single-level bungalow surrounded by some mature trees and otherwise has gorgeous views of the mesa with the mountains in the distance. It tends to get cold in the winter, because it is a bit exposed to the elements, which is probably why I was able to pick it up for a steal three winters ago. At that time I'd still been working through employment agencies, mostly short-term contract work that could take me as far as Durango on a daily basis, but

I couldn't resist the amazing bargain I was getting. During my years in Vegas, I saved up a nice nest egg. Never needing much to survive on, I was able to tuck away most of my earnings and my sometimes generous tips into savings. When I came back to Colorado, after things in Vegas turned sour, I wanted to stay as far away from Grand Junction as possible, even though I knew work was probably easier to come by there. So Durango was where I ended up first. Once I'd gotten a good gander at the rugged beauty of the mesas though, Cortez became my home.

I allow Boo to pull me along a little. I use walking to empty my mind as much as I can. It's a great way to let go of stress at the end of a long day, and today has been particularly stressful.

We turn right at the end of our drive where the paved road ends and turns into a dirt road. I often walk that way because from there we have some gorgeous trails that loop through the mesa and I can let Boo have a run. In the three years I've had him, he's never run off far or for very long. He generally just likes to sniff and maybe chase a rabbit or some other small animal before returning to me. This time of year, there can still be snow on the mesa. Not tons, but enough to give it a very wintery look. Some days the sun can get so strong, you actually see the snow slowly disappear, but the nights are cold and we still get the occasional snowfall. Nowhere near what January and February usually bring though.

When thoughts of the day's events start crowding my mind again, and the cold biting wind starts numbing my face, I call Boo and turn around. When we get close to the road, I stop and click on his leash and we make our way home.

The first thing I see is a familiar silver truck in my drive and it freezes me on the spot. Since seeing that man behind the wheel, there've been a million thoughts tumbling through my head. My first thought had been that he was a family member to the Walkers, but as far as I knew, they had no offspring. Still, could be a nephew. Next I thought he might have had something to do with the attack, but that doesn't feel right. And now that the truck is parked in my driveway, I don't know whether to be scared or excited.

Boo is getting impatient and wants his dinner I'm sure, because he's pulling hard now, forcing me to move. When I turn into the drive, I see a patrol car with Sheriff on the side, parked behind the silver truck. I couldn't see it from the road. Two men are standing under the carport where my front door is. One is wearing the sheriff's uniform and looks familiar. I've seen him in town a time or two. The second man is so much taller standing up than he was sitting down in the diner earlier. My gaze drifts over his full length, from his boot covered feet, up his long legs, thick thighs toward his broad chest and finally reaches his beautifully chiseled face. His dark eyes focus on me with such intensity, it makes the sweat break out on my forehead, despite the cold temperatures.

Boo is growling at my side and despite his giant poops and endless appetite, I'm grateful I bought a dog that big.

"Ms. Lowe?" the sheriff asks and Boo barks in response.

"Yes?" I follow more timidly, hanging on to Boo who is starting to snarl. I'm worried he'll get loose and attack an officer of the law. That would probably not be good.

With two hands I pull him back, barely containing him when the tall man takes a step forward.

"You can let him go." I don't think I've ever heard a deeper voice. Not up close anyway. I can feel the vibrations of his deep bass in my body.

"I don't think...it's probably...I think it's safer—" I stammer before he interrupts.

"Trust me. You can let him go."

"It's better if I lock him—"

"Let go." His voice is commanding which is an instant red flag.

"Really?" I'm more than a little riled now. Especially since the sheriff is just standing there looking way too amused. "You want me to let him go? Fine. Consequences are yours. Go, Boo." I drop his leash and my protector immediately lopes to Mr. Intimidating, and jumps up on his shoulders where he starts... licking? What? What's become of my hundred and fifty pound body guard?

"Boo, down," the deep voice rumbles, and to my astonishment my baby drops to all fours, sits his ass down and looks up adoringly at him.

The sheriff begins to speak. "Ms. Lowe, sorry for the interruption, but I have a few questions for you about this afternoon's events. Mr. Whitetail here was kind enough to accompany me. I understand you passed each other in the Walkers' driveway?" At this last question my eyes are pulled from my supremely disloyal pooch toward the sheriff, who still sports a smile.

Mal

"Maybe we can continue this inside? It's freezing and I have to feed my dog."

I've been struggling to keep a straight face since she came up the drive with her massive dog. I'd have picked a small little lapdog for her if any. Cats seem more her speed, but she walks up, all five foot nothing of her, with this fierce looking dog that looks like a cow and is named 'Boo.' Luckily I've always had an easy affinity with animals, as opposed to people. That's why I wasn't worried when the big pooch started growling. Somehow even the most vicious of dogs will heed me when they hear my voice. They seem to accept me as their alpha immediately.

In contrast, it takes me a long time to warm up to, let alone trust another person. I even had to learn to like and appreciate my brother again. The turning point for me was being able to help his wife give birth when she went into labor unexpectedly during a party. It wasn't just seeing how he was with Katie or with his son, it was the fact that he seemed to want me there with them. No reservations whatsoever. His trust in me bolstered my trust in him.

The moment Kimeo passes me and slaps her hand against her thigh to call her dog, I gesture for him to follow her, something he does immediately.

"She's something else," Drew mumbles to me, but with his eyes firmly on her very ample backside. That causes an uncomfortable prickle at the back of my neck.

"Back off," I snap before I have a chance to examine my rather uncharacteristic impulse. I'm pretty even-keeled and rarely get ruffled, but Drew's interest somehow strikes me wrong. My interest in the little *Nizhóní* seems to be a bit more than professional.

My words have Drew turn to me with a small smirk on his lips. "It's like that, is it?"

I try to ignore his remark, but as I'm holding the door and he walks past me into the house, I can't help myself.

"She's part of a case. You'd best remember that. Besides, from what I've seen of you, you like them young and curvy. Are you getting bored with your parade of young, leggy and thin chicks and want to try a taste of an older woman? A fat one at that?"

I don't know what possessed me to say that shit other than trying my best to distract him from her. For the case—of course. But even though I whisper it to him while still outside, I can tell she's heard—at least part of it. She's turned to the counter, her back toward us and ramrod straight, and her movements jerky. Fuck.

Drew elbows me hard. I glare at him and just catch him mouthing *'asshole.'* Yeah.

"Look," I start, wanting to... explain? Hell, I don't know what I'm thinking but I feel like the giant fuck up I am. She turns around with a forced smile on her face, pointedly not looking at me, but at Drew.

"So Sheriff, I never caught your name?" she asks him.

"Drew Carmel, Ms. Lowe. And this is Malachi Whitetail. He is an investigator for GFI, a local security and investigations firm."

Her eyes flick in my direction briefly before settling back on Drew. "Do you know if Mr. and Mrs. Walker are okay?"

"They're well looked after, Ms. Lowe. Both are expected to make a full recovery although Ezhno may be hospitalized for a while. He is undergoing some tests."

"Please call me Kim, everyone does. Glad to hear they'll be all right. I'm curious though, what exactly does a security firm have to do with the Walkers?" She bends over to put a bowl of food in front of her dog and straightens back up, determinedly avoiding my eyes.

"We'll get to that shortly, but first let me ask you a few questions." Drew swiftly detours the conversation.

"Very well, would you like to sit down?"

Without waiting for an answer, she leads us out of the kitchen and into a surprisingly spacious living room where she sits down in a large club chair. The only option open to Drew and I is the equally large sofa. Drew sits down and I opt to lean against the fireplace mantle and stay standing. This allows me to see her in profile, as she keeps her attention on Drew, while he goes over the day's events with her. I'm only half listening but closely observe her body language, more interested in what she might be hiding than what she actually shares. Yet after half an hour of detailed questioning, her body tells me nothing more than that she must have some Latin blood in her. It's the way her hands seem to fly around, emphasizing what her mouth is saying. Her small hands captivate me and each time they move I find myself thinking how they'd feel on my skin. Not sure where that comes from. She sure as hell is nothing like the women I occasionally hook up with. Just like Drew, I gravitate toward tall, leggy and preferably stacked. Not short, round and trying hard to be invisible. But she's not really invisible, is she? Not to Drew either. He seems as intrigued by the subtle hints of a bright fire underneath as I am. Still, when she describes noticing me at the diner and recognizing me in the Walkers' driveway, her posture shrinks, as if she's making herself as small as possible.

I am quickly able to deduct the fact that this woman is not knowingly involved but harbors suspicions of her own about the land sales. Two other things become clear to me though; she works hard at being overlooked, keeping her head down and her light hidden, and I've wounded her. It's glaringly obvious by her cold body language and icy demeanor. Both directed only at me. Dammit.

The only time she briefly looks at me is when Drew invites me to explain my involvement.

"Oh wait!" she cries out, scrambling out of her seat and disappearing into the kitchen. She comes back with her purse in one hand and waving an envelope in the other. "I forgot I still had this, the letter I was supposed to hand deliver."

With a quick look in my direction, Drew takes the envelope and rips it open. His face hardens before handing it to me.

Dear Mr. and Mrs. Walker,

I am writing you out of concern. I may have come across as aggressive in pursuing the sale of your property in the past, but I am not ruthless. Unfortunately it would appear that I have unwittingly thrown in my hat with a buyer who has somewhat different views on the methods of persuasion. I'm therefore strongly encouraging you to take the last offer I proposed in order to avoid undue pressure placed on you.

Yours respectfully,

Martin G. Vedica

Son of a bitch.

CHAPTER THREE

Kim

"What is it? What does it say?"

A chill runs down my back when I see the grave looks the sheriff and Malachi exchange, before collectively turning to me.

"Where is your boss?" Malachi asks, without answering my question.

"San Antonio—why? What's in the letter?"

"And he's expected back when?"

"I talked to him this morning, he says Monday. But what—" I try again but he turns away and addresses Sheriff Carmel, cutting me off.

"We need to get into the office."

"Not sure we'll be able to get a warrant signed before Monday, my friend. If there's enough here for one to begin with."

"Then I'll go in," he offers in his deep rumbling voice, but the other man shakes his head.

"Can't do that, Mal. It would make whatever you come up with unusable."

"Inadmissible maybe, but not unusable."

Tired of being ignored I clear my throat. "Excuse me—but can someone tell me what's going on?"

Wordlessly, Malachi hands me the letter, which I have to read twice to make sure I understand.

"I was right," I say out loud, with a feeling of dread in the pit of my stomach.

"What are you talking about?" the investigator asks, but instead of addressing him—the poison of his words burrowing under my skin—I turn to the sheriff. "I've had a bad feeling about this land deal. Normally everything goes through me: setting up meetings, planning trips, sorting documents, writing letters. In the past couple of months, Martin's been evasive and secretive. He's having people come in for meetings I never arranged for him. He's booking his own flights to Texas—this San Antonio trip is the third one in two months. The kicker is, other than asking me to do a title search way back when, I haven't seen any paperwork or documents, until he handed me this letter. It was the second time he asked me to personally deliver something to the Walker farm."

Looking from a set of intense blue eyes to an almost familiar, and certainly more intimidating set of dark ones, I straighten my shoulders and push on. "I can do it," I offer, lifting my chin to show my determination."

"What? What are you talking about?" This from Malachi whose eyes I meet full on for the first time since I overheard him say what's been ingrained in me since childhood.

"I have a key," I offer by way of explanation.

"Hell no."

"Was planning to do some overdue filing this weekend..."

"I said no."

His bossy tone rubs me the wrong way and I plant my index finger squarely in his chest. "Who are you to tell me what to do?"

Malachi stands unmoving, simply looking down at me with those eyes that show a lot more emotion this close up. A soft chuckle from behind me reminds me of the sheriff's presence. Maybe not so smart to blurt out my intentions when the county's top lawman is in attendance. I back away from Malachi, realizing how ridiculous I must look, my five foot three form facing off with his six and half feet—or thereabouts—leanly muscled length. No wonder the sheriff is amused.

"Hate to say it, tempting as it is since you have a valid reason to be there, but I can't let you do that," he says, his smirk disappearing. "Until we find out what we're dealing with it could be unsafe. You should just go about your business and leave the investigating up to us."

Typical brush off.

With the letter in hand and a promise to be in touch before Monday, when Martin's supposed to be back, the sheriff takes his leave.

"You heading out too, Mal?" he says when he's about to get in his patrol car, looking behind me where I can sense his friend lurking behind me.

"Yup." Comes the answer from much closer than I'd expected. A steady look is directed over my shoulder, lasting a touch more than is comfortable, before he slides behind the wheel and backs out of my drive.

Now what?

I turn slowly and am faced with the broad expanse of what is visible of his chest under the thick parka. The man is not moving, forcing me to tilt my head way the hell back to look at him.

"Excuse me." I try to get him to move.

"I can hear the wheels in your head turning, so I'll tell you again. Do not get yourself involved. Do not find an excuse to go on a solo expedition"—I bristle at the bossy tone, when he bends down and gets right in my face—"And do not go into the office until you hear from us." Then he grabs me by the shoulders and sets me aside so he can slip past me and out the door. Well.

I try to stay pissed as I watch him back up as well, but the hot tingle where his hands touched my body is too distracting.

Saturday mornings I meet Kerry for yoga at the Heart and Core Yoga Studio on Main Street. I'd told Kerry some time ago when she caught me dozing off in the middle of a conversation, that I had a history of almost constant fatigue. She immediately invited me to go with her for her yoga classes. She said it helped her sleep better at night and actually gave her more energy during the day. I always avoided any type of exercise other than walking, simply because any time I tried to do more, my joints would ache for days after. I'd been told swimming was a good way to get some movement in without putting undue strain on the joints, but that would involve wearing a bathing suit. That is so not gonna happen. I don't think I've been in the water, other than the shower, since I was maybe twelve years old. That was in 'fat-camp,' where my mother sent me to lose weight. Another childhood memory I'd rather forget. I did start going to yoga with Kerry though.

"My turn to buy coffee," she says, stuffing her arms in her coat as we walk out of the studio and to the parking lot. This is something we do after our yoga, head over to the Spruce Tree Espresso House. Kerry often has breakfast too, but I tell her I have breakfast before yoga. I don't like someone watching me eat. It's a thing.

"Sure," I tell her, getting in my car. "Follow you there."

The coffee shop is on the way to Safeway where I'll pick up my groceries after. That way I won't have to go out again.

Saturday mornings are busy and the parking lot at Spruce Tree is packed. Kerry slips into a spot right away but I have to circle three times before I spot someone leaving. By the time I get inside, Kerry already has a table and has put in an order.

"They have pineapple-almond muffins fresh this morning, so I ordered us both one." She looks at me slyly, knowing full well I don't like to eat after yoga. She just doesn't know why. "You know there's a new clinic in Cedar Tree?"

"I thought I saw that the other day when I drove past, but I wasn't sure." I know she worries about me and commiserates every time I get the standard response from yet another so-called specialist. I love her for that. I think Kerry might be the only person who doesn't hold judgement and even encourages me to eat, despite my size.

"It's actually run by a former Southwest Memorial ER physician. A woman. It's like a family clinic but she has a PT working from there as well. I hear she is very open-minded and has no problem integrating alternative medicine as well. Maybe you should set up an appointment."

"Maybe," I tell her, not sure if I want to go through another disappointment so close on the heels of the last one. But as I'm nibbling on my muffin—mostly for show—and sipping my coffee, the thought of driving into Cedar Tree for an appointment might not be a bad idea. Who knows, maybe I'll get hungry for one of those delicious chipotle chicken salads the diner offers.

My run through Safeway doesn't take long, after I say goodbye to Kerry. I haven't told her about my adventures from Friday, although she'd noticed when I didn't come back after lunch. I simply told her Martin had left me with some errands to run and she didn't ask any further. Not sure why I didn't tell her.

My standard picks barely cover the bottom of my grocery card. Greek yogurt, frozen fruit, bananas, organic peanut butter, eggs, chicken breast and two bags of spinach along with some peppers make up the contents. I'm serious about my protein, whatever way I can get it. I tried just living on fruit and salad, but it would only make me more tired. I discovered that a spoonful of peanut butter in my smoothie or a simple boiled egg for lunch would give me a little boost of energy.

I walk up to the front and push my cart to the shortest line up at the cash registers. An older lady is ahead of me, loading her groceries on the check out conveyor belt, while a younger blonde woman ahead of her leans in to the cashier and starts whispering. Trying to ignore them, I start loading my purchases on as well and am just able to pick up a few lines of mumbled conversation.

"I'd skip the peanut butter if I were her," I hear one of them say and lift my eyes to find both the blonde and the cashier's eyes on me before quickly averting them. A hot blush burns my cheeks and I try to hide behind the woman in front of me.

"Should be ashamed of yourselves. Don't hear me saying you should use a different shade of blonde in your hair, because this one makes you look washed out," the older lady in front of me says to the blonde who turns her head in shock. "And you wouldn't want your manager finding out you're being rude to the customers." The girl at the cash register, maybe early twenties, drops her eyes to her hands.

I lower my own eyes to the floor, barely able to beat down the urge to run mortified out of the store. Silently both women in front of me are cashed out. One leaves without looking back and the older lady smiles at me before she grabs her bags.

"I'm sorry." The cashier's voice is soft as she starts running my groceries through. I don't say anything back. I simply hand over the cash and without waiting for my change, snatch my bags and beeline it out of Safeway.

By the time I get home, greet Boo and put away the groceries, my mind is made up. Doesn't take much to find the number and before I get cold feet I grab the phone.

"Oh, I didn't realize there'd be someone there on a Saturday," I respond stupidly to the very friendly voice on the other side. "I'd like to make an appointment."

Twenty minutes later I'm back in my Honda, heading toward the Cedar Tree Clinic where a cancellation had just opened up a spot.

Mal

"I'll give my contact in San Antonio a call. See if he can keep an eye on Vedica," Joe says.

On Neil's suggestion, I took the information he found on the real estate agent—his flight numbers and the hotel he booked in San Antonio—to Joe. Being a former Denver cop and then the Montezuma County Sheriff, Joe had made a lot of law enforcement connections. Where Gus had friends with the FBI he could call on, Joe had them with the various police departments in Colorado and surrounding states. The moment Neil discovered Vedica's hotel, he'd been on the phone, only to find out he'd checked out yesterday even though his original reservation had been for two additional nights. His return flight Sunday night is unaltered. I'd like to know where he is and what he's up to, even though we don't have anything that would stick to him yet. I just like knowing where all my players are. Especially with a potential witness raring to engage in some investigating of her own.

She surprised me yesterday. Not quite the little meek mouse I was expecting—this one has a bit of bite. She didn't cower when I laid down the law. Instead, she tried to get in my face. Too bad she just barely comes up to my chin. The fire in her eyes was a surprise, one that makes the entire package even more attractive. Don't think I ever would've considered her my type, but I've got to admit that from the first time I saw her I've been intrigued. Judging from my body's response to her proximity by her door yesterday, as well as the feel of her soft shoulders under my hands, I've been wrong. My body seems to think she's exactly my type, but there's no way I would act on it. I've got a job to do and can't afford to let that little spark plug to get under my skin.

"Shouldn't be hard for you to get into that office," Joe pulls me from my distracting thoughts. "I've been there. Vedica did the sale of my place."

"Really? Fuck, small world." That gets a chuckle from Joe.

"Newsflash, Cortez is a small world."

"I guess. Did the guy seem okay to you?" I ask.

"Yeah. Can't say I noticed anything off. Had no complaints. He did a fine job for me, or rather, his assistant did. Kim something? Sweet little thing. She did most of the work."

"Kimeo Lowe, says she goes by Kim."

There must've been something in my voice, because I suddenly feel Joe's sharp look on me. Before he can say anything though, I step down the porch and start walking toward my truck parked out front, Joe trailing behind me.

"Not your regular plaything, Mal. She's too soft and sweet for those games," Joe says from behind me, making me turn around to face him.

"You for real? Someone like her is not for me, you should know my type by now. It's not some short, overweight secretary." I hear the sharp intake of breath behind me at the same time as Joe's face goes hard.

"Nice job, asswipe." I hear him mumble as I whip around only to see Kim hustling toward her blue Honda, which had not been there when I pulled in earlier. Fuck me.

"Kim, wait!" I try, but it's too late. She's already pulling out of the parking lot, gravel flying up.

Trying to ignore Joe, who is shaking his head at me, I get in my truck and am about to peel out of there after her when there's a knock on my window.

"Leave her be," Joe says, after I roll down my window. "From the look on her face when she overheard you, I'd say you're the last person on the face of the earth she wants to see."

Right. Even though guilt burns a hole in my gut, I curb my initial instinct to chase her down and watch the back of her little blue Honda disappear toward Cortez.

By Monday, there is still no sign of Martin Vedica. His ticket for last night's flight unused.

I just got off the phone with Drew who was going to check in with Kim to see if she'd heard from him. Gritting my teeth, I find myself telling Drew to go ahead. He seemed surprised I didn't jump in and claim the task of talking to her, but instead remained silent when he confirmed he'd be in touch after.

I pick up my sketchbook and pencil and continue mindlessly drawing. Something I've been doing since Saturday night. It's always been an outlet of sorts for me—sketching. Something I'd enjoyed doing before my sister died of an aggressive cancer that took her from healthy teenager to near skeleton in the span of three short months. I was twelve. My mother retreated and was barely living and my father, who'd descended in the bottle, took his anger out on everyone. Caleb was a year older than my sister Nasha, and we both went wild. Off the rails. Caleb pulled it together at some point and ended up with the Rangers where he got straightened out. I slid the other way hooking up with a gang of disgruntled Native kids whose sole objective was wreaking havoc. The next years the Klesh, the gang I'd gotten involved with, became a bit more structured and a whole lot more criminal as I climbed up through the ranks. From general mischief, vandalism and mayhem, the Klesh turned into a well-oiled criminal organization with its main focus being the drug trade. Two years ago we ran into some trouble with a large Mexican cartel. I was set up as the fall guy and had to go into hiding while my parents' house was burned down, killing my mom. My father, who'd been able to escape but left my mom to die, succumbed to liver failure last year. Hope he burns in hell, the way he left his wife to burn. The burden of guilt also rests on my shoulders though. If not for my involvement with the Klesh, at least my mother would still be alive. That whole episode shocked some sense into me and when I got to witness my little buddy being born—Mattias, Katie and Caleb's son—it confirmed what I already knew. No way I could ever go back to that life.

That's when I picked up the sketchbook again. Mattias was my first sketch, a day old, sleeping with his little fist in his mouth. Katie found it one day and framed it. It hangs in the living room of their big barn house.

Nowadays whenever I need to deal with emotions, whatever kind, I find solace in my hobby. I have stacks of sketchpads, most have never been seen by anyone.

These past couple of days I've found myself drawing at any chance. I try not to notice that save for a few sketches of her dog, most of them are of Kim. To acknowledge that would be akin to admitting there is something I see in her, and that just doesn't fit into my reality. Aside from the fact I've worked hard so far to avoid any kind of entanglement, I have a past any innocent woman would run fast and far from. And I think I can safely assume this one is as innocent as they come. I received a little redemption with the birth of Mattias, but I'm nowhere near appropriate relationship material. And that little mouse would deserve nothing less than a serious commitment.

Jesus. Why the fuck am I thinking about shit like this?

"Talk to me." I answer the phone, the ringing of which provided a welcome distraction.

"Need you to do a quick turnaround in Grand Junction." Gus never really bothers with niceties, which is fine by me. "Don't think it'll take more than a couple of days. Neil and I can cover the real estate case."

I want to tell him to find someone else, but I don't. Instead I ask him for details, almost relieved to be getting out of town for a bit. Justification to shove Kimeo Lowe, with her golden brown eyes and all her intriguing curves, as far to the recesses of my mind as I can.

CHAPTER FOUR

*"You cannot see the future with tears in
your eyes."*

~ Navajo

Kim

That's it. I officially hate that man.

If Dr. Waters hadn't just assured me that she would stop at nothing to find what's wrong with me, I probably would be bawling right now. As it is, I'm too excited about the prospect of getting answers to get sad over those nasty words that I've heard way too many times already. Still, coming from *him* again stings like a sonofabitch, but instead of sad, it makes me angry. Any lingering positive thoughts around him have been torn to bits. Good riddance. I do my best to forget about him and focus on the steps the doctor is suggesting.

First off, Doc Waters has ordered a complete blood screen, looking for any minor deviations from the norm. She explained that not all bloodwork results are clear when you look at them in isolation, but if you combine all screens that are even just marginal, often times a picture starts forming. She's sending me to Cedar Diagnostics for the testing and to the hospital for an ultrasound. Of course I want to get them done now, but I can't get in until Monday, and the earliest she could get me in for an ultrasound is Wednesday. Hard as it is, I'm trying not to be too optimistic, having travelled this road before, but that little seed of hope is there. It doesn't stop me from crashing on the couch for a nap after I get home, tuckered out from my emotional merry-go-round.

The rest of the weekend goes by as it usually does, with me doing a bit of cleaning, some reading and taking Boo for a couple of walks on the mesa.

When I return from our second walk of the day, dusk already staining the sky, I'm surprised to find a patrol car sitting in my drive, Sheriff Carmel standing beside it.

"Sheriff? What can I do for you?" I have to pull back on the leash when Boo starts up a soft growl.

"Can we go inside out of the cold?" he suggests.

I nod in response and pull Boo with me to open the door. He's right, it's pretty cold once the sun goes down and with the wind picking up this afternoon, my poncho is not enough to keep the chill out.

Once inside I first give Boo dinner before turning to the sheriff, who is waiting right inside the door.

"You should lock your doors," is the first thing from his mouth.

"I just went for a quick walk. I've never had to lock my doors," I answer in a somewhat defensive tone.

"Noticed that the other day. I'm thinking you should make locking your new habit."

His tone irritates me.

"I have good neighbors and nothing worth stealing anyway, so I don't see why I should start now, Sheriff Carmel." So I'm a tad snippy. I just don't take well to being told what to do.

"Name's Drew," he says as he narrows in on me.

"Very well, Sheriff Drew."

"Drop the Sheriff and we'll call it good," he says, way too close to me for comfort now.

"Reason you need your door locked is because you may have put a ding on the radar of the folks who roughed up the Walkers."

"But why? I didn't even see who was in the car." Seriously? They flew out of the driveway. Wouldn't have had a chance to see me. Would they?

"Maybe, but they might not know that, in which case they might consider you a threat," he points out, causing the hair on my arms to stand on end. I hadn't even considered the possibility of them seeing me. Yikes.

My back is against the counter in the kitchen and Drew is standing close. A little too close for my comfort. So I rephrase my question from earlier. "Why are you here?"

"Your boss never got on his flight. I wanted to know if you'd heard anything. Whether he's notified you of any changes to his plans."

That's odd.

"All I know is his original plan of returning today. Haven't had any other contact. But I could've told you that over the phone, no need to come out here on my account."

His eyes darken and a small smile tugs at the corner of his mouth. "Checking in on you isn't a hardship exactly, Kimeo. I just got off shift and was on my way home anyway. You need someone looking out for you," he says, leaning in close to tuck a strand of hair behind my ear. A low growl comes from Boo, who's finished his dinner and is sitting by his bowl, looking at the sheriff who is looking back at him.

"Your dog doesn't like me much,"

"He's just protective. Doesn't like people he doesn't know getting too close to me. And people call me Kim."

"He didn't seem to have an issue with Whitetail the other day, *Kim*" he says pointedly with an eyebrow raised.

Right. Boo had reacted differently to Mal. I'd been surprised when the dog submitted to his command right away. Perhaps it was instinctual, I don't know.

"Mal is a good investigator, but a word of warning, he's a dark horse. He has a criminal history and is someone that a sweet girl like you should probably not get wrapped up with."

"I'm afraid you're out of line, Sheriff," I tell him icily, not liking the message and not liking the fact that he's labelled me so easily. "First of all, I'm a forty-year-old woman, not a girl and least of all a sweet one. Secondly, I think it in poor taste you would make assumptions about me or Mr. Whitetail. It's simply preposterous." He has no idea who or what I am. As I turn away he puts a hand on my shoulder. Boo doesn't like that at all, as evident from the hackles standing up on his neck. Drew drops his hand and steps back.

"I apologize if I overstepped. I simply would hate to see a lovely woman tangled up with someone so completely wrong for her."

"Seriously? That is your apology? You're doing the same thing, making assumptions about me and about him that have no ground. I've answered the questions you said you came for, and now I'd really like for you to leave." I walk toward the door and hold it open for him. As he passes he bends down.

"Just keeping an eye out for you, Kim. I'd also like to ask you to refrain from any snooping at the office, since I'll be trying to obtain a search warrant tomorrow. I'll talk to you later."

I stand in the doorway, with Boo beside me, watching as the patrol car backs out of my drive and Drew waving as he drives off. Not quite sure what to think of that exchange, except that it really rubbed me the wrong way. It also got my mind churning on the small snippets of information he gave me about Malachi and I can't help but wonder how much of that is truth.

–

"That's bizarre. So you haven't been able to get hold of him at all?"

It's Wednesday night and Kerry came by the office after she closed for the day, asking me to go out for dinner with her. Her husband is out of town on a job in Silverton and has been gone since this weekend. Instead of dinner out, I'd convinced her to come home with me so I could let Boo out and promised to order something in.

I just finished telling her about my ultrasound today. The technician had mentioned the results would be with Doc Waters sometime tomorrow since she'd requested they be faxed to her. The moment I got back to the office I called the clinic to set up an appointment for Monday.

I happened to mention not being able to get hold of Martin, when I realized I hadn't informed her yet on anything that happened since I left the office early on Friday.

"Nothing. He apparently left the hotel a day early and wasn't on his scheduled flight back. It's not like him to not answer his phone or messages either. I haven't told you everything though," I tell her as we're cleaning away the remnants from Hunan's chicken lo mein and vegetable egg rolls. Kerry stops wiping the counter and turns to me.

"What do you mean, you haven't told me everything?"

I launch into a short description of lunch at Arlene's Diner, my visit to the Walker's farm as well as the sheriff and investigator showing up at my house. "Initially I thought the guy I'd seen pulling into the Walker driveway might have been part of the attack on the family, but when I saw him standing in my own driveway together with the sheriff, I realized I'd been at least partially wrong. He's involved, but as part of an investigation into my boss," I finish.

"Seriously? Martin? I mean I know you told me a few weeks ago that he hadn't been himself and seemed to keep you out of his recent business dealings, but I never suspected anything nefarious."

I pour us a glass of wine and handing Kerry hers, I lead her into the living room where I plop into my favorite chair. "Well, no one seems to know exactly what is going on, but the letter he gave me to drop off at the Walkers' indicated he was under some pressure by whomever is financing the purchase of those farms. Something big is going on. Big enough for Martin to disappear."

"Have you looked in his office yet?" Kerry wants to know.

"Can't get in. He locked the door when he left and must've taken the key with him. That alone is weird because he never used to lock it and even if he did, I'd at least have the spare key. I found out the key I have doesn't fit the lock on there now."

"If I were you I'd leave it alone. In fact, if I were you I'd be looking for another job because this just doesn't sound right to me." Her eyes on me are concerned.

"I know. It's just that the sheriff made sure to let me know that doing any snooping of my own could jeopardize their investigation, but the judge apparently doesn't want to sign a search warrant at this time. Not enough evidence or something. Carmel says Mal is out of town and to leave things in their hands. I'm sure I could find a way into his office though. I might find something helpful."

"Who's Mal?" she asks with an eyebrow raised.

"Oh, didn't I mention him? It's the name of the investigator. I think his full name is Malachi Whitetail." I try to sound nonchalant but I can feel my cheeks flush. It doesn't go unnoticed by Kerry, who leans forward, elbows on her knees and her chin resting in her hands. Her eyebrows do a slow lift.

"Sounds intriguing. What does he look like?"

"Oh, I don't know. He's tall. Long black hair he keeps tied back. I'm thinking he's Native American." I try not to let on that I seem to have his features seared in my brain.

I dare a peek at Kerry, and find her narrowing her eyes at me, a knowing smile gracing her face. "You sound different when you talk about him. You like him?"

I knew that was coming. Kerry always seems to be on the look out for a love-interest for me. I've told her many times before I'm not one for any kind of romantic entanglement, but she always brushes me off. She's also fiercely protective of me, so I know exactly how to nip this little fantasy she's creating in her head in the bud. "He's called me fat twice. Made it clear I could never be his type. So no, I don't like him. He's an asshole."

Just as expected, I can almost see Kerry's bristles go up. "He said that about you? To your face?"

"Well no, but I overheard him twice, saying exactly that."

"Forget that. Already I know he's a douche. Can't appreciate the beauty you offer? He's an idiot."

She's so riled up it makes me burst out laughing.

"Relax. I don't even know him and likely won't have to see him again."

After steering the conversation in safer waters, namely books, the rest of the evening is spent discussing our most recent, favorite reads.

It's been a week since I talked to Martin last Friday morning, and I've been fielding phone calls all week trying to cover for his absence. One man with a strong Texan accent by the name of Jacob Hartnett, has called almost every day with increasing urgency. I've had to tell him I don't know Martin's whereabouts and he was not happy. I haven't heard a thing from Sheriff Carmel or Mal, although I suspect they're keeping an eye on the office. Nothing has happened and I'm obviously not in the loop so I'm getting fed up with being in the dark.

Mal

Three days I've been stuck in my truck with a camera as my only companion, wishing I was keeping an eye on another woman and for a totally different reason. I'm silently cursing the idiot who hired GFI to get intel on his wife's so-called affair. So far I have shots of her going in and out of a restaurant to meet up with some girlfriends. I know, because I slipped in after her and caught a glimpse of her at the table, gabbing and smiling with two other women. Next up was the mall where I had to pretend to enjoy window-shopping so I could keep an eye on her. An hour and forty-five minute stop at a local animal shelter where I spotted her playing with a few dogs in an outside run and finally a visit to the grocery store before she was home again. Almost the same pattern as the past few days. Life of the privileged, where the biggest concern every day is which puppy to give your attention, which credit card to use today, or what you'll serve up for dinner. Yet so far the wife has done absolutely nothing to suggest she might be having an affair. I'm irritated as fuck that a job, which was supposed to be a simple couple of days, has already run long. I know Gus is making the client pay through the nose, it's the only way he'd even consider taking on jobs like these. Not necessarily a service GFI advertises, but he is an existing client; CEO for a large national chain of auto-parts stores we'd done some security for.

I'm about to head out to grab some dinner when I see a shadow in the alley between their house and the next. Someone is slipping into the side door. A quick look to the neighboring house shows a Porsche Cayenne sitting in the driveway. From what I've seen, the man who lives there drives it, his wife has a Ford Mustang convertible. Young couple too, much younger than our client who is in his sixties, and the wife I've been following, who is maybe ten or so years younger. Looks great for her age but still, there's gotta be at least twenty years between my target and the next-door neighbor.

Could be innocent. Could be he's simply helping to screw in a light bulb while the man of the house is supposed to be on a business trip. But somehow I don't think so. The guy's movements in the ally were too tentative—too careful. Our client is holed up in a hotel on the other side of town. His suggestion, not ours, wanting to create opportunity for the wife to stray. And by the looks of this afternoon's development he may get what he's looking for.

With adrenaline pumping and focus firmly on the case at hand, I quietly close the truck door and slip across the street and down the alley. Soundlessly, I manage to open the same side door. People are fucking stupid. So caught up in their illicit affair, they forget to lock up behind them. Idiots.

I walk carefully through an empty kitchen, following the noises that are coming from the other side of the hallway, where I know there is a laundry room and an office. I'd have expected them to head upstairs to one of the bedrooms, but it's clear they had something else in mind. From the sounds I hear, it's obvious they are getting it on. I hate this part of the job. Don't particularly get off on watching random people fuck.

Sneaking over to the office door, where it's obvious they've ended up, I see they've left the door open. Not all the way, but enough for me to pinpoint their position from the crack on the side of the hinges. The woman is leaning back on the edge of the desk, her arms behind her and her legs splayed open. The dressing gown she was obviously wearing is gaping open and hooked in the crook of her arms. The 'boy' next door is on his knees, her feet propped up on his shoulders and he is going to town between her legs. I slide the camera to the open side of the door and manage to snap off a series of shots before slipping back down the hall and out the door. They never knew I was in there, which is one of the reasons Gus likes me on these jobs. I'm silent. For good measure, I walk around the back of the house to the office window where I'm able to catch a frontal view of him nailing her from behind on the same desk. They hadn't even closed the blinds all the way. The images would have enough visible to properly identify the people involved.

Fuck, I'm glad that's done.

Once in the truck and on the road, I contact Gus right away.

"Got 'em."

"No shit? Thought the client was paranoid, but I guess he had it right. I'll give him a head's up right away. See if—"

I cut Gus off. "No offense, boss, but I couldn't care less what the guy wants now. I'll find a quiet spot, upload the pics and then I'm heading home."

I hear Gus's chuckle on the other side. "None taken. Sorry to call you away from the job here, but you are the best person to slip in and out of situations undetected. And just so you know, things have been pretty quiet here this week. No sign of Vedica and nothing happening at the office. The assistant closed the office about an hour ago and went home, so all is quiet. You can crash there and make your way back here in the morning. Get a good night's sleep?"

"I'm good. Want my own bed." My own bed, my own apartment above the diner and who am I kidding, I want to make sure myself the little mouse is holed up safely for the night. Tomorrow I'll try to get up to speed with whatever Neil may have stirred up.

A little over three-and-a-half hours later, I drive past Kimeo Lowe's bungalow. It's eleven thirty at night, and her car is not in the driveway. Whatever it is that drove me out this way is making me turn the truck around to drive along Main Street where most of the Cortez nightlife, such as it is, takes place. When I can't find her signature little blue Honda anywhere, I have one more card up my sleeve. Her voluptuous backside will be sore for weeks if I find her at the real estate office, but it's the only place I can think of.

Sure enough, a block from the office I find her car parked on the street. Thank fuck she was smart enough not to park in the parking lot. I park the truck a few cars behind hers and walk. The office is dark and the front door is locked. I head around the side alley where I find a second door. This one isn't locked so I carefully push it open, hand on my gun. I can't hear anything, but a familiar coppery tang hits my nostrils. Without hesitation, I flick the first light switch I come to. About ten feet in front of me, halfway down the hall, is the body of a man. Lying halfway out of the office and into the hallway, he is surrounded by a substantial pool of blood. On soft feet I edge along the wall toward the body, and with my gun now in hand, I swing around, crouching low in the doorway. The office is empty. It's been tossed but no one is here now. A quick check for a pulse reveals the man on the floor is quite dead. *Fuck.* Where is that woman? Is she hurt? Did she do this?

A slight sound hits my ears. Nothing much. It could've just been air through a vent, but it raises the hair on my neck. I retrace my steps down the hall until I'm standing in front of a door I passed by earlier in the dark. I note that the door is narrower than the office door and from the way it apparently hinges into the hall, I figure it's likely a supply closet or bathroom. Pressing my ear to it I don't hear anything at first, but then the sound I'd heard earlier is clear. Sounds of shaky inhalations—someone is in there. Not taking any chances, I press my back against the wall to the side of the door, carefully turn the knob and feel no resistance. Before I can pull open the door all the way it is yanked out of my hand and a short figure tries to dart past me. My body instantly recognizes who it is when my arm snakes around her from behind and pulls her into my body. Despite the tense situation, her rounded shape feels good pressed against my body. My free hand claps over her mouth before she has a chance to scream and I tuck my head in her neck.

"Hush, *Nizhóní.* Let me make sure there's no one else."

I know she recognizes my voice when she immediately stops struggling and turns in my arms. One moment I'm holding on to her to keep her from running, and the next she's clinging to me with her hands clutched in my shirt and her face buried against my chest.

CHAPTER FIVE

Kim

"I can't explain, but I need you in the office right away."

I knew coming had been a bad idea. At least coming without warning anyone.

I park the car some distance away, just like Martin had asked. The only light I'm able to see on is in the back, probably coming from his office. Instead of unlocking the front door, I walk around the side to get in the backdoor. The moment I'm inside Martin comes barreling out of his office, a gun visible in his hand stopping me in my tracks.

"Martin!" I yell, my hands up in front of me.

"Jesus, Kim. I expected you to come in the front," he exclaims lowering the gun in his hand.

Never have I looked down the barrel of a weapon and I'm pretty sure it's not an experience I'd like to repeat. I almost pissed myself.

"What the hell, Martin. You're freaking me out. What's going on? Where have you been?"

He waves his hand dismissively. "No time to explain. Here, take this and go." He presses what appears to be a flash drive in my hand.

"Wait. What? What am I supposed to do with this?"

"Keep it safe. Hide it somewhere. I have to destroy all physical evidence," he says, turning back into his office.

My head is spinning. I have no clue what's going on, but his demeanor is making me very uncomfortable. When I follow him into his office, I catch him tearing up papers and feeding them into the shredder. His eyes snap to me and I see fear and anger in them.

"Jesus, Kim, would you get out of here?"

"I don't understand."

"There is no fucking time. I'm sure they're not far behind me. Get the fuck out!"

Just as I'm backing out of the office, a loud banging comes from the front door.

"Too fucking late..." All color drains from his face when he turns to me. "Hide. Right now, hide!"

He barely has the words out of his mouth when I hear a loud bang followed by a large crash. He grabs my arm and shoves me down the hall, where my only options are the outside door—which doesn't seem like a smart option—or the supply closet. Settling on the latter, I pull open the door and turn around to see Martin disappear into his office again. I try not to listen to the voices yelling from the front office and slip inside, pulling the door closed behind me.

Footsteps come from down the hall toward me when I hear a string of curses in what I'm pretty sure is Martin's voice. I can only hear the rumble of male voices after that, until a scream pierces the air followed immediately by a gunshot.

Oh my fucking God. Oh my God.

With my back braced against the wall I sink down to the floor, my fists jammed in my mouth to stop from screaming. My entire body starts shaking and bile creeps up my throat. It takes me a few moments to register the warm flush between my legs as my bladder letting go.

How long I've been sitting here like this, I don't know. I remember the sound of crashes, maybe furniture being upended, and later the heavy tread of footsteps heading toward the front. After that, time becomes a blank. That is, until I hear someone entering through the backdoor. Did they come back? Have they realized I'm still here? When I hear the sound of the light switch and see the glare through the crack at the bottom of the door, I push myself up to my feet. My arms are wrapped around my middle, and I'm desperately trying to control my breathing.

The moment I see the doorknob start turning, I know I have to run and when I hear the latch release I throw myself against the door with all my might.

As soon as my feet start moving, a band of steel closes around my waist and pulls me into a hard wall of muscle. I don't get a chance to scream because a hand slaps over my mouth.

"Hush, *Nizhóní.* Let me make sure there's no one else."

I know that deep voice and I no sooner hear it before I swing around, burying my face in his shirt. *Mal.*

"It's okay," he murmurs, his hand on the back of my head, pressing me into his body.

"I peed myself," I mumble into his shirt. *Jesus, what the hell possessed me to blurt that out?*

He gently pushes on my shoulders to move me back a little and looks down on me. "I've got some sweats in the truck you can borrow. You can change while I make some calls." When he turns me in the direction of the backdoor, I can't resist looking back over my shoulder. Don't know what I expected to find, I heard the struggle and the gunshot, yet the sight of my boss lying unmoving in a puddle of blood is a shock. I clap my hand over my mouth to stop from tossing my cookies and a firm arm around my shoulders pulls me out of the hallway and into the alley.

The cool fresh air helps as I take in large gulps while Mal silently guides me down the block. I'm surprised to see his truck parked two cars behind mine. He opens the door and hoists me into the cab. Rooting around in the back, he comes up with a pair of grey sweatpants he tosses in my lap.

"You put these on first, before you freeze to death. I've gotta make some calls."

Slamming the door shut, he turns his back and puts a phone to his ear. I'm high up enough that no one can see what I'm doing, as long as I keep my ass lower than the bottom of the window.

It's only now, I notice the smell of urine and I cringe. His whole freaking truck will reek. As fast as I can, I strip my bottom half and pull up the sweats. *Fuck, they're cold!*

I flip the door open and quickly get out of the truck, my sodden jeans and undies in my hand. I purposely ignore Mal as I walk toward my car, pop the trunk and toss my stuff in. When I turn back, I find myself looking at the broad expanse of Mal's chest. He must've followed closely behind me. His phone still at his ear, he appears to be listening to whoever is talking on the other side, but still manages to glare at me.

In the distance, I can hear the sound of sirens.

"Gotta go, the cavalry is here," Mal says in the phone before tucking the phone in his pocket.

"Don't walk away like that again," he says calmly, yet I can hear the threat in his voice. Whatever. I wasn't gonna stink up the cab of his truck. This experience has been embarrassing enough as it is. Before I can come up with a reply, two police cars, followed by a now familiar sheriff's patrol car come whipping around the corner and drive right up to the door of the office. An ambulance pulls in behind them; I'm afraid it's too late for that.

I watch the officers go in, but just as I think the sheriff will follow them, he turns and comes straight for us. When he is about six feet away, I feel Mal step beside me, wrap his arm around my shoulders and in some kind of proprietary move, pulls me into the side of his body. I'm frankly too stunned to react, and right now, with my shakes starting back up, the heat from his big body is mighty welcome. The move does not go unnoticed by Sheriff Carmel, who raises both eyebrows in response, but doesn't say a word.

He nods in greeting. "Mal. Kimeo."

"Kim, please," I tell him, not sure why I insist on that now but somehow hearing my name from his mouth doesn't sound right. He concedes with a tilt of his head.

"Kim. Can you tell me what happened?"

For the next thirty minutes I recount everything that happened, starting with Martin's phone call, until Mal stops me with a question. "Where is the drive?"

"Oh my God...I totally forgot." I start rummaging through my pockets finding them empty. Then Mal leans in and whispers. "Your jeans?"

Shit. Shit. Shit. Bad enough to have one person witness my embarrassment. I really don't want to extend that to the sheriff. Mal seems to catch on to my discomfort and suggests that maybe I dropped it in the closet when I was hiding. That's all it takes for Carmel to go looking, giving me time to pop the trunk and check my jean pockets. Of course I stuck it in there at some point. I turn to Mal and mouth "Thank you," just as the sheriff comes walking toward us again.

"So sorry!" I wave the drive in the air. "I must've missed it the first time. It was in my pocket."

He seems to take it in stride, tucking the drive in an evidence baggie he pulls from his parka.

"I'll have someone look at this right away."

"You think maybe we should let Neil take a look?" Mal suggests. I don't know who Neil is, but apparently the sheriff does.

"I'll have a copy made and make sure it gets delivered to the GFI office."

"Thanks. Now can I take Ms. Lowe home? She hasn't seen anyone, just heard voices so unless there's something else?"

Sheriff Carmel looks back and forth between Mal and myself before nodding his assent. "Just come by tomorrow morning if you can. I'll type up a statement for you to sign."

I open my mouth to respond but Mal beats me to it. "I'll have her there around eleven."

My mouth promptly shuts. I'm pretty sure I don't like being talked over or about. Especially when I'm. Standing. Right. There.

Mal

I almost see the steam blowing from her little ears.

Her back is rigid when I try to steer her away from her car and toward my truck. She is pissed. I'm surprised she doesn't fight me. There's also something about the way she continues to avoid calling Drew by his given name. She seems uncomfortable in his presence and I'd love to find out why that is. In the meantime I find myself taking advantage against my better judgement, as I hoist her up in the truck. I don't seem to be able resisting the urge to get my hands on her body. She's so fucking short, her shoulder tucks right under my armpit when I hold her.

As I walk around the truck to get to the driver's side I feel the heat from her eyes following me through the windshield. So I'm not surprised when, the moment my ass hits the seat she lets go, full blast.

"Look, buddy. I don't know what your game is, but I won't be dragged around like a fucking rag doll and propped up for your little pissing contest. Asshole!" She spits, while I calmly slip out of the parking spot.

"Uh... language."

"What the fuck? I can use whatever the hell language I like, you self-righteous prick. Not like you couldn't use a good scrubbing with soap your-*fucking*-self."

Damned if that foul mouth of hers isn't a refreshing surprise. My cock seems to agree. Who'd have thought the little mouse was really a spitfire. Granted, it's probably the adrenaline and shock of the past hour that has her acting out of sorts, but still it's appealing. Call me an idiot but I like some bite.

"Mouth like that on a pretty little girl like you is a dangerous thing, babe."

I hear an indignant huff and turn to look at her. Her lips are pressed together and her nostrils are flaring.

"Are you kidding? Don't you think you've insulted me enough? Calling me *little* and *pretty*, when we both know I repulse you. That's like...a double insult or something."

I struggle not to chuckle at her ridiculous rant. I don't even know what she's talking about. Repulse me? Hardly.

"And what's with you and the sheriff anyway? Standing there with your teeth practically bared, pretending to be civil yet oozing aggression. He's another one who thinks he can push me around. Giving me ridiculous lines at the same time he tells me I need looking after. Bunch of cavemen." The last is muttered but what has my skin tingling is what she said before that.

"What do you mean, he thinks he can push you around? Drew? When was this?" I do my best to control my anger but she seems to pick up on it. "When, Kimeo?"

Her mouth opens and closes at the use of her full name, but she doesn't admonish me for it. "I...I think it was Sunday? What does it matter? Are you gonna beat him up? I don't know what kind of game you two are playing but I'll be damned if I'm used like some chew toy in a tug of war. I'll be the one left in tatters after you guys are done."

The knuckles of my hands on the wheel are white, I'm gripping on so tight. I have no idea about the kinds of fucked up ideas that seem to poison her mind, but I'll be damned if I let her, or any other woman for that matter, talk down about herself. "Drew picked up on my interest." I notice her stiffening in the seat beside me at that declaration, and when I quickly glance over, I can see her eyes big as saucers in surprise. It frankly surprised me too, but in for a penny, in for a pound, so I forge ahead. "I made that very clear, and still he waited for me to be called out of town to make a move on you. That's not fucking cool, babe. Not at all. I'll make sure he doesn't bother you again. I am driving you to the sheriff's office tomorrow anyway. I'll have a word."

I'll have a word all right. *Asswipe.*

The rest of the drive passes in silence. Kim turned away when I called her 'babe', and has been staring out the side window with a stubborn look on her face and her arms folded under her ample tits, making them look even more luscious than they already were. Fuck me.

The moment I park in her drive and turn the engine off she turns to me. "What are you doing?" she challenges. I choose to ignore her and simply get out, walk around and open her door. "Hey!" she complains when I lift her out of the cab and set her on her feet. "You don't have to see me to my door. It's right there." She points and I keep still. She won't be happy when I tell her so I'll stay quiet. Simple as that.

She unlocks the door and gets ready to shut it on me but I'm faster. I slip inside just in time to see her big horse of a dog up on his hind legs, the front ones on Kim's shoulders. He has her pinned against a wall and is licking her face furiously, Kim giggling under the onslaught. When he gets wind of me, he drops down and threatens to give me the same greeting. "Sit," I say firmly and immediately the big lug plops down on his haunches and looks at me expectantly, tongue lolling. I give him a good rub down before straightening up to catch Kim watching us from behind the towel she is wiping her face with. "Where's his leash?"

"I..." Startled, she looks from me to the dog and back again.

"His leash, babe. Where is it?"

"Oh fine," she mumbles as she bends down to lift the lid of a trunk sitting to the left of the door, granting me a first rank view of her ass, wrapped tightly in my sweats. Damn.

"Here." She hands me a short, sturdy strap which I clip on to his collar. "He likes the leash taught but he doesn't really pull, and—"

"Got it."

With Boo trotting in front of me I walk into the cold night. The chill in the air needed to cool off my boiling blood. I know in part I'm reacting to Drew honing in, but it isn't just that. I can't really explain what's going on, but my body seems to have no questions. That ass up in the air was like a red flag to my libido. Little mouse, my foot—sexy spitfire is more like it.

Kim

The moment Mal walks out the door the reality of what happened earlier tonight sets in with a vengeance. Memories of crouching down in the pitch dark, fists stuffed in my mouth while Martin was being murdered on the other side of the door cause my stomach to roll. So much blood.

I barely make it to the powder room where I drop to my knees beside the toilet and heave until nothing is left in my stomach. When I sit back I notice it's dark, not only in the bathroom but there is no light at all. I can't remember if I turned the lights on or not. I thought I did. At least in the kitchen, but there is no glow under the door.

The shivering starts up again in my limbs and I'm struggling not to hyperventilate.

A noise somewhere in the house startles me and my heart starts hammering in my chest. Afraid to move, I wedge myself further between the toilet and the wall. All I can hear is the sound of my blood rushing in my ears. I squeeze my eyes shut and wrap my arms over my head protectively. When the door opens I make myself even smaller.

"Fuck," I hear, before I'm yanked up on my feet. I struggle against the big arms surrounding me, but they won't budge.

"Hush, Kimeo. You're safe."

The whispered words finally penetrate when a wet nose presses against my hand. "Boo?" The responding licks and distressed doggie whimper pulling me all the way into the here and now. Back into the hallway just outside the bathroom, with Mal holding on tight and Boo pushing his head against my side. I'm home—safe. There are no guys wielding guns here, just Mal and Boo coming back from a walk.

Fuck, I'm losing it.

"Let's go clean up," Mal's deep voice rumbles. I finally open my eyes and tilt my head back to find his eyes warm and concerned.

Right. I'm suddenly very aware of the fact I probably have puke-breath. That thought alone is mortifying enough, but add that to my smelly shirt, stringy hair and whatever my face looks like now, and I want the ground to open up and swallow me. Determined to create as much space as possible, I push hard against his chest. He immediately releases his arms and allows me to step back.

"I'll be okay now. You can go home." I try to make my voice sound firm, but the little hitch in my breath at the end ruins the effect.

"Not happening." Mal doesn't seem to have a problem sounding firm. I have no energy to fight him and without another word, I turn and walk to my bedroom, close the door and peel out of all my clothes, tossing them in the hamper on my way into the bathroom. There I turn on the tap until the water runs hot and I numbly step into the shower where I scrub myself raw, the faint light of dawn slipping through my window by the time I'm done.

After a quick dry off with a clean towel from the shelf, I slip on my nightie and pad into the bedroom where I climb into bed, vaguely hearing the deep rumble of Mal's voice down the hall. He's either talking on the phone or to the dog, but I don't have the energy to wonder too long. Instead I slip into a deep, exhausted sleep.

Mal

"I want to put protection on her."

After only a brief conversation right after I pulled Kim out of the closet at the office, I called Gus back to give him the complete report.

"Absolutely. Any thoughts?" Gus easily agrees.

"I can do it," I say, volunteering myself.

"You? What about Neil? Or calling someone else in?"

"Neil will be busy with the flash drive Drew is gonna drop of this morning and I don't want to bring a stranger in. She's skittish enough as it is."

In the background I hear the water turn off, indicating Kim is out of the shower. I keep my eye on the hallway, but I don't hear anything else. I figure she's gone to bed. Good.

"I'm also going to try and convince her to come to Cedar Tree with me. It'll be safer for her. At least until we know what or who we're dealing with."

"How do you propose to do that?" Gus sounds amused. He's thinking of the women in our circle, all of who are forces to be reckoned with and not easily swayed to do anything against their will. But he doesn't know Kim—doesn't know she's different, softer, more submissive. Although, she has shown herself to be a tiger a few times.

"I'll bring her for breakfast to the diner later this morning. Maybe meet us there? We'll see if we can't convince her."

"Sure. I'll bring Emma, make it seem less like we're strong-arming her."

That elicits a chuckle from me. "Hell, Emma will do all the convincing for us."

"I'm thinking my wife can handle the task. Gonna grab a few hours of shuteye. See you around nine?"

"Yup. Later."

Just as I hang up, I hear the dog, which's been lying at my feet, whimper. When I scratch his head, he briefly flicks his eyes over to me but quickly turns them back to the hallway, where his mistress is sleeping. Again he lets out a whimper, and I find myself focussing on any sounds coming from the bedroom. Sure enough, a very soft, very low keening filters through.

Dammit.

The moment I get up from the couch, the dog is up as well, already moving toward the bedroom.

"Boo. Stay."

He stops right outside her door, where I can hear her soft cries more clearly. Gently pushing open the door, I see her shape curled in a ball under the covers. No movement, only the tortured sounds are evidence that she's not sleeping peacefully. It occurs to me she hasn't cried at all yet, other than a few sniffles. And other than the two times I ended up with her in my arms, she's also not shown much of a visible reaction to the scene at her office. I'd seen the physical effects in her shivering and later when I cleaned the bathroom after she'd thrown up, but no real emotional response.

I slowly approach the bed, not wanting to disturb her, yet at the same time, wanting to make the gut wrenching wailing stop. Carefully toeing off my boots, I lay back on the covers and roll over to fit myself against her back, curving my arm around her waist. Her hair, still damp from the shower, smells of vanilla.

Slowly the painful sounds subside and her breathing settles into a deep rhythm.

With the sun steadily rising outside, I find myself drifting off.

CHAPTER SIX

Kim

I wake up to Boo's wet nose rubbing my face and am surprised to find my bedroom bright with sunlight. I don't even register the arm tucked around me until I try to slide out of bed.

What the hell?

"Go back to sleep," a familiar deep voice sounds from my neck.

This has the opposite effect and in less than a second, I'm standing next to my bed, looking down on a sleep-rumpled Malachi in my bed. *Oh my God.*

"What are you... what happened... nothing happened, right? Oh God." I'm rambling but I can't stop myself. Embarrassment makes way for irritation when I hear Mal's deep chuckle. "It's not funny! What are you doing in my bed?" I emphasize my words by planting my fists on my hips, glaring down at the dark-haired God in my bed. Fuck. His hair is loose and draping over my pillows. *My* pillows.

"Relax. You were restless earlier, crying in your sleep, and I just held you until you slept peacefully again. Must've fallen asleep myself," he says, pushing himself off the bed, looking way too gorgeous for my liking. Certainly too gorgeous for my bedroom. I catch his eyes scanning me from top to bottom and back up again, a little smile tugging at the corner of his mouth.

I'm suddenly aware of my disheveled state. My face must be blotchy if I had been crying. A hand inadvertently lifts to my hair, which I can feel is a bird's nest this morning. Courtesy of having gone to sleep without blow-drying it straight first. Not to mention the cotton nighty I am just now remembering wearing to bed. I look down and see my treacherous nipples poking through the thin material. I slap my hands over my breasts and my eyes shoot up to meet his dark, smoldering ones. *Oh hell.* One side of his mouth twitches as if he heard me say that out loud, and he lazily scans my body up and down.

"I'll take care of the dog and make us some coffee. You'd better get some clothes on," he says in a rough voice, before picking his boots up off the floor and walking out the room.

I dart into the bathroom where my reflection in the mirror stops me in my tracks. Every curve and dimple is clearly outlined against the backdrop of sunlight, which makes my nightie damn near invisible.

I think I'll drown myself in the bathtub.

Instead I take care of business, brush my teeth, try to tame my hair to no avail, and pull some yoga pants and an oversized sweater out of my dresser. It doesn't matter. He's seen me at my worst and seeing how fast he ran out of the room, it's pretty clear he got a disgusting eye-full.

"How do you take your coffee?" His question hits me the moment I walk into the kitchen where Boo is already munching on breakfast.

"How many scoops did you give him?" I want to know, as I control Boo's diet very carefully. The intestinal tract of a large canine like him is easily unbalanced, and having cleaned up the results often enough, I shiver at the thought of another explosive episode.

"One to start. I figured you probably have him pretty regulated and didn't want to rock the boat. I had big dogs myself growing up. Now as for your coffee?"

Hmmm, very considerate and informed, and Boo clearly adores him. I have to suppress the light fluttering in my stomach.

"Babe," his voice insists and I look up at him a bit confused. "Coffee? How do you take it?"

Right.

"Black."

I actually like a little squirt of hazelnut creamer in my coffee. It gives it just enough sweetness to satisfy me and I've learned that it has less calories than sugar and regular cream, but I won't ever drink it like that in public.

"Then why do you have this in your fridge?" He's waving the bottle of fat free Hazelnut Coffee-Mate in front of me.

"For when my friend Kerry comes by," I lie boldfaced. "And for special occasions," I add lamely.

"Let's call it a special occasion then," he says, squirting a good amount in my coffee.

I want to refuse, but the cream is already in the coffee and the soothing fragrance makes my mouth water. Before I can talk myself out of it, I grab the cup from him and take a deep swallow. *Ahhh. So good.*

Then he pours a little in his cup and takes a sip. His face scrunches up and he immediately tosses the content of his cup in the sink. I can't help it, I burst out laughing. That little smile which never quite seems to break through tugs at the corners of his mouth as he watches me laugh out loud.

"That stuff is disgusting," he says, putting the offending bottle back in the fridge. "I'll take real coffee anytime."

"Real coffee?" I raise my eyebrows at him.

"Absolutely. Just beans and water. Real coffee." He pours himself a fresh cup and takes a hearty sip. "Better."

"So I'm guessing you don't ever treat yourself to Starbucks then?" I tease.

"Didn't say that. I'm partial to their Sumatra blend but without all the frills. Just black."

"I like that one too, but in a skinny café au lait," I confess with a little smile.

"What does that even mean? I hear that shit at the counter when I go in. Grown fucking men order that stuff. Don't get it."

That fluttery feeling in my stomach? Back again.

Mal tosses his coffee back and heads for the door. "Just grabbing a change of clothes from the truck."

I busy myself feeding Boo the rest of his breakfast until he walks back in.

"Gonna have a quick shower before we head over to the diner."

He's halfway down the hall when his words finally register. "Wait. What?"

"Breakfast at the diner. You have dick all in your fridge, as far as crap that is actually fit for people to eat, and we gotta have breakfast. Hence the diner. I won't be long." And with that he disappears down the hall.

Glaring at his retreating back, I try to come up with a retort, but before I have a chance, he disappears into the bathroom. Still seething, I decide to take Boo for his morning constitutional. Gives me a chance to cool of and figure out a way out of breakfast.

Mal

Jesus.

The whole time I'm bantering in the kitchen about fucking coffee with the woman whose baggy clothes do nothing to erase the image of her tempting rounded shape clearly outlined against her little nightie, I'm barely able to contain the raging hard-on behind my zipper. Worrying that the massive bulge in my jeans would send her into hiding, I keep myself covered behind the counter. Then she starts laughing and fuck if I don't get harder at the sight of her perfect little teeth, her neck arched back and the light, soft sound of her amusement.

The shower is a good hiding place, but when I grab the bar of soap on the edge of the tub, the scent of vanilla hits my nostrils stirring my blood anew. My hands slick with suds, I grab my cock and slowly pump up and down its length. Fuck if I know what she does to me, but I have to get myself back under control. If it means rubbing one out in her shower, so be it.

With her scent surrounding me, the sound of her laughing still ringing in my ears and the vision of her body barely concealed by that thin nightgown, it doesn't take long for the familiar tingling to start at the base of my spine. The memory of those twin hard peaks, slightly darker than her pale skin, poking in my direction is enough to have me coming violently in my hand. An inadvertent groan escapes my mouth. *Fuck.*

Feeling marginally better, I put on the same jeans but a clean shirt and socks, sit on the side of her bed and pull my boots up. It hits me that the house is too quiet. The kitchen is empty, the coffee cups draining in the dish rack and neither Kim nor the damn dog are there. She didn't... Lifting up the lid of the trunk where I saw her grab his leash last night, confirms my suspicions. The little fool's gone out alone to walk the dog. Maybe I need to be a little more forceful in explaining the potential danger she could be in.

"I was fine," she complains, sitting beside me in the truck. "Boo wouldn't let anyone hurt me. He's very protective."

I was standing at the end of the driveway when she came walking up the path leading to the mesa beyond. Without a word, I grab her by the arm and lead her back into the house, where I take Boo off his leash and hand over her purse, keeping the house keys that were on the counter to myself.

"Wait," she cries out when I'm about to lock the door. "I have to change my boots."

I look at her feet and see nothing wrong with the rubber boots she's wearing, but the stubborn look on her face has me give in. Whatever. I'll never understand women. We're just going to the diner, for Christ's sake. Kim is grumbling as she laces up a pair of low black boots, which I have to admit, even without much of a heel, look a lot sexier than the rubber green monstrosities she was wearing.

I just pull into the street when she starts defending herself. I haven't trusted myself to speak yet, but when she says Boo will protect her again, I snort. Loudly. That earns me a dirty look.

"It's daylight out, Mal. Nothing's gonna happen in daylight."

86

"You're not serious, right?" I bite off. "The people who shot out the lock on your office last night, and murdered your boss in cold blood, would not be deterred by a little bit of daylight. Especially not when you venture out on the mesa, where no one would hear your cries for help. That is, if you'd even have time to cry out. Fucking hell, woman. Do you have a death wish?" I know I'm yelling in the confines of the cab and I can see her shrinking away in my peripheral vision, but I can't stop myself.

"But Boo—" she tries once more when I cut her off.

"Can't stop a bullet. First thing they'd do is shoot your dog. Then what?"

Ah, fuck. My gut clenches when I hear her sniffle and when I look over, she's turned her body to the side window to hide herself.

First chance I get, I pull off into a gas station, driving around the back of the building and put the truck in park. Then I reach over, unclip her seatbelt and pull her resistant body over the center console and onto my lap.

"I'm sorry I yelled," I say softly over her head, which is tucked, under my chin. "When you were gone, it scared me. I'm just afraid you're not getting how dangerous it can be out there."

She's quiet for so long that I'm not even sure she heard me. I try to shift in an effort to get a look at her face when she finally speaks.

"Sor...Sorry," she hiccups. "I'm not...I'm just...not used to this. I s...stick to myself."

Before she totally soaks my shirt with her tears, I reach around to grab the box of tissues behind my seat. With one hand I lift her face up and with the other I grab a fistful of tissues and wipe her tear-stained cheeks. Her eyes stay downcast as she quietly submits to my ministrations. And damn if that doesn't get a *rise* out of me. She probably feels me get hard under her ass, because suddenly she starts scrambling to the passenger side.

"I'm too heavy."

"Thinking that's not the problem, babe." She doesn't answer that, but resumes staring out the window at nothing. I reach over and grab her chin, tilting it my way. "Until we get a better grip on who is responsible for last night and what your boss got himself into with those land deals, you have to be very careful." Encouraged by her little nod I press on, "Part of that includes allowing me to look out for you. The company I work for, GFI, is run by a good man, Gus Flemming, and he wouldn't allow anything to happen to you. Not on his watch. Or rather, my watch. We'll keep you safe."

She opens her mouth as if to protest, but closes it again quickly, simply nodding. Not quite the security of a verbal agreement, but I'll take it.

By the time we pull into the diner's parking lot, I can see we're last to arrive. By the looks of it, just about all of the GFI crowd is present. *Fuck me.*

Expecting a large congregation to be waiting for us, I'm surprised to see Gus and Emma off to the side in one of the smaller booths for four. Joe and Naomi, Neil, Caleb and Katie, and my little nephew are all gathered around the big round table Arlene added a few months ago. Mostly to house our crew.

"Hey!" Naomi calls out when we come in and Kim looks up in surprise.

"Oh hi," she says a little meekly, eyeing the substantial crowd at the table.

Not meekly enough to miss the ears of Mattias, whose eyes pop up in our direction. The moment he sees me, a big smile breaks through on his face. With his little arms raised toward me he starts his usual chant. "Unca! Unca!"

From experience I know that unless I give him his due attention, the chanting will turn into crying. My nephew seems to adore me, which is good 'cause the feeling is mutual. Never thought I'd be interested in kids. I generally could take them or leave them, but with the birth of Mattias that seems to have changed.

With my hand at the small of Kim's back I guide her to the larger table, shrugging in the direction of Gus and Emma who seem to be observing with amusement. They know the drill.

"Hey buddy," I smile at Mattias, lifting him from the high chair. His little hands slap on my cheeks and his smile almost splits his face in two. Bad moods never last long when this little guy is around, his sunny disposition puts everyone in a good mood.

Distracted by my nephew, it takes me a while to notice Kim is looking very uncomfortable. Of course.

"Kim, this little guy is Mattias, and he belongs to my brother Caleb and his wife Katie."

Katie, who has notably softened since becoming a mother, stands up immediately and grabs Kim's hand, smiling broadly. The hard edges her job as investigator for GFI required her to have are barely visible anymore. My brother just tilts his chin.

"Nice to meet you, Kim."

"Likewise."

I'm surprised to see Naomi also standing, giving Kim a hug. "Hey girl, so glad to see you here. I didn't realize you knew Mal."

I'm busy keeping Mattias' hands out of my hair. He loves to pull it out by hanks. But I do notice Kim's shy glance at me and decide to jump in.

"We met recently on a case," I tell Naomi with a smile before finishing up introductions. "The blond guy with the ugly mug next to Naomi is her fiancé Joe, a colleague of mine, and Neil over there is the Benjamin of the group. He's our tech specialist."

Kim lifts her hand in a small wave as I untangle myself from my nephew's clutches and plop him back in his seat beside his mom.

"If you guys will excuse us, there's someone else I'd like to introduce Kim to."

A series of *Sure things* and *Nice to meet yous* follow us to the booth where Gus and Emma are now openly smiling.

"This is my boss, Gus Flemming, and his wife Emma," I tell Kim who seems a little intimidated with all the introductions. I don't blame her, we're an overwhelming bunch. I slip her coat off her shoulders and hang it up on the hook at the side of the booth. Of course Emma immediately takes the lead when she motions for Kim to sit next to her.

"Hi there. So good to meet you, Kim. Ignore the mass of assembled muscle. We can use another gorgeous woman to balance the scales." She wraps her arm around Kim's shoulders, giving her a sideways hug.

"Emma's right," Gus rumbles, "always room for another pretty face."

Kim tilts her head down but not before I catch the slight blush on her cheeks. Having been left no other choice, I slide in opposite her, next to Gus.

"Let's order some breakfast, shall we?" Gus says beside me and I don't miss the hint of panic in her eyes when she flicks her gaze up at me. She's completely startled when Gus bellows through the diner. "Arlene! Get your ass in here. Some of us are hungry!"

Emma leans over the table and slaps him upside the head. "Gus! Are you insane? It's not like we're the only diners here."

With a big smile on her face he grabs his wife's hand before she can pull it back and kisses her palm. I notice Kim observing this interaction with a hint of shock and no small amount of interest. *She'll get used to us.* Not sure where that thought came from. I'm happy for the distraction when Arlene comes barreling out of the kitchen, a scowl on her face. She marches over ignoring all the other patrons and stops right in front of our table, setting her fists on the table and leaning in front of me until she is facing off with Gus.

"Will you quit hollering down the place already? And you," she says, turning to Emma, "you're supposed to keep his caveman antics under control. Do your job." With that she straightens up and looks at me and then Kim, her face softening with a look of recognition. "Hey there, good to see you back here. Are you gonna try the food this time?"

It was said in a teasing manner, but the reaction from Kim was immediate. Her spine seemed to collapse on itself and she looks like she's trying to disappear into the upholstery.

"Just coffee, please." If the rest of us hadn't been looking at her, we might've missed the softly whispered response.

Damn. It's a bit unnerving to see all the starch leave her so quickly. This woman obviously has some issues with food. Well—not on my watch.

"Actually, I'll have a ham cheese omelet, and she'll have the same," I tell Arlene firmly, ignoring the small gasp from the other side of the table.

"I will not."

I look at her to find the blush on her cheeks has deepened to a dark red and her eyes are shooting fire. There she is, the little spark plug.

"You've gotta eat. Can't live on coffee."

"I'm not hungry," she insists quietly, seemingly intent on not making a scene.

"Bullshit. I could hear your stomach growling when we walked in," I throw back.

It's then I notice the silence surrounding us and almost every eye in the place watching our exchange. Unfortunately, Kim notices too, and with a quietly whispered "Excuse me," she slips out of the booth and runs to the bathroom. *Well, fuck.*

"Seriously?" Emma spits out, "First you put her on the spot in front of what are virtual strangers to her"—she glares at Arlene before turning to me—"and next you stomp all over that uncomfortable moment and embarrass her even further? What is wrong with you people?"

With angry jerking motions she pulls herself from the booth, grabs her cane and hobbles in the same direction Kim disappeared, leaving me at the table with a startled Arlene, and a widely grinning Gus.

"Well, she told you," he points out.

CHAPTER SEVEN

Kim

Oh my God. I've never been so embarrassed in my life.

I'm leaning against the sink in the bathroom, grabbing hand fulls of paper towel to try and blot the steady stream of tears that have started running down my face. When the door behind me opens, I duck my head down, toss the ball of paper on the sink and pretend to wash my hands. A hand lands in the middle of my back.

"You know both of them mean well, right?" Emma's soft voice only sets off a new flow of tears. "Arlene is almost as bad as the guys. Not quite totally oblivious but getting close. And Mal? Well I can honestly say him weighing in like that is something I never thought I'd see him do, which probably means he cares. Other than for his nephew, brother and sister-in-law, there aren't many people he'd stand up for. I know it doesn't seem that way, but he stood up for you in his own limited way."

I look up in the mirror to see her standing behind me, red curls, and a sweet round face on a softly rounded body. Not quite as rounded as mine but still. And a cane. I hadn't noticed that before. She looks a bit older than me but not much. I expect the face in the mirror to hold pity but it doesn't. Concern, yes, warmth, absolutely, and even a hint of amusement is what I find in the slightly upturned corners of her mouth.

"I don't like eating in public," I blurt out when I turn to face her directly. Don't ask me why that confession comes flying out of my mouth to this virtual stranger, but somehow I feel she'll get it. Her pensive nod seems to support that.

"I figured it might be something along those lines. Hell, I still struggle with that from time to time, although Gus would put me over his knee if he knew. He likes my curves. Doesn't want me to lose any of them and frankly, I've grown to like myself just the way I am. Most of the time," she adds with a self-deprecating little smile and a shrug of her shoulders. "You know? Women with bodies like ours often don't appreciate the kind of warm protective feelings they can evoke in men. It's a known fact that most men would still prefer soft curves to hard angles. I'm not saying we should define ourselves by how men view us, but it does help. Don't you think?"

All I manage to do is nod, getting choked up again by Emma's words. And I realize something; I may have allowed others to define me, like she says. Peter, for sure, and maybe even my mom and sister too. I vow to change that, although I'm under no illusion that it will be an easy feat.

Bolstered by Emma's thoughts and my mini break-through, I force a little smile which is immediately met with Emma's bigger one. Turning back to the sink I splash some cold water on my face and dab it dry with towels. I look a mess, but there isn't a damn thing I can do about it now. Full of bluster I no longer feel, I nudge Emma. "Guess we should go eat?"

Emma giggles and hooks her arm through mine. "I have a feeling we're gonna be great friends," she says before leading me out of the bathroom and back to our booth.

Both Mal and Gus stand when we get back to the table, but I can't read Mal's face . His jaw is clenched when he moves me to the other side of the table and has me slide in before he follows. Gus does the same on the other side with Emma and puts a protective arm around her shoulders. Mal turns his back toward the diner, effectively cutting off my view, but also blocking me from the view of the other diners. His eyes scan my face before he leans in.

"You okay?" I answer with a nod and he continues, "I can change the order if you like?"

"Leave it, it's okay." My eyes slide to Emma, who's heard the exchange and gives me an encouraging nod. A moment later, Arlene slides plates in front of me and Emma, both omelettes. Mine ham and cheese, as Mal ordered, and hers mushroom. My mouth waters at the smells and as Arlene slides plates in front of the guys, I have a bite of mine, groaning a little when it hits my taste buds.

"Seb's an amazing cook," Gus volunteers, loading up his own fork. "He's Arlene's better half—"

"I damn well heard that, Gus bloody Flemming!" Arlene tosses over her shoulder while walking away from the table. Gus just chuckles.

"As I was saying before I was so rudely interrupted, Seb and Arlene own this diner jointly and since the food is always amazing, we tend to meet here instead of in my offices at home. Although..." he says with a quick glance at his wife, "my wife's skills in the kitchen are close enough."

"No need to butter me up, honey. I was already sold," Emma says, her eyes rolling mockingly.

"I wanted you to meet with Gus, since he's the one who took on this real estate job to begin with. All the others," Mal says taking over, indicating the larger group sitting at the big round table in the corner, "they weren't really invited, but as you can see, it doesn't stop them from showing up anyway." I peek around Mal at the group at the table, finding only Naomi's eyes on me. The rest are deeply engaged in conversation. Naomi smiles and winks before she too turns her attention to whatever is being said. Must be something funny because everyone bursts out laughing.

These people are close. Closer than just co-workers from the looks of things. More like friends.

A pang hits my chest when I'm once again reminded how much I've missed. Hell—*am* missing. All because of some warped sense of self-protection. When it is ingrained in you, since childhood, that you're not enough, that you fall short of expectations, only to have experience after experience confirm those words, into adulthood, eventually, you start to believe it. The harsh words spoken randomly over a lifetime become the soundtrack to your reality.

As a result, I've held myself back from socializing, from making myself vulnerable to another person. Not until I met Kerry did I even come close, and still something holds me back from exposing myself all the way. I don't know why it is Emma's words that actually penetrate. Well, maybe I do. When I look at her I see someone very similar to myself. Even though I don't walk with a cane, I'm crippled by my body in a different way. Both by self-perception and by pain that regularly rages through my body without explanation.

My eyes slide back to Naomi. There is another woman who has broken through somehow. Just by quietly listening to my issues last week, and instead of sending me home with another diet and exercise regime, immediately ordered tests to get to the bottom of it. I can't wait to find out what the results were on Monday. It's almost sick when you think about it, wanting for something to be *wrong*, but struggling a lifetime knowing your complaints are not a figment of your imagination. Beating down doors of doctors and specialists, only to be told it's all in your mind and if only you lose weight, you'd get better. It gets old. It's demeaning. It's absolutely debilitating.

"Where are you?" the whispered rumble comes from Mal who I find leaning toward me. "You seem miles away. You haven't even really started eating yet."

I look around the table and notice everyone's plate is empty while I have an almost complete omelet still sitting on mine. "Sorry," I mumble, forcing another bite in my mouth and feeling like a zoo animal at feeding time.

This eating in public is definitely gonna take some work. If it was easy to stop thinking everyone is judging me, I would've done it a long time ago.

Mal

Despite the disastrous start to breakfast, Kim finally manages to eat half the omelet, and Arlene offers to pack up the other half for her. For a minute there she'd been lost to her thoughts and it was almost comical to observe a complete range of emotions play out on her face. I'd love to have a peek inside that head of hers.

Gus used the time she was eating to tell us Neil had discovered that the deeds to the two farms bordering the Walker farm were now in the name of some obscure not-for-profit organization apparently devoted to preserving historic sites. The farms certainly weren't of any historic value but as is not uncommon here, the land often surprises us in revealing remnants of the days of the ancients. A partial kiva, some pottery, an occasional arrowhead. Some of that stuff is just lying there for the taking. So having a charity with a focus on preserving the history of the area is not too far fetched. But, as Gus explains, the fact that nothing, not an acting executive, not a board, not any living breathing person can be connected to this so-called philanthropic organization, is cause for suspicion. Enough suspicion that Neil and Gus are eager to get their hands on the flash drive, hoping it will bring some clarity on what we are dealing with.

"One of the reasons the entire team is here is because we're committed collectively to finding answers," Gus says to Kim, "and keeping you safe. I'm sure you get that you might be in a dangerous situation here?" When she nods quietly, I put a hand on her knee under the table. She seems to need the assurance.

"From what we can tell, no one knows you were there last night, but as his only employee, which I'm sure is a known fact, you would also be a loose end to them."

"So no more going off to walk Boo alone. Even in broad daylight." I can't help reminding her of that stupid move earlier this morning.

"Who the hell is Boo?"

Arlene is back with a styrofoam container holding Kim's leftover omelet.

"My puppy," Kim says and I throw my head back laughing.

"Hardly a puppy, babe. More like a cow. Actually, he's exactly like a cow. He's got the spots and he's so gangly he can't walk a straight line."

"He can too walk a straight line!" I'm glad to see the fire back in her eyes. She doesn't seem to have a problem challenging me, even though she can barely look anyone else in the eyes. Except maybe Emma, who is observing us with a little smile on her face.

"Love dogs," Arlene offers. "Always wanted one but never had the time...still don't really."

"My point was," Gus interrupts the talk of dogs. "That in order to keep you safe, it would be best for you to stay somewhere where it isn't so easy to find you. I'm thinking here in Cedar Tree where you'd have all of us at your back."

I can tell she is moved by what Gus says but as soon as the reality of what he is saying penetrates, a crease forms on her forehead.

"But where would I stay? I have all my stuff at my house, my dog."

"There are a few options, actually. There is a fully self-sufficient guesthouse at the back of Emma and my place. You'd be welcome to bring your dog. Neil is staying there now but he can move to the motel easily for the time being."

"Oh no. I couldn't do that. Put him out. No, I'll just stay at the motel?"

It doesn't surprise me that she is not going for that option, but the motel is not an option for her.

"They don't allow pets at the motel. Besides, it's only more difficult to watch out for you there. Motels and inns are the first place they'd look," I explain.

This time Emma pipes up, "A friend of ours never sold her house when she moved in with her man. Her son was living there for a bit, but he's currently in training in Quantico so the house is empty. It's not big, but has a fenced back yard and is not too far from us."

"That's too much trouble," her mouth says, but I catch the little spark of interest on her face, so I push a little harder.

"Gotta stay somewhere, *Nizhóní*. Beth's house is actually perfect. Like Emma said, it's only a few streets over from her and Gus's place and it has a second bedroom, which means I won't have to sleep on the couch."

At that, her head snaps up. "Why are you staying there?"

"I live in a small apartment over the diner. There's no room there and one of us will have to stay with you at all times. At least until Neil has a chance to install a better security system. Can't take any chances if we don't even know who we're up against."

"It's the smart thing to do, Kim. Trust me, I know how it feels to have your world turned upside down and alpha men sprouting on the spot, all wanting to protect you, but in the end what matters is that they do. It's worth a little discomfort while their doing it," Emma says and I notice Kim carefully takes what she says in carefully.

"No shit," Gus says, as he smirks at Emma. "I never noticed I made you that uncomfortable?"

"Oh hush. No one asked you," she says, punching him in the shoulder, which only makes him laugh harder.

"But what about work?" Kim says to me, ignoring the interaction between the two people across the table.

"Honey, I'm sorry, but with your boss dead, there is no job, right?" I suggest gently, watching her face as she swallows hard before lifting her chin in defiance.

"That may well be, but I can't just leave our clients hanging. I at least have to notify them."

"Shouldn't be a problem to haul whatever you need, computer and files, over to Beth's. We'll clear it with the Sheriff's Office first. We can't just walk in there, it's a crime scene. Which reminds me, we have to head down there to sign your statement. We should get going."

I slide out of the booth and grab hold of her hand, pulling her with me. When she starts rooting through her purse and pulls out a wallet, I take the wallet from her hand and stuff it back in the bag.

"But I need to pay for breakfast."

"No you don't. Here, put on your coat and grab that take out container."

"I pay my own way," she says stubbornly.

"Fine. Then how about this, this one goes on my tab and the next one you can cook for me. Now say goodbye."

Kim

"Yes hi, Ms. Lowe, the sheriff is waiting in his office."

Smiling at the older lady at the front desk, I see a door open on the other side of the barrier.

"Thanks Carol," Mal mutters as he opens the gate to let me through.

The moment I walk into Sheriff Carmel's office, he is out of his chair, coming around the desk.

"Kimeo. Hope you slept okay after last night's events? Come sit down."

"It's Kim," I say, uncomfortable when he puts his hand on my shoulder to guide me to the single chair in front of his desk. "I believe I mentioned that a few times already." I sit down hoping to dislodge his hand, but his grip stays firm.

"Right. I keep forgetting. We won't be long, you can wait outside, Mal," he directs behind me.

"Not a chance. And Drew? You may wanna take your hands off her. I don't recall her inviting you to do so." Mal's voice sounds even deeper than normal and there is no mistaking the underlying bite to it. The sheriff does immediately pull his hand back and takes a step back.

"I want him to stay."

His eyes flick from Mal to me and back before he nods his head once and retreats behind his desk.

After that, it's a pretty straightforward procedure. The statement I gave last night is read to me, I'm asked if there's anything I'd like to add and then I sign. Mal asks when we can get my files and computer from the office, and the sheriff arranges to meet with us there on Monday. The whole thing lasts about thirty minutes.

The sweet lady at the front desk, Carol, waves as we pass her, the phone at her ear.

"So what now?" I ask, as soon as we're back on the road.

"Now we go grab the dog and anything else you need from your house, pick up some groceries and head back to Cedar Tree to get you settled in."

Settled in, that's a joke. There's no way I'll be able to settle with this man around. I'm far too aware of him and too self-conscious to be able to relax. I really don't want to be cooped up with Mal, but I get what everyone was saying at the diner this morning. The knowledge that they were all there in support says a lot about the kind of people they are, and I really don't want to cause anyone trouble.

I'm just going over a checklist of things I need to pack, when Mal disrupts the surprisingly comfortable silence in the car.

"Expecting visitors?"

My eyes search out my driveway where Kerry is standing beside her car. *Shit.* Her angry eyes spot me through the windshield and don't let go until Mal pulls in beside her and turns off the engine.

"My friend," I say by way of explanation. "We go to yoga every Saturday morning and for coffee after. I totally forgot about it." I jump down from the truck before Mal has a chance to come around and lift me down, and quickly move to Kerry whose mouth is set in a firm line.

"God Kerry, I'm so, so sorry!"

"Let me tell you about my morning," she starts, but Mal interrupts.

"Let's move this inside," he says, ushering us both into the house where I'm almost bowled over by Boo who is quickly pulled away by Mal. I look over to Kerry who is standing at the kitchen counter, observing his movements as he grabs Boo's leash from the trunk, mouths a "be back" to me and takes off, my dog in tow. I can tell she is holding back on the shit storm she's about to unleash on me.

"Seeing as it's Saturday morning, I headed over to the yoga studio, expecting to meet up with my friend, who I've been meeting there for the past year. *Every* Saturday without fail. I called her and didn't worry too much when she didn't answer, thinking maybe she was in the car, or perhaps in the shower and couldn't hear. I tried calling again after yoga, and headed over to our coffee place, hoping she'd show up there. Then I considered that maybe her boss had finally shown up and called her into the office. Odd that she wouldn't let me know, but still I was willing to give her the benefit of the doubt." When Kerry takes a breath, I discover from the search my hand conducted through the content of my purse, that said phone is probably somewhere here in the house. Sure enough, it's not a foot from Kerry's hands resting on the counter, where I forgot it this morning. I feel guilty when I see Kerry take a deep swallow and blink back tears. *Oh boy.* "I got worried when I was greeted by miles of yellow caution tape cordoning off her office building and the parking lot. It was then I got worried. So worried that after yet another unanswered call I popped into the nearby convenience store and found out there'd been a murder..." Kerry's voice has steadily risen during her diatribe and I wince when I think of how scared she must've been. I try to reach for her hand, but both hers come up in a defensive gesture. "It took me twenty minutes to find out it hadn't been you, lying somewhere on a cold steel slab, but a man instead. Then I got mad. Really, really ma—ad." She hiccups, losing the battle with her tears which are now rolling freely over her cheeks.

"I'm so incredibly sorry, I didn't think..."

"Well that's clear," she snaps, while wiping furiously at her cheeks. "Because I got here, and to my astonishment, you showed up ten minutes later with the guy I recognized from your description as the douchebag who called you fat—twice! Am I right?"

"Well yes, but..."

"There are no buts when it comes to men like that, Kim. Like I said before; he's an idiot if he can't see how gorgeous you are. Yet here you are galavanting around town with him."

"But you don't understand," I try once more.

"Worse," she interrupts me again, "You're ditching me to do it."

"If you'd quit browbeating her for one second, she could explain things to you." I swing around at the sound of Mal's voice behind me. Fuck. How long has he been standing there?

"I thought you were walking Boo," I say stupidly. "How long have you..."

His eyes bore into mine. "Long enough, and your friend's right, I'm an idiot, but as to why, that is something I'll save for you."

"You've got some nerve," Kerry jumps in. "What are you doing here? Cutting this woman down twice not enough? You wanna embarrass her some more?"

"Please Kerry, if you'll just let me explain—"

"You know what? Guys like you are all the same, too shallow and dumb to be able to *handle* a real woman." Kerry just continues as if I never spoke and now Mal is right beside me wrapping his arm around my shoulders and pulling me tight.

"I'm thinking it's three times now that you've either missed what Kimeo said or you just plain ignore her. Now you tell me? How are *you* not a douchebag? For fuck's sake she's right here, let her explain." With that he presses a kiss to my head and walks out of the kitchen. Kerry's looks at me with her mouth hanging open and I'm frozen in the spot. Seriously, I can't move or think.

Kerry leans over the counter and stage-whispers,

"He calls you Kimeo? You don't let anyone call you that."

My only answer to that is a shrug of my shoulders. I *don't* let anyone call me that. My father was the only one to ever use my full name and I loved it when he did. Made me feel special.

"Kim?" Kerry pulls me out of my head. "Wanna tell me what's going on?" she asks softly. I pull out a stool, sit down, and tell her everything that's happened over the last twenty-four hours. I never notice Mal rummaging around my house, gathering all my stuff and my dog's.

Kerry does, her eyes never miss a beat.

CHAPTER EIGHT

Mal

"I can't believe you went through my things."

Kim is moping beside me as we head back to Cedar Tree. Boo is hanging over my shoulder, his tongue lolling from his mouth, surrounding me with his doggie breath. Lovely.

We'd stopped at Safeway to get some supplies, most of which I added to the cart since if I'd left it to her, we'd have had a bag of dog food, the makings for salad and a bottle of fizzy water. Christ that woman can be stubborn. She tried to pay at the cash register and got in my face when I pushed her wallet back in her purse.

"That's the second time you've done that. Third time is gonna cost you your hand," she hissed at me.

Now she's on my case about getting some of her shit together so we could get out of her house. She hadn't even noticed me grabbing things until Kerry left, after finally hearing Kim out. She made both her and me promise to keep her informed and wasn't satisfied until I exchanged numbers with her. I didn't mind. Good friends are hard to come by and despite a shaky start, I could see Kerry was looking out for her friend. The moment she left, Kim went to her bedroom to 'pack a bag,' apparently not appreciating the fact that I'd already unearthed a duffel from the bottom of her closet and had tossed some stuff from her dresser and bathroom counter in there.

"You need stuff and I packed it. Quit turning it into a big deal. At least we got out of there in no time, despite Kerry's interruption."

"Yes, but you went through my underwear drawer—that's just not right," she complains, making me chuckle. "It's not funny!"

"It's not a big deal. Stop obsessing."

I can see her pressing her lips together from the corner of my eye. Stubborn girl. I used the time to put a quick call in to Beth, whose house we're moving into, to let her know we're on our way.

"I'm gonna need a new job," she mumbles under her breath, and I realize she may well be picking arguments to avoid thinking about the state her life is in. That kind of turmoil is something I can understand, as well as needing to find a new direction as fast as possible, before slipping into dark apathy. Much harder to claw your way out of that. Keep moving is what she needs to do to be able to roll with the punches.

"I'm sure you'll find one, no problem. You're intelligent, capable, caring and loyal. In the meantime, you still have some work ahead of you in closing down the office, so you won't exactly be bored."

"Shit!" She suddenly blurts out. "That's right—what time do I have to meet the sheriff at the office on Monday? I forgot I have an appointment at the clinic at two."

"First of all, there's no way you're going anywhere near your office or Drew by yourself."

"I can handle him on my own."

"Actually no. He's the one who worries me most. I want you to stay away from him unless I'm with you."

"I can't believe you. First you pack my stuff without asking and now you think you can dictate what I do and who I'm with?" I notice how her hands tend to fly around when she is animated. Or just angry, which is the case here.

"Drew is interested in you."

"I don't care. I've been handling myself just fine before you came along and I'll continue doing so when you're long gone."

I roll my eyes to the ceiling, praying for the patience that is eluding me right at this moment.

"Drew is a player, Kim. He throws his badge around and plays the big protector and women fall at his feet. He has a new flavor almost weekly and for some reason he's decided you are next in line. He cannot be trusted."

"You are so full of shit, Mal!" she yells at me as she throws her arms up and turns away. Instead of blood rising to my head, it seems to pool in my cock, making me harder than steel with the taste of her temper. "I heard you. Both times, the first time when you were warning Drew off and the second time when you were talking to that Joe guy. What is it you want? You obviously are repulsed by me so what does it matter to you? Besides, it's ironic how each of you tries to warn me about the other."

My head swivels to face her. "Warn you about me? Drew did that? What did that prick have to say?"

"He said you were a dark horse and had some kind of criminal history. Said a 'sweet girl' like me shouldn't get wrapped up with you. For your information, I told him what I thought of him, and that I didn't appreciate it."

"Fucking asshole." I can't stop the growl rolling up from my chest. "He's not lying, but he has no right to say that to you. I'll have to remind him of the meaning of sealed files." I'm furious with him now. Information surrounding my not-so-law-abiding history is supposed to be sealed up tight and for him to use the information against me to make himself look good is below even him. I might've shared my past with Kim at some point, but I would've liked to have had that choice.

"Look, I don't mean to cause trouble," her timid voice sounds beside me. "I'm not even sure I like him much. He's too pushy."

All at once I feel myself having to hide a chuckle. She thinks he's too pushy? Has she not noticed me moving into her life? I won't bring it up, though. I'm just gonna file that interesting tidbit for future reference—along with the fact she seems to allow me to call her by her full name, yet corrects everyone else who does it. Interesting to say the least.

"Right. Now there are two more things to address," I tell her as I pull into Beth's old driveway and shut off the engine. I turn in my seat to face her. "One being what you heard me say— twice. In both cases I said it to ward off unwanted attention. Drew's attention on you and Joe's attention on me. It doesn't excuse what I said, and trust me, if I could take it back I would. That would be so much easier than trying to convince you I don't think that. At all." I reach over to grab one of her hands on her lap. "Babe, I was way out of line. It was a knee-jerk response that I never had a chance to pass through my brain before it left my mouth. I'm so sorry." I lift her hand to my mouth and kiss the back of her hand.

She immediately pulls away and faces me full on, her brows drawn together. "Why? I mean, it's the truth, right? It just so happens the truth hurts for me, but I know I'm fat." The sheen of tears in her eyes is killing me. Fuck. Her mood swings are hard to keep up with but if I'd known this ran so deep, I'd have never... Ah, who the hell am I kidding. I'm an asshole. I was so intent on keeping my distance I tossed her under the bus. Last laugh is on me—since there is no way for me to deny my attraction now.

"I know you'll likely not believe me when I say I don't think you're fat." She keeps her eyes downcast, but I see her head shift in my direction, so I know I have her attention. "I'm not done. I prefer the term plus-sized, which is far less harsh and unattractive sounding than 'fat.' And I'm finding neither you nor your body unattractive in the least."

The little snort coming from her is a sure tell sign she's not buying it, but I also don't miss the little flush creeping up her cheeks.

"You may not believe me now, but trust me, you will."

She offers me an almost imperceptible nod, which I would've missed had I not been studying her cues with rapt attention. I figure it's as much as I am going to get for now, so I'll take it.

"Now, I said there were two things," I continue. "I noticed you seemed to know Naomi. Is it her you have an appointment with on Monday?"

"Why do you need to know," she tries to evade, but I'm not having it.

"Because if it is with Naomi, I'm glad. She's a fabulous doctor and an even better person. I also want to know what's wrong that you'd need to see a doctor. Are you ill?"

She turns her head away and mumbles as she stares out the window. "I don't really want to talk about it."

I figure I could probably push it, but I'd rather she tell me of her own accord. "Fair enough. Just know the subject is not dropped, only postponed. And as to your earlier question; we meet up with Drew at noon, so we'll have plenty of time to get you back here for your appointment," I say, watching the door to the house open and Beth walk out, keys in hand.

Kim

It's cute, Beth's house. It's very cute. More like a back split than a two-story house with an unfinished basement, where the laundry is housed. The front door is set to the side of the house but it has a little porch that goes halfway around the front. A wooden porch swing hangs from chains right at the corner where the porch wraps around to the front. Perfect spot for morning coffee. Coming into the house there is a powder room to the right and then a few steps to the two bedrooms right beside it. On the left is an L-shaped living/dining room facing the front and the kitchen fits right in the crook of the L, complete with a small table and chairs. Off the kitchen is the stairway going down another few steps to the basement. Compact and cozy. It doesn't have quite the views or the secluded feel of my little house, but it's not a bad place to hang out for a little bit.

There's one thing that has me a little nervous, though. There is only one full bathroom, and it so happens it is wedged between the two bedrooms upstairs. Both with access doors. Yeah, that's a little unnerving.

Mal greeted Beth with a hug and a kiss on her cheek and she turned to me immediately with a warm smile on her face. I liked her instantly. Especially since she took her time to give Boo a good ear scratch, before putting her arm around my shoulder and walking me straight through the front door.

"Let's have a look at your new digs, shall we?" Which we did, with Boo and Mal trailing behind us quietly.

I'm in the kitchen holding on to the counter, suddenly swaying on my feet, feeling unbalanced with the speed at which my normally predictable life seems to be spinning out of control. Beth left a short while ago and I don't know where Mal went. I'm clearing away the bags of groceries he carried in.

"You all right?" Mal's voice comes from behind me as I feel two big hands landing on my shoulder. It's not helping. If anything, I feel even more shaky with the heat of his body behind me.

"I'm okay," I lie. "My head's just spinning a little."

"Why don't you sit and let me finish putting away the groceries."

Before I can answer, he's already moving me firmly over to the kitchen table where he pulls out a chair.

"Sit," he dictates, "before you fall down."

Throwing him a dirty look, I grudgingly sink down in the chair. As usual, stress seems to leave me tired and sore. I watch him store our supplies into the fridge and cupboards, eyeing the ripple of his muscles underneath his long-sleeved shirt and the firm twin globes of his ass in those washed out jeans. *Damn.* Tearing my eyes away from his mid-section, they slowly move back up his torso to his broad shoulders, only to find his eyes catching mine over his shoulder. Busted. The small pull at the corner of his lips only intensifies the flush I feel creeping up my face.

I clear my throat. "Where is Boo?" It's the first distracting thing I can come up with. He doesn't answer right away, his scrutiny making me feel buck-naked. After what seems like an eternity, he finally turns his attention back to the fridge before answering.

"Put him outside. Yard is fenced, so he can't go anywhere."

"Thanks," I say, struggling to push up from the chair as inconspicuously as I can. Sitting for too long only makes me hurt more. Besides, I'm eager to escape the uncomfortable tension that seems to hang thick in this kitchen. Not looking at him again, I walk into the hallway. "I'm just going to unpack." I'd wanted to claim the guest room after noticing the feminine decor in there, but Mal insisted I take the master. Beth's son had obviously taken over that space and it had a decidedly masculine feel to it. I wasn't going to bother arguing.

"Kim." His voice stops my feet on the stairs. "Why are you limping?"

So not a topic of conversation I want to get into so I try evasion. "Think I have something in my boot. I'll take them off upstairs."

Lame. I know he probably won't buy it, but I'm not giving him a chance to respond. I'm up the stairs like a shot and quickly close the bedroom door behind me. There I lean with my back against the door and try to get my heart rate under control. *He spells heartbreak, Kimeo*, I tell myself. A man who personifies everything that would not be interested in someone like me. Sure, he's said some nice things after saying a few not so nice things, but my life experience is such that it is safer to go with the negative expectations. Far less of a chance of getting hurt that way. I've managed to steer away from any entanglements and keep myself safe for the last twelve years. Not about to let a pretty face and a drop dead gorgeous body mar my impeccable record.

With that I firmly push away from the door and start putting away my things, suppressing any lingering thoughts of *him*. Once done, I tuck my bag at the bottom of the closet and lay back on the bed. It's only four o'clock in the afternoon and yet it feels like a week's worth of things have happened since this morning.

Just gonna close my eyes for a minute.

The cold floor of the closet offers no comfort and does little to stop the persistent trembling in my limbs. What was I gonna find outside of this door? The yelling had been unnerving, but then Martin screamed and the bang after that, a gunshot I'm sure, had been so loud the sound of it still rings in my ears.

If I thought the noises had been bad, they were nothing compared to the thick silence that followed. My heart jumps in my throat when I hear soft sounds coming from the hallway. New sounds—different from the earlier mayhem. Part of me wants to see if maybe Martin was just hurt and was trying to get to me. Another part has me curl into a tighter ball.

I can see the light go on and push to my feet, just in time to see the knob turning in the soft light filtering through the crack under the door. The moment I hear the click of the latch, I throw myself against the door, flinging it open wide and make to run. Except, instead of Mal's face, I can just make out two gleaming eyes glaring at me from a mask, before the sharp burn of a knife cuts at my throat and I scream...

Mal

The little wench was checking me out, I'm pretty sure. I know I noticed the way her eyes were fixed on my ass, as was clear to see even in the reflection from the window. The deep red blush on her cheeks only confirmed it when she discovered she was caught. Yup, there is definite interest there as much as I know she doesn't want there to be. Fuck, that's gonna make things more complicated. Not that I don't want to go there, because hell yes, I want to go there, but I'm also supposed to be keeping her safe. And frankly, until we get a grip on who's behind this, I have to stay sharp. Rolling around on the sheets with what I suspect will be a little fireball of a woman, would seriously dull my edge. Not a good idea. For now.

The moment she gets up from the table I see confirmation of what I had only suspected before, she's hurting. Don't know from what, but I was damn well gonna find out. Except she hides in her bedroom before I have a chance to dig deeper, since she doesn't seem eager to share.

That's where she's been the last hour or so. I ended up pulling out my laptop after getting the dog in and feeding him. Got a few emails sorted and received one from Neil who apparently received the flash drive earlier that afternoon and was starting to pick away at the information on there. So far he is pretty sure it's related to some natural resource, since he found what looked to be a geologist's report referencing prime locations for drilling core samples. Oil or gas would be my guess, since there was known to be plenty of untapped energy under the soil and rock of Colorado. Natural resources were big money and big money often meant dubious or even lack of morals. Wars have been fought over oil, and there are some who wouldn't think twice about taking out anyone who even looks like they might stand in their way. If this is true, Kim could be in major trouble.

Suddenly Boo gets up from where he's been laying at my feet and clambers up the stairs. Curious to see what he's up to, I follow behind and catch him laying down outside Kim's bedroom with his nose practically stuck under the door, whimpering.

She's in trouble.

That's the first thought that jumps to mind and before I can stop myself, I have the door open, one hand on my gun at the small of my back. My eyes scan the room darkening with the loss of daylight, but nothing seems off until I hit the form in the bed. She's thrashing about, not making any sound, but her mouth is stretched open in a silent scream. *What the fuck?*

"Kim, honey." I approach the bed carefully, keeping Boo back who appears ready to jump on. That would scare the shit out of her since she seems deep in the clutches of a nightmare.

Sitting down carefully on the edge of the bed, I try again. "Hey, Kim? Wake up, babe. You're having a nightmare." Softly I use the back of my fingers to stroke down her cheek, clammy with tears and sweat. Her hair is plastered against her head. A strand of hair seems to be wrapped around her throat and with my index finger I pull it free. Immediately a bloodcurdling scream bursts from her mouth and Boo, unable to hold himself back, jumps on the bed. This seems to be a trigger, because immediately she scissors up, almost knocking my chin in the process, then starts clawing at her throat. "Kim!" Despite the fact that I virtually shout her name, it doesn't seem to penetrate.

Her nails are digging into the skin of her neck so deep she draws blood, spreading it around as her hands work frantically against...something. When I grab her wrists to stop her from doing more damage, she struggles against me. "Kim! Knock it off, you're hurting yourself." She stills for a second, which lulls me into gentling my hold on her. Immediately she wrenches a wrist free of my hand and claws at my face.

As a last resort, I push her down in the mattress and roll my body on hers, trying hard not to notice how softly it cushions mine.

"Kimeo, you've gotta snap out of this."

At the mention of her full name her eyes finally snap open, looking wild and disoriented. It's Boo's soft whimpers from where his head is perched on the pillow next to hers, that seem to pull her back into the here and now.

"What?" Her voice sounds hoarse from the screaming. Turning her face away from Boo, her eyes finally focus on mine and she repeats, "What?"

"You were having a nightmare. Pretty bad from what I could tell. Do you remember?"

The confusion seems to disappear from her eyes only to be replaced with horror as she scans my face.

"Oh my God...did I do that?" Her shocked whisper has me raise a hand to my cheek where I feel a slight burn. It comes away bloody and instantly Kim's eyes fill with tears. "I am *so* sorry..." Her fingers skim over my face, leaving a cool soothing trail in their wake.

"It's fine. Just a scratch, honey. You did worse damage to yourself. Let's get you cleaned up."

Without waiting for an answer, I reluctantly push up from her body and get off the bed, before pulling her off too. My hand firmly on the back of her neck, I guide her into the bathroom where she stares in shock at her reflection.

"I did that?"

"Mmm." I grab a washcloth from the shelf and wet it under the tap before gently wiping her throat while lifting her chin up with my other hand. "It's not that bad, have a look. Just a scratch," I reassure her.

"I was in the supply closet and the door opened, but it wasn't you. Just two eyes behind a mask. He had a knife." Her body does a full on shiver and against my better judgement, I dump the washcloth in the sink and wrap her tight in my arms. "Just a dream," I mumble in her hair.

"Yeah, but you rescued me again," she whispers in my chest before tilting her head back to look at me. "Thank you."

Fuck me. Those big liquid eyes, plump pouty lips, hell even the red blotches on her nose are impossible to resist. Keeping her gaze trapped with mine, I slant my mouth over hers and on her gasp of surprise, sweep my tongue inside for a taste. Sweet, hot, with a hint of spice—*damn.*

Big mistake.

When I feel the vibrations of her moan against my tongue I know I have to pull back or I'll lose all control. That moan travels all the way down to my cock and I know there's no way she missed that pressing in her belly.

Rather abruptly, I push her back by the shoulders. She has a dazed look on her face and I know exactly how she feels. In a last indulgence I run my thumb over her soft bottom lip before completely letting go of her.

"Have a shower. It'll make you feel better. I'm gonna whip us up some dinner."

With that, I leave a not quite coherent Kim in the bathroom.

So much for staying away from her...

CHAPTER NINE

Kim

This is crazy. I have to get these dreams under control.

I lean my head back to rinse the conditioner from my hair. With my eyes closed, the memory of Mal's dark ones loom over me as his mouth slid over mine. I can still taste his flavor and my body tingles... *Holy frig!* I force my eyes open, and am immediately assaulted with a flood of hot water and conditioner burning them. Dammit! Furiously rubbing and blinking I try to get the remnants out of my eyes. It's one way to stop thinking about that kiss. Instead, I spend a little more time than necessary on shaving, surprised Mal would've even thought to drop my razor in the bag, but he seemed to have a better grasp on my needs than I'd have given him credit for. He remembered to grab all the necessary supplies as well as a selection of clothes geared more toward comfort than class. Not that I had many classy things. Except for some of my underwear. It seems he managed to find the best pieces in that drawer. The soft pink and white lace set I only wear when I need to feel secretly powerful. The black set with shelf bra and thong that Kerry gave me for my birthday last year and I'd never worn. Well the bra I did, the thong however was still brand new. My underwear drawer is like my little secret. I like lingerie. I just don't like others to know about it. Especially not *him*.

By the time I've dressed, dried my hair a little and open the door of my bedroom, the enticing food smells coming from the kitchen have my stomach rumbling. Mal looks good behind the stove. I swallow a giggle that pops up at that thought. I must've made some sound, because he turns around and spots me in the doorway.

"Hey. Feeling better?" His observant eyes scan my face before narrowing on my own. "Were you crying?"

"What? No, I got some conditioner in my eyes. Probably rubbed to hard." I curse myself for not putting on some make up, suddenly feeling rather 'exposed.'

"Ah." He turns back to the stove.

I walk up behind him to peek around him. "What are you making?" I ask, seeing two halves of a squash upside down on a baking tray. The pan he's stirring in appears to have bell peppers, corn, onion and chicken.

"Quinoa and chicken stuffed squash. Something my *amá sáni* used to make. Except she did it with rabbit." He chuckles when I wrinkle my nose.

"Bunnies? You eat bunnies?"

"Wild rabbit. My *amá sáni* had several snare loops in the fields behind her trailer. Caleb and I had the job of checking them every morning to see if we'd have rabbit for dinner. Wild rabbit is actually very tasty. Do you like venison? Deer?" he asks, a smile on his face as he scoops the quinoa from the pot on the back of the stove through the chicken mixture with his hand. He sees me watching him use his hands as utensils. "My hands are clean, promise," he says with a wink.

"I've eaten it. Deer I mean, a few times actually. It's very flavorful."

"Exactly. Most game has a more intense flavor than the regular meat or poultry you buy at the store."

I watch his long fingers work the quinoa through the pan and a small shiver runs down my spine. Who'd have thought a man cooking could be so...erotic? His hands are nimble and strong.

"What are those?" I point out the almost black raisin-like kernel in the mixture.

"Those are dried juniper-berries. The Navajo used them both for medicinal and cooking purposes. Smell them." He indicates a small cheesecloth bag on the counter.

It's full of the little dried berries and smells woodsy—a bit earthy, but fresh.

"When cooked with meat, it seems to enhance the flavors. I put it in because it makes me think of home. The days when everything was simple."

A dark look settles on his face and I can easily detect the presence of not so good memories. Liking the companionable mood in the kitchen, I try to distract him.

"What is a sam...sama—"

"*Amá sáni?* She was my grandmother. My mom's mother. She died when I was ten."

Shit. Afraid I'd only made it worse I watch his face from the corner of my eye, but it would appear memories of his grandmother are happy ones.

"Sorry," I mutter.

"Can you flip the squash over? I think they're cool enough."

He takes a step to the side so I can reach. When I flip the squash over I notice it's seeded and a caramelized layer has formed on the cut side. With deft fingers Mal fills the halves pressing the filling down in the hollow space.

"Are there cloves too?" I ask, sniffing the amazing fragrant blend wafting up.

"Ground cloves, nutmeg, fresh ginger root, and juniper berries. You'll have to wait ten more minutes while I quick bake it in the oven, but wait until you taste it." He smiles at me and I realize he seems to be doing an increasing amount of that. Just like talking, something he barely did at first, but doesn't seem to have a problem with now.

"I'll set the table," I offer, and not once do I think about my usual anxiety over eating in front of someone.

Not even fifteen minutes later, when we sit down at the table, a beer in front of each of us and an entire half squash on his plate, and half of one on mine. Not a thought as I put fork after fork of the most interesting food I've ever tasted in my mouth, while Mal tells me small anecdotes of his *aná sáni.*

It isn't until much later, after I'm in bed, exhausted from the roller-coaster ride this day has been, that I realize I've broken two of my firm rules for self-protection. One being that I don't eat in front of someone, anyone, so they can't use it against me. Second is to let no one close enough to where they can hurt me.

The kiss may not have felt like a mistake, but I know it was. I know because the feel of his mouth on me, his tongue stroking mine, after this many hours, still tastes like hope—and hope is dangerous.

Mal

"Hand me that Phillips screwdriver, would you?"

I locate the tool and slap it in Neil's hand.

He got here this morning just after cleaning up the breakfast dishes. Breakfast that Kim had insisted on making me.

Good thing he came when he did, because watching Kim all morning, covered in her signature oversized clothing, but all ruffled and rosy from sleep, was becoming a temptation I had a hard time resisting. I wanted nothing more than to grab her the moment I walked in the kitchen and saw her barefoot and with her hair piled on top of her head in some kind of bun thing, a pencil sticking through. My gut told me to go slow with this one. Rather than trying to bulldoze those walls down, I think removing them brick by brick might be the way to go.

Ironically, it would seem she's doing some wall breaking of her own. I'm a quiet guy, but around her I seem to feel the need to talk. Telling her about my grandmother was out of the blue, but felt natural. It's been a long time since I've allowed those good memories, the happy ones, to surface. They were usually fast replaced by the not so great ones, and there are a huge number of those. That's one of the reasons I want to find out why she's seeing Doc again on Monday. I don't like medical surprises. They don't invoke good memories. Actually thought about calling Naomi myself, but aside from being out of line, it would piss Naomi off.

It's pitch black in this part of the basement now that Neil's turned off all the power. The only light we have is from a small penlight that I'm trying to keep aimed at what he's doing. Which is disconnecting the old alarm system from the main feed and installing a brand new one that runs through a PSU which has it's own battery resource should the power be interrupted. The old system didn't have that, so if someone managed to cut the power from outside the house, they'd effectively disarm the alarm too. A very out-dated system that was in need of upgrading anyway. It'll be state of the art when Neil is done.

"You guys want more coffee?" Kim shouts down the stairs.

"Would love some, but you may find it easier to brew once we have the power back on," Neil shouts up, making me chuckle.

"Right!" Is the answer, but I can hear her berating herself for not thinking of that herself.

"Give me five minutes and you'll have it back."

"Thank you!"

"She's really cute," Neil says, raising my hackles a bit. "But I thought Kendra was more your type?"

The question is loaded, I can feel it, and suddenly a few things become clear to me as to why Neil had seemed more than a little antagonistic with me.

"Kendra looks like the type I've always banged."

The air temperature dropped by ten degrees. Even if I couldn't really see him well, I could feel the angry tension radiating off him. *Bingo.*

"You better have a good explanation for what you just said," he says through clenched teeth.

" She and I went out a few times and nothing happened because we both realized we were better friends than lovers. But, aside from that, I have recently discovered that I likely have been wasting my time looking at the wrong types of women."

"Is that so?" There is still an edge to his voice but a lot of the tension seems to have left him.

"Yup. And for your information, had I known you we're interested, I wouldn't have made a move on her."

His answering silence tells me he's mulling over my words. "I'm not interested," he bluffs, "but that doesn't mean I wouldn't lay down for her if she was being badly treated. She's a friend. Besides, she's gotta be eight or nine years older than I am."

Right. I'm not gonna push it. Not my place, but apparently Neil doesn't live by that conviction.

"So Kim?"

I growl in response, making him chuckle and that serves to clear any remaining tension from the air. I'm glad. It'd been awkward working along side each other, knowing something was off but never being able to put my finger on it. Now I know. Our little boy wonder, who would shoot me on the spot if he knew I called him that behind his back, has eyes for our local new PT. Well, well, well.

Fresh coffee in hand, I sit at the dining room table and fire up my laptop. The installation is almost done, except for some outside floodlights. Neil wants to make them dual purpose so that they have a sensor, but they're also wired into the alarm, so that when it goes off, every damn light on the house will flicker on and off. He wants to make the whole house light up like a Christmas tree. I like the way that kid thinks. So he's off to Cortez to pick up the odds and ends he needs, including the lights. Kim is on the couch, curled up with her electronic reader, and Boo is cuddled up beside her, his massive head in her lap, effectively pinning her down. Right now she's not reading, though, her body completely still.

I can feel her eyes on me as I log into my computer. Just minutes ago I set down a fresh cup beside her on the side table and leaned down to kiss the top of her head. She froze in her seat. I ignored it, grabbed my own cup from the kitchen counter and sat down here.

"Why are you being so nice?"

My eyes come up from the screen to land on her still shocked face. "Nice? I'm not being anything specific. I'm just...just being me. Why do you ask?"

"I'm...I don't know. You confuse me." Her eyes lower to Boo's head which she is absently stroking with her hand.

"Don't think so hard," I tell her. "Things are not as complicated as you think they are. Quite simple actually."

"Whatever," she mumbles, flicking her eyes to me briefly before resolutely picking up her e-reader and pretending to be engrossed in her book. I turn back to my emails with the hint of a smile on my face, pretending not to notice the way her eyes keep wandering to me.

The next two hours or so are spent just like that, only interrupted by Neil's return with his supplies and a giant bag of take-out from Tequila's—a favorite Mexican restaurant on Main Street in Cortez. He just bought half the menu instead of calling for preferences. When Kim makes a comment about the mass amounts of waste in doing that, Neil calmly states, "It's not a waste when there's enough leftovers for dinner." Spoken like a true man.

I notice Kim barely eats while Neil is around, carefully cutting a burrito and only putting half on her plate. When Neil is done stuffing his face and heads out to hang floodlights, Kim gathers up the plates and takes them to the kitchen. When I walk in a few minutes later to grab a beer for Neil and myself before joining him outside, I catch her with the remaining half of the burrito half-eaten in her hand. A dark blush steals over her face and she immediately drops the remainder back in the container.

"I'm...I was..." she mumbles around her mouthful.

"Hungry?" I finish for her. Seeing the struggle she wages to swallow down the bite in her mouth, and the way she seems to be fighting tears. I decide it's time to try and knock a couple of bricks off this particular wall.

"Look at me?" I wait for her eyes to lift up, take both her hands in mine, and entwine my fingers with hers before continuing. "I don't know what happened to you to make you scared to eat in public. What makes you starve yourself half the time."—she opens her mouth to protest, but I shut that down right away—"Just let me get this out. Please. I don't know, but I'd like to. I have a feeling that no matter how much I tell you there is *nothing* wrong with you and your gorgeous curves, I won't get through to you until we tackle what is at the root of this obsession with eating. Or rather, not eating."

Her eyes fill with tears at the same time her head shakes in denial. Of course Neil picks that time to walk in the backdoor.

"Can I grab a beer? I'm parched. All that spicy food has me thirstier than a camel after a month-long trek through the desert." Totally oblivious to the emotions swirling around the kitchen, he dives into the fridge and comes up with one, waving it in my face. "Want one?" he asks, before finally appearing to clue in that something is going on. "Right," he mumbles, looking briefly at Kim before coming back to me. "I should know better than to walk blindly into a kitchen. I have a knack for hitting it at precisely the wrong time. I'll just take this outside." And with that he disappears out the door.

Kim jumps on the opportunity to try and make it past me out the kitchen, undoubtedly to run up to her room where she can block me out, but my arm is faster. I wrap it around her waist and pull her back to my front.

"Don't run," I mumble, my lips pressed against her ear. "I'm not gonna let you."

Whatever struggle she had in her disappears in an instant, as she sags back against me. Keeping my arm loosely around her waist, I use the other hand on her shoulder to turn her around, before lifting her up on the counter.

"Wait! I'm too—"

"Don't say it." I interrupt her, sliding my hand along her jaw to lift her face to mine. "I bench press nearly three-hundred pounds. Picking you up barely strains me. So don't go there."

"I'm still too heavy," she whispers. "At least according to the scale in the clinic."

"And?"

"It's a lot. Too much."

"Says who?" I lean in, my eyes scanning the emotions clear on her face. "I'm two-hundred and twenty pounds."

I watch her mouth fall open in surprise. "You don't look it," she says incredulously.

"No, I don't. But I'm tall and heavy-boned. That's not my point, though. I'm just trying to illustrate how deceiving it is to let yourself be defined by a set of numbers on a scale. By charts made up by some 'genius' to show what is acceptable as a weight in an average person of a certain height, when you and I both know there is not a single average person out there. The numbers are not a concern, but what is, is the fact that you feel the need to hide consuming the barest of sustenance, because you are somehow ashamed your body needs it. *That*, is not okay, Kimeo."

"I can't help it." I can barely hear her voice when she buries her face in my shirt. "It's all I know."

That hits me in my gut. Telling me that this is much deeper than her own hang ups about size.

"Tell me," I prompt her.

After a few minutes of silence that leave me to think she's never gonna talk about it, she takes a deep breath and starts.

"My dad married the prom queen, but he was not the king. He was a gentle, kind and sweetly attractive five foot seven portly guy. My mom towered over him at five foot nine and outshone him with her beauty, and he—he adored her. Had her on a pedestal. He adored all of his girls like that."

"All of his girls?" I interrupt.

"Mom, my sister Britta and me."

I knew from the research I'd done when I was still unsure how she fit into the land deals that she hails from Grand Junction and her dad, a well-liked judge, passed away when she was barely out of school. Her sister, a successful lawyer in her own right. But I wanted her to tell me herself.

"Dad didn't care about the food rules Mom enforced on all of us, he'd hide food in the desk in his office and would sometimes share something with me. Telling me not to let Mom see me eat. Something I didn't like doing anyway, since she would usually admonish me on the first bite not to 'over-do it.' "

I don't think she realizes that her body language is enough to tell me her feelings about both her parents. Face softening and body relaxing when talking about her father, but in contrast her shoulders pull up high and her lips tighten when discussing her mom. I have one hand braced on the counter beside her hip, but the other is alternately stroking her back or playing with the ends of her hair. She doesn't seem to notice that either, lost to her memories.

"Britta is my older sister and the spitting image of my mother. When I was maybe only five or six, I already knew I was abnormal."

I have to bite my tongue not to object, but I don't want to stop her words. I can object later.

"It doesn't take much for a child to start believing what they're told enough. It wasn't until I was about to graduate high school that my dad encouraged me to go see a doctor. Find out what was causing my constant sleepiness, the persistent weight gain and the pain in my legs. He never agreed with Mom that I was just lazy. He died two weeks later of a massive heart attack." The last was said on a sob and I cup her face to wipe the tears from her cheeks.

"I'm so sorry," I tell her, understanding how that grief could still live so close to the surface when losing someone who you loved and who loved you in return.

"Was a very long time ago. More than half my life," she admits shaking her head slowly before lifting her red-rimmed eyes up to me. "Still hurts to lose the one person who ever stood up for you, who always accepted you unconditionally. That loss stays...somehow."

I bet it did. "What about your sister? Britta? Did you get along?"

The loud snort I get in response is answer enough, but still she explains. "Britta is three years older, was always the image of perfection. Class valedictorian, cheerleading squad, and the ultimate crowning to her high school years was following in our mother's footsteps and becoming prom queen. She was a tough act to follow, with my average grades and less than athletic abilities. I certainly never had the looks to match hers. No," she says as she shakes her head. "We lived in separate worlds, she and I."

"So I gather you don't have frequent contact with them?"

"Left home right after graduation and moved to Vegas. Worked as a nanny for a wonderful family for years before working as a croupier at the Bellagio."

My eyes shot up to my hairline at that information. Not sure if it wasn't part of the background file, or whether it just didn't register at the time, but the thought of Kim in a little black and white getup, battling wits at some card table was more than just a little hot. Damn. Her soft giggle pulls my mind out of my boxer shorts, and I find her smiling at me.

"Surprised?" she asks a little unsure.

"Yes," I tell her honestly. "But mostly because it seem such a forward kind of job. Shows a side of you that you don't seem to let out much. One I'd really love to see more of."

Oddly, her face shuts down. "I left Vegas twelve years ago and never looked back. And to answer your earlier question, I get the occasional card from my mother, wishing me a happy birthday or merry Christmas, but I haven't spoken to her in two years. And that was over the phone. My sister, as far as I know, is a successful lawyer in Grand Junction. Other than the occasional call while I was still living in Vegas, I haven't spoken to her either."

I feel I have a clearer picture of Kim now. A better idea of the minefield I'll have to traverse to get inside. And I'm starting to discover that I really do—want to get inside.

"Appreciate you sharing, babe. Don't think I haven't noticed that on top of what you grew up with, Vegas somehow left a hole big enough to drive a Buick through. But I'm not gonna push you on that." The look of relief that flits over her face almost makes me chuckle.

"That doesn't mean we won't get to it at some point."

Still, I'm reminded of something my *aná sáni* used to say. Something about words being like arrows and once you let them find their mark, their power may come back to haunt you.

I wonder how true that might be.

CHAPTER TEN

"Coyote is always out there waiting, and Coyote is always hungry."
~Navajo

Kim

"How are things?"

Kerry has called me three times since Saturday to check in with me.

"Quiet. Boring. Even Boo seems to sleep all day," I complain.

"Boo probably sleeps all day every day, you just never saw it," Kerry points out. She may have a point.

"I guess, but that doesn't mean it's not excruciatingly tedious. Ever since a weekend full of all kinds of action, this... quiet is driving me nuts." For some reason Kerry finds this hilarious as I hear her snort into the phone. "Not funny."

"Oh, but you're wrong, it's so very funny. I remember not to long ago when I wasn't even able to get a certain someone to get out of her house for Saturday yoga," she chuckles.

"Shut up. You know what I mean. It's this suspended tension. Waiting for something to happen but nothing does."

"Well, I hope not! Except of course if it's those six feet whatever of ponytailed deliciousness you're talking about, maybe you shouldn't wait for him to make something happen."

"Kerry! You know that's not what I mean. He's just doing his job. Besides, I haven't seen him since Monday morning after he followed me home from picking up my computer and my car at the office," I lie. Well, partially, because I do secretly wish for him to be around. Even though it was me who, after spilling my sordid history to him on Sunday afternoon, has tried to close the door on him. But I was actually referring to wanting these people found so I could go back to my own home and enjoy the warm early April afternoons on the mesa with my pooch.

"I need to find new work. It'll take another few days for me to refer all Martin's clients elsewhere and get the accounting in order so I can hand everything over to the lawyer for his estate, but it's a couple of hours a day at most. I need to have something more to do than twiddle my thumbs the rest of the time."

"Well, how about this? I have to go to Vegas for a five-day book convention. I already have the room. Why don't you come with me? We could easily drive it if we do it together. What do you say?"

The chance to get out of town for a little while would be amazing. Clear my head. Get some distance from Mal, who takes up too much headspace and sees far more than I'm comfortable parting with. And I'd love to see the hustle and bustle of the city again. The only thing holding me back is even the remotest chance of seeing either Peter or Mia again. There's a reason I haven't been back there in twelve years, but maybe I've been allowing it to have too much control over my life. Odds are I'll never see them again, so why would I keep myself from doing something I can get excited about?

"Okay. Provided I can find a solution for Boo."

"Ohhh, I'm so excited! That was the most pregnant pause ever. Don't know what all went through your mind to reach that conclusion, but I'm pumped! As for Boo, I'm sure Greg would take him."

That almost makes me laugh out loud, but I just manage to hold it in, because I don't want to insult her. Greg is a kind man, but Boo absolutely runs circles around him. Quite literally at times.

"Let me see what I can come up with and if that doesn't work, I'll let you know. When are we leaving?"

"I want to be there on Wednesday in the early afternoon. So maybe start driving at dawn? We'll be heading back Sunday midday. Home some time after dinner."

We hang up shortly after that, with my promise not to skip yoga again on Saturday.

I'm excited. I haven't told Kerry about my appointment with Doc Waters yet and frankly, I don't know if I will. Seems silly to worry her when there's likely nothing to worry about. I was glad I'd convinced Mal I could go by myself after he'd helped me bring in my computer following our meeting the sheriff at the office. I have to admit, it was not easy walking back into that building without feeling the terror crawling back up my throat, but I managed to tamp it down. Mainly because of Sheriff Carmel's presence. Don't know why I can't bring myself to call him by his given name. Doesn't seem to stop him from trying to call me Kimeo at every turn. Except this time Mal reminded him in no uncertain terms that I'd told him on numerous occasions not to call me that and that if Mal heard him do it again, he'd have his fist down his throat. That threatened to escalate the situation, because the sheriff accused Mal of threatening an officer of the law. I had enough at that point and simply walked out. Of course Mal came running out after me, angry at me now for 'exposing myself to danger,' his words not mine, and I had a good reason to shove a little wedge deeper into whatever had been bubbling between us. Wouldn't pay to get my hopes up over something that was so clearly a mistake. So it wasn't that difficult to tell him I was quite capable of seeing the doctor by myself, since I now had my car and the clinic being a two minute drive from the house.

It was with reluctance and a lot of jaw grinding that he finally gave in.

Naomi was lovely, and that was nice after spending the moments before observing all the beauty of Kendra, who obviously is way more in Mal's league than I am. Harsh but necessary lessons to learn if I want to get through life without many more scars to my name.

She took me in her office, sat me down and explained in a very matter of fact way that she thinks she may have a reason for my lethargy and aching. Maybe even for my disproportionate weight to my daily calorie intake. She was very gentle when telling me there were a few more things she wanted to test for, but that it would appear something is wrong with my thyroid.

"I wonder if that could cause restless sleep, nightmares, or even the up and down moods I've been experiencing lately," I questioned out loud.

"Generally any problems with thyroid or the nearby pituitary gland have an impact on hormones, and any imbalance could be at the root of any or all of your symptoms. Including those."

"I don't get it. They did several TSH tests, all of them came back within the margin," I pointed out. She explained that it wasn't unusual for those not to show any large deviations. The results of the Free T4 test, however, showed a lower count than normal and my ATA was through the roof. On top of that a faint shadow on the thyroid was detected on the ultrasound. I walked away with assurances not to worry unnecessarily and an appointment for an MRI was scheduled for April twenty-eighth. That would be the Tuesday after I come back from Vegas which suits me just fine. The timing for this trip actually couldn't be more perfect.

Maybe I'd sleep while in Vegas. I haven't had much over the past few days, in part because of nightmares, and the rest of the time worry would keep me awake.

Part of me wishes I hadn't sent Mal packing on Monday, but that easy dependency only confirms how dangerous that fixation could become. Not now. Not when I have my life crumbling apart on all sides.

Mal

It's been tough keeping my distance from Kim. I could feel her defenses go up the moment I told her how revealing her story was to me. I should've kept my mouth shut, but I wanted to let her know I could see her clearly and it didn't matter to me. Wrong thing to do. She did everything from that moment on to negate any headway I might've made with her. Monday morning she refused to let me come to the clinic with her, which I didn't fight very hard. Everything in me screams to grab hold and force her to deal with me in her space, but from what I understand about her now, that could spin in a direction I might not like in the end. She did answer my call Monday night but would only say things were *fine. Fine*—how I've come to loathe that word. It is the ultimate lie almost every time it is used. It's a convenient one-syllable answer for anything you might want to hide. A word I had shoved at me for months until it was suddenly not *fine.* It was very much *not* fine when my sister died so suddenly, I didn't have time to get my head around it. The twenty-five or so years after that I spent angry. Wasted time over '*fine.*'

"Mal?"

Kim's voice is unsure when I answer the ringing phone with my usual "*yeah?*"

"What's up?"

"I uhh...was wondering if you could take Boo for a couple of days?"

"What do you mean? What's going on?"

All kinds of thoughts bombard me, the most persistent one a vision of Kim, sick, and alone.

"You okay?" I ask before she has a chance to answer.

"Yes, I'm fine. It's just that Kerry is going to Vegas for a few days next Wednesday and asked me to come. I mean, her husband can take care of Boo but he's, well—"

"I can take him. But Kim, I don't know if now is a good time. I mean, we're getting a better idea of who we're dealing with, but you'd be hard to keep an eye on in Vegas."

We actually have a really good idea in which direction to look, since Neil discovered the geologist's drilling suggestions.

That led to an unreleased report which is being hung up by the Natural Resources Conservation Service, NRCS for short, describing the locations of suspected oil fields in the state of Colorado. Apparently a shitload as evident from the map enclosed, depicting a number of them in Montezuma County. One name keeps coming up, that of an aggressive Texas oilman who has made himself a name with his less than above-board tactics in procuring land on top and around newfound oilfields elsewhere in the state of Colorado. There is no real evidence tying Jacob Hartnett to the Walker ranch and its neighboring properties yet, but the quick forceful sales through a third party, often a realtor, is too similar to other cases to be a coincidence.

"...Are you there?" Kim's voice breaks through my train of thought.

"Sorry, yes. What were you saying?"

"Just that if it's difficult for you to keep an eye on me, how could it be any easier for someone who doesn't even know I'm going to be there? I mean, we don't even know if I'm really in any danger, right? Vegas is like a haystack and I know it like the back of my hand," she says, reminding me she lived there for many years.

"Right. Still, let me talk to Gus and get his take."

"I need to go, Mal." Her voice is almost pleading. "I need to get out just for a couple of days. I'm going nuts."

"Let me talk to him. We'll figure out a way."

I didn't tell her that I'd pay someone to watch her ass if I had to.

Turns out Gus has a better idea.

"When is she going?" Gus wants to know when I sit down again in the chair across from his desk. We'd just finished discussing the case when my phone rang.

"Next Wednesday morning. Driving with her friend from what I gather. Back on Sunday. She's going nuts with nothing to do, Gus."

Without a word Gus gets up and opens the door. "Emma!" he hollers down the hallway.

"You bellowed?" Emma's voice can be heard coming down the hallway between their house and the office wing. Gus grins unashamed at his wife's words, pulling her into his arms and laying a wet one on her.

"How long have you been bugging me about Las Vegas?"

Emma raises an eyebrow. "Only forever."

"Right," Gus chuckles. "Well, I have a proposal, but I need your help. I'll kill many birds with one stone," he says, and proceeds to tell Emma about Kim and her friend's trip.

"Since Mattias turned two, Katie has been eager to get back into a bit of action. Caleb is working on an Internet fraud case with Neil, who is also helping us with this land deal one. Caleb could keep Mattias since most of his work he can do from home. We can't afford to send anyone to Vegas to keep an eye on the girl, but Katie can get her feet wet again with an active assignment, and you can do whatever it is you do that makes everyone love you. To make that arrangement go over more easily." He sits back and watches his wife.

"So let me get this straight. You want Katie to be the muscle and me the soft shoulder? For Mal's girl?" She turns her head to me. "I assume we're talking about Kim, right? I've gotta say, compared to what I've seen you with before, it's refreshing. Just don't hurt the girl."

"Not exactly my girl, Emma." I feel I have to clarify.

"Well, why the hell not?"

"Haven't quite gotten there yet."

"Bullshit. I heard you called off Drew a few times. Sounds like your claim is staked," Gus contributes and I stifle the grin that wants on my lips.

And to Emma he says, "Yes, that's what I want. You know Katie can get abrasive at times. It would help if you were there to smooth the way, so to speak."

"I'm going to Vegas?" A big grin crosses her face now that things are settling in. Emma makes to stand up right away.

"Where are you off to?" Gus calls after his wife who's already halfway out the door.

"Vegas baby, I've got nothing to wear!" she calls over her shoulder.

I throw my head back and laugh when Gus grabs his hair with both hands. "At least wait until we have it all confirmed!" he yells after her.

Of course Katie jumps at the opportunity when Gus calls her. I had no doubt she would. Kim would be another matter though, and one I think I better go handle in person.

"All right, I'm off to clear all this with Kim."

"You don't want to send them in and make this a 'chance encounter'?" Gus asks.

"Fuck, no. From what I know, Kim's got some trust issues. And she's smart as a whip. Emma 'happens' to show up there with my sister-in-law in tow, she'll know I had a hand in it and that would be one black mark against me. No thanks. Besides, how long do you think Emma could keep up a lie?"

"Not even a minute," is his immediate answer. We all know out of everyone, Emma is the most straightforward, honest person who doesn't even know how to hold a grudge.

"Exactly. I want a chance to get in with this woman. It's not gonna happen after I set her up blindly."

"You're already a fuck of a lot smarter than I was when I met my wife. Took me a while to figure that one out."

Boo is at the door, barking, when I walk up the steps. No sign of Kim though. I punch in the code on the new touch pad lock Neil installed.

Boo almost slams me into the door when I come in, charging at me the instant he recognizes me.

"Down." Obediently he immediately drops down on all fours, even though his clumsy tail never stops wagging. "Good boy."

Walking into the kitchen, I find it empty. As is the living room. Her car is in the drive so she has to be home. I call her name a few times, but there's no answer.

Heading down to check the laundry room, I hear the patter of bare feet on the stairs above me and turn just in time to see Kim coming around the basement door. She lets out a scream and slaps a hand over her mouth when she spots me at the bottom of the stairs. The other hand is desperately trying to hang on to the towel wrapped around her midsection. Looking up the stairs I have a perfect view of the tidy patch of hair at the apex of her soft white thighs. All that is in my mind all of a sudden is wedging my shoulders between those thighs and breathing her essence in before tasting her. Which is why I totally miss what Kim is saying.

"Mal!" she yells, finally catching my attention, but also propelling my feet into motion, climbing those stairs two at a time. This causes Kim to back up against the kitchen counter. "You scared me half to death," she manages, her ample chest heaving, tits threatening to spill free from the flimsy hold the barely clutched towel provides. I stop two feet away from her, breathing at least as heavily as she is.

"I called out." My voice sounds hoarse and I swallow.

"I was blow-drying my hair," she whispers, her eyes big and round.

I don't even try to hide my hungry scan of her body. Didn't expect her to look so soft, so downy. Cute toes, a touch of turquoise on the tips, tapering out to full legs and round hips. A soft belly and high waist underneath a set of tits that have my mouth watering. *Jesus fucking Christ.*

I can smell her...fuck, that smell. Something fresh: a hint of citrus and rich spices underneath. Shampoo and... arousal.

By the time my eyes reach her cute as hell face, her teeth are worrying her plump bottom lip and her eyes are dark and hot. The pressure of my surging cock behind my zipper has me wince and I press the palm of my hand against my fly. Her eyes inadvertently follow the movement and at the sight of my crotch, they pop open even further. Her mouth falls open.

"You do that to me," I growl. "Don't need to be almost naked either. You come near me, I see you or smell you, this happens."

She looks at me with a mix of surprise and panic clear on her face. Before she has a chance to make a run for it, I take the remaining two steps to box her in against the counter, an arm on each side of her. Her scent is stronger and my head dips down to take her mouth. Slowly. Thoroughly. Her lips open immediately allowing my tongue to sweep in. I can't stop a deep groan as the heady combination of her smell, taste, and her softly receptive body pressed against me, hits my senses from all directions. Her hands that were clutching at the towel earlier, are now holding on to my shoulders. Wrapping one arm behind her, I use the other to push back from the counter without losing her mouth, press her body closer and turn us both. With my back to the counter, Kim is in between my spread legs. It's easier for me to reach her mouth now—and other places. Sucking on her lower lip, I slowly let it slide from between mine before kissing her jaw, along her neck and down to her shoulder. She automatically tilts her head away to allow me access. The moment I pull my chest from hers the towel slides down, exposing a surprisingly small, dark pink and very hard little nipple. Ignoring her sharp intake of breath, I bend my head and suck it hard against the roof of my mouth. My nostrils are flaring, sucking in air while I feast on her breasts. The small whimpering sounds escaping from her have my cock leaking pre-come like a teenager.

"Malachi..." Her soft voice pleads, hands grabbing on to my head pressing me to her.

The shrill ring of the doorbell bursts the erotic bubble and with a pop, her nipple slips from my mouth.

"Don't move," I tell her, my voice ragged. "Be right back."

I set her back a little and walk to the front door to find a teenager selling newspaper subscriptions in the neighborhood. Assuring the kid we're not interested I return to the kitchen, only to find her gone.

CHAPTER ELEVEN

Kim

"I'll be there at ten thirty to pick you up."

Surprisingly excited at the prospect of a little shopping, I quickly check my bank account. My savings are substantial enough to take a little dent. I've never enjoyed shopping much, but when Emma called to see if I wanted to head into Durango with her, to her favorite plus-size boutique, the prospect of some new threads suddenly seemed like fun.

Nothing to do with the beautiful tall man who seemed irritated after I ran into my bedroom after our hot and heavy make-out session in my kitchen. In broad daylight with every bump and dimple of my body on display. My God, I'd never been so mortified once the blinding fog of sex was lifted by a simple ring of the doorbell. I have no idea what possessed me. Sure, there was no doubt he had a reaction to me. A pretty intense one, but I convinced myself the moment his mouth and hands left my body that he'd come back into the kitchen, take one look, and realize the mistake he made. So I ran. Even though he had ordered me to stay put, I beelined it up the stairs. By the time he came after me, I was already dressed in my most comfortable sweats. Safely unappealing.

His eyes darkened when I finally opened the door to him, and his mouth drew tight. His disapproval obvious. He didn't like it when I told him it was all a mistake. Didn't like that at all.

"Bullshit," he said. "You're scared. You don't want to see what's right in front of you and is so obvious to everyone else. You're a gorgeous woman. All of you. You look good, you smell great and you taste even better."

Embarrassed at his candor, I pushed past him and went downstairs, Mal close on my heels.

"Mouse, I'm not gonna push this, but what happened just now, my mouth and hands all over you and you whimpering with need? That's only the beginning. It *will* happen again, and next time I'll want to taste that pussy that got so wet for me I could smell it."

I remember the combination of disgust at myself and instant arousal at his words, but other than the blush I could feel on my face I pretended to ignore his words.

"Why are you here?"

When he finally gave up on the intense stare-down, he told me about Gus's plan to have Emma and Mal's sister-in-law, Katie, come with us to Vegas. We'd go in two cars, so Katie could make sure no one follows us. Apparently Katie had been an active part of the team until she'd had her baby and wanted a chance to go back 'into the field.' My first reaction had been negative. It felt like an intrusion. But after a little consideration, I had to admit it was probably the best compromise. Why Malachi had stepped up as my protector, who knows, but he was determined to look out for me and I had a choice of either going with his plan, or not going at all. And I wanted to go to Vegas. Besides, Emma had made me feel really comfortable the first time we met at breakfast, and to be honest, the idea of maybe making some new friends felt good.

Mal left shortly after that, but not without bending low to press a soft kiss to my lips. "You go have some fun with the girls, but babe, when you come back, we're gonna see where this goes."

For the last two days I haven't seen him, but his words have been rolling around in my head. In fact, I haven't been able to think of much else until Emma called. She's so excited about going to Vegas and some of it is spilling over to me.

"I absolutely *have* to have some new clothes. All I own is sweats, yoga-pants and a few stray jeans. Nothing soft and summery. It's gonna be warm there already, you know?"

Yes I know, I've been all over my own closet with little to show for it. It tickled me to hear Emma's wardrobe is much like mine. Although I do have a few business outfits, they are mostly aimed at hiding, not showing off. For some reason I feel like showing off a little. I try to deny it has anything to do with the hunger in those obsidian eyes as they scanned over my near naked body a couple of days ago.

And still...

"So funny that I lived in Durango for years and never knew this place was here," I point out to Emma who is leading the way into what appears to be a historic brick building along Main Avenue. It probably had more to do with the fact that I never considered the boutique would have anything for people my size, so I never even bothered to look closely.

"This is awesome!" I blurt out when I look at the mannequins scattered around the store in all shapes and sizes. Both Emma and the plump sales lady smile at my outburst.

"Hi, I'm Leslie," the woman says. "Why don't you have a look around and if there's anything you need to know, ask me.

We have tall, regular and petite sizes in most items and certain things are grouped by body shape."

"I'm in fucking awe, pardon my French," flies out of my mouth when Emma and I start moseying around. Emma bursts out in a deep belly laugh, so infectious, I have no choice but to join her.

"Never would I have guessed you knew how to swear," she says, a smile still playing on her face.

"Oh, I know how, I just rarely do," I admit. "Here though, I feel like I can totally let it all hang out. This is *such* a great place. I don't feel I have to make myself 'small' to blend in. But I'm sorry about the swearing."

Emma's eyes on me have turned pensive. "I'm afraid you and I are gonna have to have some talks," she says seriously. "I have more than just a few years on you and you'll have to forgive me when I feel the need to impart some of my hard-earned wisdom on you."

"Okay?" My tentative reply makes her smile.

"Just be prepared to get a good swift kick in the booty, every time you hold back the real you. Promise you'll not suppress a damn thing today. Enjoy it with me without worrying about whether you can or you should, just grab on. Got me?"

I'm actually not quite sure I do, but I nod anyway. I'm gonna try and go with the flow.

I start roaming the racks around me, completely lost in the vivid colors and gorgeous materials. My colors of choice have always been black or grey. Occasionally I would 'dare' to venture into a dark navy or brown, but actual color? Very rare and those pieces hang mostly unworn in my closet. But I'm going to Vegas—and black in Vegas is just...wrong.

"Honey," the kind voice of Leslie has me turn around. She's standing with her arms folded, hip cocked and her face wearing a lopsided grin. "You do realize you're in the wrong section, right? This is for apple-shapes, which you're not. You have a lot of shape you should be happy with. I'm thinking somewhere between hourglass or pear."

I look down at myself and back up at her, not quite understanding. She reaches out, grabs my hand and pulls me in front of a mirror in the section where Emma is browsing around. Stepping behind me, she puts her hands on my shoulders. "What do you see?"

I shake my head to clear it. "What do I see? I see me?"

"When you look at your body, what do you see?"

I snort. It's a funny question, especially because I don't look at my body. I avoid it at all times. Even when I accidentally catch a glimpse, I turn away from the mirror quickly. So I tell her, "Hardly anything. I avoid it."

Her head tilts to the side, observing me quietly. "You shouldn't avoid it. You've got it going on with all these rich curves. Look here." She lifts my arms up to the side and sets her hands on my hips. "You've got these hips that are made for showing off. A nice long curve from your knees all the way to your waist, where you dip in. You've got a waist. Apples don't have waists. They need clothes that make it look like they have one. But you, you've got one, right here." She grabs me firmly where she claims my waist is. With her hands on there I can see I actually do have a bit of an indent. Hmmm. "Now from the waist up, you have a set of knockers that when displayed properly, would knock any man off his feet."

"She's not lying." Emma is leaning on her walker, watching us. "You hide your shape."

I step away from the mirror and turn to face them. "I don't, I hide my rolls."

Wrong thing to say. Emma squints her eyes and Leslie clucks, shaking her head.

"Honey, there'll be no hiding here and those are not rolls. We call them curves and we're gonna show those babies off. Now come with me."

An hour and forty-five minutes later, feeling more like a full day, I dump my selections, or rather, Emma and Leslie's selections *for* me, on the counter. Soft flowy tops, three quarter-sleeved A-line tees in three colors, some stretchy jeans with bootcut legs that are so comfy, I want to live in them, and finally, black shoes and a dress. I haven't worn a dress since I was twelve years old and my mother forced me into wearing one for my First Communion. An experience that caused me to stay far away from dresses, and church, ever since. Leslie picked it out, telling me every woman needs an LBD—little black dress. The only good thing I saw when pulling it into the dressing room with me, was that it was black. It took Emma and Leslie half an hour to convince me that the dress was made for me. Fifties retro style, with a fitted bodice ending right under my breasts and a roomy skirt that falls right on my knees. A deep swooping neckline with a saucy little slit for some added cleavage and straight three-quarter sleeves. I had a hard time looking away from my dimpled knees, but when Leslie put some black, very narrow black pumps on my feet with a slightly blunted tip of the toe and reasonable heels so I won't break my neck on them, I was sold.

"That was the most fun I've ever had shopping," I tell Emma honestly when she drops me off at my house, with my four bags stuffed full of purchases. "I'm in desperate need of some tea, though. Would you care to come in for a cup?"

"Would love to. And I had a blast too. Shopping is not usually something I enjoy, but when I discovered that place a couple of years ago, it became much less painful." She chuckles at her own words.

We end up outside on the back deck with our coats on so we can enjoy the warm afternoon sun, a steaming cup of tea in our hands.

"So I'm curious," Emma starts, turning to face me. "You mentioned something about that sexy black number Leslie forced you into—which by the way, looks stunning on you. That was the first dress you've put on since you were twelve? What's the story with that?"

The question has me wince and I take a quick sip of my tea, delaying the answer, which would expose more of myself than I've ever been comfortable with. Emma patiently waits, and nothing about her suggests she'd be anything other than understanding. I take a deep breath and a leap of faith.

"My mother insisted I wear this hideous dress for my First Communion. So unflattering that some guy in church compared me to a bride on her way to a shotgun wedding. Mom was angry with me, although I could never figure out the reason why. So every time my mom tried to force me into a dress after that, I threw a tantrum. Vowed never to wear one again. Instead I started wearing anything black and oversized to her abject horror." A sour little snort escapes me when I think of the way she would scold me for not even trying to be pretty. I shrug my shoulders in an attempt to shake it off. I promised

154

myself I was done with that—done with letting it spoil the gain I made this morning alone.

"I see," Emma says quietly and even with sparing her most of the details, I believe she does.

We sit quietly for some time, sipping tea, thinking our own thoughts, while watching Boo chase imaginary flies.

Mal

"Drew just called," Gus says the minute I walk into the office.

"You're going to want to head over to Kim because he's on his way there. A neighbor called the cops early this morning, reporting a possible break in at her place. Cops found the door broken open and her place rifled through. Took them a while to figure out this was possibly connected to the murder and so Drew didn't find out until this afternoon. He wanted to know where she was, Mal. I had no choice but to tell him. You know he's a good guy."

A good officer of the law, yes. A good guy, I'm not so sure.

"I'm on my way," I tell Gus before heading back out the door.

"Call me when you have a chance, we'll talk about moving up this Vegas excursion," Gus yells after me and I wave my hand in acknowledgement.

I'm surprised to find Emma's SUV in the driveway behind Kim's blue Honda. I end up parking on the street and walk up the drive when I can hear voices trailing from the back of the house. I recognize both Kim's and Emma's. Instead of going in, I decide to intercept Drew before he has a chance to barge in like a bull in a China shop. Standing there, leaning against the side of the house, I can't help picking up some of the conversation from the backyard and what I hear angers me. Additional evidence that her mom is a piece of work, and all the more reason for me to prove to Kim how wrong that woman was.

The moment Drew's patrol car pulls in tight to Emma's bumper, I'm up on my feet and approaching him. He shakes his head on a little smile when he sees me coming. Bastard.

"Are you trying to piss me off?"

"Doesn't take much, apparently," the smartass fires back.

"Something happens to my girl's place and you don't think to call me first? I'm gonna take that as a challenge."

"Keep your shorts on. Gus mentioned you were on your way in when I called to notify him. I didn't feel the need to double up our efforts in getting word to you. As for *your girl,* did you have a chance to talk to her?"

"No. I wanted a chance to get some more information first." I consciously let go of the anger I've nursed since getting the news.

"Original call came in at five this morning. On duty officers went to check it out, found the side door kicked in. They gained entrance and found the place tossed."

"How bad?" I want to know.

"Just came from the house. Looks like a mostly methodical search. The tossing part is mostly pillows thrown around,

156

contents of drawers and cupboards pulled out. And they emptied her freezer. That's what tells me they were looking for something specific."

"You think her boss mentioned something? Right before they shot him? Doesn't make sense, they would've come after her sooner," I point out.

"Maybe. Could be he told them he had left information with someone in case anything happened to him, trying to save his ass. First place they'd look would be close family. He has a sister in Houston I talked to earlier this week about the release of his body by the coroner. She wants to bring him back out there for burial. I haven't heard anything since but it's possible someone's been sniffing around her, got nothing and is moving on to the next candidate. His assistant."

It's possible. And with Kim not showing up at her house for days, it would make them impatient and possibly reckless.

"Anything traceable? Fingerprints, tire tracks?"

"Still working on that. We do have a pretty decent description of the car from the neighbor who called in. Said it was a maroon Ford Edge, looked brand new."

I nod, taking in the information. "Figure it's a rental?"

"Likely. I've got someone checking car places to see if anyone rented it out." Drew looks at me, his head tilted to the side. "You think maybe it's time to talk to her now?"

Before I have a chance to answer, the side gate opens and Boo slips through, bounding up the porch steps to try and jump on me. Following closely behind are Kim and Emma.

"Talk to me about what?" Kim asks Drew right away, alarm etched on her face. I leave it to him to answer, but step down the porch and put my arm around her in support right away.

Her face lifts briefly to me and I give her what is supposed to be an encouraging smile, but it doesn't take the panic from her eyes.

"There was a break in early this morning." Drew holds no punches. "Your neighbors called it in."

Immediately she tries to pull away from me, but my hand grabs her far shoulder, preventing her from moving too far. "My neighbors? Are you... you mean at my house?"

"It doesn't look like much, if anything, was taken, but they left a mess." Drew informs her, looking apologetic. "We have some good leads based on the information your neighbor was able to give us, but I'm thinking it's good you're staying here for the time being. Best not to go anywhere for a bit."

This is when I jump in. After half a word from Gus, I already know he's wanting her out of harm's way and set up in Vegas until we can get a decent grip on this case. "She has plans to head out of town next week, and I'm thinking those plans just got moved up by a few days, Drew," I tell him firmly, before looking down in her face. "Gotta get you packed, babe. That little trip of yours is gonna start earlier than anticipated."

One look at Emma and it's clear she's clued in when she gives me a nod and pulls out her phone. Dialing either Gus or Katie before she steps off to the side a little.

"I don't know if—" Drew starts before I cut him off.

"Not staying here until we have a good idea of what we're up against," I say firmly, holding his glare.

"I have to insist she does a walk through of the house. We've gotta know if anything is missing," he fires back.

"Don't like it, but I hear you. We'll be there at nine tonight so we can get her in and out under the shadow of darkness. No lights on until we get inside and all blinds closed. Don't need to make things easier."

With a curt nod, Drew turns to Kim. "I'm sorry, honey. We'll get this sorted—I promise."

I bristle at his use of an endearment when she's fucking clinging to my side, but I swallow it down. I'll have a chance to deal with that later.

A final smirk in my direction, the ass, and he's off.

"My husband wants me to come home and pack," Emma announces before walking over and pulling Kim in her arms. "Listen to Mal, honey. It'll be okay."

With Emma backing her SUV out of the driveway I finally turn Kim in my arms. She looks to be in shock. "This just got serious, didn't it?"

I can't help the chuckle escaping me, but she's so damn cute. Stumbles on a violent scene at the Walkers' place, witnesses a coldblooded murder—but just now it got serious?

"What the fuck do you mean you've got nothing?"

He sits behind his massive desk, looking out at his sprawling ranch just outside Austin, his knuckles white around the phone.

"She's a fucking secretary. How far can she go?"

He grinds his jaw listening to the man on the other end. "If she's disappeared, you fucking find her, you moron. That information gets out, it's millions if not billions down the drain and my ass is on the line. I'm gonna fucking hold you personally responsible... You know exactly what I mean. Time is of the

*essence. You have a week or I'll send someone else... Damn right."
He slams the phone down on the desk, and tosses back the glass
of fifty-year-old Chivas Regal like it's plain tap water.*

*Those incompetent idiots had burst into that motherfucking
traitor, Vedica's office, like a bunch of Keystone cops. They shot
the idiot and grabbed whatever they could find on the land deals,
instead of torching the damn place to burn whatever evidence
that prick had amassed, like they were supposed to. Claimed the
computer was clean but was displaying a pop-up screen alerting
that an external drive had been removed incorrectly. Vedica
must've made copies before deleting everything from the hard
drive. No disk or flash drive was found in the office, which can
only mean he'd already handed it over to someone.*

*The man's only living relative, a sister, is clueless, but we're
keeping an eye on her mail delivery. That little bitch however—
the one who was working in his office until the day my boys paid
him a visit. The one who was less than forthcoming on the phone,
when he went off grid in San Antonio. That one might know
something. The fact that she can't be found tells me she does
know something. Now our job is to get to her—and fast.*

CHAPTER TWELVE

Kim

"I'll see you in the hot tub in a few," Emma calls out as Katie and I make our way down to the pool level.

I couldn't believe the luxury of the three-bedroom timeshare Gus managed to snag for us. A complex with three separate buildings. The main one held the lobby—the tallest of the three—and offered three different outdoor pool levels flanked by the second building and a smaller one that had its own pool and hot tub surrounded by gigantic palm trees. That's where we were staying.

When the Vegas trip had gone into overdrive at the insistence of Mal and his boss, I really had no time to think. On Mal's instructions, I packed, while he called Kerry and got her up to speed. She would meet us in Vegas on Wednesday as scheduled and I was surprised to find that GFI had even arranged a flight for her so she didn't have to drive by herself. These guys didn't mess around.

Going over to my place after, under the cloak of darkness, to find it in shambles was not a fun experience. Again, under Mal's steady lead, it was dealt with quickly, having found nothing missing. My work computer and laptop were both at Beth's house in Cedar Tree. Other than leaving a house that would take days to straighten out and a front door that needed replacing, there wasn't much I could do right then.

This morning after a surprisingly restful sleep, perhaps because I knew Mal was sleeping in the guest room, I woke up to the sound of the shower. Burrowed under the blankets, and still lazy with sleep, I didn't stop my mind from visualizing what he would look like with his long hair wet and loose around his strong angular face, and water sliding down the hard planes of his body. All I had to go by is that same body fully dressed, but the promise of what's underneath was enough to have me clench my thighs under the covers. Before I gave in to the urge to slip my fingers between them, I flicked back the blankets and resolutely got out of bed, banning all thoughts of the tall, olive-skinned beautiful man currently naked just a thin wall away. By the time I had coffee ready, he walked into the kitchen, hair wet but tied back and completely dressed. Dammit. He was no less tempting like that and before the blush that crept up into my cheeks became too visible, I darted around him with a quick 'morning' and aimed for the stairs. Two steps up, an arm snaked around my middle and I was turned around, my hands grabbing onto his shoulders for balance. Dark smoldering eyes with a sparkle of amusement met mine.

"Running?" The rumble of his deep voice sounded good in the morning and I squirmed a little.

"I have to get dressed, and I still need to... um, shower."

The humor in his eyes was immediately replaced by something more intense, and a hell of a lot hotter. A low growl coming from deep in his chest sent a shiver up my spine.

"Hard enough standing in the hot spray trying not to imagine you sprawled in bed just a few feet away. Fucking impossible not to think of you, naked and covered in soapsuds." Another groan, this one pained, escaped his lips as he leaned forward to rest his forehead against mine. "Better head up there, baby. Before I take you right here on the stairs."

I was absolutely paralyzed and even the hard press of hot lips to my forehead before he turned and walked into the kitchen barely registered. Yet the moment his back disappeared, I whipped around and ran up the stairs.

I barely looked at him the rest of the morning as he loaded my case into his truck and we drove over to pick up Katie and Emma at her place. Transferring all the bags into a huge Yukon belonging to Gus, who is apparently driving us to the Durango airport, took all of two minutes. Before I knew it, it was time to say goodbye. I was ready to climb in the backseat and leave with only a wave, when Mal grabbed my wrist and pulled me toward the house, telling Gus over his shoulder, "Gimme a minute." Once inside he dragged me into the bathroom and closed the door behind him. My hands grabbed the counter behind me in an attempt to hold me up. My traitorous knees threatened to buckle as my heart pounded an erratic rhythm in my chest. I guess I looked scared, because the look on his face morphed from a scary dark intensity to a much softer version. Cupping my face in his hands his forehead landed on mine again. "Promise you'll be careful and listen to Katie," he whispered, his breath fanning my face, smelling of toothpaste and coffee.

"Y-yes," my voice croaked.

"Need a taste of that mouth before you go, *Nizhóní*," he said before dipping his head down and licking—*licking*—the crease of my mouth. So warm and wet, my lips opened on instinct to allow him inside. I don't know what I expected, perhaps a sudden invasion of my mouth, but not the sweet stroke of his tip along the inside of my lips. Not the gentle probing caress of him against my tongue, luring me into languid play. It felt like

I'd stopped breathing, the mechanics of it had left me along with everything else in my mind. The warmth that spread through me at the tenderness of his touch, brought tears to my eyes.

Good God, I'm drowning.

By the time his mouth pulled back, I was gasping for air. His cheeks were ruddy and from the ragged breaths he pulled in, I could tell he was affected too.

"That was a mistake."

Everything inside me froze at those dreaded words, although why they surprised me I don't know. I was ready to push past him to get out the door, but his next words stopped me. And confused me even more.

"It only makes me crave more," he mumbled before pulling open the door. Taking my hand in his, he led me back outside, past Gus who was looking up with a smirk on his face. Mal got me settled beside Katie in the backseat. Who, by the way, was sporting a similar smile on hers.

"You're miles away," Katie says and I open my eyes to find her staring at me. That smile still on her face half a day later. Submersed to our necks in the softly bubbling hot tub, I take a minute to appreciate the cool night air and the surprisingly crisp Vegas sky.

"Mmmm." I opt for a wordless response, cause really— what can I say?

"Did you know Malachi helped deliver my Mattias?" she asks, taking me by surprise. No, I had no idea. More layers to this intriguing man. I shake my head in response.

"He did. Along with Naomi and Caleb. It was unexpected and very fast, but Mal kept a cooler head than my husband." She smiles at the memory before turning to me and her face softens. "He's a good man, Kim. He may look dark and have a hint of danger around him, but despite the tragedies and mistakes in his life, he's the real deal."

"Why are you telling me this?"

"Because I've seen you together only twice and each time you look at him I see a combination of heat and fear in your face. I don't know you well enough to judge where that fear is coming from, but I do know that Mal is the last person to deserve that. He deserves a chance."

A chance?

Despite the butterflies dancing in my stomach, I'm determined to let reason do the talking.

"I don't think we're at all compatible. I mean, look at him; he is in a different league. Maybe he sees me as a nice diversion, but ultimately I don't think I'm really his type." Katie surprises me when she throws her head back and laughs heartily, just as Emma pushes her walker to the edge of the hot tub.

"What's funny?" she asks as she uses the railings on the stairs to help her down in the water.

"Kim thinks she's not Mal's type." Katie snorts and my mouth falls open when Emma chuckles right along with her. These women are nuts.

"I went shopping with her yesterday, and I can confirm that the woman is clueless when it comes to valuing herself."

I honestly don't know whether to be embarrassed, insulted or shocked.

"Honey," Emma says grabbing one of my hands and clasping it between hers. "It's clear to me you see yourself in a much different light than the rest of the world does. Including Malachi. For all intents and purposes, that man has claimed you as his. It's clear to everyone but you."

My eyes flick from her face to Katie's who nods in agreement, but Emma's not done.

"That little bit of yourself you shared yesterday was enough to paint a pretty clear picture. It speaks volumes about why a pretty girl like you would have such a warped body image and be so insecure about her own appeal. My guess is your mom is tall and never carried an extra ounce of weight?"

Surprised at the accuracy of her guess, I blurt out, "My older sister looks just like her."

"Right." Katie grimaces.

I don't know if it is the relaxing hot tub, the fact that apparently my safety is in question, these inquisitive women who don't shy away at asking real questions, or a combination of all of it. They seem intent on picking at my defenses, albeit in the kindest possible way, and so I just keep talking. I tell them about growing up with a 'perfect' mother and sister, being constantly chastised for my weight, my laziness. I tell them about Dad who was sweet but weak. I even tell them about my endless doctor's visits, trying to find a medical reason for the pain and fatigue I'd lived with since I could remember. I shrug my shoulders, pretending the constant put-downs and doubts by my family and the medical community didn't affect me. It's obvious they don't believe me and I'm oddly grateful for that show of sisterhood.

"I hadn't seen a doctor in years when my friend Kerry convinced me to see Naomi," I tell them.

"She's wonderful," Katie says convincingly. "She was pivotal in my recovery from a brain injury. She is amazing with Mattias and will take good care of you. I promise." She looks at me sincerely.

"I know, I've already seen her twice."

"Yeah?" This from Emma who is still hanging on to my hand.

"She thinks she may have an answer."

"That's amazing!"

"Yeah. Maybe... I'm not sure. I'll need more tests," I volunteer, not sure whether I want to address this here—now.

"What kind of tests?" Katie asks, her forehead creased.

"An MRI, the week after we get back." I take a reinforcing sip of my wine. "The ultrasound of my thyroid showed a shadow they want a better look at." The fear of what they might find has been tucked away deeply. Years of doctors, specialists and testing does that to you. You could live your entire life paralyzed by what ifs if you let it consume you. So I stomp it back down, each time it threatens to surface. Except I can't seem to push it back now. Not with a few glasses of wine, a hot tub and genuinely compassionate women to soften me.

"It could be just that, a shadow," Emma suggests but I can see in her eyes she is worried. I don't even make an effort this time to battle the tears.

"So you see, even if I would allow myself to dream a man like Malachi could honestly have an interest in me, I can't. It's almost easier to think he's only copping an occasional feel to change up what I'm sure is his usual fare of slim beauties. With so much uncertainty, hope just hurts."

"I guess he doesn't know, then? You haven't told him?"

I turn to Katie, a little confused. She sounds almost angry. I haven't told him anything, really. So I shake my head.

"It's just easier."

"For who? You? Because I can guarantee it won't be easier for him."

"Why?" I want to know but this time Katie shakes her head.

"It's not my story to share, but please trust me on this, if there's even a remote chance you might be seriously ill, you have to tell him." With that Katie gets up out of the tub and grabs a towel.

Emma finally lets go of my hand, but not before giving it a reassuring squeeze. "She's right, you know. He should have the right to be there for you."

Not sure how to respond to that, I get out of the tub as well. "I think I'm going to bed. It's been a long day." I take the cowardly way out and with the big towel wrapped around me, I grab my room key and flee the hint of disapproval in the air.

Mal

"Drew just called," Neil says as I walk into the conference room at the GFI offices.

"Yeah?"

"Rental came from Durango Airport. Avis car rentals. They actually had a credit card on file. They won't rent without one."

"Whose is it?"

"Company name, Hart Holdings." He smirks at me, obviously pleased with himself over something.

"Yeah? Should that mean something to me?" I impatiently bite off.

"It might, if you'd have gone over those damn files on that flash drive ten thousand times like I have. Hart Holdings was on two separate documents in the small print. And..." He lifts one eyebrow to dramatic heights. "The only thing I was able to find out about Hart Holdings is a post office box."

"And that is why you're excited?" I ask him pointedly.

"The post office box is located in Austin, Texas," he says smugly, as the puzzle starts to slowly take shape. "And Hart is spelled without an 'e.' "

"You're saying—"

"I'm saying it seems more than just a coincidence that the one name that's jumped out at us from the start is one Jacob Hartnett—without an 'e'—and his main residence is 60 miles outside of Austin, Texas."

Adrenaline spikes my blood and I point my finger in Neil's grinning face. "Dig, pretty boy. Dig fucking deep. There's gotta be something tangible to tie him in. Payments, previous cases of forceful land transfers; follow the money. I'd bet my left nut that he's behind this."

"Feel free to hang on to your nuts. I've got a fully functioning pair myself, thank you very much." He's still smiling when he turns his back on me and starts furiously tapping the keyboard of his laptop. Leaving him to do what he's good at, I head over to Gus's office to make a call.

I haven't talked to Kim since Sunday morning when I kissed her knees weak of her in the small bathroom down this same hall, but she's never been far from my mind. I purposely have gotten updates from Katie, instead of directly calling. From the sounds of it Kim has opened up a little with the women and although I'm glad she's opening up, something Katie said gave me pause. A remark made in a flippant way, but I know Katie well enough to hear the underlying concern. Something about hurrying up the case because Kim had to be back for Thursday next week. An important appointment on April twenty-eighth. It was slipped into the conversation in such a way it shouldn't have stuck, but it did. I'm an investigator. I'm trained to notice hairs out of place, and April twenty-eighth stuck up like a damn hair out of place. Did she have a job interview? Meeting someone important to her? I don't know and don't much like being out of the loop of anything to do with Kim's life. I was already uneasy about her going to Vegas when from what I gather, something pretty significant went wrong there for her. I was surprised she wanted to go back there after all these years, but her wanting to leave town for even a few days had seemed like a good way to get her out of harm's way. I needed to focus and work to get her safe on a more permanent basis, and her mere presence proved to be very distracting for me. The unease was back in full force, however. I've survived forty-two years relying on my instincts and right now they were sending up red flags everywhere.

Gus is not in his office and I slip behind his desk and pull out my cell.

"Hello?"

"Kimeo," I say simply.

"Hey Mal," she replies softly, a hint of a smile in her voice. Enough to make the ball of tension sitting on my chest release a bit.

"Having a good time, baby?"

"I am, but I miss Boo."

"Just Boo? He's fine. He's taken to sleeping on the bed with me. You never told me he's a cuddler."

The sound of her laughter does something to me and I feel a responding smile cracking my face.

"He is, but he's got a bad case of morning breath," she jokes.

"No shit. I opened my eyes this morning to his head on your pillow and almost passed out when I caught a whiff."

"My pillow?" she asks softly.

"Master bed is bigger, babe. I like to stretch out. Besides, until the dog decided to join me last night, it smelled of you."

"Oh." Her voice sounds breathless and a little surprised.

Wanting nothing more than to keep the conversation going in this direction, the faster I get my answers, the faster I can get her safe and in that big master bed beside me. Fuck the dog.

"Have you heard the name Jacob Hartnett before? Texan?" I jump right in.

"Yes I have,"Kim says, surprise evident in her voice. "He left a few messages for Martin when we couldn't find him. Was quite persistent too, seemed very eager to find out where he might be. Why? Has he shown up at the office? I'd looked for any kind of agreement with him after we picked up the office files, thinking I should probably let him know what happened, but there was nothing. No contract, no notes and I couldn't find the message slip I'd left for Martin to call him back."

I let her ramble on while the puzzle pieces slide home in my head. Along with the excitement over our having confirmation now, comes the realization that Kim holds a real threat for

Hartnett. It's not just the files on the flash drive he's wanting to get rid of, it's Kim herself.

She's been witness to too much and it would appear she's the only one who can confirm his personal connection to Vedica. She's in even more danger than I thought.

CHAPTER THIRTEEN

Kim

I'm giddy.

I don't know if it was the conversation with Mal this afternoon or the two glasses of wine we had earlier, sitting at the bar by the pool, but I find myself putting a lot of effort into getting dolled up tonight. At Emma's insistence I pull out the black dress. She was thrilled to find I brought it with me and I have a suspicion she planned a fancy night out, simply so she could get me to wear it.

I feel fantastic, despite the fact the fabric is skimmed tight over my chest, the light flare of the skirt underneath seems to hide most of my flaws. I leave my hair down and spritz some of my favorite Light Blue by D&G in the air in front of me before walking through the mist. I almost convince myself it isn't because Mal mentioned 'my smell' on the pillow that I pull out the Light Blue.

"You look amazing!" Katie blurts out behind me and my eyes find hers in the mirror. "Holy shitballs, Mal would have a coronary if he could see you. Wait, let me take a picture." She runs out of the bathroom, leaving me in a state of panic. I don't do pictures, I hate them. Hate looking at myself in them. But before I can make up a decent excuse, Katie's back with her cellphone, snapping shot after shot from behind me.

"Uhhh, I'm sure you don't need pictures of my ass, do you?" I point out, to which she has a ready response.

"Ass, hair, and in the reflection in the mirror, your gorgeous face and tits. Man would I kill for a rack like that."

"A rack like what?" Emma's voice sounds from behind Katie, as she tries to peek over her shoulder.

"Check Kim out here. She's rockin' her LBD," Katie says, stepping aside to let Emma in.

"Amazing."

Emma's soft words and little smile fill me with warmth. Both her and Katie have dressed up too. Katie is wearing a wrap around dress with short sleeves and a full skirt, while Emma is looking positively Bohemian with her floral tunic over black leggings and the cutest little orange flats on her feet.

"Dresses and heels do not play well with my walker," she explains. "I gave those up a while ago. These days I aim for *interesting* rather than pretty.

"Well you're more than interesting—you look stunning. Both of you do." I smile at these women who have made me forget everything these last few days. Well, almost everything. After my escape from the hot tub that first night, any tension disappeared with the morning sun the next day. We've had a blast and I can't wait for Kerry to get here. She's set to arrive tomorrow, but tonight Emma has made reservations at Tao, an Asian restaurant and club at the Venetian. She wants the full experience there including taking a gondola ride. Yesterday was a quick look through Caesar's Palace, then we hit the Bellagio with the gorgeous Murano glass ceilings in the lobby, and we ended up outside on the pathway along the manmade lake where we stood for an hour and a half and watched the fountain show three times. Emma is like a kid at Disney and it's fun to experience Vegas through her eyes. Much has changed over the past twelve years, but the anything-and-everything-is-possible atmosphere is as strong as ever. Some time ago I had thought that would be true of Vegas for me.

Looking at my lonely Kindle staying behind on the kitchen counter, I pull the door shut behind us and follow the girls for a night on the town. With a line up of taxis already waiting by the front lobby, it takes us all of five minutes to get dropped off at the Venetian. The sound of slot machines is almost deafening, even just in passing on our way to the elevators that will take us to the second floor where Tao is located. Emma is in front and after she tells the hostess we have a reservation, we are immediately led to a reasonably quiet booth.

"Your server will be right with you," the friendly tattooed girl with a pink and auburn pixie haircut says as she hands out menus.

I'm engrossed in the food on offer, mentally calculating calories as I skim the ingredients, when someone approaches the table and starts speaking. A voice I recognize, even after all these years.

"Hi, my name is Mia and I'll be your server tonight. Can I get you ladies started with a drink?"

I freeze instantly, my mind trying to grasp the fact that fate is cruel enough to place her in my path. What are the odds? Last thing I knew she was working at the Bellagio. If anything we could've bumped into her there. I certainly would've been less surprised. Even kept half an eye out. Finally I look up and as I watch her, Mia smiles around the table before her eyes snap back to me and get big. For a second, all I think is how fast I can get out of here, but then I watch her face change from surprise to guilt before shutting down completely.

"I'll have a white wine, please," I manage, pretending to be cool as a cucumber, but shaking inside—not wanting to spoil the night with a scene.

"I...uhh...sweet or dry?" she stammers and I find myself getting a small amount of satisfaction from the fact my presence is rankling her.

I smile and ask for dry before diving right back into my menu as the others place their drink orders. This may be one of those unique times where I have an opportunity to kill with kindness. It's not usually my way to face a possible uncomfortable situation head on, but the last few days with these women have been so much fun, I don't want a blast from the past spoiling our fun nights. I convince myself it has nothing to do with the fact that I happily partook in a little pre-drinking at the condo before we left.

"Who was that? Do you know her?" Katie hisses at me across the table as Mia walks away with our drink orders.

My response is to snort. "You can say I know her well. Well enough to tell you her boobs are fake and she wears the same size shoe I do." The confusion on their faces is priceless and I burst out laughing. "Mia once professed herself my best friend. Of course I believed her until I found my boyfriend banging her on his couch on my birthday. The birthday she had earlier insisted on wanting to celebrate with me. I didn't stick around long enough to find out whether she'd always intended on Peter to be a part of the celebration, but I didn't really care to find out at the time."

"Ohhh, this is gonna be interesting, seeing karma in action," Katie says with a pleased little smile, but Emma still seems to be in shock.

"She did what? Oh hell no. When she comes back I'll tell her exactly—" She's virtually steaming from the ears before Katie cuts her off.

"I'm thinking Kim's got this one, Emma. No violence needed."

By the time Mia comes back with our drinks, her mask is back in place and she continues to pretend she doesn't know me. I let her, smiling big when she sets my wineglass in front of me. "Thanks, Mia. I think we need a few more minutes with the menu, if you don't mind?"

Her lips draw in a straight line. "Of course," she forces through her tight smile and walks away.

"I know what I want," Emma says.

"Me too." This from Katie who had already collected Emma's menu and along with hers, stacked them at the end of the table.

"I know," I say, feeling for once in absolute control with my little black dress on, my face and hair done up and two *real* friends by my side. "I just wanted her to come back to the table that one extra time."

This time it's Katie who busts out laughing, Emma not far behind and I can't hold back a smile myself.

"You are positively evil."

"Remind me never to piss you off."

I just shrug and play with my menu some more. When I see Mia tend to a table next to ours I wave her over. She's not happy, as is evident from the dirty look she sends me.

"Are you ready to order?"

"I think we are," Emma says, still snickering, while placing her order. Katie is next and I'm left for last. Perfect.

"So, *Mia*," I say her name with emphasis after I give her my order and she's about to walk away. "How *is* Peter?"

Her body stiffens, her face pales and I'm instantly regretting calling her out. I've experienced it enough myself to recognize the hit of a painful blow. "I don't know," she bites out. "He didn't—"

I cut her off with my hand up. "I'm sorry. That wasn't nice of me. Forget I said anything."

"No," she says softly. "I'm the one who's sorry. I can't even blame it on him. He was a dick, albeit a charming one. I don't regret causing you to get rid of his ass, since it's obvious you have found bigger and better places. But I betrayed you in the worst possible way. Don't even know what I was thinking. I realized it that moment, on that day and it was already too late to do a damn thing about it." With that she turns and takes our dinner orders with her.

"Well," Katie pipes up after we collectively watch her go, her shoulders slumped. "That sure didn't have any of the fireworks I was expecting."

"I feel sorry for her," I say, watching as the other two swing their gazes at me.

"Say what?"

"I mean, she's right. I did go on to bigger and better things, even though I'm technically unemployed right now. I own a nice house, drive a car that's only four years old and well-maintained and I have good friends. She doesn't look like she's that lucky."

Our food is served by another waitress and we don't see Mia the rest of the three hours we're there. I manage to eat most of mine, which is a small victory in itself, but after we pay our bill and the girls are ready to hit the club, I'm suddenly hit with overwhelming fatigue.

"Guys, I'm gonna head back to the condo. I'm wiped. Why don't you guys go on ahead?"

"Can't," Katie says, "I'm supposed to be here looking after you—not painting the town while you walk the streets alone."

Without warning a large hand clamps on my shoulder.

"I've got her."

Mal

It had taken me less than five minutes to make up my mind. Another five to track Gus down and get his support. It took me longer than that to gather up Boo and his stuff, and pack a bag for myself. Luckily Boo and my brother's dog Blue hit it off right away when I dropped him off.

It had taken me all of half an hour to get sorted and on the road. The trip that would take any normal person at least seven and a half hours to make, took me six. This is one of those times when having a gadget geek for a colleague pays off big time. With Neil's 'upgrades' to my truck it was easy to steer clear of any speed traps. A good thing since I was doing at least eighty miles an hour for most of the trip.

By air it would've taken me at least as long. Also would've been easier to track.

When I get to Vegas, I head straight for the condo, but when I check my missed messages quickly before getting out of the car, I spot one from Katie that came through about three-and-a-half hours ago. A picture and a message.

This girl is smokin'. Should draw some attention at Tao.

When I pull up the image, my mouth goes dry. Kim with her hair all shiny and big around her pretty face and her body perfectly displayed in a black dress that looks fucking amazing on her. Katie must've taken the picture in the bathroom. Kim is leaning forward doing something to her face and the reflection in the mirror shows her curvy front, and with the shot coming from behind, I have an even better view of her splendid ass.

I immediately toss my phone in the console, start the car and turn toward the Venetian.

I have no trouble spotting the three of them as they stand right outside the restaurant chatting. The only one spotting me is Katie, but like the trained operative she is, her only 'tell' is a slight pull at the corner of her mouth. Oh yes, my sister-in-law is playing some game. She knew exactly the impact that snapshot would have. _Minx._

"I've got her," I say as I sneak up behind Kim and put my hand on her shoulder. She smells fucking fantastic when I lean in and stick my nose in her hair. She stiffens at my touch, but I can tell the moment she realizes it's me, her entire body seems to relax prior to turning around with a big smile on her face. I let my eyes roam her body up and down, before coming to rest on her face.

"Never had cause to complain before, but babe, tonight you look especially stunning."

A deep blush appears on her cheeks and she looks at the floor, but with a little smile still lingering.

"Something wrong?" Emma says once she gets over her shock of seeing me here.

"Not a thing. Decided it's been a long damn time since I've been in Vegas."

Lame excuse, but I only wanted to make it very clear that I'm not gonna talk here on the sidewalk inside the Venetian. A message both Emma and Katie seem to receive loud and clear.

"You guys go have some fun. I'll take Kim back."

"You sure?" Katie directs the question more at Kim than at me. When she nods, Katie gives her a quick hug as does Emma, before they head off.

Despite outward appearances, as fine as they are, Kim does look tired. She also doesn't object when I put my arm around her shoulders and start walking her toward the valet station.

Once inside my truck, she doesn't hesitate to turn to me. "What's wrong?"

So deceptively docile, she is, but her perceptions and instincts are sharp. I tell her the truth.

"A combination of things. Mostly because I'd feel better if I could keep my eye on you myself. Especially after our call earlier this afternoon. Seemed like a good enough excuse to come check on you."

Her mouth twitches as she tries to hold on to a smile. I'm glad I have that effect on her and I hate bursting her bubble.

"See, after you told me you'd actually spoken to Hartnett on the phone, I realized we may have underestimated the threat you pose to him. Jacob Hartnett is a very powerful man. He is one of the largest Texas oil barons, but with the least scruples. He's used to getting what he sets his sights on and doesn't mind paying whatever the cost to make sure that happens."

I see a light dawning in her eyes. "He's behind the land deals. I'm guessing he was the one Martin was meeting with in Texas when he disappeared. You think something went wrong at the meeting?" She looks at me expectantly like I hold all the answers, but her guess is as good as mine.

"Looks that way. Vedica made a mistake coming back to the office because they obviously had been keeping an eye out. Tracked him down quickly and killed him in an attempt to get rid of loose ends. Only thing is, if they haven't already, they will soon realize you are another loose end."

I pull back into the same spot outside the condo building, turn the engine off and turn in my seat just in time to see Kim take a big swallow.

"That's not good news," she says looking solemn.

"It is and it isn't. Yes, he's powerful but now that we have confirmed his connection to Vedica, we know what we're up against. Drew is calling in the FBI. I've no doubt they would've swarmed in at some point, considering what we're dealing with, but with Drew beating them to the punch, it becomes more of a collaborative effort than a turf war. In the meantime, my focus becomes keeping you safe until they can pin him down."

"Haven't you been doing that from the start?" she points out smartly, making me smile.

"Yes. But now I get to devote all my time to it." The implication is thick and she gets it. Gives it away with the sharp inhale of air and the quick look down at her hands.

I slip out of the truck and move to the passenger side to let her out, craving the opportunity to put my hands on her to help her down. Her body is so soft and warm, I can't resist wrapping my arm around her waist and pressing her against the door. With the back of my fingers I stroke the skin of her cheek.

"So soft," I murmur. "Every bit of skin I've touched on you so far has been softer than anything I know. Can't wait to explore every last inch."

Her eyes grow large at my hungry words, and I'm sure the raging hard-on pressing into her belly is not going unnoticed either. I lean in for a taste of her mouth, but before I have a chance to explore too deeply, someone clears their throat nearby. I look up to see an elderly couple patiently waiting to get into their car. The one parked right beside my truck.

With a smile of apology, I move from between the vehicles, pulling Kim along with me.

"Where is Boo?" she finally asks as we step into the elevator.

"With Caleb at his place. He's got a big mutt, Blue. I thought the two might get along. Seem to be so far."

"Blue?"

"Actually Katie's dog. Walked up to their house a stray and he kind of adopted Katie. Has proven to be very protective of her and Mattias. He is very alpha, which didn't seem to bother

Boo much. I'm sorry to say, your dog rolled over on his back the moment those two met. Totally submissive."

Kim giggles out loud, despite the hand she puts over her mouth. Love that joyful, unrestricted sound. When the elevator doors open, I grab her hand and walk her to the door, where she stops. Pulling her hand from mine, she starts digging through her purse for the key card. I reach around and take it out of her hand, sliding it in the lock and pushing the door open.

Without a word, she drops her purse on the dining room table, and turns around to face me.

"Do you want a drink? We don't have beer, only wine. Or coffee? I could make some coffee." She wrings her hands nervously as she slips past me into the kitchen.

I don't let her get far before I come up behind her and cage her in between my arms leaning on the counter. With my head bent down I breathe in the scent of her, my lips skimming the shell of her ear. I can feel a shiver running down her body.

"Turn around, *Nizhóní*."

Her body turns slowly, before her luminous eyes make it all the way up to mine. I make no effort to hide the hunger I feel for her and I can see a touch of fear and a whole lot of uncertainty in her face. But the moment her small white teeth bite down on her bottom lip, I put my hands under her arms and lift her on the counter. As her eyes widen in surprise, I put my hands on the outside of her knees, pushing her dress up as I go. Her skin is so fucking soft and smooth. Wedging my hips between her legs, my hands find her luscious ass and I press my hips into her heat at the same time my mouth slams down on hers. A small sound of protest escapes her but in the next instant her hands come up and curl around my neck. The small grunts she makes in the back of her throat drive me wild. So fucking responsive. I can feel her nipples pebble against my chest. I revel in the feel of the soft stroke of her tongue against mine, the lush flesh of her ass pliant in my hands. I have to have her. With one hand on her ass, I bring the other around to stroke over her thigh up to the slick evidence of her arousal.

"God," I pull my mouth from hers, "you are so ready for me." I look down and watch my two fingers slide inside her tight channel and pull away slick. "Lean back," I tell her before pulling her ass to the edge of the counter and sinking down to my knees. In one swift move I have her panties down her legs and her feet propped up on my shoulders, her shoes discarded on the floor beside me. The view is fantastic. The trimmed patch of soft dark hair stark above the flushed deep pink of her pussy. Her scent is even better and I lean in to have my first taste.

CHAPTER FOURTEEN

*"There is nothing as eloquent as a
rattlesnake's tail."*

~ Navajo

Kim

"Mal..."

His name slips from my mouth when the heat of his tongue touches me. My feet are up on his shoulder and my knees fall open wide when he presses the inside of my thighs with his hands. His thumbs spread me open and the long rasp of his tongue along my crease, just shy of my clit has my back arc up off the counter. Another stroke, firmer, this one also stopping just short.

"You're delicious," he mumbles as he licks me a third time, but this time he flicks just the tip of his tongue over the little bundle of nerves, already screaming for his attention. My thighs clench around his head, my clit already almost too sensitive to the touch.

How did I go from zero to a hundred in an instant? I've never enjoyed oral. Not on me and not by me. But I'm starting to think it wasn't in the experience but in the execution, because this is fucking phenomenal. I feel a sense of abandon, lying here spread out like a banquet while this gorgeous man feasts on me. The two fingers he slides back in stretch me to the edge of painful. Only for an instant though, before his lips and tongue flicking and sucking my clit bring me back from that edge. I've read about G-spots and only had an abstract idea until his fingers curl inside me and press up. It's like a magic button. With the strong tug of his mouth, and his fingers' firm pressure, I come apart. My vision blurs and my head is light as my hips inadvertently twist and jerk against his persistent mouth.

"My God..." I manage, barely coherent. When I look down between my legs, his dark obsidian eyes are watching me.

"Fucking glorious, watching you come apart for me."

With a simple kiss between my legs, he stands up, wraps my legs around his hips, and with his hands firmly clasping my ass, lifts me up.

"I'm too heavy," I protest, grabbing on to his shoulders.

"Which one is yours," he growls, not responding to my words, but simply carrying me in the direction I wave my hand. The door is open and he walks right over to the bed where he gently lays me back. I instinctively close my legs and roll protectively on my side, but he won't have it.

"Do not hide yourself. I think your body is fucking amazing—don't you dare hide it from me," he says as he turns back to shut the door.

Well. Okay then. I try not to think about how I must look to him when I roll to my back, my jelly belly on full display. My attention is immediately drawn to him. He stands by my feet, looking at me like a starving man and I'm the last slice of bread in the basket. Without taking his eyes off me, he grabs the edge of his T-shirt and whips it over his head, pulling his hair tie out along with it. His almost black hair falls around his shoulders. He looks magnificent. Strong angular features, dark arched eyebrows and a slight bump halfway up the bridge of his shapely nose, nicely shaped full lips and a square jaw down to the strong column of his neck. I let my eyes drift lower and take in the wide shoulders and muscular arms, the tattoo of three arrows pointing up to his shoulder and a tribal band around his arm. I focus lower, on the ridges of his abdomen and the fine dusting of hair narrowing toward where his hands are working on the buttons of his fly. With swift movements he pushes his jeans and boxer briefs over his hips, pulling a condom from the pocket as he shoves them down his legs. I can't help my gasp when his formidable cock is released. As strong and long as his physique, it juts out from his body proudly, like the man. A bead of pre-come visible at the tip and I inadvertently lick my lips. He tosses the condom packet on the bed beside me.

"Uhh..." I mumble when he sets a knee in the bed, coming toward me. "Don't know if that will fit."

One side of his mouth tilts up into a cocky little smile. "Oh, it will fit. Don't you worry." His movements are predatory and I'm not sure if I shouldn't be feeling a little concern. Damn.

Sitting back on his calves, he pulls me up to a sitting position before finding the zipper to my dress, which is bunched up around my waist.

"You can leave that," I try, but again, my protests go unheard. Instead, he pulls the dress over my head and off. And just like that, I'm sitting, buck-assed naked across from this virtual God.

"Lay back, *nizhóní*," he says softly, mesmerizing me.

"*Nizo*... whatever. You've called me that before, what does it mean?"

"*Nizhóní,* it means beautiful. Not just a description, but more a concept. Now, Beauty, I believe I told you to lay back. Let me look my fill before I bury myself inside you."

With a little shiver at his words, I do as he asks. Even if he hadn't just called me beautiful, the expression on his face is clearly one of appreciation. He reaches out a hand, spreads his fingers wide and drags them from my hairline, gently down my face, over my chin and neck, between my breasts and over the soft swell of my belly to the hair between my legs.

"Open for me," he whispers, barely making a sound and without thinking I find myself opening wide.

In that moment I would do anything he asked. I'm so entranced by his focus, his words, his touch. With legs open, eyes open and my heart open as well, I watch him roll on the condom before lowering himself on top of me.

Ahh, the feel of his skin against mine. So incredible. My arms immediately go around his shoulders and my fingers tangle in his long strands. His mouth takes mine and when his tongue slips inside, I can still taste myself on him. The blunt head of his cock teases my slick entrance before slowly advancing inside. The stretch burns and I inhale sharply through my nose.

"Relax honey, let me inside. Trust me," he mumbles against my mouth. I let my legs fall open wider and slowly breathe out as he slides in. All the way in.

He's careful, very gentle when he first starts moving inside me, but despite having come minutes before, I quickly become restless.

"Please, Mal, I need to... Harder, please," I plead with him, needing more. My hands grab on to his firm ass, encouraging his movement.

He slips an arm around my back, pushing me up the bed against the headboard, stuffing a pillow under my ass.

"Brace yourself." Is all he says before grabbing the back of my knees and pulling my legs around his hips. With one of his arms propped up against the headboard, the other hand guides his cock as he slams home, balls slapping against my skin. The pace is fierce, furious, and I find myself bracing both hands above my head, bucking my hips in tandem with his. Sweat glistens from his face to his chest, showing the straining tendons in his neck.

"Close," I breathe, "so close..."

The moment his thumb presses on my clit, he takes my mouth in a plundering kiss, swallowing my cry of release. His own movements become erratic and ripping his lips from mine, he throws his head back and roars out his own orgasm.

Absolute beauty.

Mal

"Stay," I mumble when Kim tries to slip out of bed. "Too early."

Actually, a quick glance at the clock shows it's seven in the morning. After we both came hard last night, fatigue took over and she'd been asleep on my chest in minutes. It had taken me a lot longer, listening to hear deep breathing, my fingers trailing up and down over her soft skin, until I finally dozed off well after I heard Katie and Emma come in.

I sit up, wrap my arms around her midsection and pull her back down on me.

"Mal, I need coffee," she mutters, struggling a little but without much conviction. I flip us, so she is on her back and I'm half on her, my leg keeping hers trapped and my head up on my elbow so I can look at her. With daylight filtering in, I'm able to take in the tousled hair, slightly swollen eyelids that give her a sultry look and a red spot on one cheek, from sleeping on it. She lies perfectly still while I let my eyes wander to her ample breasts, pink tips tightening under my scrutiny. I can see the moment she tries to suck in her stomach and I guess it's instinctive for her, but I don't like it. Putting my hand on the soft pillow of her belly, I look back to her face.

"I like this belly. I like how it welcomes my body when I rest on you. Love how my fingers can sink into your flesh, making me feel like we're melding. You're soft and round all over, in perfect contrast with my angles and hard lines. Nothing I would change about you. Not a thing."

I see her swallow down her reaction before she visibly relaxes under me, her big shiny eyes on mine when she starts talking.

"I'm ashamed that I'm ashamed of my body. Does that even make sense? I mean, I was raised to believe it was a shameful thing to be bigger than average. It's all I've known. Even as an adult I equated success with slim people and failure with fat ones."

I don't bother rejecting that notion, because it's ludicrous.

"I'm starting to understand that makes me as judgmental as anyone out there." Her eyes trail off to the side and for a moment I think I've lost her to her thoughts, but then they snap back to me. "When I left Vegas twelve years ago, I'd just found my boyfriend and my best friend naked on the couch in his apartment. On my birthday. He said some things that hammered home what my mother had been telling me for years. It didn't help Mia was tall and svelte and gorgeous. Her betrayal was almost worse than his."

"What's his name?" I find myself grinding out through clenched teeth, but Kim just chuckles, lifting her hand and stroking my face. Soothing.

"He doesn't matter. But I did see Mia last night. She pretended not to know me but since she was our waitress it was difficult for her to keep the act up. Especially after I made it clear I remember her quite well. All these years I'd been thinking that the pretty girl won. And all this time she'd been thinking I was the lucky one. Ironic, isn't it?"

"Is that why you didn't want to go out after?" I ask, lazily stroking her stomach.

"No. Maybe partially. I was really tired. I tire easily and didn't want to wake up hurting today, with Kerry coming in tonight."

"I may have tired you out more. Are you sore?" I feel only a hint of guilt for almost attacking her last night. Wanting to sleep with her wasn't why I had to come, but it had taken only one look at her luscious body in that deceptively seductive dress, one whiff of her unique scent, and being inside her was all I could think about.

The smile on her face softens her words. "I am, but only because I was out of practice. Twelve years out of practice, so trust me when I say, I welcome this kind of sore."

Twelve years of abstinence? I mean, I haven't been with anyone since before I took Kendra on a date, but prior to that I would occasionally hook up with Serena when the mood hit me. And before that—before I changed my life around—I'd tap anything willing. So I can't say I've been a choirboy, but since settling in Cedar Tree my priorities have started changing. Now that I've met Kim, I know they're in the right place. I might not have recognized all she has to offer back then.

"Holy shit," comes out of my mouth and I watch her eyes go big in response before she bursts out laughing. Fuck—I love hearing her laugh. Just as fast her face turns serious again.

"Not that I'm...I mean, I'm not assuming...I don't have expectations, if that's what you think. I didn't say that to put any pressure on you. I mean, I don't want to sound like—" I shut down her stammering by closing my mouth over hers and kissing her until I feel her hands tangle in my hair and her breathing turn choppy.

"Kimeo." I barely make a sound when my lips move against hers. "Not going to take that gift lightly and most definitely coming back for more. I played—plenty. Can't lie about that, but I'm not playing with you. Pleased as fuck you trust me with you, and I'm right where I want to be. Don't doubt my intentions, *Nizhóní*."

For a moment she simply stares at me, a war of emotions raging in her eyes before she finally nods. "Okay." He voice is a mere whisper.

"Okay," I whisper back. "Now I believe you mentioned coffee?" I add on a smile, getting a timid one in return before she comes up, swings her legs over the side, leans back to me and kisses my lips lightly. I watch her as she—still a little uncomfortable in her skin—moves over to her suitcase and pulls out a shirt and some stretchy pants. Clothes clasped to her chest, she darts into the bathroom, giving me a splendid view of her jiggling backside.

By the time I've pulled on my jeans and tugged my tee over my head, I head into the kitchen where Kim is bent over snatching her shoes and underwear from the floor. I'd forgotten we'd left them discarded on the floor. Poor Kim looks mortified when I take the items from her and gently nudge her back into the kitchen.

"I'll take these to your room. Relax."

Her eyes shoot fire when she hisses, "Relax? You realize that would've been the first thing they saw coming in last night?"

As if she summoned them, one of the doors on the other side of the living room opens, revealing a sleep tousled Katie. Complete with a Cheshire cat smile.

"I'm guessing it's a good morning?" she teases.

"Katie..." I warn her when I notice Kim's look of mortification.

"Chill, little brother. I'm nothing but happy. For both of you."

The little brother remark almost has me laughing because by my count, Katie is still younger than I am and certainly a shitload smaller. Katie's focus is on Kim though, walking straight up to her and putting her arm around her, squeezing her shoulder.

"So. You do coffee and I'll cook breakfast when Emma wakes up?" I hear her say to Kim when I walk into the bedroom and toss Kim's stuff on the bed, before taking my turn in the bathroom. I left my bag out in the truck, so after my shower I slip into my jeans sans underwear and use Kim's toothbrush. Hope she doesn't mind.

When I resurface, Emma and Kim are sitting at the counter, chatting away and Katie throws me a wink from behind the stove, where apparently breakfast is cooking.

Kim

"We have to go."

Kerry is arriving in less than half an hour and I want to meet her at the airport. Emma and Katie are arguing about the little Elvis outfit Emma spotted in the store window that she wants to buy Mattias for next Halloween. Katie isn't having it. Mal is leaning against the wall, his arms crossed over his chest looking bored, but his eyes are always scanning.

I finally throw up my hands. "Fine you guys, you stay here and shop. I'll go pick her up."

"Wait!" Emma cries out when I turn to go. Mal pushes off the wall to follow me. "We'll come."

"I'm serious, why don't you guys hang around here in the mall for a bit? Mal and I can pick her up and bring her back to the condo and we'll figure out dinner then?"

"I'm good with that," Katie says, shrugging her shoulders, but Emma still looks unsure.

"But that seems rude."

"Doesn't make sense for all four of us to sit at the airport waiting, especially since she's not really expecting anyone at all. Go. Do your thing. We'll see you later."

Mal loops his arm around my shoulder and tucks me to him when we start moving in the direction of the parking lot.

"You know it's a real turn on when you get all bossy," he rumbles by my ear. I slap his chest in mock reproach but can't stop the little smile from forming. I'm elated to introduce Kerry to Emma and Katie.

Half an hour later, I've lost the smile.

There's a notice on the screen when we enter the airport terminal, that the flight from Durango, via Denver, was delayed by half an hour. That wasn't an issue, we simply grabbed a coffee and found a spot to sit and wait. Mal next to me, his arm tucking me close, and a decent cafe latte in my hand is not a bad way to spend half an hour. No, the problem starts when two women sit right across from us, ignoring the plentiful number of empty seats all around us. It's not a stretch to figure out why they pick those seats in particular. He's a beautiful man, but dammit, I'm not invisible am I? Reminding myself I'm the one sitting here with his arm around me. I try to focus on his thumb stroking my hip, when suddenly I feel his body freeze. My attention peaked, the hushed conversation the two women have carried on starts penetrating.

"....there's something wrong with that. Only thing that makes sense is if she's rich."

"Still, look at her, she's gotta know there's no way she can hold on to a man like that. Not looking the way she does."

I'm stunned—and mortified but mostly stunned. Mal, who must feel the shift in my body language, leans in and whispers, "They're blinded by their own bullshit. Don't let it get to you."

But it's too late, they have gotten to me, and when Mal turns to them, apparently ready to lash into them, I put a restrictive hand on his chest. This is my battle and I'm sick of cowering to people who think it's okay to belittle me because I'm not perfect. Fuck them.

I stand up and walk over to stand directly in front of them, looking each of them in turn, in the eyes. One of them snickers nervously while the other tries to look anywhere but at me.

"Is there something you'd like to say to my face, ladies?" I challenge, only to get a stupid little giggle in response when they turn to the other for reinforcement, I imagine. Both sets of eyes suddenly fly over my shoulder and I know Mal has walked up behind me, not saying anything just standing there, letting me fight my own battle. Still, I'm grateful for feeling him at my back. "You seemed to have plenty of an opinion just now, I'd love to see if you have the guts to say what you did out loud, but you two are obviously the cowards I already knew you were. Sitting there, judging people from a distance. You know nothing!" I spit out the last sentence before I turn away from the bitches.

"No way someone like you has what it takes to hold on to a real man like that. It's clear to anyone who looks, you're out of your league," one of them pipes up and stops me in my tracks.

My eyes find Mal's and his are filled with anger. Not at me, at the women behind me. I grab his hand and turn back to face them.

"It's no wonder you two have to put up with each other, with personalities that ugly. It's no wonder I'm the one standing here with a good man, a decent man"—I lean in for more emphasis—"and yes, a gorgeous man at my side. There isn't a man worth his salt who would put up with such ugliness." Mal tugs at my hand but I'm not done. "You think you can tell from the outside what a person represents? What their life is like? You think you know by just one look? Well feast your eyes as my fat ass walks away with my amazing boyfriend. And in case you were wondering? He's hung like a stallion and knows how to use it." I feel no small amount of satisfaction as my last remark seems to resonate, when one claps her hands over her mouth and the other gives Mal another look once-over. I don't care. I'm done. Done with them, done with this, done with me feeling less than anyone else because of vile words spit my way. I'm done.

I march away, not quite sure where the hell I'm going but I don't care, as long as it's away from those venomous tarts. I'm forty, not twenty. I should know my worth by now and am determined to start living it.

"Whoa," Mal's voice rumbles behind me, his hand still in mine as I drag him through the terminal. Okay, drag is possibly a slight exaggeration since his long legs could easily overtake my stumpy ones, but still. "Slow down, tiger." Pulling me in, he releases my hand and with his arm around my shoulders keeping me close, he directs us into a hallway leading to the bathrooms. He backs me into the wall and turns me to face him, and before I can voice an objection, he has his mouth on mine in a blistering kiss. My need for air soon has me pulling away, and I lean my head back to look him in the eye.

"What brought that on?"

He holds my chin between his thumb and fingers and with fiery eyes scans my face.

"The mouse in you is already sexy as hell, but babe, when you let loose that tiger you keep hidden, you are fucking phenomenal. So hot, I almost came in my pants."

I'm in a public hallway outside the bathrooms at an airport, and all I can think about is dropping to my knees and making him come in my mouth.

"Killing me here, honey," he growls. "You lick your lips like that, like you want to have me for dinner, and my control is gone."

The passing of an elderly gentleman on his way to the bathroom, doing his best to ignore us, brings me resolutely back to our situation. "Let's check the board," I suggest and stand up on my tiptoes to kiss him softly.

It's an hour after Kerry's plane finally landed that I start to get worried.

She hasn't come through the gate yet and the earlier flow of people has dried up. I pull out my phone to call her but there is no answer. I then try Greg, her husband, while Mal gets up to check with the airline. When he comes back I tell him what Greg told me: he dropped Kerry off at the Durango airport an hour before her plane was scheduled to leave and assumed she would've arrived by now. He's been waiting for her call.

"She would've called him or me if she missed her connection in Denver, I'm sure of it," I tell Mal who immediately pulls out his phone.

Another hour later, after several phone calls back and forth with Greg and with Gus, who Mal contacted right after finding she'd never boarded the plane, I know I have reason to be afraid. Kerry's suitcase was found abandoned in the bathroom at the Durango airport, but there was no sign of her.

Kerry's disappeared.

CHAPTER FIFTEEN

"You did what?!"

He jumps up from his chair, knocking a stack of papers off his desk. In his rage, he picks up the glass paperweight and hurls it at the door, where it leaves a dent before bouncing, intact, to the floor. Fighting to reign in his anger, he takes in a few deep breaths before he starts talking again in a deceptively calm voice.

"I thought I explained that we can't afford to draw anymore attention. You think that maybe snatching someone from an airport might stand out?" He pulls his free hand roughly through his hair, making the decision right then and there, he will have to go and take matters in his own hands.

"No. That is not what I told you to do. I told you to see what you could find out discretely. This hardly constitutes as 'discrete.' I don't want any blowback on this. My silent partner is getting restless and we don't need to aggravate him more. At least tell me she won't be able to identify you... Good. Damage control. I want you back here tomorrow."

He sits back down in his chair, feeling his control of the situation slipping like sand through his fingers. The instant the phone rings on his desk, he knows who's calling and for the first time he feels the cold chill of fear squeezing his airway.

Mal

"Give us five minutes," Katie says as she follows Kim into her room to help her pack her things. I'd called her right away to fill her in. She suggested canceling the flights, and proposed we'd be home faster if we all piled in my truck. With the extended cab we'll all fit and not needing to drop them off at the airport and arranging for a pick up on the other side would save some serious time and manpower.

Kim had been reluctant to leave the airport and spent the short ride back to the condo quiet and withdrawn. I suspect she's barely hanging on.

While the girls pack, I head back down to the truck to clear any junk out of the backseat and make room. I'm just pulling some empty discarded coffee cups from under the seats when my phone rings.

"Caleb, what's up?" I answer, after checking to find the familiar number on the screen.

"Got a witness who saw a woman being carried out of the bathrooms by a big man, bridal style. When she approached the man he told her his wife was unwell and he was taking her to the hospital. She offered to call an ambulance, but he told her that would take too long. She's given us a detailed description of the guy. Identified what sounded to her to be a slight Texas twang and she watched them get into a maroon Ford Edge."

"These guys aren't too smart if they're still trucking around in that same rental," I point out. After the break-in at Kim's, everyone had been on the lookout for the maroon Ford. Only yesterday we'd manage to trace it to an Avis location at the Durango airport. I thought they would have ditched it somewhere by now—that probably would've been the smart thing to do.

"We've got Durango police on the lookout, as well as the state troopers. And Mal? Just a head's up, the feds are coming to town." The way my brother says it sends warning flags up.

"Great. Don't tell me, Damian Gomez?"

GFI had several run ins with Special Agent Gomez fairly recently on a case that involved Beth's son Dylan. The only good thing coming out of that was that Dylan had been given a chance to turn his life around, and he'd joined the FBI.

"Bingo. Breezed into town maybe an hour ago. He's been in with Drew ever since. At least according to Carol."

Carol worked the front desk at the Montezuma County Sheriff's Office and since Joe left the sheriff's position in Drew's hands to come and work with GFI, we were kept up to date on all goings on. Woman is older than dirt but has bigger balls than many men I know.

"I have no doubt he'll be hitting Gus next to get his take. Better be on standby in case there's any bloodshed, brother," I caution him.

Caleb's deep chuckle warms me. It still surprises me that after almost a lifetime of being considered the family's black sheep—a grim albeit justified label—I was so easily forgiven and accepted by my big brother.

"I'd better grab the girls and get on the road. Keep me informed. I'll be on hands free, though, so watch what you're saying."

"Drive safe, Mal, and tell Katie to give me a ring when she has a chance."

"Will do. See you in a few."

Tucking the phone back in my pocket and throwing out the last of the garbage from the floor of my truck, I head inside to grab the bags.

Kim

"Hey... wake up, Kim."

The combination of a hand stroking my face and the low rumble of Mal's voice makes me want to linger here in that half-conscious state, which seems to keep all negative emotions at bay. Reality sneaks in anyway, and I suck in a deep breath and shoot up straight in my seat.

"Any news?" I want to know, rubbing sleep from my eyes and surreptitiously wiping my mouth to make sure no drool marks are visible. I look at Mal who smiles at me gently before turning his eyes back to the road.

"They're tracking down a lead on the Ford, just north of Durango. That FBI agent I told you about? Gomez? He's on it with his team, but keeping Gus informed. So far nothing, but it's early yet. In the meantime we've just passed Cortez. We're almost home."

I look at the vague landscape passing outside my window. It's dark outside, must be getting on midnight, and I can barely see what I'm looking at. We'd stopped at a gas station just before crossing the Utah border and stocked up on some drinks and food, since none of us had had a chance to eat anything. By now though, the threshold of my bladder has obviously reached its limit and I'm squirming in my seat.

"Me too," I hear Katie quietly talking to Emma from behind me and I look around at her. "Bathroom," she clarifies and I nod.

"Ahhh, don't say the word," Emma complains from the backseat. "I'll take the bushes at this point, I don't care!"

"Two minutes, ladies, and you can all breathe easy." Mal's mouth twitches, fighting a grin. To me he says, "We're meeting Gus at Caleb and Katie's. Easiest, since Caleb has the baby and the two dogs.

We pull into a tree-lined driveway that opens up to a beautiful old barn. A rather massive structure with a red steel roof and big arched windows in place of the barn doors I'd expected. A door is opened to the side and I recognize Caleb stepping in the doorway, a large dog by his side and my Boo trying to sneak a peek from behind him.

Mal is still getting Emma her walker when Katie starts pulling me inside, yelling over her shoulder, "You grab the downstairs bathroom, Em!"

I barely have a chance to say hello to Boo or look around me, before I'm being dragged up the stairs and pointed down the hall to a bathroom. Boo is still miserably wining at the bottom of the stairs when I come back down, so I give my baby the attention he deserves. He responds by promptly knocking me on my ass.

"Boo." The firm use of his name does little from me, but when Mal says it, he immediately responds. Traitor. With a firm yank of Mal's hand, I'm back on my feet before the other dog comes sniffing. This thing may not be quite as tall as Boo, but looks a whole lot fiercer. Dark grey unruly fur and a lanky build, but the bright blue eyes scrutinizing me show a high level of intelligence. Not a dog to mess with. I'm obviously deemed acceptable when he saunters and plops down in front of a fire in the massive stone fireplace. It's much colder here than in Vegas and I'm drawn to the heat of the fire.

"Anything?" I ask Gus, who's settled in with his wife tucked closed and a steaming mug of coffee in his hand across from me.

"Not yet. Neil is back at the office, monitoring the scanner. If Gomez doesn't call, Neil will let us know when something happens. Waiting is the worst part, honey. Hopefully we'll know something soon."

The words no sooner leave his mouth before the phone starts vibrating on the table in front of him.

"Talk to me."

His forehead creases and his eyes flick to me as he listens to what's being said on the other side. Cold starts penetrating my body again and I shiver. The look on his face is not promising.

"Have you notified the husband?"

Mal's arm pulls a little tighter around me.

"No offense, don't mean to tell you how to do your job, but find the second guy and make fucking sure you don't put holes in this one. We need him alive." With that, Gus ends the conversation and looks around the room, his eyes coming to rest on me.

"Found your girl. She's alive, but worked over. She's on her way to the hospital. Her man's been notified and one of Damian's guys is driving him up."

I jump up and plan to go straight for the door when Mal grabs my hand and pulls me back down. "Where are you going?"

"I've gotta get to Durango. See Kerry—be with Greg." I struggle to get my hand loose but he won't let go.

"Kim, look at me," Gus says and I lift my head to face him. "I'm sorry, honey, but one of the guys who was willing to shoot at FBI agents, got killed as a result. There's a second guy out there somewhere, probably pissed as hell, and we don't even have a good take on who they are or who they work for. They want you. That's clear. They went after Kerry to find you. Trust me when I say it's very likely they'll have eyes on her, which means if you go near, they'll have eyes on you too."

Realization starts sinking in. They took her...because they wanted me. I'm not a stupid person, but this is so far out of my comfort zone, it takes me a while to grasp the crazy turn my sedate and safe life seems to have taken.

Mal

"Sleep, baby. It's almost two in the morning, and as soon as they know more we'll get a call."

Kim had gone very quiet after Gus shut down her plans to go to the hospital to see her friend. I'm not sure what's going on in her mind, but I'd rather have her cry it out than watch her shut down. When I tried to get her to talk though, she only gave me perfunctory answers. Short and for the most part, monosyllabic. We left the barn at the same time as Emma and

Gus, who wanted to get back to the office and monitor things from there. Boo seemed reluctant to leave his newfound buddy but once we got back to Beth's house, he plopped on the floor in the bedroom and was out like a light. I'd gone back out to grab our stuff from the truck and spent some time locking up the house before coming back up to the bedroom to find Kim already in bed.

"I don't understand any of this. I mean, I know on a practical level what's happening, but I just don't get it. This is not me. This is not my life. She's hurt, Mal, because of me?"

There they are, the tears I've been waiting for, rolling down her face as she turns to me. Without a word, I pull her in my arms. Nothing to say. Softly stroking her hair, I hold her until the tears finally subside and other than an occasional sniffle, she falls asleep on my chest.

I realize I must've dozed off too, when a few hours later, my phone buzzes in the pocket of the jeans I hadn't had a chance to take off. Kim is still in deep sleep and not wanting to disturb her unless I have to, I slip out from under her body, which is still draped over me. I watch her curl up on her side and walk out of the bedroom, pulling the phone from my pocket.

"Yeah."

"Thought you might want an update," Gus says. "She's got a broken arm, a few broken ribs, a body black and blue from the beatings and a nasty cut on her neck from a knife held to her throat. They expect her to make a full recovery though. Physically. Not sure how 'fine' she's going to be emotionally, but Damian says she's a tough cookie. She'll likely be released tomorrow or the day after and Damian is sending both her and her husband to a safe house."

"Kim will want to see her, at least talk to her," I point out.

"You and I both know seeing her is out of the question. At least if we want to keep both of them safe. Talking to her can probably be arranged in a few days."

"Any word on the second guy?" I suspect he would've led with news of any capture, but it doesn't hurt to ask.

"The rental was found in the airport parking lot, keys left in the Avis drop box. He must've slipped through before the FBI could get there, but the only possible flight he could've gotten on is one that stops in Phoenix before flying through to Austin. They're scouring the passenger manifest right now to see if anything pops up and have a team standing by at both airports. We nab this guy, it may be the break we need to tie it all together."

"Good. Not enjoying sitting on the sidelines while this plays out, Gus," I confess, my frustration growing with the inability to control the situation. I'm actually torn. The need to protect Kim obviously outweighing any urge to go out and try and get this case resolved. But that doesn't mean I don't want to be out there making sure that bastard can't do anymore damage.

"I hear you, my friend, but with the FBI now actively involved it would be difficult sticking our noses in anyway. Not just the state of Colorado, but the federal government doesn't take kindly to our natural resources being held hostage. And from what little information Damian has fed me, there is a strong suspicion the buck doesn't stop with the Texas oilman. There are indications the real power comes from outside our borders."

"Damn."

"Exactly. Too big for us to take on. So we worry about our little slice of that pie and make sure Kim stays safe." After a moment of silence, Gus continues, "And Mal? She seems like a sweet woman who is able to roll with the punches so far, showing a lot of grit, but this is a lot for her to process in a really short time. Be careful. If the events of the past month don't break her, I get the feeling that you easily could."

He hangs up before I can respond. I know I'm having an effect on her. Hell, I'd be lying if I said she wasn't having an effect on me too. Living without any emotional connections for many years was necessary to survive the criminal and often violent people I used to associate with. Since then my hard shells have started cracking under the influence of my brother and his family, but also the acceptance and friendships I've found here in Cedar Tree. Kim seems to be peeling away at the hardened shell, piece by piece, and she doesn't even know she's doing it.

The clicking of nails on the stairs announces Boo is awake and in search of relief. I unlock the backdoor and let him out. A quick glance at the clock shows it's almost seven—time for coffee. With a pot brewing I start pulling some things from the fridge: eggs, cheese, ham, spring onions, salsa and a roll of Pillsbury biscuits. I find a baking dish in the cupboards and butter the insides. While the oven heats, I split each of the biscuits in two. After covering the bottom of the pan, I add some ham I cut in strips, some chopped onions and top it with a pile of grated cheese. A couple of eggs poured over top, followed by chunky salsa, a bit more cheese and with the remaining biscuits I finish it off.

Kim

I startle awake when one side of the mattress dips down under the weight of Boo, who is apparently tired of waiting. He's not supposed to be on the bed, but I still take a minute to snuggle with my arms around his neck.

"Boo. Down."

It would seem Boo didn't come alone. A shirtless Malachi, with his jeans hanging loosely on his hips, is standing in the doorway. Of course, Boo listens to him and immediately jumps down. But a second later, the dog's place is taken by the man. The man smells a hell of a lot nicer, like food and Malachi. Both probably not very good for me.

"Your face just scrunched up. Do I smell?" he asks, chuckling as he lays beside me, his elbow in the mattress and head propped up on his hand. The other is pushing the strands of hair away from my forehead and tucking them behind my ears.

"Yes... " I say without thinking, watching his eyebrows shoot up. "Shit. I mean no, well... technically yes, but in a good way." One of Mal's rare smiles stretches wide on his face.

"A good way, huh?"

"You smell better than Boo."

"God, I sure as hell hope so. That dog smells like the bottom of a dumpster," he deadpans.

"Ew. Gross." I wrinkle my nose at the analogy before explaining. "You smell like comfort food and you. I was just thinking how it's quite possible neither is good for me."

The amused expression on his face dulls and I get the feeling I said something wrong. When he moves to roll away and get up, my hand shoots out to stop him. The confirmation that my words stung comes when he turns his now impassive eyes on me.

"I've got to get breakfast out of the oven," he says as he pulls his arm from my hold and walks to the door.

"Wait..." I call out after him, clambering off the bed to catch him. "I said something wrong, I know it, I can see it, but I'm not sure what it was."

He stops at the top of the stairs and turns back to me. At least I can see some emotion in his face, not that bland mask he seems to wear in public a lot. He doesn't speak though, making me a little nervous so I blunder on.

"I like the way you smell." I try to remember what I said exactly. "Maybe I should've worded it better. I obviously didn't do a good job." Then suddenly it occurs to me what else I said and how that could've been perceived the opposite way in which I intended. With the heat of a blush burning my cheeks, I walk over to where he stands and put my hands on his chest. "I said neither is good for me." The spark in his eye—ever so brief, but there nonetheless—tells me I've hit the bullseye. Confession time.

"Food is a hang-up for me. You know that. So I don't think that requires explanation, but you...you are not bad for me. You're good for me, and that's bad." Once again his face registers confusion. I'm not sure how to explain without exposing more than I had planned. "I'm afraid you could really hurt me when it's time for you to move on."

I can feel the sharp intake of breath under my hands and looking up, I see the confusion is now replaced with anger. "When?" he asks in a deceptively soft voice, but I can feel heat bubbling underneath. "*When* it's time for me to move on? Not *if* but *when*?"

I open my mouth to respond, but before I have a chance he bends down, flips me over his shoulder and marches me right back into the bedroom where he tosses me down on the bed, landing squarely on top of me. "Didn't think I'd have to explain this," he growls as he cups my face in his hands, forcing me to keep eye contact. "I'm not going anywhere. I don't know where you get this *when* business from, but it's complete bullshit."

"I'm sorry..." I mumble, a little unnerved.

"I care for you. Know I'm balancing a dangerous line between professional and personal..." He closes his eyes and shakes his head. "What the fuck am I saying? I crossed that line the moment I saw your pretty brown eyes looking straight into mine. You've burrowed in deep, *Nizhóní,* and you don't even realize it. This doesn't end with the job. Fuck no, it's barely even started."

Who knew that hope could be so painful and beautiful at the same time? I can barely breathe as his words start to sink in. The girls told me in Vegas. Heck, under their encouragement I even believed it when I told off those two bitches at the airport. I trusted it then, but in the hours since so much has happened, I seem to default to self-protective mode. But this time I insulted, maybe even hurt Mal.

"I wish for that," I tell him lamely. "I'm falling and I'm scared."

There is a light tug on the side of his mouth when he leans in and skims my lips lightly with his, before dropping his forehead to mine. "Don't be scared. I promise you a soft landing."

CHAPTER SIXTEEN

Kim

"Would you stop blaming yourself? You have no responsibility in this."

Kerry has apparently had enough when I apologize once again for getting her involved in my mess.

"You didn't ask for this, nor could you have predicted it. I'm fine, there's nothing that won't heal and although I've been made to swear not to disclose our location, it is quite beautiful where we are. I'm just a little nervous about the store being closed for so long."

"I'm glad you like where you are, but I'll be happier when you can come home. As for the bookstore, one of Mal's colleagues went over the other day and put a notice on the door saying it's closed due to a family emergency. That should give you some time. And once we can all breathe easy again, I'll help you get back up to speed. It's the least I can do," I offer.

"You know what? That's actually a great idea—you can come work for me. We'll have to sit down at some point and hammer out details but there's so much I've wanted to do with the store and never had time for. I have all kinds of time to plan now, and with your help once we're up and running I could have the time to implement. This is awesome!" Her enthusiasm would be contagious if not for the angry voice in the background that I know belongs to her husband Greg. He is none too happy with me and unlike Kerry, fully places blame on my shoulders for her attack.

"Doesn't sound like Greg agrees with you," I point out sadly, but Kerry instantly waves it off.

"Don't worry about him. He's just pissed he's missing his weekly bowling league. He'll have to get over it."

Far be it from me to get involved in their business, but I'm not too sure about their future together. Greg has been more concerned about how inconvenienced he has been than about his wife's kidnapping and injuries. Odd duck, that one.

"My *handler* tells me I have to hang up," Kerry interrupts my thoughts, "but promise me you'll think about it? The store I mean?"

After vowing I will and saying goodbye, I hang up.

"That Kerry?" Mal asks, walking out onto the back patio where I'm having my morning coffee. I've had to 'borrow' one of Mal's big hoodies to keep the chill off, but other than that it is a gloriously sunny early spring morning and I'm loving it.

"Yup. She's wanting me to come help her at the bookstore. You know... after?"

"Be perfect for you," he says with a nod, before leaning over my chair and pinning me with an incendiary kiss that momentarily blanks my mind.

He's been like that a lot these last few days. Ever since he assured me he was falling for me as well, he's gone out of his way to show me. I've never had such singularly devoted attention before. Of course that is in part because he is keeping me safe, but I have a feeling that even without this immediate threat, he wouldn't venture too far. Katie told me the other day when we were having lunch at the diner again, that she'd never seen him look this relaxed. She claims it's me and I'd love to think I have something to do with his much easier smiles. He has everything to do with the fact that I feel cherished. I'm almost at a point where I can look in the mirror and catch a glimpse of what he claims to see in me. At the very least I'm happier than I can remember ever being, although it's disturbing I can feel that way when my life has been completely uprooted. The fact someone is out there, trying hard to find me, still boggles my mind. Not to mention the upcoming MRI that might make my life go totally tits up. I shake my head slightly to get rid of that terrifying prospect. It'd be just my luck that just as I start believing the possibility of a beautiful future, my health threatens to take it away. Not ready to face that possible reality yet. Certainly not ready to put it out there in the open, so I firmly shut the door and instead focus on the obvious threat. Fuck my life.

Yesterday we found out through Gus's contact with the FBI, that guy Damian, that they still haven't found the second suspect in Kerry's abduction and Jacob Hartnett has gone off grid. They can't find either of them. Hartnett's staff both at the house and at his offices is providing a solid barrier, claiming he's gone overseas for some important business meetings for an undetermined period of time. Gus mentioned that Damian seems to think Hartnett was feeling the heat and went underground. The other guy seems to have slipped past the agents waiting at both the Phoenix and Austin airports. They do have a name based on the passenger manifest but by the time they eliminated all other passengers and were able to zero in on one Philip Winters, he'd already disappeared. They did manage to find this guy has quite an extensive list of suspected prior offenses. He's apparently well known within the Austin PD. That doesn't exactly make me feel safe and secure, but the constant presence of Mal and the involvement of the rest of the GFI crew sure helps.

I look over at Mal who's stretched out in the chair beside me, his legs up on the side of a planter. He is resting his arm next to mine with our fingers entwined. It's on my lips to thank him for sticking with me when the phone in my other hand rings again. Mal's head turns to me as I answer the call.

"Hello?"

"You couldn't call to remind me?" My mother's voice rips right through my fragile sense of security. Mal's fingers tighten around mine and I realize he's able to hear her grating voice from where he's sitting. Not wanting to have him be witness to what I'm sure will be a dressing down of some kind, I try to get up from my seat, but I'm stopped by his hand grabbing my wrist. Resigned, I sit back down and without looking at him, answer my mother. "Remind you of what, Mother?" My voice sounds weak and my mother is on it like a vulture.

"Your birthday was last month. Forty, wasn't it? I know you probably prefer not thinking about it, given that age is likely not helping your looks much, but it's a milestone nonetheless. Would've been nice to hear from you."

I almost laugh out loud. My age is more of a milestone for her and not in a good way. When Britta turned forty a few years ago, my mother had needed a two-week stay at a spa to 'help her through it.' But as usual, this time it's easy to focus her negative energy on me. As if it is in my power to avoid turning forty. She's in her sixties now and although I haven't seen her in years, I have no doubt she looks as flawless as she ever did. The biggest compliment she'd occasionally receive was when asked if she was Britta's sister. Even more ridiculous is the notion that it is my responsibility to remind her of my birthdays. But that is my mother. She likes confrontation, at least with me.

"Didn't celebrate, Mom. Haven't for years. It was just another day." I don't tell her about the events shortly following my birthday that ensured my mind had been otherwise occupied anyway.

"I can imagine. Probably best to stay away from celebrations anyway. They tend to come with an overabundance of calories that you know you can't afford."

The angry heat is coming off Mal as I can sense him sitting up straight. He heard. Just lovely.

"What can I do for you, Mom?" I try to steer away from the inevitable discussions around my weight and lack of male companionship. Although for once, the latter doesn't apply to me. I had companionship, and it was very male, but better to avoid feeding that tidbit to my mother.

"I wish to come and visit."

The thought of my mother in a place like Cedar Tree with all its *normal* people is laughable. I have to press my lips together not to snicker at the image of Mom facing off with let's say, Arlene or Emma. Even Katie. My mother doesn't hold a stick to any of these women but I doubt she'd see it that way. To her they'd be nothing more than working class and far beneath her. Heck, I'm far beneath her and I'm her daughter.

"What is the occasion? I haven't seen you in years." It's true, it's been years and the lack of contact has been as much my responsibility as hers, but then I don't like volunteering for the type of abuse she tends to rain on me.

"All the more reason. Britta has an appointment with an important client on Friday in Durango. I thought I'd come along for the drive and pop in."

"Haven't lived in Durango for the past three years or so. I believe I told you I bought a place in Cortez?" I know I did. I sent her the listing and pictures of the house and surroundings, but she never responded. Don't know what I'd hoped to gain by that. The woman had never been proud of anything I accomplished. I think that was when I stopped hoping to gain her approval.

"I don't remember anything of the kind," is her acerbic response. "Cortez you say? Is that nearby? We could perhaps stop in after her meeting."

"It's not a good time, Mom, and besides, I'm not at my house right now. I'm staying with friends while my place gets repainted." I lie through my teeth, making big eyes at Mal who continues to boldly listen in. The result is a slight tilt of his lips. He is completely unapologetic in his eavesdropping.

"Friends? I didn't know you had any." And there we go, my mother's sharp tongue comes out for another lashing. But before I can respond, Mal's hand shoots out and takes the phone from me.

Mal

Just the sound of that woman's scathing voice has my hair on end. The belittling tone and condescending choice of words she uses with her daughter is infuriating. Yet Kim sits there quietly taking it all, sometimes even with a ghost of a smile on her face. That does not sit right with me.

She'd admitted a few days ago she was in deep enough that I could seriously hurt her if I left. At long last, she had made herself vulnerable to me and that meant a lot. It meant enough for me to do a little confessing of my own. Her telling me she was falling for me had settled deep in my chest. I couldn't tell her I was falling, because I was already gone. I'm in deep, but the words to tell her exactly how deep are hard for me to say, so I spent days showing her in every way possible. I've let my body do the talking, showing her how beautiful she is to me, making her look me in the eye as she falls apart under my mouth, my hands, my cock. I watched her slowly start believing and I'll be damned if I let that piece of shit excuse for a mother of hers break down that little bit of confidence Kim's started building up. Hell no.

"Mrs. Lowe? I'm Malachi Whitetail, Kim's boyfriend." I watch as her eyes open wide at my use of that defining term. I would've introduced myself as her "man," but have a feeling her mother doesn't get the concept of that term so I keep it simple. "Like Kim said, her place is not accessible at this time, so she's staying with me for the time being."

"I don't know who you are, but I'd like to speak to my daughter." The bitch sounds seriously pissed. Good, 'cause so am I.

"I don't think so. No man worth his salt would allow for his girl to get spoken to the way you just did, and I don't care if you gave birth to her, that's not the way a mother treats her daughter."

Kim's eyes almost roll out of her head as she motions furiously for me to hand her back the phone. Fat chance.

"Well, I'll be... You have no right to talk to me like that. I see my daughter hasn't learned a thing, she continues to make the wrong choices. I—" When I see tears forming in Kim's eyes I've had enough.

"Mrs. Lowe, let me stop you right there. If you would like to see your daughter, I'm sure we can figure out a way to make that happen, but let me assure you, she will be surrounded by friends, none of whom will take kindly to her being talked down to. And yes, Kim has a large number of very good friends. I suggest you discuss with your other daughter if coming to Cortez is something you can fit into your schedule and let us know. We'll set up a time and place to meet then." Without waiting for a response I hang up on the woman.

I look over to find Kim with both her hands over her mouth in apparent shock. "I can't believe you just did that," she whispers. "She thrives on confrontation. Lives for it."

"She can bring it on. I wasn't gonna sit back and allow her to tear into you like that, *Nizhóní.* Best she gets used to that right away." I tell her, cupping her face in my hands and wiping the tears streaking down her cheeks with my thumbs.

"You don't understand. I would've been fine never seeing her again. These past years I worked so hard to stop looking for approval when it comes to my mother. I can handle the rare phone call but face to face? I don't know if I'll hold up." She pulls my hands away from her face and pushes up from the chair, but I don't let her get far.

"Babe, I'm sorry if I upset you, but your mother still has power over you. You struggle with the garbage she's filled your head with every day. I see it. And she'll continue to push your buttons until *you* stop allowing her to treat you that way. I figure with me and your friends behind you, there's not a chance in hell she can continue to convince you you're not good enough. We'd all be evidence to the contrary."

She stops at the door, but still has her back to me. I get up and move in behind her, slip my arms around her waist and rest my chin on her head. "Circumstances suck, baby, but this is a chance for you to get rid of that persistent voice inside your head. The one that tells you, you aren't worthy when the rest of the world sees easily how amazing you are."

She drops her head forward and moves out of my hold and inside. Looks like I fucked that up. I'm calling myself all kinds of stupid. Serves me right for thinking I can give someone else advice on how to handle parents. My own had been fucked up beyond salvation, and the way I 'handled' it almost cost me my brother and my life. It ultimately cost my mother's.

"I'm taking a shower, are you coming?" Kim's voice filters down the stairs and interrupts my thoughts. I'll be damned.

It takes me only seconds to get up there, two stairs at once, just in time to see her very naked, very juicy ass disappear behind the shower curtain. My clothes are off in a blink and when I step into the shower with her, she lowers the arms she had crossed over her chest and finally shows me all of her. Her chin high, the slightest hint of shyness still lingering in her eyes but completely exposed. Beautiful. I lift my hand, spread my fingers, and starting at her hairline I let my touch memorize her brow, her nose, mouth and chin, and down. With only the soft contact of my eyes and fingertips, her body responds beautifully under my hand. Her eyes shiny, mouth slightly open, a light blush on her chest and those perfectly dark pink nipples standing at attention, show me the effect I have on her. No words needed. There is no hiding what she does to me. My heart is pounding in my chest and my cock is so hard, one touch will be enough to make me lose all control. I'm learning her as my fingers glide softly over the gentle swell of her belly and she lets me. She makes no attempt to suck it in or even as much as flinches at my touch. I'm so fucking proud of her. With my free hand I grab hers and put her hand over my face. Immediately clueing in, she slides her hand down, letting her fingers caress as she learns my body.

Wordlessly we stand in the hot spray and with no other connection than through our eyes and the lightest of touches, we bare ourselves.

I almost lose control when the palm of her small hand strokes along my throbbing cock. I completely lose it when she sinks down on her knees and tentatively licks the head, her little pink tongue darting out and tasting. She manages to slide me inside the wet heat of her mouth once before I step back, and with my hands under her arms pull her up and push her against the tiles. My mouth slams down on hers as my body rubs against her wet, slick skin. Fuck, this feels phenomenal. She's wet, warm and slippery all over and when my fingers slide down between her legs, I find her ready.

"Wait..." she says breathlessly before turning herself around, bending over and presenting me her ass. Fuck me. Magnificent. She is magnificent. I can't pass up the opportunity to do a little tasting of my own and sink down behind her. Grabbing hands full of the soft flesh of her ass and spreading her cheeks, I plunge my tongue in her pussy, absorbing her scent and flavor all at once. With a few strong laps of my tongue, I can feel her quivering under my touch and when I close my mouth on her clit and suck, her knees buckle and she cries out her release. "Mal!"

"Can't wait. I have to be inside you," I growl as I stand up, hold her firm by the hips and drive myself inside her to the hilt.

"Fuck, beautiful. So good, so sweet. I've never known this before," I mutter, as I reach deeper inside her with every thrust of my hips. No longer in control of anything, I buck a few times before I come in long jerks. "Fuck!"

"I'm on the pill, you know," Kim's soft voice brushes over my chest.

We ended up back in bed, her body is draped over mine and my hand is stroking her backside. All movement freezes when I register what she's saying. Fuck me. That sure as hell has never happened to me before. Not ever have I had unprotected sex. When I feel Kim's body start to roll away, I pull her back into my arms, realizing she may have misinterpreted my sudden stillness. My hand resumes touching and finds its way back to the ass I've grown very fond of.

"I'm sorry, *Nizhóní.* It's not like me to lose control like that. Pretty sure I never have like that before—never went without a condom." I watch as she lifts her head and rests her chin on my chest, looking at me with regret in her eyes.

"Just as much my responsibility, Mal. Last thing I want to do is saddle you with an unwanted pregnancy," she says so sincerely, it makes me smile.

"I was thinking along the lines of your health more than anything. And for the record, who said anything about unwanted? Timing is off, but the thought of you pregnant wouldn't necessarily be a hardship." I chuckle when surprise at my words makes her eyes almost bulge out of her head.

"Are you for real?"

"Last time I checked." I laugh. "My preference would be to have both of us fully involved and aware when we get to that point, but there wouldn't be a pregnancy that involves you and me, that could ever be considered unwelcome, baby."

CHAPTER SEVENTEEN

Kim

"Do you need anything while I'm out?" Mal asks.

I look away from the window to find him standing by the door, his hand on the knob.

"Boo is almost out of dog food."

"I'll pick some up. We'll be back in a couple of hours."

The days are getting long and tedious with only my Kindle to keep me company. Not that I mind reading, not at all, but I'd rather be doing it by choice than because there isn't anything else to do. I'm bored out of my mind, and although Mal keeps me occupied at least a few times a day, I can only do so much cleaning and I hate having to ask someone to come with me whenever I want to walk my dog. Idle hands are the devil's workshop, as my mother would say. Her phone call this weekend has occupied me to where I'm starting to think Mal may have made a good point. I'll never get her voice out of my head unless I face up to her. Show her that her words don't affect me the way they used to. She hasn't called back again, and I wonder if she even will. I might go another few years without getting another call, because I won't be the one calling her. Part of me hopes she will call back, though. I want to actively take control but I can't when the ball is in her court. That's part of what's been eating at me until Mal announced this morning that were heading over to Gus and Emma's because he had to head into town with Gus, and Emma wanted to see me. I was just excited to have a plan—any plan—one that involved getting out of the house.

"Penny for your thoughts," Emma jokes as she hands me a fresh mug of coffee. We're sitting at the counter in her awesome kitchen which has a view of the guesthouse and the landscape beyond. It's another beautiful spring day and I'm itching to go out on the mesa.

"They're hardly worth a penny." I smile at her, deciding I really enjoy her company. Emma probably has close to ten years on me but I've rarely met anyone who I've felt totally at ease with right away like I do with her. She has that quality. "I was just thinking about the possibility of my mother and God forbid, my sister, descending on us sometime in the near future."

"Why? I mean, why now? You mentioned it had been years."

"It has. Not a clue other than what she said when she called on Sunday, out of the blue. My sister apparently is meeting a client in Durango and Mom is coming along for the ride. She thought I was still living in Durango and was planning to pop in. She couldn't even remember the pictures I sent her years ago when I bought my house in Cortez." I shrug my shoulders, noticing that my mother's lack of real interest in my life already has lessened in impact. "Mal talked to her," I confess, watching Emma's eyes light up.

"Really? Oh, I'm gonna love this. What did he say?" Emma's virtually bouncing in her seat with glee.

"He could hear her doing her usual thing with me and he got pissed off, so he took the phone out of my hand and proceeded to lay it out for her." I can't help but smile at the memory.

"No shit? I've gotta say, I already hate your mother, but I absolutely love the way Mal is coming out of his shell. He's been a quiet one, ever since he turned his life around. I've worried about him, but you've brought out this side of him we all knew was there, but was carefully hidden."

"I've heard mention of him turning his life around, but he hasn't really opened up much about it. I want to know, but am afraid to pry. Words can be damaging if not chosen the right way. I know that all too well. I said something to him the other day that was supposed to reflect on me but he didn't hear it the same way." I smile at the memory of what followed, though. The make-up sex after clearing the air had been amazing.

Emma's chuckle pulls me from my thoughts. "By the look on your face, I'm guessing he didn't stay mad long. You know, we grow up learning that women are the complicated gender, when really it's the men. They have this whole tough outer layer that they hold up on display, but it's only there to hide the same fears, insecurities and struggles inside. Don't get me wrong—they have a very different way of looking at the world at times and seem to be able to compartmentalize things better, but when it comes down to it they are as emotionally fragile as we are. At least we tend to let it hang out for the world to see. Nothing complicated about that. Most men never really make themselves that vulnerable."

I think about that while I quietly sip my coffee. Unfortunately I don't have a lot of experience with the opposite sex, and what I do have is probably not reflective of men as a whole. But what Emma says strikes home. I look at the guys I've met thus far in Cedar Tree, Mal specifically, and I can often sense a bubbling cauldron of emotion underneath that unflappable exterior. Unnerving at times.

"I think you're right."

"I know I'm right," Emma doesn't hesitate in pointing out. "Gus was sitting on some pretty heavy things for the longest time, and I swear he probably would never have told me if I hadn't pried a little. Trust me, if anyone can get Mal to open up, it's you." With that Emma gets up to get the coffee pot. "Refill?"

My cell starts ringing in my purse as I'm holding up my cup for more coffee. I quickly set it on the table so I can answer the damn thing before the ringtone drives me nuts. Much like my mother, who I know is the one calling. *You're So Vain* is interrupted when I swipe my finger across the screen and watch Emma stifle a laugh.

"Mom."

"Is that horrible man with you?" I knew she'd open with that. I know her better than I care to.

"That man's name is Malachi and he is far from horrible, Mother."

Emma is now full out chuckling with her hand over her mouth and I widen my eyes at her.

"What kind of name is that anyway? Please tell me this isn't some bible thumping farmer. I don't think I could handle that."

I can't hold back, the giggles bubble up from my chest hearing Mal described as a bible thumping anything. Silence on the other end tells me I've pissed her off. Oh well. Moving on.

"Were you calling to let us know you're gonna stop by?"

"Yes. Britta says Cortez is a little over an hour from Durango. She expects we can be there after her meeting, sometime mid afternoon. I'll need your address."

My test is scheduled for the morning, in Cortez, but I'd hate to have to hang around town waiting for them. "I'm staying with friends, remember?" I say, making a snap decision. "I'm actually staying in Cedar Tree. It's a small little town not fifteen minutes outside of Cortez. Real easy to find."

My mother is surprisingly mild and I start to give her directions to Beth's house when Emma puts her hand on my arm.

"Diner..." she mouths with a wicked little glint in her eyes. "Let them come to the diner."

"You know what, Mother? I have a better idea. If you follow County Road G like I said, don't turn off at the first stop. Keep going half a mile up the road and you'll see a diner on the left side. *'Arlene's Diner.'* They have excellent specials on Thursdays. I'll see you there at five? We'll have an early dinner, so you can get back on the road while it's still light," I ramble on to avoid the reaction I'm sure is coming.

"A *diner*? Good lord, you've turned into a real country bumpkin. Please tell me you haven't doubled in size since the last time I saw you?"

And there it is.

I jump in. "Yes, Arlene's Diner. I'll see you there at five." And before she has a chance to say anything else, I hang up.

"Holy shit—she's a piece of work," Emma says, having heard every word. Hard not to, my mother's last words were delivered at full volume in her customary high-pitched shriek. "I already understood it, but now I really get it." She shakes her head and looks at me sadly. "She doesn't know how lucky she is to have you as a daughter, although I can't figure how you ended up so wonderful. I'm sure it wasn't her loving influence."

Both of us have a good chuckle at that, but on the inside, Emma calling me wonderful settles me with warmth. Just like all the other bits and pieces of self worth I've picked up here and there since meeting these people.

"Why did you suggest the diner?" I want to know.

"Not a chance in hell she's gonna miss the kind of friends you've made for yourself, because they'll be all over her the minute she starts spouting her venom. We'll all be there for you," she says with a squeeze of my hand and I swallow the lump in my throat.

And right there is another piece.

Mal

"Got a call from a Detective James this morning."

We're meeting in Drew's office, and Damian doesn't hesitate to take the lead.

"Late last night a body was found in a parking lot just outside of Austin next to an unregistered vehicle, with his only identification a receipt for a coffee from Sky Harbor airport in Phoenix. The general description fits Winters, but until the coroner has a chance to do the autopsy sometime this week, he can't give us a firm identification. Luckily the APB on Winters caught his eye and he put two and two together. Coroner will have to confirm, but it was pretty obvious the cause of death is a gunshot wound to the head. Large caliber, from the looks of what's left of his head and confirmed by a rifle round found earlier this morning. Someone picked him off. There was no cellphone, no luggage, nothing. Both the man and the car were stripped clean, except for that coffee receipt tucked in the coin pocket of his jeans."

"Any ID on the shell?" Drew asks.

"Hope to get that confirmed later today, but whoever pulled the trigger was a crack shot. The cartridge was found around three hundred yards away, on the other side of the road beside a one-story building. I'm thinking he was on the roof, lying in wait. He must've lost it off the side of the building or otherwise he dropped it on the way to his vehicle. Can't imagine someone who takes enough care to strip his victim and car clean would be so careless as to knowingly leave any trace."

That rings true to me. I don't have the military or police training the other guys in the room have, but three hundred yards in the dark sounded like someone with some serious training was at the trigger.

"Could be a link with something I picked up on," Neil offers. "I dug up a membership to an outdoor gun range just north of Austin. Jacob Hartnett has held a membership for over fifteen years. Ever since he demobilized."

"Can you access his military records, Damian?" Gus asks. "My gut says our boy was part of an army sniper team. He's taking out loose ends. Something's got him spooked."

That is not good news for Kim. You don't want someone talented with a long-range rifle to get spooked, especially when there's already a bullseye on your back.

Turning to me Gus says, "I'm adding Neil to Kim's detail. He has experience in the field."

I nod. I don't know a whole lot about Neil's history but I do know he was military at some point. My suspicion had always been special ops. The fact that Gus finds him most suited to deal with a potential sniper only strengthens that suspicion. The youngest of the team, and the jovial one, on the surface, Neil is by far the most intelligent one and has the poise of someone much older.

"I best get back." I'm restless about being half an hour out of reach from Kim. Especially with this bit of news.

"Caleb's keeping an eye out," Gus reminds me. I knew that. He told me on the way here that he'd asked him to look after the girls from a distance. I realize he must have done that after Neil found out about the rifle range. "Let's finish this brief and we'll head out."

The next hour is spent laying out any and all information. The content of the flash drive, the geologist's report on the oilfields, the name Hart Holdings which, as confirmed by the FBI, is a known front for Hartnett Oil and Vedica's role to obtain the real estate. Gus assures us that the Walker Family is being looked after by the Ute community, and that there have been no further incidents on their farm.

I'm fucking frustrated as hell at the threat of the unknown, and our inability to plan for it. At not having any idea where our suspect is, although the discovery of Winter's body would seem to indicate that Hartnett was in the Austin area as recent as last night.

Lastly we get security for Kim hammered down. Unfortunately I'm the who has to tell her she'll be even more restricted in her movements and that's not going to make her happy. But I can take the heat if it means she'll be safe.

"Well that's nice. I've just told my mother to meet me at Arlene's for an early dinner on Thursday."

Just as I thought, Kim is less than pleased to hear that unless she's willing to brave the outdoors with an entire entourage of armed men, she's to stay inside at all times.

"Meet *you* at Arlene's? You don't for one minute think I'd let you face that woman alone, right? And whose brilliant idea was Arlene's anyway?" I notice a light twitch of her mouth when I bring up the location.

"That would've been Emma, who seems to think I need a show of force. My mother will hate it," she says, the smile finally surfacing on her pretty mouth. "As for the other, I didn't want to presume you'd want to be there."

I curse her mother for putting that hint of insecurity back on her face, and don't hesitate to get rid of it. I cup her face in my hands and have to bend down to touch my forehead to hers. "You, are the only person who's allowed to freely *'presume'* when it comes to me. It can't have escaped your notice that I like being around you. And I certainly won't give up a front seat to the big parental take-down."

The smile is back on her face and my heart beats a little faster when she stands up on tiptoes and reaches to touch my lips with hers. That's a first.

Keeping my mental fist-pump to myself, I quickly take over the kiss with one hand tangled in her hair and the other firmly on her lower back, pressing her body close. Reluctantly, I pull my mouth away from hers. "You know I'd love to take this where we both know it'll lead, but there are some other things I want to update you on."

We'd just walked in after I picked her up at Emma's, where the two of them had been chatting away like old friends. She seemed happy and relaxed and I hadn't had the heart to lay everything on her right away. At least not until we got home.

Then Boo had demanded our attention with his boisterous hellos and I'd taken him for a quick walk before giving Kim an update. I know a lot of people would want to protect their loved ones from worry, but in my experience it's better to know what's at stake. So I want to give that honesty to Kim.

Loved ones. I have to admit to myself I'm at that place—the place where certainty slips into your awareness. I'd seen it happen before to my brother with Katie, that moment there is no longer any hint of insecurity about how you feel. You *know.* It's as simple as that. Maybe it's the voluntary kiss she initiated, or maybe I've known it all along, but this moment seems to bring it home for me. I'm it for her, and as unexpected as it may be, she's it for me. In her I see a future I never thought possible. One I never even looked for or strived toward, but now that I have it in my sights, I'm not going to let go. I'm certainly not going to risk it by keeping information from her.

"There's a reason for us needing to tighten up security around you for a bit." And with my arms holding her close and my nose almost touching hers, I tell her everything I found out this morning.

I feel her shock when she finds out Winters was found murdered, and again when I tell her we suspect Hartnett might be responsible and why, but I hold on tight when she tries to pull away.

"I can't believe someone else is dead because of me."

"Stop that," I tell her with a little shake until she lifts her tear-filled eyes to mine. "You did nothing but show up every day and do your job and show loyalty to your boss. You planning to take the blame for everything bad that happens? None of this is your responsibility and you know it. So knock it off."

Perhaps not the most sensitive way to handle her self-recriminations, but fuck, this woman lives inside her head so much, she's bound to get lost in there. Along with her self-doubts and blame. I'm grateful to see the flash of anger on her face.

"Don't you tell me to knock it off, Malachi Whitetail," she bites out. "I know it's not really my responsibility, but I can't help feeling bad. Even if he was obviously not a particularly upstanding citizen."

Her fire is like an aphrodisiac for me. My already half-hard cock grows to full attention with the heat she glares my way. Leaning in I skim my lips over her tightly clenched ones before moving my mouth to her ear. "You have no idea how turned on I get when you let your temper fly," I grumble. "And the words *upstanding citizen* from your cute little mouth has my cock stand at attention and salute."

I'm rewarded with a soft chuckle from her. "That's ridiculous," she says, smiling.

"Oh yeah?" I press my hard-on into her stomach. "Does that feel ridiculous, *Nizhóní*?"

"*Mmmmm*, no. It feels like it deserves a little attention of its own."

And in broad daylight without any hesitation, she sinks to her knees on the kitchen floor, and proceeds to give my dick her thoughtful and thorough consideration.

CHAPTER EIGHTEEN

*"You can't wake a person who is
pretending to be asleep."*

~ Navajo

Kim

I woke up with butterflies in my stomach this morning.

That feeling of an impending storm you can't really prepare for.

My appointment is today and I haven't yet broached the subject with Mal. I don't know what I was thinking. It's not like he would let me out of his sight long enough to sneak out to Cortez, get the MRI and sneak back without him noticing. I've just been avoiding. I had plenty of opportunity yesterday when we just hung around the house most of the day, watching a movie, putzing in the kitchen and spending an ungodly amount of time in bed. A great distraction in clearing negative thoughts from the mind.

I don't want to think about a potentially bad result, so I haven't brought it up because that would only highlight that possibility. I've always stuffed shit I don't want to think about far down, but I get a feeling in this case, it might have been prudent to share with Mal at some point. Not to mention the impending dinner with the '*fam*' after. Should make for a great day altogether. No. It's not a surprise my stomach is queasy.

"You're not eating," Mal points out.

I've been pushing the scrambled eggs he made us around my plate and I can't even remember if I've taken one taste. I demonstratively put a bite in my mouth and chew. It should be delicious but right now it tastes like rubber.

"Don't like it?"

It's obvious I made some kind of face, because Mal is looking at me with mild amusement. Time to face the first challenge of the day.

"It's not that. I should've told you about an appointment I have today. I...it's nothing, just routine, but I... Well, I need to go to Cortez this morning. I'm scheduled for a MRI. Just routine," I quickly add when I see the worry I've been trying to avoid, on his face. "It's just, before Naomi can make a proper diagnosis, there are a few tests she ordered for me." I don't tell him about the shadow the ultrasound had revealed. I convince myself I'm not lying when I tell the truth, even if it isn't complete. Let's face it, after today I might be able to forget about it too, when the MRI comes back clear.

"I'm taking you," Mal says, pushing himself away from me, his face dispassionate, but I can feel anger underneath.

"I'm sorry, I know I should've told you. I'm not used to... having someone care so much. I'm really sorry." I wrap my arms around his waist and hold him as tight as I can. His body feels like a stone column under my hands. I feel more than I hear a big breath of air expelled, before his body relaxes.

"Sorry," I mumble again for good measure and his chin drops to the top of my head while one hand holds me to his chest.

"Hush," is all he says.

I'm having a panic attack. I swear this contrast dye they're running through me intravenously is crawling under my skin and making me nauseated. If this fucking strap is not taken off my head very soon, I'm gonna lose it. My fucking body is lying on a metal 'bed,' wide enough to hold about half of one of my goddamn legs, but no—they want my whole body on there. Then they shove me inside a tube I just about feel brushing up against me. And *then* they tell me to lie still with my arms and legs slipping off the side of the bed and my stomach about to explode. Fuck this.

"Ma'am? You have to lie still, ma'am, or we'll have to start over." The disembodied voice can barely be heard through the headphones they plopped on my head. The noise is too overwhelming.

"Ma'am? Slow down your breathing, you'll start hyperventilating soon."

No shit, Sherlock.

With the threat of having to do this again right from the start, I dig up every ounce of control I have and with Mal's face as my focus, I manage to get through the final five minutes of this hell. Serves me right to refuse the sedative I was offered earlier. Next time they're welcome to knock me the hell out.

"Are you okay?" the hapless technician asks me as he removes the contraption that was holding my head in place like Hannibal fucking Lecter, and looks concerned at my tear-streaked face. Really?

"No, I'm not. I need a—" And before I can finish my sentence, the nausea churning in my stomach wins and I puke all over his shoes.

He screams like a girl.

My torture reaches its peak when Mal, who was grudgingly confined to the waiting room on the other side of the doors, bursts through. "What the fuck is going on?" He takes one look at me and rushes over. Lovely. "You okay, babe?" he says, grabbing a corner of the sheet that was supposed to keep me warm in this sub-zero room, and starts wiping my cheeks and mouth. Giving up, I bury my face in his chest. At this point, what's the point of resisting. "I thought it was you screaming," he mumbles in my hair and despite the totally embarrassing situation, I burst out laughing. What else are you gonna do?

The technician unhappily cleans off his shoes and dismisses me, saying the radiologist will have results to my doctor as soon as possible. Mal leads me to the nearest patient bathroom and deftly cleans me up. I'm beyond caring and just let him do his thing.

"Be back in two seconds, baby. Close the door behind me?" he says before darting out the door.

A few minutes later, I let him back in and he hands me a packaged toothbrush and toothpaste. "Thought this might make you feel a bit better," he says.

That's when I burst into tears again.

"Thank you," I tell Mal as we are leaving the hospital parking lot, followed closely by Neil, who'd been our 'tail' into

Cortez. I was mortified to find out he'd been standing guard outside the patient bathroom, while Mal was making his purchases in the small gift shop in the lobby. Mal whispered in my ear as we walked right by him on our way out the door to just ignore him. Not to draw attention to him. So I shoved it from my mind, as I have a tendency to do with unpleasant things.

"No problem, Kimeo." He smiles a little without taking his eyes off the road, but his hand finds mine on my lap and for the rest of the drive home, he doesn't let go.

Mal

I recognize them the minute they walk in the door. Both bottled blondes, compared to Kim's rich brown color. Tall and skinny. Too skinny, that much is clear. The older woman's face is gaunt with skin drawn too tight for someone her age. The younger one looks a bit more fleshed out but wears an ugly distasteful scowl that takes away any attractive appeal she might otherwise have. Kim's mother and sister.

I shouldn't be surprised to see their eyes skim right over Kim to take in the diner before coming back to rest on me, not Kim, who's shrunk in her seat beside me. I'd purposely blocked her in the booth by sitting down next to her before Arlene appeared and took our drink orders. The older woman's eyes are the first to glimpse Kim sitting beside me and shoot right back to meet mine. The younger one never moved her gaze and with a small shiver of disgust I register the veiled heat I see there.

Not gonna happen, blondie. Not on your life.

The moment Kim's mother starts walking toward our table, her other daughter looks confused before she too finds her sister sitting in the booth next to me.

"Seriously, Kim?"

Kim's back straightens underneath the arm I've casually slung around her. I've got to bite my fucking tongue not to take this woman down right this minute, but I'd promised myself I'd let Kim fight her own battle, just providing her security. She needs that.

It helps that Emma stood true to her promise. Everyone, including Clint, Beth and their grandson Max, were sitting at the big round table in the corner. All of them knowing full well what was going down. Only Neil and Joe were outside somewhere, keeping an eye out.

"Mother. Britta. Good to see you both," Kim says as the other two slide into the booth across from us.

"I see you haven't changed much," her sister says with a sneer. No hello from either of them. Un-fucking-believable.

"Thank you. You look well too," Kim says smiling and I can't stifle the chuckle at how she puts them in their place by being deadly polite. They don't even realize it. All eyes shoot to me, Kim's warm and appreciative, the other two irritated at my intrusion.

"And who might you be?" Britta holds out her hand while batting her eyelashes. I reach out my free hand to shake her limp one, letting it drop right away when I feel her thumb brush my palm. Fucking piece of work.

"Sorry, this is Malachi Whitetail, my boyfriend. Mal, this is my mother, Elaine Lowe, and my sister, Britta," Kim says in a strong voice and I have to restrain myself from kissing the stuffing out of her right here and now.

Elaine's lips are drawn in a tight line and Britta's mouth falls open in surprise before she lets out a snort.

"Kidding me, right? This is your boyfriend?" she asks Kim incredulously. Elaine says nothing and before either Kim or I have a chance to respond, Arlene shows back up with our drinks.

"Here you go, lovebirds, a beer and a tea. And what can I get you two ladies?"

Britta's eyes move fast as lightning between Arlene, and Kim and I.

"I'll have a tea also. No milk, no sugar," Elaine says as she watches with disapproval while Kim doctors her tea with both.

"Honey, you ask me, you could do with a little sugar. Both of you," Arlene says, waving her hand between the two blondes. "You've gotta know, real men like a little meat on their women. Just you wait, my Seb will get you set up. He's made one of his specialties tonight: a good hearty shepherd's pie with home made applesauce. That stuff'll stick to your ribs, all right. I don't even have to ask these two, but how about you? Ready for some good country food? Shall I make it four specials?"

The smile Arlene sports is as fake as a three-dollar bill and I can't be positive she won't spit in their food given the chance.

"Just water for me," Britta bites off. "And a house salad, with a light vinaigrette."

"As you wish," Arlene grinds her teeth. "And you, Madam?"

Kim snorts when her mother flinches at the title.

"Just the tea. I'm not very hungry."

"Tea it is, and I'll say a quick prayer that wind they promised for tonight holds off a bit. You're bound to be blown away otherwise."

The chuckles from the table in the corner are evidence the interaction was observed by quite a few eyes, and I'm having a hard time keeping a straight face when Arlene turns on her heels and disappears into the kitchen.

"That woman is rude. I'm surprised you'd invite us to a place like this." Elaine is not good at hiding her distaste, if she even tries.

"What is rude is seeing your daughter after years and the only thing you manage to say is 'Really?' What is rude is sitting down at a table with someone without introducing yourself. What is rude is not responding to your daughter when she welcomes you anyway. And lastly," I say, turning to Britta, "it is extremely rude to not only ignore your sister's existence, but to then come on to her man and to laugh in her face when she gives you the facts. Now, I thought you wanted to have a visit with Kimeo."

With that I turn to Kim and kiss her at the hairline. "Sorry babe, I couldn't hold back," I mumble.

"No problem," she says softly, her face turned to me with the brightest smile before turning to her sister. "So—tell me, how did your meeting go?"

It takes a few seconds before Britta answers. I tune her voice out and let my eyes wander over the table of friends. A wink from Caleb, a thumbs up from Emma and Gus can't hide his chuckle. Beth, Katie and Naomi all smile big. It hits me, *fuck* I'm lucky. Shitty fucked up background, yet I have these people who have my back *and* Kim's. No questions asked. Caleb is my blood but I don't count that against him. These people are all the family I need.

Slowly my attention is drawn back to the conversation at the table and I just catch the last of what Britta says.

"...Charming man. I guess my reputation stretches over state lines because he called the firm and asked for me specifically. It'll definitely be rewarding to work with someone of such good standing." Britta babbles on and I notice how quiet Elaine has gotten when Arlene carries a large tray over to our table. The two women are served their respective drinks and Britta her salad, before Arlene sets two small, steaming oven dishes in front of Kim and I. Two small bowls of chunky applesauce are placed beside them and with a slightly sarcastic *Bon Apetit,* Arlene leaves.

This is the big test.

From the corner of my eye, I see Kim spread her napkin on her lap and pick up her fork. She scoops up a bite, brings it up to her mouth but stops before she turns to her mother. Elaine's eyes are slits as she watches every one of Kim's movements.

"And how did you like Durango, Mother?" she asks, right before closing her lips over the fork and closing her eyes at the rich taste of the food. She deserves a standing ovation.

My girl—she's a goddamn goddess, and she's holding her own. Actually, she's wiping the floor with them by not having said one untoward thing. The epitome of class.

"It was fine," Elaine says distractedly, watching every bite that disappears in Kim's mouth. Britta is just toying with her plain salad, not particularly interested in the conversation.

"Pretty drive isn't it? Did you guys see Mesa Verde? Gorgeous right? You should take some time and look around there. It's amazing." Kim babbles, trying to keep the rather awkwardly stilted exchange going. "I've been there several times. I think the last time was last summer, when my friend Kerry and I went for several hikes. There are some great trails to walk."

Her family may not be paying much attention to what she is saying, but I am. I'm taking her into the park this summer if it's the last thing I do, and I can think of a few more spots I'd love to show her.

"Refills?" Arlene stops at our booth, before leaning over and whispering to me, "Trouble coming in the door, I'll try to head her off."

My eyes immediately go to the front, but all I see is Arlene's back, blocking the view of whomever she's trying to warn me about. I have a gut feeling this 'family meal' is about to get a whole lot more uncomfortable.

Kim

Oh my God.

How messed up can one day get?

After my lovely MRI from hell, we'd come home to find Boo on the bed, chewing the styrofoam container that had held ground beef we cooked earlier in the week. He'd dug that container out of the garbage, which was now spread all over the kitchen. When he was a pup he'd sometimes get into the garbage. Usually when I would go back to work after a weekend. We've spoiled him and now he's regressing. I almost cried when I explained to Mal that this was Boo's version of a temper tantrum, but he calmly called Boo, clipped on his leash and took him for a walk, telling me to leave the mess for him. Of course I didn't and by the time he got back I'd cleaned it up.

And now, only two hours after scraping the garbage off the kitchen floor, I'm sitting here with a damn smile plastered on my face, struggling hard to stay polite. That's my plan, no matter what they throw my way, I'm ignoring what they say and staying friendly and polite. Not how I feel, let me tell you. I'm so riled up after this fucked up day that I'm itching to smack someone, but that would not help. I keep reminding myself of the saying '*you teach someone how to treat you.*' I'm trying. My hair may go completely grey with the effort by tonight, but doggone it, I'm trying. Other than Mal's little intervention, which seems to have had some effect, it feels good to have him there. A warm glance, an acknowledging hand on my knee—he makes sure to let me know he's there with me.

Right up until I feel him tense up beside me and mutter something under his breath. When I follow his glance which seems to be focused on the entranceway, I notice Arlene talking to someone. A woman with long blonde hair, teased all the way out there, and a body much like my sister's. I don't know her, but when she moves past Arlene and starts walking toward our booth, the mumbled "*Shit*" from Mal tells me he sure does.

It's like watching a car wreck happen. You know it's coming, you know it's gonna get ugly, but there's not a damn thing you can do about it but brace for the impact. And boy, what an impact it is.

"Hey, honey!" The blonde twitters as she stops beside the table, leaning into Mal for... for what? A kiss?

"Not your honey, Serena," he says, holding a hand out to stop the progress of her pursed lips. "Made it clear to you months ago that was not gonna happen."

"Pfff, lover's spat, that's all." She waves it off with her hand before resting it on Mal's chest.

I don't know if she's really conniving or simply that stupid when her eyes finally scan the rest of the booth. "Hi," she half waves to us with the hand Mal just resolutely removed from his chest. Or rather, she waves to my mother and sister who, by the looks of it, are frothing at the mouth for the inevitable drama. The moment her eyes hit mine, I can feel the negative energy rippling my way. Oh, she knows.

"And you are?" she directs at me, and only at me. *Challenge accepted.*

"I'm having a quiet dinner with my family. This is our table, and I believe you're the one who walked up and interrupted. That means *you* don't get to ask that question and frankly, I don't give a rat's ass who you are."

Whoops and hollers from the corner table where my new fan club sits and a deep chuckle from Mal beside me tell me I did good. But then I look back at her and I know she's ready to come back with a zinger.

"Oh honey, honestly? Look at me," she says, running her hands down her body like a two-bit hooker. "If I can give him this, and all you have on offer is...*that.*" She waves her hand in my direction. "Do you really think it'll be a hard choice for him to make?"

"Hey! That's my sister you're talking about."

My eyes about bulge out of my head when I turn and see that indeed, Britta has her angry glare focussed on Blondie. But before the situation has a chance to deteriorate into a bawdy cat fight, Mal stands up and grabs the woman by the shoulders.

"Enough. Don't know what you thought you'd accomplish coming here, but you knew months ago there was no chance for anything between us. Not a chance, Serena. And you know why? Because I knew someone like her would come along one day and that kind of quality? A man goes down on his knees to get a shot at that." He drops his hands from her arms and I feel almost sorry for the woman as I watch her shock turn into embarrassment when her gaze darts around the diner, taking in every pair of eyes turned her way. But she walked in here with her head high, looking for a scene. She just didn't count on walking out with her tail between her legs after a public dressing down.

"He loves you," Mom whispers and my eyes find hers wet with emotion. And at that, the heavy fist that had been squeezing my heart painfully since her first call on Sunday, suddenly releases.

"Lucky bitch."

Britta's words are soft and filled with a longing I understand well. She actually smiles at me and a lump gets stuck in my throat. I'm so wrapped up in this unfamiliar feeling of warmth around me, that I don't even notice Mal marching Blondie to the door, or Arlene clearing away the plates from the table.

"Your mouth is hanging open, *Nizhóní,*" Mal's voice rumbles right beside my ear, just before his lips press a kiss at my hairline. "Time to get you home."

I'm still a little stunned when I wave goodbye to a table full of smiling faces and follow my mother and sister into the small front lobby. Mal calls out to wait right there while he goes to take care of the bill.

"I'll be in touch," my sister says. Something I haven't heard her say in the longest time. Not quite a hug goodbye yet, but in comparison to the more familiar cold dismissal, it sure feels like one.

Mom turns to me and grabs my face. "I...I'm..." That's all she manages before shaking her head and turning to leave. The sudden shattering of the glass front door freezes everyone followed by the sound of Mal yelling from behind me.

"Get down!! Get the fuck down!!"

I'm dazed, trying to grasp what is happening when my mother turns and throws both of us down on the ground. Mayhem ensues, yelling and screaming from somewhere behind me, but it all fades into the background the moment I look down to find my mother's eyes closed, her head resting on my chest.

CHAPTER NINETEEN

That was fucking brilliant.

Finding that file on Kimeo Lowe in that idiot Winter's car was a stroke of luck I hadn't counted on. The name of the law firm in Grand Junction, where her sister was an associate, stood out like a beacon and my plan started taking shape.

The woman had been so eager to land a big client, she'd not even questioned his need to keep their meeting under wraps. She'd been the one to bring up her sister, mentioning she thought she lived in or near Durango. I didn't correct her, but instead suggested perhaps she use the opportunity to look her up. Emphasized how important family is. The idiot woman fell for it.

Setting up the appointment for the Thursday gave me enough time to drive the back road and avoid being spotted. The sister didn't even question the back room in the restaurant I'd rented out for our 'meeting.' Staff left us alone—enough cash made sure of that. Money always talks.

With only a little prodding, she spilled that her sister was currently staying with friends—in some hick dive called Cedar Tree outside of Cortez, and that they were meeting her later for dinner. Bitch had been right under our noses the entire time.

My phone buzzes in my pocket. I turned the sound off to avoid being heard the moment I left the truck on the other side of a wooded area outside of the diner Ms. Lowe and her mother pulled into. Doesn't matter, I know who is calling and I'd call him back as soon as the job is done. As soon as I deal with Ms. Lowe, now squarely in my crosshairs.

It takes me a second to register the bullet that tears through my thigh, the impact enough to throw off the shot I had just aimed at my target's forehead.

Mal

I don't know why, but right as I walk Serena to the door, the hair on the back of my neck stands up. After watching her get in her car, I scan the parking lot, but it looks as it did earlier. Still, something tells me it's time to take Kim home. Time to put this fucked up day behind us.

I'm not sure what I was expecting when I get back to the table, but it certainly isn't the highly emotional charge hanging around the three women at the table. They barely notice my approach and it's only after I kiss Kim that she looks at me. The three of them get up without complaint and I have time for only a quick glance at my brother who's got his thumb up and is smiling, before I have to call to stop the three from walking right out the door. I turn to Arlene at the counter to pay, but she waves me off.

"You kidding? I couldn't buy the kind of entertainment you bring with you. People are gonna flock, waiting for round two."

I start to smile at her when something has me turn to the front door, just in time to see it shatter. I know I yell out for them to get down, but after that things become chaotic. The only thing I see is Elaine and Kim both going down. *No.*

It's Gus barking out orders that unglues me from my spot and, the next instant, I find myself on my knees beside Kim and her mother. Both are covered in glass but only Kim's eyes lift to meet mine. I expected Elaine's would be lifeless under her closed lids, after seeing the size of the hole between her shoulder blades.

"What the fuck happened out there?"

Gus is yelling, pacing back and forth in the parking lot of the hospital I just left a few hours ago. Seems ages ago already.

With the arrival of ambulances and law enforcement vehicles, there hadn't been time to go over details. I'd been too busy holding on to Kim and her sister, as first Naomi and then the EMTs worked hard to revive their mother. It had taken everything to get Kim in the second ambulance. She had lacerations all over from the flying glass, but thank God no bullet wounds. Thanks to her mother.

Britta, who had just stepped through the door when she'd heard it shatter behind her, came away without any injuries. I left them with a couple of Drew's deputies standing guard outside the room.

Leaning against Gus's Yukon, I wait for him to be done tearing a strip off whomever he has on the phone.

"Clusterfuck," he says when he finally stops in front of me. "Total clusterfuck. Shots came from the woodlot. Neil was on that side scanning the tree line when he was intercepted by the fucking feds. They'd picked up Hartnett's lead and fucking followed him, but with their heads up their assess that far, they didn't think to give a head's up. He managed to get off two shots before they took him down."

"He dead?"

"No. They wanted him alive. They want whoever is pulling Hartnett's strings. They whisked him off to 'an undisclosed location.' " Gus sits down on the curb and drops his head in his hands. "You know? This situation is exactly why I had to leave law enforcement. Agencies so focused on the big picture, they forget to do what they're here for—protect the individual." He seems dejected when he lifts his eyes. "Kim's mother?"

My headshake is enough of an answer. She'd been whisked away to an operating room by the time Kim was wheeled into the ER, and I'd frankly been surprised she'd survived the ambulance ride. They'd miraculously been able to get her heart going. Still, Kim seemed numb and Britta was pale and in shock. I chose my words carefully to explain the situation to Britta, who was at a complete loss as to what just happened. She wordlessly went to sit beside Kim on the bed and drew her into her arms. Feeling useless here and eager to get more information, I left them sitting side by side on the bed, staring into space. Hanging on to each other for dear life. Kim didn't even register my kiss and the promise I'd be right back.

The slow clip of heels on the parking lot pavement had both Gus and I turn our heads to see Britta hesitantly making her way toward us. Her face even paler than earlier.

"I...I'm not sure..." she starts nervously. Gus stands up and gives her shoulder a squeeze.

"Is Kim all right?" I want to know.

"That woman doctor is with her, Naomi?"

"A friend of ours."

"Right. So I'm not sure if this has any bearing on what you just told me in there, but that new client I met in Durango earlier? He's in oil." She shakes her head dismissively. "I'm sure it has nothing to do with what happened, but a few things occurred to me. His call came out of the blue and he seemed insistent to meet with me. He also insisted I mention nothing about our meeting to my firm yet. Claimed he needed time to get his business freed up from his current firm. It seemed...odd, at the time, but he appeared very interested in my family, my sister in particular. You don't think..." This woman, fiddling the edge of the elegant shawl draped around her neck is nothing like the fire-eating bitch I met a few hours ago. She's uncertain, an unspoken question in her eyes.

"Hartnett," Gus says. "Jacob Hartnett. He's responsible for at least two deaths, as far as we know."

The confirmation of what she obviously feared hits her hard, as she folds her arms around her waist and doubles over, as if punched in the gut. I know the feeling.

I leave Britta in Gus's care, who is trying to glean as much information from her as he can, although I doubt Hartnett would've discussed anything with her that would be of value to us. He'd had one objective in mind and that was finding Kim.

When I walk into the treatment room in the ER, Kim is lying curled up on her side, her back to the door. She doesn't even move when I walk up to the bed. Only when I lift her hair away from her face does she turn and lift her eyes to mine. They're dull. Devoid of any real emotion and that concerns me more than if I would've seen pain or confusion there. She looks like she's shut down. There's nothing I can say, so instead I toe off my boots and crawl into the narrow hospital bed behind her, scooping her body close. Initially she's stiff as a board, but after a few minutes I feel her sinking into me. When I feel her take in a shaky breath, I roll her body onto mine and she buries her face in my shoulder as the first sob rips free. She cries until her tears must've dried up, before I notice Britta sitting on the single chair in the room.

"Hey," I greet her softly.

"Hey," she says back, a hitch in her voice.

Kim

"I'm sorry."

Boo's big head is on my lap, his big body splayed out over the couch I've tried for the past few weeks to keep him off, as the memory of my sister's parting words play through my head.

She's on her way back to Grand Junction where my mother was transported by helicopter this morning. Gus apparently offered to drive her, but she'd been adamant about needing time to process and thought that driving would be good for that. It's been two days since my mother was shot and although the surgical team at Cortez Memorial had managed to pull her back from the brink, they'd made it clear that her survival would take more than stopping the active bleeding and fixing her collapsed lung. The bullet had torn through Mom's spine, leaving her spinal cord almost severed. The surgeon enforced on us the importance of moving her as fast as possible to either Grand Junction or Denver where a specialized neurological team would be able to try and repair the damage. For now, they'd kept Mom in an induced coma, until the neurosurgeons have a chance to assess her. We opted for Grand Junction. The team there has a high success rate repairing damaged spinal cords as Britta discovered when she immediately researched our options. Of course it was also the more convenient option, although that was clearly a secondary factor.

I'd felt useless as Britta had spent most of yesterday making phone calls to Mom's friends. People I don't even know. It was hard for me to admit how little I have to offer my mother. I've been so far removed from their life for so long. I can't help wonder how many real friends she has. I can't really recall any from when I was growing up. Other 'society ladies' yes, but not the kind of friends you'd chat with for hours at a time over a cup of tea, or that you'd go hiking with. Not the ones who would laugh and cry with you through your ups and downs. I realize how fortunate I am to have that, and it makes me sad for her. Her carefully toned and honed body that she put so much value on is almost a shell now. For so long the memories she left me with were mostly painful. Not joyous, not sweet, but bitter and hurtful. Except in those last few moments before she was shot, the wonder in her eyes when she told me "He loves you," and the sacrifice she made, putting my life ahead of hers. I recognized her as a mother in those moments and I will treasure them.

"Hey."

I feel the couch shift when Mal sits down on the other side of me, curling me into his body. I willingly drop my head on his chest, where his hand finds my hair and starts stroking. "You okay, baby?"

"Sad," I mumble into his shirt. "Just so sad about... everything. But also very blessed in a way. My mother has given me more in those last moments before all hell broke loose, than she ever did before. Those are warm and unexpected."

"Mmmm." The rumble from his chest is comforting and I snuggle in deeper.

"It just feels so empty—wasteful, you know? All these years, all that hurt and disappointment and I'd resigned myself to it. But now all I can think of is what we missed out on and whether it's too late to make amends or work things through."

"I hear you. Believe me, I hear you. Just remember this though, whatever happens to her, hold on to those glimpses she showed you. They may have been very raw and uncensored, but also very real in a way that no amount of analyzing and working through history would've been able to accomplish. She may not even have realized the gift she was giving you."

I lift my head and look up at his words. "A gift?"

He nods his head seriously. "Your sister. She brought you your sister. Reconnected you. Hell, for all I know, the two of you may never be close, but I wouldn't let her disappear from your life again."

I snort in response. "I don't think I could stop her if I tried. Have you met my sister? She has a successful career and kicks serious ass for breakfast. If she chooses to stay away, she will."

"I don't see it that way. You're the strong one, the one with the power. You're the one with the friends who care for and accept you just as you are—not for your success, your money or your looks, but simply for you." He shoves Boo's head off me and lifts me to straddle his lap, taking my face in his hands. "You're the one who wakes up every day to a man who loves you. All of you. For your strength, your beauty, your honesty, your body, and your heart."

The lump in my throat has grown to massive proportions and I struggle to swallow around it. The beautiful swelling in my chest so overwhelming, it's to the point of painful. I don't even try to hold back the tear that forms and rolls down my cheek, leading the way for the next one to follow, and the one after that.

Mal smiles one of his rare and stunning smiles as he wipes at my cheeks with his thumbs.

"I love you, Kimeo—my *Nizhóní,*" he says, right before he slants his mouth over mine and kisses the pain from my heart.

Deep and thoroughly his tongue explores and tastes, and before long I'm squirming in his lap, my hands tangled in the thick silky strands of his hair. I can't stop myself from moaning in his mouth, when his hips rise up and I feel the hard ridge of his erect cock rub against my core. I shamelessly rock myself against him, whimpering when I'm already close to exploding.

In one move, he is up and my legs automatically wrap around him. I'm too far gone to question his ability to carry me as we make our way upstairs to the bedroom where he slams the door behind us, effectively locking Boo out. My hands are already under his shirt, running through the sparse hair and over his hard chest. The charge that builds when my skin touches his is almost tangible and makes me feel alive, free, beautiful.

Our touching is intense, almost frantic. In no time I'm stripped bare under his skilful hands and bent over the dresser, my hands bracing me.

"Stay just like that." His voice sounds jagged as I hear, more than see, him remove his clothes. My breathing is erratic with anticipation and the moment his large hands caress my ass cheeks I inhale open-mouthed. A tiny fragment of self-consciousness lingers until I feel his groan of appreciation vibrate against my pussy. The firm, rough rasp of his tongue licking me deep brings out goosebumps all over my skin and the shiver that follows is one of utter bliss. With my eyes closed, the sensations are multiplied tenfold and I shamelessly grind myself against his mouth.

"Watch yourself when I make you come," he growls against my skin, and I open my eyes into the mirror leaning against the wall on top of the dresser. My face is a shock. Eyes glazed, lips wet and plump and a deep red flush on my chest and cheekbones. I look... vibrant, very unfamiliar, and when I feel Mal's touch disappear, almost lost. In the next instant he rises up behind me, his hands firm on my hips and his eyes boring into mine in the reflection of the mirror. His chin is shiny with my juices and I should be ashamed, but I'm not. The sight is arousing, with his long hair dark around his shoulders, his eyes devouring me and his body dark and muscular against my white and plump one. He slips his arms around me and pulls me up, one dark hand sliding down to cup me between my legs and the other one up to cup my breast.

"I love the way you overflow my hands, the way our contrast balances me. You balance me."

His words, his skin against mine, his cock hard with promise against the small of my back, I'm almost delirious with need. "Please..."

One finger on the hand cupping me shifts and slides over my clit and I detonate on a sharp intake of breath and loss of orientation. I drop forward on my hands to catch my breath, but before I can even find my legs, Mal has the head of his cock slowly sliding through my folds.

"Sweet Jesus," falls from his mouth as he seats himself deep inside me. My eyes find his again in the mirror. He's beautiful. We're beautiful together. He pulls out slowly before surging home again, and again, and again, until I see his jaw clench and his body bend over me, jerking his release. With his mouth latched onto my neck, I follow him over.

Mal

"You love me?"

Her almost timid voice filters through my post-coital haze. After coming so hard I thought I'd go blind, I was able to maneuver us onto the bed, where Kim draped her naked and sated self on top of me. We've been lying here, tangled up in each other—touching—for at least ten minutes when she responds to my earlier declaration. For a bit there I thought she was purposely ignoring my words. Fuck. That would've hurt.

The relief at her question bubbles out of me in a laugh and she pushes herself up on my chest.

"I was afraid I might've misunderstood. That maybe it was a joke."

"Fuck no. No joke, just worried. When you didn't say anything, I thought I'd fucked up." I spread my hand over her face, softly drag my fingertips over her features and watch her eyes flutter closed.

"Thought maybe I'd been dreaming, or wishful thinking or something," she mutters almost to herself. "I never... I feel so much, sometimes I think I can't breathe, my chest feels so full. It's terrifying to feel so vulnerable to one person, but at the same time so very good. Almost too good to believe..."

Her words trail and although she hasn't really come out and said it, what she does tell me is enough. I feel exactly the same way and trust me, vulnerable is not something I like feeling. Yet with Kim it feels safe—I trust her completely.

CHAPTER TWENTY

Mal

It happens on the way home from Grand Junction, where we'd just spent yesterday waiting in the hospital while the surgical team spent almost ten hours trying to repair Elaine's spine. They won't know for a while yet how successful their efforts have been. Kim's mom will be kept in a coma for a while to allow her body to heal. It may be a week or more before they even attempt to wake her up, so Kim had wanted to come home. She misses her dog, which is staying with my brother and Katie, and wants to move back to her house in Cortez. I'm not sure whether that is safe yet, but hate to bring that up with her. She's been through enough. That's why when I called Gus earlier this morning, I made sure Kim was still sleeping in the spare bedroom in her mother's house.

I wanted to get an update because Hartnett had not been talking at all so far, but with warrants in hand, the FBI was peeling apart his home and his offices, and questioning his staff. They were bound to find something at some point. A couple of days ago, we'd had a meeting with the Sheriff's Office and Damian Gomez. It didn't go so well. When put on the spot about his lack of communication when they realized Hartnett had been en route to Cedar Tree, Damian had tried to pass the unwritten 'need-to-know' rule off on us. That resulted with me up in his face, explaining in no uncertain terms that I held him personally responsible for putting my girl in danger.

"We were waiting for Hartnett to communicate with his contact, but when he headed to Cedar Tree, we figured we'd have some leverage to make him talk if we could catch him red handed," he said, trying to justify his decisions.

"So you used Kim and her family as bait?"

When he shrugged his shoulders in response I lost it.

I got exactly one hit in before Gus and Drew were pulling me back. And then Gus was sending me home. He told me although he didn't think Kim would be in danger from anyone but Hartnett, to keep a close eye on her. And I have—not letting her out of my sight for anything.

We've just passed Monticello when Kim's phone rings.

"Hello?...Oh hey, Naomi...Yes thank you, we're on our way back now. It was okay. They'll try to wake my mother in a few days, but Britta has it all under control...Yes, Mal's driving."

I watch from the corner of my eye and see Kim pulling her eyebrows together as color seems to drain from her face.

"They did? What does that mean?...Okay, I'll meet you there."

I pull off the road, first chance I have, shut the engine off and turn in my seat. "What's going on?" I ask Kim whose face is turned away from me. I cup the back of her head and turn her toward me. A cold fist grabs me when I see the stark fear in her eyes. "Kim? Talk to me."

Kim

So I hadn't exactly lied to Mal, but I hadn't told him everything.

At the time, I felt I was enough trouble already and was afraid he'd go running in the other direction. In hindsight, I should've given him that choice. I can't explain this one away with vague references and blatant omissions.

"That was Naomi," I point out the obvious in an attempt to delay and his raising of one eyebrow high, tells me he knows it. "She, uhh... got a call from the radiologist's office. They apologized, said my report had been misplaced, that they should've called sooner." The intensity of his eyes on mine and the tight clench of his jaw make me hesitate.

"Go on," he prods.

"She wants me to meet her at the hospital in Cortez. She's set up an appointment with a surgeon."

"Why?" he bites out, struggling to maintain his composure and frankly, mine was gone five minutes ago. My entire body is shaking like a leaf and I'm afraid if I don't cry soon, my eyeballs will explode.

"They found something growing on my thyroid." Naomi had actually used the word 'tumor' but I can't bring myself to say it.

I'm so lost in my own head that it takes me a moment to realize that Mal has gone silent. A glance in his direction finds him looking at me studiously, as if waiting for me to give him more information. There is none. "Let's get you looked after." That's all he says, turning the key in the ignition and steering the truck back on the road. I'm confused and mostly want to puke, but I'm holding it together. Barely. It doesn't help that Malachi seems as far removed from me as he was that first time I saw him in Arlene's diner. A stranger. The only emotion he's showing is the slight twitch of a muscle by his jaw. I feel utterly lost.

I have no idea how long the drive to Cortez was, but I haven't really seen or registered anything until I notice us pulling into a parking spot at the hospital. Mal walks me in, with his hand at the small of my back. The moment Naomi sees us walk in, she moves away from the nurse's station where she was chatting.

"So glad you're here. Dr. Mitcham is just finishing in the OR but suggested we use his office. Come with me." I start to follow Naomi right away but notice Mal's hand is not at my back anymore. Stopping I turn around to find him standing by the nurse's station, looking after us.

"Hold up," I call out to Naomi as I retrace my steps and stop in front of a stoic looking Malachi. "Why aren't you coming?"

He looks pained, his mouth a thin line, and his face good enough to beat out a poker game, but his eyes—his eyes swirl with dark emotion. "I don't think—" he starts, but I don't want to hear it. I need him with me.

"Please..." My plea sounds breathless, terrified of having to face what is coming on my own. Mal rubs both hands over his face before he reaches out for mine and interlocks our fingers.

"Let's go," he says resolutely.

"Have a seat." Naomi gestures to the couch against the wall of the office she just showed us into. She turns one of the visitor's chairs in front of the desk around and sits down, facing us. "I'll start with the good news. You have what I suspected, Hashimoto's disease. It is an autoimmune disorder that affects your thyroid gland and wreaks havoc on your hormone levels. It is the culprit for many seemingly unrelated symptoms, but it can most definitely be regulated. Unfortunately, it is also a condition that leaves you prone to other autoimmune disorders, and some cases, to tumors. Thyroid lymphoma is a pretty rare complication, but it happens."

My hand has stayed clasped in Mal's while Naomi is talking, and at her last words, I feel his fingers clench around mine. I'm not really processing what I'm hearing. My mind is stuck on tumors and lymphoma.

Naomi pauses and looks at both of us. "So far any questions?"

Neither of us move, too stunned, too scared, too confused. Any of those or all.

"When we spotted a shadow on the ultrasound, I was already suspecting Hashimoto's but was thrown off a bit by that result. The MRI was necessary to confirm a mass and the placement of that mass." She leans forward and grabs my free hand. "You definitely have an abnormal mass on your thyroid, but we can't identify what it is or how to treat it unless we do a biopsy. Now because of the placement of the tumor, it may be difficult to do a needle biopsy, which is why I've called in—"

A very tall, thin, older man in scrubs, with grey hair and glasses walks in and straight over to shake hands. "Hi there, I'm Dr. Mitcham. Dr. Waters filled me in on your case. Did she have a chance to go everything with you?"

"I was actually just going to explain why a needle biopsy is not necessarily helpful for her," Naomi tells him.

He sits down behind his desk and turns to us. "Where the mass is located is a difficult area to obtain an accurate needle biopsy from, so I recommend surgically removing it. For two reasons, actually. To be able to send all of the tissue for a proper pathology to be done and because even if the tumor turns out to be benign, it's size and location would likely interfere with the proper functioning of your thyroid. We need to get it out, and I'd like to do it soon."

I'm struggling to catch up with this wave of information when I hear Mal speak up beside me.

"How soon?"

"In four days. I have a Tuesday eight AM slot that just opened up and I've pencilled you in."

Mal

I hate fucking hospitals.

That's flashing in my mind as Kim and I walk, dazed, toward my truck. Neither of us has said much, although her hand is clutching mine like it's her lifeline. Numb would probably be a better description for what I'm feeling, but underneath, I can feel anger and fear fighting to break through. Without a word, I help Kim up into the passenger seat, get myself behind the wheel and drive off.

The trip back to Cedar Tree is made in silence and when we pull up to Caleb and Katie's place to pick up Boo, Kim is out of the truck and rushing to the front door before I have a chance to get out of my seat. When I catch up to her she's sitting on the floor of the entrance, her arms around Boo's neck and her face buried in his fur. My brother and his wife look a little shocked, watching her.

"What's going on?" Caleb mouths at me when I bend over to pick Kim up off the floor. It takes a small battle of wills when Boo decides that moment to become protective and growl at me. With hierarchical balance restored, Boo tentatively looks on as I pick a sobbing Kim up and carry her to the couch. Katie is there in an instant, wrapping Kim in her arms. I tuck my hands in my pockets, not sure what I'm supposed to do next. Up until about an hour ago, I had been so sure of what my role is, where I belong. Now, I'm at a loss.

"Come with me," Caleb firmly orders as he walks past me outside. I follow him to the picnic table under the trees where we sit down and stare out at the beautiful view. "Talk to me," he urges. "What is happening here? Did things not go well with her mother?"

I shake my head, not sure how to explain. Not sure if I want to say the things I'm feeling out loud. Makes it too fucking real.

"Mal," Caleb softly pleads.

I take a deep breath and just like that, the shield of numbness cracks and the pain, fear and anger bleed out. "She lied." My voice cracks on emotion. "She said the MRI was just routine, but she lied. I knew something was off, I fucking knew it." I drop my head in my hands and instantly feel Caleb's hand come to rest on top of it.

"Brother," he says softly, instant understanding in his voice. He would, he lived through it just like me. "She has can—"

"Don't fucking say it!" I yell, snapping my head up. "I can't...I just can't." I push away from the table and start walking to the truck. I can't talk about it or it will be real. More real than I can handle. But before I have a chance to open the door, I'm swung around and pinned against the door by my brother's weight, his face right in mine.

"You're not doing this. You're not running. Not this time, Malachi. You're not twelve, this is *not* history repeating itself. You hear me? Neither of us are running. This time we're gonna stand together and fight. You with me?" He slams my back into the side of the truck with every new sentence and it feels like every emotion inside me is dislodged. A raw yell bursts free, and instantly, I'm folded into my brother's arms. His voice firm in my ear. "She doesn't know, does she? Your Kimeo, she doesn't know how your life—hell, our lives—got ripped apart when cancer took Nasha How our family was left raw and seeping like a festering sore in the aftermath. How love was turned into a destructive emotion and something to be feared." I hear the emotion tear at my brother's voice as he remembers too, watching my sister slip away so quickly, we never had time to adjust.

"I haven't had a fucking chance to."

"Talk to me," Caleb says, slinging his arm around me and walking me back to where we were sitting before.

So I do. I tell him about the MRI and how sick and scared she'd been and how I should've clued in it was more than *routine.* I tell him what little I've managed to glean from her in terms of her health issues and how she's been very reluctant in sharing. Of course, Caleb points out that what goes for the goose, goes for the gander and that I can't in all fairness expect her to be an open book when I haven't even told her about my own sordid history, my family, my sister's death, the dark path I followed after that. And he's right, of course he's right. Then comes Naomi's phone call and our meeting with her and the surgeon.

"Wait. So let me get this straight, they don't know if it's cancer yet?" Caleb asks, surprise on his face.

"They need to remove the tumor in order to do a reliable pathology, the surgeon said. But I have this gut feel—" A sharp jab on my shoulder cuts me off mid-sentence.

"Fuck your gut feeling," Caleb bites off, his face angry now. "For once, feel with your heart, not your head or your damn gut. When it comes to people you love, your 'gut' seems to be in a constant state of denial. You know this. Smarten the fuck up and start praying instead of picking the worst goddamn scenario possible!" He emphasizes that with a smack upside my head.

"She lied," I try, but Caleb's right on top of that.

"She omitted some details. Minor infraction compared to you keeping your whole fucking life from her."

I lower my eyes from his challenging glare. Truth is, I know this isn't really about lying, or omitting or whatever. I'm scared—of more than just cancer. I'm scared I won't be able to give her the support she needs if that's what this turns out to be. I'm scared I can't live up to the man I want to be for her. I'm scared she will be alone worrying about her mother, about herself, when I fail her. I'm scared to lose her...

I can deal with the people who are out to harm her. But how do I fight an enemy I can't see, don't understand and can't control?

Kim

"*Shhhh*," Katie's voice quiets me as deep sobs have turned into silent tears that don't seem to want to dry up. She sits down beside me on the couch, pushes a mug of something warm in my hands and instructs me to take a sip. Warm, sweet tea with milk. It soothes and slowly relaxes the hold panic has on my chest. "Now talk," she says.

I do. I tell her everything and before I'm even done, she's called Naomi, Emma and Kerry, who's been back at home since last Friday. I tell her about the drive to the hospital, Mal's reaction or lack there of—I still can't quite put my finger on it—and about the surgery scheduled four days from today.

"Holy shit." Are her exact words. "That's exactly it, the cherry on top of an already steaming pile of shit you've had on your plate. Good news is, there is no other direction to go but up, 'cause honey, there's no way this can get any worse. No way in hell."

I can't stop the snort that escapes at the visual and that sets us off giggling.

"I have to laugh, otherwise I'll just start crying again,"I manage breathlessly.

"Oh, honey,"Katie whispers, wrapping me into hug.

CHAPTER TWENTY-ONE

Kim

The universe must've taken Katie's words as a direct challenge, because the days to follow are brutal.

It hadn't taken long for Katie's living room to fill up with people I now comfortably called friends. It was a heart-warming gesture, but my eye kept wandering to the door, waiting for Mal to come in. About half an hour after the girls had arrived, though, it was Caleb who walked through the door. Alone. I caught up with him in the kitchen at one point and asked him where Mal had gone.

"He loves you, you know," had been his somewhat non-responsive answer. "He needs a little time to come to terms with this."

I started backing out of the kitchen, completely in shock. What does that mean? Come to terms with what? Tears welled up in my eyes as the hurt of having him walk out at a time like this tore through my soul.

Caleb watched me, moving toward me the moment the first tear rolled down my face. He pulled me into his arms and simply held me. "My brother will be back, Kim. I promise. There is so much about him you don't know yet, so much you should know. But I have faith he'll find a way to tell you. It's not you," he assured me when I tilted my head back to look at him. "It's that he doesn't open up to people. Not ever. This afternoon was the first time the two of us talked about stuff we should've talked about a long time ago. Things that happened in our childhood. I've learned to talk through a lot of that with Katie, but he hasn't had anyone in his life he trusted enough. Until you."

"But—"

"Give him a little bit of time. I'd like nothing better than to tell you what you need to know, but that's not mine to share with you. It's his. Trust me when I say my brother is worth waiting for, no matter how bad it looks right now."

With a kiss on the top of my head he walked out of the kitchen.

That was Friday. Today is Monday and I haven't heard from him yet. I even sent him a text, but he hasn't responded. The girls haven't given me a chance to drown in my worries. Just this morning Naomi was over before her clinic hours started. She'd brought a book about Hashimoto's for me to read. I'd done research online already and cried so hard when I discovered every one of my symptoms listed. Every last one, including my weight, the joint pain, the fatigue and the nightmares. They're all directly related to a poorly functioning thyroid. Naomi told me that there is medication to regulate the symptoms but that we had to wait for the surgery and pathology before we work on a treatment plan.

How ironic is it that the moment arrives in my forty years on this earth when I finally receive a diagnosis, and I can't even be happy. I want to be. Hell, part of me is elated, but that doesn't last long. The threat of cancer is too real. Naomi mentioned that the longer the condition goes untreated, the more likely the chance is of developing some kind of abnormality. Sometimes in the form of a cyst, which is relatively easy to get rid of, but sometimes in the form of a solid mass.

I try hard to keep my mind on what I can control right now, and that is absorbing as much information as I can about Hashimoto's. Knowledge is half the battle. I miss Mal though. Miss talking to him, touching him. I'm fighting to keep persistent insecurities at bay, reminding myself constantly of Caleb's words.

"Mind if I make a pot of coffee?" Neil interrupts my thoughts, as he saunters into the living room where I'm curled up on the couch, with the book Naomi left me.

"Of course," I tell him, wondering why he had no one to go home to. He'd picked me up at Katie's place on Friday afternoon and hadn't left my side since. Any hopes of going home to my own place in Cortez off the table for the foreseeable future. Gus's decree. He said I had the choice of an FBI safe house, until Damian Gomez and his crew could make sure there was no further threat to my life. Gus had offered up the alternative of my staying in Beth's house under GFI's protection. Since I was able to keep Boo with me here, I chose to stay. I didn't volunteer that I needed to be here in case Mal returns.

"Actually, I think I changed my mind. I'll be out back with the dog," Neil says, his eyes focused on something outside the window.

Mal

I grab for the bottle, the only thing I brought with me into the kiva, and take a swig. The water is cold and helps wake me up.

I've been holed up here for three nights and they've been cold ones. With nothing more than the clothes on my back, it's been a bit of a challenge to fight the cold and the inevitable hunger. Not sure what drew me here when I left Caleb sitting at the picnic table outside his house. I guess I needed the quiet to sort through my messed up emotions. Pain, anger, fear... love.

More than once I'd been tempted to walk the forty-five minute trek back out to the parking lot to see if I could catch a signal so I could call—hear her voice—but each time, fear held me back. I'm still terrified. On a good day I'm not worthy of Kim's love, not the way I've lived my life before coming to Cedar Tree. Sure, I can blame it on circumstances, but the truth is, both Caleb and I came from the same fucked up nest. A nest that used to be a loving family until cancer ate its way through. Not just taking my sister in an ungodly short amount of time, but tearing through the very fabric that had made us a unit. She was gone and my parents left shortly after, my father drowning in a bottle and my mother drowning in her grief. No room remaining for Caleb or I. No place safe from the loss of not only my sister, but our family too. I'd been the only one making the wrong choices though. Caleb joined the Rangers, moved away and found his path, when I persisted in sticking around, taking my anger out on the world and keeping my wounds raw. Cancer had become my number one enemy. One I still have no defense against. Which is why the thought of going another round with that bitch scares the fuck out of me. Why I needed to come here to find my courage. I'm a coward.

This is where Caleb found me last time. Where I had holed up when my previous life chewed me up and spit me out. I still carried a huge chip on my shoulder then, one that I'd been able to whittle down bit by bit since I've started over in Cedar Tree. Maybe that's it, maybe that's why I needed to come back here. To find the right direction again. Another crossroads. Another choice. But the three nights in the dark stillness of the kiva has made it clear there is no choice. There is no walking away from the first person I have dared give my heart to voluntarily. The pain that would come with the prospect of losing her to cancer is no more substantial than the pain leaving her altogether would cause.

The cold sip of water seems to have cleared away any lingering uncertainties. Life is just like that, unpredictable, painful at times, but with possibilities so heartbreakingly beautiful, it would be a sin to leave them behind.

Suddenly I'm in a hurry. I've left my girl to deal with a lifetime of nightmares all by herself. When she needed me most, I snuck off like a coward. Fuck, I'm an idiot. I can't blame her if she turns me away. Not that I will go. I'm ready to fight this time. Fight for the life she deserves. The life we deserve.

I scramble up the ladder out of the kiva and am momentarily blinded by the mid-morning sun warming the day ahead. This place, this haven in the middle of the Arches National Park that we discovered many years ago on a family vacation when life was still simple, has worked its magic on me once again. A little weak from lack of nutrition and reeking after days without a shower, I start my trek to the parking lot, where I hope my car is still parked.

"It's me."

"Finally," Caleb says on the other side of the line. "I was about to come and drag you out of that hole in the ground again."

"Figured you'd know where I went."

"Brother, I know you as well as I know myself. If I didn't believe you would come out of there with your priorities sorted, I wouldn't have been so patient. How are you?"

The simplicity of his straightforward honesty hits me. My brother trusts me to do the right thing. He trusted me before I trusted myself.

"I'm good. A bit rough on the edges, but good."

"Need a pick up?"

"Nah, I'm on my way. Just coming through Monticello. How badly have I fucked up?" I ask tentatively, trying to get a lay of the land before I wade in. Caleb's responding chuckle is kind of reassuring in itself.

"Nothing that can't be fixed, but buddy, you best come all the way clean with this woman. Despite her shy ways and soft little body, that girl is made of strong stuff. Katie and her posse have not given her a chance to be alone much, but from what I hear and can see for myself, she is hanging tough."

"I love her, Caleb."

"Not news to me, Malachi. No other reason for you to struggle so hard. She's worth it."

"I know," I admit softly.

When I pull into the driveway, I see Neil framed in the window, staring at me, before he disappears from sight. I thought about stopping at my apartment for a quick shower, but ended up driving right by. I need her to see she is first and foremost on my mind—in my heart.

Neil is hanging over the back gate when I get out of my truck, waving me over.

"Done communing with the universe?" the smartass asks.

"Yes, not that it's any of your business," I bite off, but it only makes the idiot smile bigger. "How's she holding up?"

"The women-folk have not let up much. They've run down the door. When no one's around, she's either at the computer, researching the hell out of her condition or she sits staring out the window. Other than the cry-fest she had on Friday, she's been quiet."

Guilt churns in my stomach at the thought of having caused her further pain and I know I have some work ahead of me. "Think she'll kick me out?"

"Nah man, figure you've got a bit of grovelling to do, but she's not gonna kick you out. Unless maybe cause you stink and look like shit."

I back away from the gate and straighten up, taking a deep breath in. "Thanks. You're a pal. Still, best stick around until we're sure. I want to get an update too, but first I have some crow to eat." With that I turn toward the house.

"Get out!"

That's Kim's first reaction when she looks over her shoulder to see who walked in the door. Next she gets up off the couch where she's curled up with some mammoth sized book, which she carelessly tosses aside as she turns toward me, hands on her hips. Her eyes squint down to slits as she looks me up and down and slowly I see the anger in her eyes change to concern. I can't get a fucking word out. I'm just standing there gaping at this beautiful woman who I'd gladly lay my life down for and still no words will come. A thick lump is stuck in my throat and it takes everything from me not to bawl like a baby at the thought I'd walked out on her.

"Mal? Are you okay?"

I watch her slowly moving toward me and I stand dead still until she's within reach. My hand shoots out and I pull her to me, sinking down on the floor, taking her with me. Lack of food and sleep, and emotional exhaustion finally taking its toll. Kim simply twists around on my lap until we're face to face, her hands on my neck.

"What happened to you?" she whispers, confusion in her eyes.

"You." My voice cracks. "You happened and I can't..." I curl my body around hers and shove my face in her neck, taking a deep breath. "I had a sister, Nasha. She was the middle one in the true sense of the word. Always stepping in when Caleb and I would fight, which happened quite a bit." I allow myself a few happier memories before I plow on. "At first I guess they hadn't wanted to worry me, and then it was too late. I was worried already when she just got sicker and sicker, but by the time my parents finally told me Nasha was dying, her spirit had already left. A week after that she was gone, and I never really had a chance to say goodbye."

My eyes lift to find Kim's eyes wet with tears, but it's only when she reaches to wipe at my cheek that I realize I'm crying too.

"She had cancer, right?"

When I just nod at her question, she gets off my lap and stands, pulling me up by my hand. Wordlessly she leads me upstairs to the bedroom and pushes me to lie down, curling up beside me. I roll over to face her, stroking my fingers down her profile and letting them rest between her breasts. On her heart.

"Nasha's death devastated all of us. Mom, Dad, Caleb, as much as me. We were so broken individually that none of us had it in them to hold the other up. Mom's grief turned into apathy, where she would wander around the house, a picture of Nasha clenched in her arms. As if she was searching. My dad wasn't much better, except he numbed himself with alcohol. Caleb and I...well we raged for a bit and then Caleb left. Joined the armed forces, and I... I couldn't tear myself away from the anger. I was twelve when she died and I was barely fifteen when Caleb took off. I don't blame him. We all had to save ourselves or we'd all go down together. But it was hard."

I want to look away. I know I can't avoid letting her in completely, but I hesitate showing her the darkest side of me. The risk is not insignificant.

"I made choices that weren't the right ones."

"That's understandable." She smiles and I love her for it, but she has no idea.

"I've done bad things, Kimeo. Things that should've landed me in jail for a very long time. Bad things that have harmed others." I see her wince, before she regroups and smiles a tremulous smile in encouragement. I'll take it. Even if it's all I'll get. "Ending up in Cedar Tree, I saw the family my brother had built for himself, and rejected it at first. But there's no way to keep these people at bay, as I'm sure you've now learned. Once they decide you're part of the family, there isn't a damn thing you can do about it." She chuckles at that and smiles, almost nostalgically. "I didn't stand a chance," I continue. "But really trusting? Real trust, where you put your faith in someone, give yourself completely? I never wanted that. Never believed in it.

And then you happened, " I say and reach out to cup her face, because I need to feel her soft skin. "Like a fucking tsunami you wiped out my carefully constructed barriers until every last emotion was floating around aimlessly." I can't hold back the chuckle of self-derision that slips out. "To think I thought I was beyond feeling seems funny now. Truth is, I'm a fucking mess, *Nizhóní.* I spent the last almost seventy-two hours holed up in a kiva in Utah with only a bottle of water for a companion. I probably stink, am dirty and the only thing I was able to get clear in my head is that nothing is worth anything if it doesn't have you."

I roll Kim over on her back and brace myself over her. "So you see, I'm not anything like the man you thought." I see emotions swirling in her eyes and hold my breath for what comes next.

"No, you're not. You're more."

Kim

My voice comes out whispered and for a minute I think he hasn't heard me.

I didn't think there would be anything he could say that would make me understand why he up and left on Friday. I was wrong. Now that he's lifted a veil, there is so much unresolved pain and grief visible, it's a miracle he's able to function the way he has. I'm no stranger to the kind of damage that can be done to a child. With actions just as much as with words. But words can heal too, when weighed carefully and given without reservation. Mal has shown me that. He's used his words as a balm on the wounds left by others. Time and time again. It's my turn.

Finding his eyes with mine, I stroke my fingers over his unshaven jaw until I know I have his complete focus.

"I love all of you, Malachi. Each part, every nuance, the dark, the light, the protective, the vigilant, the tender, the wounded—I love them all. Each separately and all combined. There isn't a part of you I want to hide from or want hidden from me. I love you."

His eyes grow darker above mine and he opens his mouth as if to say something before closing it again, clenching his jaw. He inhales sharply through his nose and then buries his face in the hollow of my neck, his arms banding tightly around me.

And I tighten my hold on him, making the same silent vow without words, the message infinitely stronger.

CHAPTER TWENTY-TWO

Kim

I'd been dozing off with Mal's body pinning me to the bed when my phone started ringing. Exhaustion must've felled him, because he'd fallen asleep with his head on my chest. Poor guy. When I tried to ignore the insistent ringing, he'd woken up and mumbled for me to get it.

"Might be something important. Could be your sister. Go grab it, I'm gonna wash the kiva off me." With a stroke of his fingertips over my face and a soft press of his lips on mine, he disappeared into the bathroom. I just managed to get to the phone before it stopped ringing.

"I mean it, Kim. I've been giving this a lot of thought while I was stuck in that damn 'safe-house' with my very cranky husband. I don't care what he says. This store is my dream, and with your help, I think we can make it something truly unique."

"I don't want to be the cause of a rift between you, though."

That makes Kerry laugh bitterly. "Honey, trust me, it's got nothing to do with you. It's something I guess has been a bone of contention between us from the start. It just has been driven to the surface in the past few weeks. Greg's never been a fan of me starting my own business. Never quite voiced why, but I get the feeling that it somehow threatens his sense of male superiority. He is a simple, hard-working man, who doesn't understand my passion. He doesn't even read, for God's sake.

It's frivolous to him. The sad part is, he can't even bring himself to be excited on my behalf. He's never really had much of a reaction to what I've built so far. Not even when the local newspaper did that write up—he just tossed it aside. What he wants is not who I am. It never was, except I'm only just now realizing it. All the years of research I did before I opened the store, he thought of it as a hobby. Never took it seriously. Ever since the store opened he's been increasingly unhappy that it takes my attention away from him."

"I'm so sorry, Kerry. I had no idea it rooted that deep." My heart aches for my friend. I knew her marriage wasn't all bliss, but I hadn't realized how brittle it really is.

"Nothing to be sorry for, sweetie. We'll just have to deal—and we will. In the meantime you get yourself sorted until you feel ready to jump in with me."

I say goodbye to Kerry when I hear the shower turn off upstairs. She'd initially called to offer to take me to the hospital tomorrow. She was happy for me but cautious when I told her Mal had come back. Without going into details, I assured her his reasons for leaving so abruptly were enough for me. She did insist on being in the hospital waiting room with him. There wasn't a thing I could say that would sway her and I have to admit, it makes me feel better to know she'd be there.

"Kim?" Mal's voice travels down the stairs. "Everything okay?"

I get to the bottom of the stairs, look up at him and my stomach does a silly twist. With his hair still loose but washed, and naked but for a towel wrapped around his hips, he looks like a fearless warrior. It only makes me feel more blessed that a man so strong and powerful valued me enough to bare his soul.

"Everything is fine. That was Kerry inquiring about tomorrow, but I told her you'd be taking me."

He slowly starts moving down the stairs and stops on the last step, looking down on me. "I am?" he asks and for a minute I feel unsure. Maybe I assumed too much?

"Well, unless you'd rather not. I didn't mean to presume..."

"I want to," he says gruffly, lifting a hand to wipe a wayward strand of hair out of my face. "Wherever this journey leads, I won't let you take another step alone."

Mal

"That's a new one," Neil's voice sounds from the kitchen door where he stands, hands in his pockets and shivering slightly. "It's usually the kitchen where I seem to have a habit of walking into evidence of my coworkers' primal urges. This time it's the stairs. Maybe I should write this down for posterity?"

Kim takes a few steps back immediately and turns a pretty shade of pink. I pull the towel off my hips, ball it up and toss it at him.

"You're a pain in my ass, boy," I call over my shoulder as I march bare-assed up the stairs to get dressed.

"I'm fucking blind now!" Neil yells dramatically which has Kim burst out in giggles behind me.

Once dressed, I find Kim on the couch, her nose deep in her book, and with a soft kiss on her lips, I wander into the kitchen to find Neil.

"Catch me up. What did I miss?"

He looks up from the laptop on the counter. "Not a hell of a lot. They've got Hartnett en route to a safe house, but they haven't managed to get anything useful out of him. Other than that, there seems to be a tug of war going on between jurisdictions. Everyone wants a go at this guy and since he's got charges pending in different states now, the FBI is taking control. For the moment."

"No chance of getting this resolved any time soon, is there?" I observe and I can tell Neil appreciates my sense of urgency. It's two-fold; I want both clouds of uncertainty removed from looming over our heads. Gomez has made it clear he intends to use Kim's testimony to help tie Hartnett to the murder of her boss, and that has become even more pivotal to the case now that they don't have any other witnesses left, with Winter and his partner dead. And then there's the concern over the outcome of the surgery scheduled for tomorrow. Too many balls in the air, and all are connected. A heavy feeling settles back on my shoulders but this time I'm not running away from it. I'm standing firm.

"She'll be okay," Neil offers, making me wonder how he can read me so well.

"Yes she will, but get the fuck out of my head, boy. You're freaking me out."

With a chuckle, he turns back to his screen and leaves me to pour myself a coffee.

"Is this another recipe from your *amá sáni?*"

Kim walks up behind me and leans around, her hand on the middle of my back and her nose over the pan.

"Sort of. It's just a beef stew, but she used to make it with deer meat. Venison."

"Smells good. What's in this?"

"Cubed beef, carrots, onions, a few bay leaves and black pepper. Oh, and some wine."

"That's what I smell, the wine and the bay leaves." She turns and smiles at me, lifting her face for a kiss. "Makes me hungry."

I chuckle at her suggestive words. "It does, does it? Too bad Neil is in the other room and I can guarantee he won't be leaving on an empty stomach. For all his size, the guy is one big hollow leg." I lay the spoon on the counter and wrap my arms around her. "But once he's fed and I close the door behind him, I plan to feast on you."

"Incoming," Neil walks into the kitchen, sniffing the air. "When's dinner?"

Kim and I look at each other and burst out laughing. It feels fucking great.

Neil takes kitchen duty after almost clearing out the pans, and Kim and I are just sitting back on the couch, watching the news for the first time in what seems like forever, when the doorbell rings.

"They wouldn't let me bring booze!" I hear Arlene's near bellow from the front door, when Kim gets up to answer.

"Not a good idea to thin the blood of someone who is going under the knife tomorrow, you twit," Emma points out and the banter between those two makes me smile as it always does. Goes a long way to soothe the irritation of seeing my plans for the evening evaporate with their arrival. When I turn in my seat, I find three angry pairs of eyes staring at me.

"Decided to come back, did ya?" Of course Arlene is the first one to attack. "Your girl gets bad news and your solution is to slink off to wherever you went and let her face that shit alone? Never expected that of you, Mal."

"Arlene!" Emma tries to shush her but doesn't take her accusing eyes off me.

I'm about to respond, because she's right. The two of them plus Naomi have cause to be angry at me, but Kim doesn't give me a chance. She walks over to stand in front of me and turns to the three women. "You've been amazing friends, better than I've ever known and I'm so grateful for that—but—you have no right to come barging in and go on the attack when you don't have a clue what you're talking about."

"But, honey, he left you..."Arlene persists.

"I saw you this morning, you were barely hanging on," Naomi points out. But Emma's eyes go from me to Kim and back, and the faintest ghost of a smile tilts her lips.

"She's right."

"He had good reason and that's all you need to know. He explained to *me* and that was good enough," Kim says firmly with her hands fisted at her side fierce in her protection of me.

I stand up and slip my arms around her waist from behind. "Down, tiger," I mumble for her ears only, but in current company that's an impossible feat. They all heard, but I ignore them. "They're just looking out for you and that's not a bad thing."

Kim turns in my arms, looking up at me confused. "But it's—"

"Shhh." I put my finger on her lips before turning to the group assembled.

"Did I miss the cat fight? Dammit, I was just putting the last of the dishes away when I heard the commotion." Neil walks into the room, having obviously heard the raised voices, and looks at all the players in this impromptu stand off.

"Neil!" Emma, who at times was more of a mother to Neil than anything else, scolds him.

"What?" he feigns innocence. "I'm a great purveyor of mud wrestling, but I'll never turn away from a good cat fight."

I bury my face in Kim's hair to stifle my laughter. The kid really is a nut, although I've come to know him enough to realize he's spouting idiocy just to diffuse the tense situation. He's so much smarter than the young pup demeanor he puts on.

"I really wish I'd brought that bottle," Arlene pouts. "Could've used a drink just about now."

Emma snorts and Kim giggles. Naomi stays silent and just observes the woman in my arms before lifting her eyes to mine and giving me a single nod. As much as it conveys her acceptance, it also holds a threat that I better not fuck it up. I nod back, letting her know I got the message. Loud and clear.

"Where's Katie? Or Beth? I would've thought you'd bring the entire wild bunch for a smack down," I say, trying to lighten the lingering mood.

"Beth and Clint are in Durango for the weekend visiting with Clint's brother who just bought a house, and Katie is looking after Max for them," Emma says fiddling with the handle of her cane.

"My brother couldn't look after the boys for a few hours?"

"Uh, Katie actually didn't want to come. She said she trusts you," Arlene admits grudgingly and that sets Emma off again.

"You never told me that. You said you weren't able to get through to her," she accuses Arlene.

"Yeah well, I didn't lie. I *wasn't* able to 'get through' to her," Arlene answers, her finger quotes rather dramatic.

"Enough. Please tell me there's booze in this house. I'm sorry, Kim," Naomi says apologetically, "but I need the numbing buzz of alcohol to block out these two."

"Hey!" The two women in question exclaim simultaneously.

Crazy, overprotective, impulsive but oh so loving bunch of nuts. I look down at Kim's smiling face and in that moment, I feel like the luckiest bastard in the world. Not at all deserving, but fuck if I'm gonna throw back this gift of ultimate trust she's given me.

However long I can have it for.

CHAPTER TWENTY-THREE

*"A rocky vineyard does not need a prayer,
but a pick axe."*

~ Navajo

Kim

"Hey Kim, how are you feeling?"

I don't know the nurse whose face is leaning over me. She's not the same one I saw when I closed my eyes.

I try to answer, but there's no sound when I open my mouth, just a sharp burning in my throat. My mouth snaps shut.

"Don't try to talk," she says and my first thought is *Then you shouldn't have asked me a question to start with.* My second thought is *I want Mal,* but when I mouth his name she doesn't have a clue.

I must've dozed off again because the next thing I know, the surgeon is beside my bed. Dr. Mitcham starts talking but I hold up my hand to stop him mid-sentence. I really need Mal here for support. Again I try to speak, with much the same result. Finally the nurse clues in and hands me a piece of paper and a pen. *Please get Mal FIRST.* I write out.

"Is Mal the tall dark gentleman with the ponytail?" she asks and I nod."I'll go grab him. He's been pacing a hole in the floor and I almost had to call security on him when I told him only family was allowed in recovery." She looks my way and smiles weakly. "Anyway... I'll just be a minute."

Thank goodness Dr. Mitcham takes that time to check the IV drip on the side of the bed. Not a minute later, the door slams open and Mal is at my side in two strides, grabbing my hand in one of his and wiping tears I didn't realize were running down my face away.

"Hush baby, I'm right here," he mumbles as he leans down to brush his lips lightly over mine.

"Right." The surgeon draws our attention. "Surgery went as expected. The tumor was lodged against your thyroid making it impossible to remove without sacrificing the entire gland. We were able to confirm the presence of abnormal cells in the first sample we took and decided not to muck about and took your thyroid gland entirely."

Mal's hand holding mine is gripping me tight, but I welcome the mild pain, needing to feel something.

"So it's cancer?" Mal asks the question I can't ask.

"PTL or primary thyroid lymphoma, yes. You were lucky, we caught it early. This would've likely gone undetected for a while yet if Dr. Waters hadn't been so thorough. We removed generously, to make sure we got it all in one go, but it's likely you'll need follow-up treatment to make sure it hasn't spread. We're not taking any chances. What you should know is that PTL is very treatable. Usually a combination treatment but your oncologist will go over your options with you. You will need to start on hormone replacement therapy right away. I will let Dr. Waters know the outcome of the surgery and about the dosages we'll start you out on. Best of luck to you."

And with a handshake for each of us, he's gone, leaving us in a shocked silence that neither of us seems willing to break. Instead, Mal squeezes himself on the bed, careful not to bump any of the wires still attached to me and pulls me in his arms.

We're still wrapped around each other when a while later the door opens and Naomi walks in.

"Hey," Mal's voice rumbles in his chest.

"I hear we've got some cancer ass to kick?"

I try smiling at her but it's a pathetic attempt, I can tell when she winces.

"You don't get to talk yet, just listen," she says pointing a finger at me. "Mitcham tells me he's pretty sure he got it all. He took out the entire thyroid and some lymph nodes, all of which have been sent to pathology. That report will be sent to an oncologist at the Mercy Durango Cancer Center and we'll get you in there within the next few days. This is going to be fast and furious, folks. Very intense for a relatively short period of time but then you're done. Well, other than that without a thyroid, you'll have to take hormones for the rest of your life, but I'm thinking in the grand scope of things, that's a minor glitch. Let's get this big sucker taken care of first. Deal?"

I nod, smiling a little at the pep talk that makes Naomi sound like a football coach. I'll kick this. My entire life I've known there was something wrong with me. In a perverted kind of way, this almost feels like justification for all the clinic doors I went through hopeful for an answer, and walked out again discouraged and sad. Perhaps I should send each and every one of them copies of the Hashimoto's diagnosis and the pathology report. Assholes.

Mal

"Hey, how is she doing?"

I've just left Kim in a regular room, where she'll get to stay overnight. Naomi is with her, talking to her, trying to calm her down 'cause she's pissed. Angry at the cancer, angry at the army of doctors she'd seen before who never took the time to listen. Her anger is fueling mine and I was already barely hanging on, so I told her I'd go grab a quick coffee. I didn't expect to bump into Caleb in the hallway.

He's leaning against the wall next to a waiting room and the moment I walk up to him, I notice the room is full of familiar faces. Damn. Looks like Cedar Tree closed its doors today. Even Arlene and Seb are both there. Slipping his arm around my shoulders, my brother sidles up to me as I look around the room dumbfounded.

"Tried to keep them away. As you can see that was a complete failure."

I have to swallow hard at the sudden lump in my throat before I move into the room. "Thank you guys," I manage, but barely. "She's...awake. Naomi is with her." I fall silent, not sure how to proceed. Not sure if I can give voice to something I've hated for so long, threatening to take the one woman—hell, the only woman—I've ever let in. Fate wouldn't be so cruel, would she?

"Just spit it out, brother," Caleb says softly behind me, but instead of talking I take a deep breath in and swing my fist full force into the wall by the door. Caleb's arms slip around me from behind, pinning my arms to my side, but he doesn't have to worry. I needed that out of my system. The throbbing pain in my fist gives me momentary distraction until a little voice pipes up.

"Unca owie?"

I look down to see Mattias toddling over, eyeing my hand with worry on his little face. Fuck me. "I'm good, little man. Just a Band-Aid and I'll be fine." His head tilts to the side as he looks at me, before reaching for the offending hand and pressing a slobbery kiss on it.

"Me kiss Unca owie bettuh."

"Thank you, buddy—that helps." My voice cracks. "It's cancer." I focus on Katie's face when I spit it out and when she squeezes her eyes shut at the news. I can feel it in my gut.

"Brother..." Caleb mumbles behind me. The two of them are the only people who know exactly what this means. Katie knows, because Caleb opened up completely with her, just like I've now done with Kimeo.

"She'll kick that bitch, just you wait," Arlene says blinking furiously.

"Arlene! Language..." Emma points at Mattias who has found his buddy Max playing on the floor.

"Damn right!" Kerry says at the same time.

I fill them in on the rest of it. The wait for the lab to type the cancer, the appointment at Mercy Durango, the aggressive treatments that will follow. By the time I'm done, I'm drained, but when I look around the room, all I see is hope on the faces of our friends, and just like that, the heavy load on my shoulders lifts a bit. Whatever happens, we're not in this battle alone.

"Please, Mal, I need you."

Kim's voice is still hoarse from surgery almost a week later. She was warned that in some cases, the type of surgery she had could alter the voice permanently. I would hate not hearing that sweet melodic sound again, so I scold her when she talks too much. Her sister had been down for a visit. Left again the same day after a tearful apology when she heard Kim had likely always had a thyroid condition. Harsh to learn that her entire life she had berated Kim for things she never had in her control. I couldn't help but hope she felt like shit at the discovery that her small-mindedness and judgement were always unfounded. Not that it's ever okay to treat another person like that. I knew she was hurting. Good. She could afford a little hurt after all Kim incurred. After assuring Kim that their mother appeared to be recovering slowly, but surely, Britta left. She cried and promised to make up for lost time which got Kim going. Pissed me right the fuck off, because crying is painful for her and it doesn't do her voice much good.

I'm staying with Kim in Beth's house. Nowhere else I want to be, and Gus agreed to the leave of absence until we had her back on her feet. His words, not mine. It's not like money is going to be an issue. I've built up a nice nest egg over the past few years of going straight and hardly any expenses.

I need to be close to her at all times. To sleep with her in my arms, feel her breath on my chest when we wake up together, although I haven't dared move beyond kissing her and holding her. Until now.

Kim is awake when I come to bed and her eyes follow me around the bedroom as I strip my clothes off and drop them on the hamper. "If you can drop them on it, I'm sure it wouldn't be much extra effort to drop them *in* it," she points out with an eyebrow raised. I love seeing a bit of fire back, as I ignore her remark and crawl up the bed and on top of her, my elbows bracing her head on each side.

"You being a smartass?"

She wiggles a little, her legs spreading wide to allow for my hips to settle down between them. That's when her eyelids go half-mast and in her croaky voice she begs me.

"Please..." she repeats, lifting her hips and mouth simultaneously, reaching for contact. "I need to feel you. Need you to make me feel alive."

That I can do, and with swift, gentle moves, I strip her nightie off. She's blessedly naked underneath. Wearing nothing more than my underwear. It's only a second before I too am naked, but instead of fitting my hips between her legs again, I slide back down the bed to wedge my shoulders there. The soft flesh of her inner thighs pillowing my ears, muffling the sounds she makes when I close my mouth over her pussy. My tongue flat against her folds, her taste and scent invading my senses. She's so slick and primed, it doesn't take much to send her soaring with the pulsing suction I keep on her clit. The moment I feel her legs relax and loosen their hold on my head, I kiss my way up her body, making sure to include a careful press of my lips against her incision. When I reach her lips, I plunge my tongue in her mouth, and at the same time I slide my cock into her sweet heat. Nothing like it.

My eyes lock on hers and in them I see everything I feel reflected. We knew sleep would be hard to find tonight and we both need this affirmation. This physical expression of every emotion we're feeling. This confirmation of life, right now, in this moment.

Our lovemaking is slow and as intimate as I've ever experienced anything, lasting deep into the night.

Tonight nothing but the two of us exist, but tomorrow we learn our enemy—and then we fight.

CHAPTER TWENTY-FOUR

Kim

"Want me to wait out here?" Naomi asks as the nurse waits to show us in to a private room.

Joe and Naomi had followed us into Durango this morning. Joe had an appointment with Damian Gomez and Naomi offered to come along so she could be here if we came away with questions. I would've asked her if she hadn't offered. Both Mal and I have been trapped in our own minds this morning. Thoughts of what was ahead preoccupying us both. Thoughts often too scary to voice. We seem to be too conscious of not upsetting the other. Ironic, that we both realize that but still find it difficult to open up to the other. Cancer is a bitch and having it out there as something that affects others is not the same as having it invade your life, like an unwanted and uninvited guest at your holiday table. Alien and uncomfortable. Scary even, like something separate from you intent on living in you, living off you, at your ultimate demise. The thought of fighting this...*thing* that has invaded me, by fighting my own body seems so unnatural. Which is why I don't really trust my own mind. Or Mal's for that matter. He would be inclined to want to avoid anything that is uncomfortable or painful for me.

Naomi is the perfect person to have with us. She cares, but is knowledgeable and removed enough to be able to give sound, fact-based advice. We'll need that.

"Hell no. You're coming in," I tell her, grabbing her hand and dragging her out of her chair. Mal chuckles from behind us. "And don't you dare bail out on me either," I throw at him for good measure.

"Talking too much," he warns me teasingly.

When the three of us walk chuckling through the door the nurse indicates, a very surprised doctor is already waiting for us. "Hi," she says, sticking out her hand. "I'm Dr. Jennifer Healey, I'm an oncologist here at Mercy Durango. I'm sorry, I'm a little startled. I'm not used to too much giddiness on a first visit but it sure is a nice change." She smiles at me, having somehow pegged me as her patient. "See you brought reinforcements too. That's good. You'll need the support, this is not gonna be a cakewalk. But make no mistake—you will kick this."

Over the next forty-five minutes, she amasses a team of different specialists to hammer out a treatment plan, which will span six weeks and will include three chemo treatments, immunotherapy, radiation and hormone replacement therapy. Apparently this is not uncommon with non Hodgkin's lymphoma, which I apparently have. Two of the lymph nodes they took had also been affected which is why they appear to be throwing the book at me. My head is spinning as Mal keeps his arm firmly around me. I'm so grateful Naomi is here to ask all the pertinent questions, because I swear I've forgotten seventy-five percent of what I've been told. All I can think about is my hair. How sick is that? As if that's the worst thing that can happen to me, losing my hair.

"So we'll see you tomorrow for your first chemo treatment, and Thursday we'll start with the first set of five consecutive days of radiation." Dr. Healey offers her hand again and when I grab it, she holds my hand in both of hers. "It's gonna be fast, my dear, but you have a great team here and we'll get you through it."

After Mal and Naomi say their goodbyes we make our way to the coffee shop in the lobby, where Joe is already waiting. I'm so exhausted. I can't even think let alone speak but I do notice the serious look he sends Malachi.

"You girls grab a coffee and I'll just borrow Mal for a second, okay?" He gives Naomi a quick kiss while Mal hugs me tight.

"You gonna be okay for a bit here?"

I nod my response forcing myself to open my fists, which are clenched in his shirt.

"Come on." Naomi grabs my arm and pulls me to the counter. "Since they already warned you that nausea might become a problem in the next few weeks, we might as well gorge ourselves now, right?" She points out the pastries behind the glass of the counter. My knee jerk instinct to say no almost makes it out of my mouth but at the last minute I forcefully shove it away. No fucking way. Not a minute longer am I going to cave to the hurtful conceptions planted in my brain. If I am starting to understand anything, it's that I've let that kind of thinking restrict me for forty fucking years. Not a moment longer.

"I'll have that one, and that one." I point to a scrumptious looking jelly-filled donut and a cream cheese Danish. Haven't tasted either of those since my father was alive and would occasionally sneak me off to the bakery around the corner. "And I'll have a full fat latte with cinnamon," I add rebelliously, making Naomi laugh.

"That's the spirit, girlfriend," she snickers, throwing her arm around my shoulder. "You heard the woman, and make that a double order," she tells the kid at the counter.

Mal

"What's going on?"

Joe takes me out the front door and over to a bench under a couple of trees where we sit down.

I don't have a good feeling about this. He wouldn't have picked this moment to pull me aside if it wasn't something serious.

"Hartnett's gone."

"What?" I shake my head, not quite grasping what he's saying.

"Jacob Hartnett disappeared from the safe house in the mountains this morning. One FBI agent was knocked unconscious, another was shot in the stomach. We don't know yet what the exact sequence of events was, but the result is the same—he's gone."

"Did he have help?"

"Looks like. He was shackled the entire time he was there, but when they found him gone this morning, his shackles had been cut off with a bolt cutter. They don't generally keep bolt cutters around for convenience. So yes, I'd assume he had outside help, although how the hell they were able to find the house in the middle of nowhere, I have no idea. Shit, we didn't even know where it was until this morning."

"Fuck! This is not what we need right now," I bite off, knowing full well Joe can't do a damn thing about it either.

"I know, bud. Believe me I know."

"I can't take Kim away now. Her treatments start tomorrow. And starting Thursday she has to be in daily for radiation. I was already thinking about finding a short-term lease here in Durango. She's likely gonna feel pretty miserable and I don't want her to have to drive back and forth for hours every day."

"That might not be a bad idea, you know? Let me see if I can get a hold of Jed. You remember him? Clint's brother? He stepped in when Clint was injured and finished Naomi's clinic."

"Yeah, I remember him. He moved here, didn't he? To Durango?"

"Yup, but I just heard from Clint he's working on a massive property outside of Ouray. So he's out of town. Let me make a few calls. See if you can't crash at his place for the time being. It's a nice log home just out of town. Pretty secluded, but I'm guessing only fifteen or twenty minutes from the hospital." Joe looks pretty pleased with himself and I've got to admit, it seems like a pretty solid plan. Question now is what to tell Kim.

"Tell her," Joe says as if I voiced my thoughts out loud. "Seriously—I would. Secrets kill relationships. You love her, right?" I just lift my eyebrow and Joe chuckles. "Right, I figured. That woman in there is stronger than she looks, my friend."

I know that. Of course I know that. *Jesus. All these guys are in my head. It's creeping me out.*

I glance over at the coffee shop, spot her sitting at a window seat with Naomi and I burst out laughing. Joe looks at me oddly, before following my gaze and when he starts chuckling himself, I know he's seeing the same thing.

The moment she spots Joe and I laughing, I see her put the donut down and wipe furiously at her mouth and chin which are covered in icing sugar and jam. Next she throws me a dirty look, which apparently Joe finds even more hilarious.

"She doesn't get out much, does she? She looks starved," he snickers, which earns him the sharp end of my elbow as I get up from the bench to try and make nice with my girl. She had looked pretty ridiculous, sitting there with both hands on that giant donut obliterating half of her face. "She's starved herself for decades. It's only recently I managed to convince her to eat. I'm thinking she's doing some catching up."

"Right," Joe says, suddenly serious. "I can see why she would—now."

By the time we get inside, Kim has shoved the plate with the half eaten donut and an untouched Danish to the edge of the table. She refuses to look at me.

"Sorry," I try as I slide onto the seat beside her, draping my arm around her shoulders which she is holding stiff. "I wasn't laughing *at* you, per se." That earns me a glare from the corner of her eyes, before she focuses on the table in front of her again.

That went well.

Kim

"We'll come back here after your treatment tomorrow and I will pack us up. Thursday morning we drive back to Durango, drop Boo off with Caleb, and settle into Jed's place after we stop for your radiation."

We just got back from Durango and are taking Boo for a much needed walk. Neil is following behind. Something that apparently is necessary again with Hartnett on the loose. Mal filled me in on the way home and after the initial shock, I got pissed. I never asked for any of this, yet I seem to get handed one pile of shit after the other. Damn that Hartnett. God only knows where he is now. I don't even know if he would bother coming after me at this point in time. What's the use? Am I not the least of his worries now that he's escaped federal custody? The anger feels good—productive. I know I overreacted when I saw Mal and Joe laughing at me. I guess it must've looked ridiculous, but I've always been sensitive when it comes to how I look and it doesn't help to know that I'll likely be losing my hair sometime in the near future too. Now that's gonna be something to see. I swallow down the tears that are threatening. I have no time or energy to spend crying over the little things right now. I should save my energy for more important things—like beating this thing. I don't even know if it would be wise for Hartnett to get close to me, I might just use him to take my anger out on. I can't use Mal for that, he's suffering enough already.

"I don't think that's a good idea. Hartnett knows I'm in Cedar Tree. He doesn't have a clue about my treatments. Last place he'll look is back in Durango. He'll come here first."

Mal stops and turns toward me. "Then what do you suggest?"

"Easy, we'll spend tonight here, and tomorrow we'll leave for Durango early, *with* Boo. Drop him off at Jed's house, go to the hospital and just stay there. Why come back here?" I don't want to even discuss Boo. He's coming with, whether Mal likes it or not.

"Babe, it's much easier to leave Boo at the barn with Caleb. We're gonna be in and out of Jed's place and it'll just be a new place he needs to get used to. He's used to hanging out with Blue."

I shake my head no, even though I know what he says makes sense.

"Gonna need Boo, Malachi. I need him there with me." My voice sounds fragile even to me. It's true though, if I'm going to be miserable, I want Boo around. He's always so sweet when I feel off.

Mal bends down trying to look me in the eyes, which I'm trying to keep averted because I. Don't. Want to cry. Noticing my struggle, he folds me in his arms. "Okay," he says simply. "Boo comes. Maybe what we'll do is see if Neil can bring him later. He was going to head up there anyway."

"Neil? Why?"

"For extra safety. In case we run into anything unexpected. In case I have to attend a meeting at some point or leave you alone for groceries or whatever. Two of us are better than one, and I figure you're already used to Neil being around."

My first instinct is to protest. These people have done so much, already there's no way I can ever repay them. But as we make our way back onto our street, with Boo happily lifting his leg on every blade of grass, it dawns on me that having Neil around might be as much for my sake as for Mal's. I'm pretty positive he wouldn't see it that way, but considering what lays ahead, he is in for a rough ride as well. So I swallow back what was on my lips to say.

"Okay," I agree instead, my reply catching him a little by surprise. He curls his arm around my neck, draws me close and presses a kiss to my forehead. Slipping my own arm around his waist, we walk up the driveway to find a big Yukon parked there. Gus and Emma are waiting on the porch.

"We're not staying long," Gus says with his hands up, "I just need a minute of Mal's time and Emma has some stuff for Kim."

Sure enough, when Mal opens the door and we all pile in the house, Gus comes in last with a box full of containers.

"What is all this?" I want to know, taking a peek at what's inside.

"I did a bit of research this morning to see what you should and shouldn't eat while you're getting treatment," Emma starts but Gus interrupts her.

"She was going to cook you pies, silly woman."

Emma slaps her hand in his midsection. "Hush, you know I need to feed. Anyway, as I was saying, after Gus so graciously pointed out that pie might not be the best choice of food in your case, I found some great stuff on the Internet. It says there are ways to minimize nausea for instance, so I made you a bottle of ginger tea syrup that you only have to add hot or cold water to, whatever your preference. It's supposed to prevent or soothe nausea. It also say you should make what you eat count in terms of nutrition but that some things may be difficult on your stomach, so to eat small meals or snacks." She holds up the large square container. "These are Powerballs, made with sunflower seed, oatmeal, almond butter, coconut and cranberries. Supposed to be great energy boosters and are full of healthy protein." She hands me a ball from the container and I try it.

"Ohmigawd," I mumble through my half-filled mouth. "That is so good."

"I know right?" Emma smiles.

"This is amazing, Emma. I don't know what to say." I'm getting a bit misty-eyed at the incredible support I'm getting from people I didn't even know a couple of months ago.

"Not much we can do but try and make this battle a little easier for you. You're still gonna have to do all the fighting yourself, but let us do what we can to cheer you on."

At a loss for words, I wrap Emma in a tight hug, which the older woman returns with equal force.

"How the fuck did you find that place?"

The one man who has the ability to scare me simply shrugs his shoulders. "Got my sources, esé. Not that difficult if you buy the right people."

Figures he would have law enforcement in his fucking pocket too. I was shocked when he just walked in behind the two guys who took me from the FBI safe house. From what I understand, he never sets foot on US soil anymore. That's why I entered into this oil field deal, because I had expected him to be a silent partner. He turned out not to be so silent, dogging me every step of the way during the land negotiations and upping the pressure when the Walker family held out.

Ernesto Duarte was the head of the Mexican Agave cartel and a man whose reputation for being ruthless in his business dealings made me look like Santa Claus. He was also standing across from me, forcing me to tilt my head back, since I'm tied down to a chair. Not a position I particularly enjoy.

Especially not when Duarte motions one of his men forward, carrying an old-fashioned doctor's bag.

"Hey, what's going on?" My voice squeaks as panic closes up my throat.

"You've tried and failed, esé. Time for the professionals to take over."

"All I need is a day, I'll find her," I plead to deaf ears.

The man simply shakes his head, almost making me believe he's regretful, but I know better. "Jacob, Jacob, Jacob—you still don't get it, do you? You've lost focus, my friend. The oil is the primary objective and you've lost sight of that."

"But the girl knows too much—" I try before he cuts me off with a blow of his fist that snaps my head back. I can taste the blood in my mouth and my eyes tear up, blurring the sight of him.

"What's her name?" he barks.

"Kimeo—Kimeo Lowe, I almost had her. I...I think she knows more than she's let on." In a last ditch effort to get out of this, I throw the bitch under the bus. She's the one who's caused trouble from the start. She'll get what's coming one way or another.

With a dismissive wave of his hand, Duarte turns and walks toward the door and for a moment I feel elation at having dodged that bullet. That is, until he stops and turns at the door. "I'm done with him."

It takes the cold steel of a barrel against the base of my skull and a single moment of terrified realization before it all goes black.

CHAPTER TWENTY-FIVE

Mal

"Joe obviously called."

I watch Neil pick up Boo's ball and toss it to the back fence. Gus had lead us straight through the house and out the backdoor. Of course Boo wasn't gonna be left behind.

"He did," Gus says easily. "Gonna have to get used to everyone wanting to look out for you, my friend. Your girl's been adopted by our significant others and they demand we do our part, so suck it up. Jed's place is secure, but not as secure as Joe'd like, so I'm here to pick up Neil and we're heading out there to tweak it a little."

"Right now?" I'm surprised and a little peeved that I hadn't even considered that.

"Yes, right now—and stop beating yourself up for not thinking of it first," he chuckles and Neil joins him.

"What the fuck? Since when are all you guys in my head?" I ask, making Gus laugh out loud.

"You fell in love, dufus. The moment you did your mind became predictable. All of us guys, except for maybe young Neil here, have been there. You focus on her and let us worry about the rest. Oh, and by the way," he says picking the ball up that Boo drops at his feet. "May wanna fire up that BBQ. I won't be here long, but prepare yourself for an invasion. It's Monday, the diner is closed and the telephone tree was active. Cookout here and supplies are coming."

"Save some steak for me," Neil contributes before following Gus through the garden gate.

At the same time, I hear the doorbell. The invasion has begun.

"Are you scared?"

Kim's back is tucked into my front, her hands holding my arms around her in place. I lean in and kiss the exposed skin of her neck. "I am," I confess.

We spent a loud and rambunctious, but fun evening with even Clint and Beth. The two little monsters, Mattias and Max, gave Boo a good workout. After a little initial shyness on the boys' and Boo's parts, they were thick as thieves as soon as the first ball was tossed. Seb and Arlene had shown up with coolers full of dinner fixings: steaks, hot dogs, a macaroni salad, green salad and baking potatoes. Naomi and Joe hauled in a few gallons of ice cream, a case of beer and a big bottle of wine and Emma made an apple crumble appear while dinner was cooking. We had that with ice cream after dinner.

Kim and I had been so exhausted when we made it to bed that we wrapped around each other and promptly fell asleep.

It's early morning now, light filtering through the blinds and I am surprised Boo hasn't come begging to be let out yet. I'm halfway between sleep and awake when Kim asks me and maybe had I been fully awake I wouldn't have been so direct.

"I'm mostly frustrated, angry that I can't protect you from this—can't take it on for you. But there's a small part of me that is scared of even the most remote possibility of losing you to something I can't control."

She turns around in my arms to face me, her hand immediately reaching up to touch my face.

"You won't lose me. God wouldn't be so cruel. I won't let him." Her eyes are sincere, but they have a sparkle.

"Won't let him, huh? You've got that kind of clout with the big guy?" I tease her, chuckling.

"I do. I think we're both due for some happy. This is just the last hurdle before we get to it." She scoots closer and I lay back when she rests her head on my shoulder. My arm tucks her tight.

"Whatever happens, if this moment, right here, is all we'll have, it's still the happiest I've had. I love you, Malachi." Her voice is soft but firm, and I'm amazed again at the strength and light this woman is no longer afraid to share.

"Love you. Heart and spirit, *Nizhóní.*"

Forcing everything but her smell, her touch, her love out of my awareness, I grab a handful of her hair and press her even closer.

Kim

"I'll be right behind you," Mal says as he leans into the car and gives me a kiss. "Just going to give Boo a quick walk and then I'll head into town. Neil's gonna be following right behind you guys."

Mal's brother had some business in town and Katie had driven up with him yesterday, leaving Mattias and Blue with Beth. I was actually relieved to hear they were coming, the mood in Jed's beautiful house was getting more strained by the minute. I don't know what I expected, shacking up with two guys who seemed to only tolerate each other, but this past week and a half has been a test on everyone's nerves. After my first chemo, I hadn't felt ill at all, at first. It was the second day, the Wednesday, that my system raised protest. I spent a lot of time in the bathroom that day and both Mal and Neil had fluttered around, trying their best to make me comfortable. I hadn't even been able to muster up any feelings of shame for my upset stomach or bowels. I'd been too miserable. But it was clear that as much as this wouldn't be easy for me, it was perhaps even worse for these guys, who with all their protective instincts at peak level, couldn't do a damn thing for me.

Radiation had been a cakewalk in comparison. In and out in twenty minutes and only the last round yesterday left me with a slight burn and a scratch in my throat. Merely uncomfortable in comparison to what I know this next chemo session will be for me. I've been holding back on voicing my anxieties around Mal, because it only seems to enflame his need to make me feel better. That, in turn, is starting to eat at me. Guilt. I know it's unreasonable and out of my control, but still, I feel responsible for bringing this on everyone. Which is exactly why the timing of Caleb and Katie's visit couldn't have come at a better time. The moment they arrived, Katie's direct and pertinent approach felt like relief. No careful and cautious questioning, but a blunt statement that had me doubled over laughing.

"You look like crap." Was the first thing out of her mouth and I could've kissed her for being real. Mal started to react but I surprised him when I burst out howling until tears ran down my face. I missed having my friends around to distract me and lighten the mood. Being excommunicated to a log home in the middle of nowhere had fast lost its shine.

The building tension in the house dissipated into thin air over the dinner that Caleb and Mal cooked. Lean protein, softened vegetables and a peach cobbler, sent up by Emma who couldn't resist. I didn't eat much but enjoyed every bite, if not for the flavor, for the company I shared it with.

This morning, for the first time since I started this journey, Mal won't be glued to my side and I was glad for it. Not that I don't want him there, but I'm starting to worry more about him than about me. We both need a little break. Both Katie and Neil are fully trained security specialists, so I'm not worried about that. In fact, nothing has happened in the past week and I'm starting to think this may all be over. In any event, having Katie drive me this morning is a great distraction from what I know is coming. She chatters about Mattias and his antics, and tells me she's been in touch with Kerry, who is planning to come up next week.

"I offered her to tag along, but she said she has a few things to sort out this week, but she'll call every day and promises to be there for your last chemo. She wants to celebrate with you."

Tears burn my eyes, but I'm willing them not to fall. Noticing my struggle, Katie quickly changes direction. "So any hot doctors I need to look out for?" She wiggles her eyebrows, making me snort.

"Not hot enough to be any kind of distraction from the fine set of brothers we've got our claws into."

"Ain't that the truth," she says, turning to me with a wide grin.

The moment we pull into the parking lot my anxiety is back. If she notices my sudden quiet, Katie doesn't seem to miss a beat, but simply continues to chat about...well, I don't really know about what, since my mind is on what is to come. It's welcome though. The sense of normalcy she tries to inject when otherwise I would probably be asked if I was holding up all right constantly.

"Hey, Kim," Chrissy, one of the nurses greets me. "You brought new reinforcements today?"

"Hi, yes, this is Katie, Mal's sister-in-law."

With introductions out of the way, Chrissy settles me in one of the large recliners in the treatment room, pulling up a visitor chair for Katie before taking off to prep my cocktail of poison. The curtain is closed around us, giving us an illusion of privacy, even though the door to the hallway is always open. Still, it's enough to leave me with a bit of dignity without making me feel isolated. With the nurse's station right across the hall, all it would take is a sniffle or a clearing of my throat for someone to come check.

"I brought you something. Well, actually, Caleb brought it. Something his grandmother made for him." She pulls a beautiful afghan out of her tote. Rich earth colors brace a set of intricately detailed wings. Angel wings.

"It's beautiful," I say in awe.

"She gave it to them after Nascha died, with the wings representing their sister watching over them. It's the only thing he took with him when he left home."

I'm overwhelmed as she tucks the blanket around me.

"Caleb is convinced of its powers," she smiles indulgently. "Every time Mattias has even a simple cold, he wraps that boy up in this thing, summer or winter, doesn't matter. Anyway," she says, looking a little red-eyed herself, "we figure both Nascha and *amá sáni* would be honored to provide you with some comfort—and who knows, maybe some protection too."

"That's gorgeous!" Chrissy steps around the curtain, pushing a cart with all the 'tools of torture.' I can't help but chuckle at my own melodrama. I run my hands over the soft texture of the afghan and smile up at her.

"Isn't it? Mal's grandmother made it and Katie and her husband brought it in."

"It's perfect. Gonna keep you nice and cozy. You know this stuff can give you the chills." She indicates the IV bag on the trolley. "You know," she turns to Katie, "If you want to grab a drink or something to eat quick, this would be the time."

I see the hesitation on Katie's face. "Go, it'll be a long sit without any sustenance. Grab something, I mean it," I add when she still seems unsure.

"Okay. I won't be long," she says, squeezing my hand in passing.

The moment Katie is gone, Chrissy pulls a chart. "So tell me—what if any symptoms did you have after your first chemo? Any nausea, diarrhea? Excessive hair loss?" she adds carefully.

"Yes, yes and..." I hesitate because saying it out loud makes it more real. It may be vain, but losing my hair is something I've not been able to bear thinking about. In my mind it has always been my best feature and losing that is like losing myself. I swallow hard before continuing, I need to be realistic about this. "And yes, not so much the first couple of days, but I've noticed when I wash my hair or brush it that it's coming loose easily. I actually tied it back in a ponytail, naively thinking that maybe I'll keep it on my head a bit longer that way."

She doesn't say anything, but spends the next few minutes in silence, scribbling her notes before closing the binder. It takes her only seconds to find a good vein for the IV needle. She eases it in, securing it, before she hooks up two bags, hanging them on the stand. When I'm all set to go, she sits down beside me grabbing my hand. "You know—I imagine for most, the hair loss, when it does happen, is a very harsh reality check. I'm guessing it makes the cancer so much more real—visible. But I also know for those who are incredibly strong, like I know you are, it can be a badge of honor too. A sign of strength, of an ability to fight without leaving a stone unturned. The new hair that will grow eventually will be an affirmation of your victory. I really believe that." With a smile and a hand ruffling my, still present, hair, she disappears through the curtains.

I'm allowing myself to drift off a little with my eyes closed, when I hear the curtains pull back. It must be Katie, who's come back and I wait for her to say something.

"You don't look like you'll be too much trouble," the unfamiliar deep rumble stops my heart.

Mal

"How are you holding up?"

Caleb slides into the booth across from me. We're just grabbing a quick bite at a diner on the outskirts of town before

Caleb heads off to meet a new client. It's been hard for me to eat around Kim, not because she has a problem with it, but because I feel guilty with every bite I put in my mouth. Her stomach has been easily upset and I've seen the weight coming off already. Not something I like seeing.

"It's tough—being so powerless—it's not something that sits well. I lie awake forever at night just looking at her, you know? Wondering—"

"Don't even go there. Don't draw comparisons to Nascha. Kim is going to beat this and you've gotta start believing it." Caleb grabs my wrist and squeezes before letting go.

"She's starting to lose her hair," I reveal, remembering the soft strands I found on her pillow when she rolled over last night. "She loves her hair."

"It's gonna grow back, Mal."

"I know..." I let my words trail off, because really—what is there to say? Rationally I know it's part of the treatment, just like the nausea and the weight loss, and yet I want to pick her up and take her away from all of this. Totally irrational, and still I feel that urge.

A cheerful waitress slides some mugs in front of us. "Coffee I assume?" she says with a smile as she dumps a hand full of creamers on the table. "You ready to order? Or do you need a minute?"

"Two eggs over hard, bacon, home fries and if you have it, rye bread," Caleb says, going first.

"No rye, but we have a nice sourdough?"

"I'll have that."

I order the same.

Caleb's phone rings a few minutes later, when I'm about to put the last of my toast in my mouth.

"Talk to me." I see his eyebrows shoot up before his eyes hit mine. "How long do you figure he's been dead? —Don't give me that coroner crap, you must have some idea."

The hair on the back of my neck stands up. Who the fuck is he talking about? But his next words really concern me.

"Shot to the base of the skull can't be a coincidence. You have anything else? —Right, then let me fill Mal in. I'll be in soon."

The moment he hangs up I'm on him. "Cartel signature execution. You talking Hartnett?"

"Got it in one, little brother. Found this morning by someone chasing after their dog up in the woods on the north side of town. Tied to a chair, shot in the back of the neck. Not a lot left of his face but from a few other identifying marks they could make a good guess at his identity. At least Gomez did. Looks like he'd been dead for close to a week. That was him on the phone by the way, Gomez. Looks like his hunch about Hartnett not playing alone was dead on. With any luck this will be over for Kim now. She doesn't know anything beyond Hartnett's involvement."

I shake my head, even as Caleb is trying to convince me otherwise. "Not the way they work, Caleb. They don't leave loose ends. Never." I should know—a few years ago I got tangled up with a Mexican cartel and they were relentless in their pursuit. If not for an unexpected family connection to Katie that had them back off, I'd probably still be on the run. Or dead. At the time I ran into trouble with the cartel, Katie had been unaware she was actually the illegitimate half-sister of the current cartel boss. Something she struggled with at the time, but had not hesitated using to get me off the hook with them.

Caleb pulls out his wallet and throws some money on the table. "I best head over to meet up with Gomez. He's set up a briefing at the police station. If you could drop me off there? I'll get a ride to the hospital when I'm done, or I can call Neil."

Mercy Medical Centre is clear on the opposite end of town and since Katie used their vehicle to take Kim this morning, Caleb drove into town with me. We settle in the truck when an uneasy feeling that started in the diner quickly grows into an anxious sense of urgency.

"Call Neil," I tell Caleb as I turn the key in the ignition and pull out of our parking spot into traffic. I can feel his intense glance in my direction.

"What are you thinking?"

"Just call him."

I listen to Caleb dialing and wait.

"No answer. Reception could be bad in the hospital. Let me try Katie."

Again I hear him dial, my knuckles turning white on the steering wheel.

"Hey little one, are you with Kim?—Okay. Look, we've had some development. Hartnett was found dead this morning.—Yes. It looks execution style.—You've got it. Anyway, I can't get a hold of Neil.—Please. Call me when you're in the room with her."

We stop at a traffic light and I look over at him. "And?"

"Katie was grabbing some breakfast. She left Neil outside the door to the room and the nurse was just getting Kim set up."

Our eyes lock just for a moment before Caleb simply nods. No words needed. I slam the gas the moment the light turns green and with squealing tires I yank the wheel, making a U-turn in the middle of the intersection under a concert of honking. Caleb is already dialing and I vaguely hear him talking to Gomez, but my focus is on getting to the hospital. The closer we get, the tighter the cold fear squeezing my chest.

CHAPTER TWENTY-SIX

Kim

The tall man standing in front of me, casually lifting his shirt to display a gun tucked into the waistband of his scrub bottoms. He looks nothing like a doctor on closer inspection. The scrubs and white coat might do the trick at a quick glance but his appearance is almost regal. Dark, with an olive complexion and distinguished grey threading through the almost black hair by his ears. The laugh lines around his mouth and by his eyes put him somewhere between forty and fifty, but it's his eyes that look ancient. Dark, black and devoid of any emotion. The mild amusement shifting over his face doesn't seem to reach his eyes. He exudes cold power and that is more frightening than the weapon in his hand.

"I'm afraid we'll have to take a little trip, my dear," he coos, his voice soft and deadly silk with only a hint of an accent. "The good news is, you won't need that any longer." He gestures to the IV pole and the bags hanging from it.

"What do you want?" I manage to squeak through an airway constricted with fear. My eyes flit to the door, wondering why Neil isn't barging in.

"I'm cleaning up. Our Texas oil baron was kind enough to provide me with your name. A simple search by a talented information expert is all it takes these days to flag anything with a name attached, floating around the ether. It took him two days to follow a trail of medical reports here. It's so—"

A sharp intake of breath from the direction of the door has the man swinging his gun around, and without even thinking, I am out of the chair and duck down behind it like a shot, accidentally yanking the IV from my wrist.

"Ernesto!"

I'm confused when I hear Katie apparently call the man by name.

"*Hijo de puta*! Ekatarina..."

"You were the force behind Hartnett, weren't you?" Katie says, accusation thick in her voice. "I thought you'd vowed not to set foot in the US again? You're taking a big risk coming back here."

"*Mi hermana*, don't involve yourself in this."

I don't remember much Spanish, but I know *hermana* means sister. Katie is this man's sister?

"That woman is my family. She's going to be my sister-in-law."

"*I'm* your family, Ekatarina. *Tu hermano.* Don't you forget that."

"Half-brother, and I never knew of your existence until a few years ago. We are on opposite ends of the law, always have been, always will be. No amount of blood between us is going to change that. But what binds me here to these people—to my chosen family—is love. And guess what, Ernesto, love is much, much thicker than blood."

"*Madre de dios.* I cannot risk leaving loose ends."

I'm surprised to hear exasperation in the man's voice where before it was flat, and a small niggle of hope that Katie is getting through to him surfaces.

"Listen." I hear her say in a strong voice. "This woman is Malachi's and you and I both know that if anything happens to her, he will not rest until he has you six feet under, and my husband will be right behind him closing the hole."

"Jesus fucking Christ! Of course that *hijo de puta* has to be involved. I should've killed the bastard when I had the chance."

"Hey!" I stand up and yell. "Mal is not an *hijo de* whatever the hell that is and you don't stand a chance of hurting him."

The man, Ernesto apparently, turns around and looks me up and down, but I stand my ground. I even ignore Katie when she softly pleads for me to stand down. Instead I lift my chin, tuck Mal's grandmother's afghan around me and look him straight in the eye. To my surprise he drops his shirt back over the weapon in the front his scrubs, straightens the white coat over top and chuckles softly, the smile reaching his eyes this time.

"Figures that son of a bitch found himself a little *bola de fuego*."

A ruckus in the hallway draws my attention. The heavy tread of boots comes closer and suddenly, Malachi is in the doorway, a wild look in his eyes, with Caleb right behind him.

"Fucking Duarte," Mal spits out after looking at me for a split second, and launches himself at Ernesto. Luckily Caleb manages to grab his brother around the waist, doing his best to hold him back. Chrissy squeezes in between the two big bodies and the doorway, takes one look at me and immediately turns to take in the crowd assembled.

"Out!" she commands, her hands on her hips. "Out right now, or I'm calling security."

I'm stunned with this bizarre turn of events and watch open-mouthed as Katie grabs Ernesto's arm and Caleb follows closely behind, keeping his arm firmly around Mal. At the door he pulls away and walks toward me.

"You're bleeding. Are you okay?"

I look at my hand and notice some blood dripping down my hand from where I'd accidentally pulled the IV out. "I'm fine, just...confused. Very, very confused."

"I'll be right back and I'll try to explain, okay?" he asks, stroking my hair from my face before kissing me lightly on the lips.

"Lucky girl," Chrissy mumbles as she bends over my other arm with a fresh needle.

"From what I picked up you have gained a...let's say 'unique' family. But honey? Watching Mal with you? I totally get it." She smiles at me as she tapes the IV lines down securely. "Lucky," she repeats softly, before leaving the room.

Lucky, not necessarily a term I would ever have thought to describe me, but—she's right. Even without any explanation as to what just went down here, all it takes is the sight of my beautiful Malachi leaning against the doorway, staring back at me, to know she's so right. I might be battling the biggest fight of my life, but I'm doing it *lucky*.

Mal

I almost beat the snot out of Neil when I saw him talking to an old man at the front desk. He was supposed to be keeping an eye out on the hallway outside the treatment room. When I yell his name, his head snaps up and he looks surprised. A sharp snap of my head in the direction of the oncology wing has him following us to the stairwell. As soon as the door closes behind us I turn on him.

"What the fuck? Thought you were going to be by the door?"

"Did something happen? There was an old woman who slipped and fell by the elevators. I was the only one close and had to call the nurses to help. That was her husband down there." A pale Neil pushes past me and talks while taking the stairs two at a time. I catch up with him before he slips through the door on the second floor.

"Hartnett is dead," Caleb blurts out beside me and Neil's eyes immediately focus on him.

"How?"

"Shot to the base of the skull," Caleb offers.

"Cartel." The statement is made matter-of-factly, as if there isn't even a question in his mind. "Fuck. FUCK!"

Pulling his arm loose he barges through the door and down the hall, where I catch up with him again.

"Stop the fuck running. You're either gonna give Kim a heart attack or you're gonna warn whoever is in there with her off. Back up."

Without waiting for his answer I walk at a normal pace down the hall toward her door. The moment I spot the man apparently in a stand off with Katie and a bleeding Kim, rage courses through my body.

"Fucking Duarte."

The smug smile on his arrogant face works as a red flag and if not for Caleb wrapping himself around me from behind, I would've torn that smug face off his fucking skull.

Kim's nurse comes in and with a show of some serious sass, she kicks us all out of the room. When I look back and see Kim standing there, a bit forlorn, I pull out from Caleb's grasp and walk over to her to see if she's all right. I want to stay, but the damn nurse is shooting daggers and I can see the blood dripping from Kim's hand. She needs looking after first, so I promise I'll be back to try and explain what just happened—as soon as I can figure it out myself.

Caleb, Katie and fucking Duarte are standing to one side and Neil is glaring death daggers at the leader of one of Mexico's most dangerous cartels. Passing by them, I lead the way into a blessedly empty waiting room on the other side of the hallway, closing the door behind us.

"Hartnett was found this morning," I start, keeping a close look on Duarte who doesn't even blink at the name. "My guess is you used his obsession with expanding his oil empire to gain a semi-legitimate solid source of income on US soil, to fund your other endeavors."

The only response is a slight shrug of the man's shoulders, but his face remains unaffected by my words.

"You never intended to let him live, did you? I bet you ever only intended to use him as a pawn, use his expertise in the field to get to a certain level of production before you pulled the plug on him. Am I in the ballpark?"

Another noncommittal shrug, but this time accompanied by a slight tilt of his mouth. Cocky motherfucker. Time to move this along, since Caleb's call to Damian will likely result in the local PD and FBI alike flooding the hallways in short order. "You're done here. Kim never knew anything about you anyway. We let you leave, you cross back over that border and we don't see you in the neighborhood again. Deal?"

This time his eyebrow almost hits his hairline. "Who's to say you can keep me here if you tried?"

"You wanna play pissing games? Special Agent Gomez, I'm sure you're familiar with the name, is less than ten minutes behind us. Your choice, Duarte. We're done here, or one way or another, you're going down," I bite off.

Slowly he pushes away from the wall he's been leaning against. "I want to see my nephew," he directs at his half-sister who pulls herself up to her full height. It isn't much but the steel in her spine all but makes up for it.

"I'll email you pictures. That's it. Take it or leave it and don't for a minute think that I'd hesitate taking you down if you even think of threatening my family again."

For a few tense minutes they stare each other down. Surprisingly it's Duarte who drops his eyes first. "Fine. Take care of my sister and her boy," he directs at Caleb almost in a challenge.

"My woman, *our* boy. He's my blood and that's my wife you're talking about," Caleb doesn't hesitate to point out.

Duarte starts moving to the door, stopping right in front of me, his eyes boring into mine. "I had no idea until five minutes ago that this had anything to do with you and your woman. It wasn't personal," he says as if that should be explanation enough for why he came tearing into Kim's oncology unit. Duarte lets his glare hit each of us in turn, with his final glare landing on his sister, before he opens the door and closes it behind him

We release a collective sigh, except Neil, who has smoke coming out his ears. "You're gonna let him fucking walk? We could've taken him down, handed him over!"

"It's like this, grasshopper," Caleb says calmly. "We take him in, there are ten other, more dangerous, motherfuckers waiting to take his place. Ten others we have no leverage with, any one of whom could and likely would launch a full out war simply for revenge, to gain respect and solidify their position of authority."

Neil is grinding his jaw, trying to reconcile his strong sense of justice with the blind eye we're asking him to turn.

Caleb puts a hand on his shoulder. "Look, this way we can at least ensure our little corner of the world stays safe—our families, our friends, our home. You know what they say, keep your friends close, but your enemies closer."

Without another word, he grabs Katie's hand and walks out of the room, and into Damian Gomez barreling down the hallway with two agents by his side.

"Did you get him?"

This time I beat Caleb to the punch. "Bastard pulled a gun, took off on us. No way we're gonna shoot up in a hospital."

"Tell me you at least got a good look?" He looks at me hopeful.

"Sorry, man. Latin dude, but I didn't recognize him. You?" I turn to Katie who shakes her head, the regret on her face almost believable. The rest of us deny recognition.

Frustrated, Gomez turns to walk into Kim's room, but I hold him back. "Where the fuck do you think you're going?"

"The chick saw him, maybe he said something."

I stretch to my full height which puts me over Gomez by about three inches when I answer him. "That 'chick' happens to be my girl you're talking about, and if you think for one second I'd let you go in there and upset her while she is fucking fighting for her life, you've got another goddamn thing coming!"

Gomez's compatriots step to his side in support when I raise my voice—hands on their weapons. Just as Caleb, Katie and Neil have obviously closed ranks with me. Ridiculous, in a small hallway in the cancer wing of a hospital, but I will risk prosecution for attacking a federal officer if he even looks at her door twice.

Sensing my resolve, Gomez lifts both hands in the air. "You guys are a fucking constant pain in my ass, you know that? Bring her in when she's done..." Unsure of what to say next, he just waves his hands around. "...With all this." And with a head tilt to his team, he turns on his heels and walks off.

"I'm going in," I announce and walk into Kim's room where I see a familiar afghan wrapped around her legs. My sister's wings.

Kim

Oh my God. Mexican cartels, oil conspiracies, unexpected family connections and execution style killings. It's all a bit much for my weary brain to comprehend, but when Mal sits down at my feet and lays his head on my lap, I feel as light as a feather. Granted, some of that might be the chemo, but I swear most of it is the relief when Mal tells me I won't have anything to worry about again. He's firm on that and I believe him. I even understand the tenuous truce GFI seems to have with the Agave cartel, as Mal tells me they are known. But the fact that Katie, who'd grown up without parents, never knew she had a father who was head of one of the most violent cartels in Mexico, was probably the most mind-blowing. Mal told me in gross outlines, promising to fill in the blanks when I'm not yawning every second. I don't have the heart to tell him it's not just fatigue, but a way my body is trying to fight off the nausea I already feel. Dammit.

"Time to go home, *Nizhóní*"

Mal's voice pulls me from a heavy nap. Three hours is a long time when you're not really able to roam around at will. Chrissy comes in, unhooking me from the now empty bags and the moment I turn my head, a wave of nausea hits me out of the blue and I slap my hand over my mouth in a futile attempt to stop from vomiting. All the water and weak tea I've been sipping comes up and I'm mortified when I see I've not only thrown up all over myself, but managed to dirty the beautiful afghan and the bottom of Mal's jeans. I hate this part. It didn't start until a few hours after we'd gotten home the first time and I was prepared. This time I'm obviously not. I close my eyes and block out the room, only feeling Chrissy's gentle fingers removing the needle from my arm and sticking a Band-Aid on, as if I hadn't just puked up my guts all over the place. The moment Chrissy's touch disappears, a warm, wet washcloth is wiped over my face before Mal's hands, that I've come to know very well, clean off my hands as well. Without saying a word, he takes the afghan off my lap and brushes at the wet spots on my lap with a towel. My eyes now open, I follow the movements of his hands and can't help but wonder where I'd be if I'd never met him. If I'd dropped off that envelope the day I was supposed to, I might never have stopped at the diner, or been a witness in the assault on the Walkers. So many ifs, and most of them leading to a reality I don't even want to contemplate.

"Thank you," I whisper, trying not to breathe on him.

"Look at me," he urges and I slowly lift my eyes. "Let's go home. I want to take care of you."

I just nod and let him lead me from the room.

Once home he helps me strip and settle into the tub, with a bucket close by—just in case.

"Going to look after Boo and send Neil to pick up something for us to eat so you don't have to smell cooking, okay? I'll be right back."

I lay my head back on the edge of the tub and breathe deeply. One more round of chemo, one more session like this and I can start healing. And as I run my fingers through my hair I feel a large chunk coming away in my hand.

CHAPTER TWENTY SEVEN

Mal

"Have you guys talked to Gus?" I ask Caleb.

He and Katie hung around Durango for the day and popped in to say goodbye on their way home, but ended up staying for dinner.

I'd made sure Kim was still sleeping, something her body seems to need a lot of these days. I'd found her asleep in the tub when I'd come back upstairs, and carefully got her up, dried off and dressed in one of my old shirts she's taken to sleeping in. Once in bed, her bucket right beside her, she looked up, her eyes shiny. "You're an intensely good man, Malachi, and I love you so much."

Those words carry so much more weight than just their face value. With that one line, she seemed to have wiped away any lingering doubts about whether I'm good enough for her. I'm fucking great for her and I will prove it every day for as long as she'll let me.

When I emptied the tub, I saw the strands of hair she'd left on the edge of the bath and I was hit with a sharp pain. Her hair—her pride—her sacrifice, which seems insignificant in the grand scope of things, but is a poignant, painful loss for Kim. I can clean her when she's been ill, hold her when she feels weak, but that is one thing I can't give her relief for. Back in the bedroom, she'd rolled on her side with her knees drawn up, her head resting right on the edge of the mattress. I crawled in behind her and loosely held her until I heard her breathing even out. When Boo stuck his head around the door after greeting Neil when he returned, all I had to do was pat the bed and the big dog clambered up. He inched closer until his body was snugly against Kim's back and I left them resting together.

"We filled him in. He was as shocked as we were, finding out the Agave cartel was involved. Oil doesn't fall under their usual 'business' interests. Took us all for a loop." Caleb sits back and takes a sip of his coffee before turning to his wife. "How do you feel about staying in town for another night? I'll call and see if Beth can keep the 'kids' a bit longer, but since we're meeting with Gomez tomorrow for a final brief we may as well hang around."

"I'll stick around with you, but I'll call Beth—if I'm lucky, Mattias is still up, I just want to hear his voice," she says, standing up from the table and taking her phone into the kitchen.

The moment she disappears I turn to Neil. "Did you pick one up?"

"Yup. Are you sure about this?" he says, grabbing a shopping bag from the sideboard.

"Sure about what?" Caleb wants to know, leaning forward, elbows resting on the table.

"Ask him," Neil motions to me.

"Well?"

When Katie walks into the room five minutes later, she stops in her tracks, taking in the scene and claps a hand over her mouth. "Oh Mal..."

It's not like I had to think about it for very long. When the idea first popped into my head this morning, my first instinct was to fight the impulse, but it seemed like such a small thing to do. A silent vow of support and commitment. Kim would probably be one of the few to understand it's full significance. Caleb and Katie as well, but the truth is, I hadn't felt the need to carry my heritage like a shield for a while now. And whatever the size of the remaining chip on my shoulder, it was easy to push off.

Katie walks over with tears streaming down her face and runs her hand over my remaining hair. Caleb's reaction when Neil had pulled the necessary tools from the bag had been similar shock, but without the tears. When I put the scissors in his hand and asked him to do the honors, he didn't hesitate to step behind me and make the cut.

Katie eyes her husband who is holding out my hair, still tied together in his fist. It's long enough to be used for making a wig.

"You want to help shave the rest?" I ask her as I point to the clippers Neil is holding.

"Hell, yes." She smiles through her tears as she takes them from him.

Kim

I wake up to an unfamiliar distant buzz, before a wave of sudden nausea has me reach for the bucket. My sudden movement sets Boo, who apparently cuddled on the bed beside me, scrambling off the bed. *False alarm.* I slowly roll on my back and breathe through my nose, trying to will my stomach to settle. With the door open a crack after Boo toddles off, I can hear the deep hum of voices and the occasional laugh. Sounds like Katie and Caleb are here and I wish I was down there with them, visiting.

With a desperate need to pee, I gingerly sit up, trying not to make any sudden moves. I can't help but notice when I finally stand beside the bed, that I left a little nest of hair curled on my pillow. Well shit. Snatching up the clump, I dump it in the wastebasket, relieve myself and run a quick washcloth over my face. I quickly brush my teeth and pull on a pair of yoga pants hanging on the back of the door before returning to the bedroom where I find Mal sitting on the edge of the bed. It takes me a minute to register something is significantly different, and another to pinpoint what it is. As my hand reaches out to the doorpost to keep me up, I'm thinking how funny it is that a change that significant takes a while to compute. His head is bald. So bald, it's shiny. His beautiful hair is all gone.

"Don't worry, I still have it, it's going to Beautiful Lengths campaign. Katie is printing off the donation form." His voice sounds gruff as he holds out his hand.

I automatically start walking toward him, slipping easily between his legs as he holds on to my hips. Reaching out, I run my hand over the smooth warm skin of his head, smiling, before I bend down and press a kiss on his crown. His arms slide around, pull me tight, and his head presses into my belly.

We don't need words—I recognize his gift and he feels its importance to me.

Boo nudges his big head, trying to insert himself between us, letting us know he has needs too.

"All right big guy. You want to go out?"

His uncoordinated tail starts whacking me in the leg in reaction to Mal's voice. Grabbing my hand he walks me out of the bedroom and downstairs, Boo trailing us excitedly.

Another surprise waits in the dining room, where the rest of them are gathered around the table. It's not just Mal, but both Caleb who normally has pretty close-cropped hair, and Neil, whose 'do' is more like a surfer, who each now sport a shiny globe as well. I can't help it, I burst out laughing and crying at the same time. Katie walks up to me to give me a hug.

"You know I tried to bribe Neil to shave my head too, but Caleb threatened to hack off his balls with a butter knife," she semi-whispers in my ear. "The butter knife won."

"You know?" I tell them with a watery smile, "You guys make everything so much better. Thank you. I'm blessed and I know it."

"Last one, babe."

Mal is spreading some aloe gel on the skin of my neck and upper chest with gentle fingers. The skin there is almost purple and hot to the touch from the treatments. Yesterday was my last radiation and chemo will be done after today. I was supposed to be done last week, but the blood counts were a little on the low side.

Today will be the last one. We've been in Durango now for a little over five weeks and in that time I've become almost unrecognizable. My hair is officially gone—the last remaining strands were shaved off lovingly by Mal—my face looks hideously swollen from the chemo cocktail and the rest of my body is pasty and quite a bit slimmer. Mal says he hopes I'll put it back on when I point out the weight loss. He hadn't even really registered the changes in my body and face.

His bald head is sporting a little dusting of fuzz now and when he tried to get me to shave it smooth again a few days ago, I refused.

"Mine will start growing back soon as well—at least I hope it will—and I really like running my fingers through yours"

"You do, do you?" he growled in my ear, which spurned on a whole other reason for me wanting him to keep the slight stubble. Our hunger for the other hadn't really lessened. It was just that it seemed to feed from a need to be as close as two humans could possibly get, instead of lust-fueled passionate coupling. It often started with Mal doing incredible things with his mouth between my legs.

"Don't." His low voice threatens as he looks at me from under his heavy brow, pulling me from my thoughts. "I can hear you thinking and we need to get going. Bags are packed and in the truck and we'll head straight home after that."

Neil had stuck around with us, even after it was clear I was no longer in any danger, and I'd been happy for it. Excited even, to see the initial palpable tension between the two men transform into a solid friendship. I'd grown to love Neil too. In a purely platonic way of course, even though I can't deny the man has a serious hot and flirty vibe going on. No, he feels more like a loving brother to me, someone who is not afraid to show he cares and will always look out for those he cares about

Still, can't wait to get home. My own bed, my own kitchen. My own mesa. Oh, and my Boo. Katie brought him over for a visit last week and I bawled for the first hour. Poor dog was beside himself. I just don't know how I'll manage not having Mal around twenty-four/seven. I mean we've shared more in the last few months than many do in a lifetime but still... I'm sure he can't wait to settle down in a normal routine again—in his own place again. A normal routine, which for me right now is a little vague. I'm sure I'll need some time to get my strength back up but sitting at home twiddling my thumbs is going to get old soon. I'll want to get back on my feet, especially since my savings have taken a hit, being without regular income now for well over two months. There is also my mother in Grand Junction, whom I'd like to go see soon. Britta has kept us updated on her progress, which has been quite steady since the doctors slowly allowed her to wake up. She'd likely be spending a long time in rehab, trying to strengthen her spine and regain as much of her mobility as possible. I feel a bit guilty for not having gone to see her, but I was busy fighting my own fight.

We are meeting Kerry at the hospital. She's been adamant about coming so she could celebrate the final leg of this journey with me. I'm excited to see her, but at the same time a little anxious at her response to my appearance. It's something I haven't really cared about while here. The time has felt like living in a bubble, but going back home is a different matter. I'm not sure I can deal with all the questions and curious glances once I'm ready to resume my life.

When Mal pulls the truck into the hospital parking lot, he turns off the ignition and swings around to face me. "So quiet,

Nizhóní. And yet I can still hear those wheels turning," he says, running his widespread fingers down my face, as I've come to experience as his signature show of affection.

"Why do you do that? Stroke down my face? Don't get me wrong," I hurry to add when he threatens to pull away his hand. "I really enjoy it—makes me feel...treasured. I'm just curious."

He lifts his hand back and does it again. "My sister used to do that to me. Each time I was angry or sad, or she thought I was frowning, she would run her fingers over my face. Used to drive me nuts. I was convinced she was teasing, but after she died, I...I found I missed it. Missed what it meant—that she could see me. Me. She always did, even when I was a bad-tempered fledgling adolescent, she never lost sight of who I was to her. Took me a while to understand."

His smile is soft and although the pain of his loss is still there, in his eyes, he talks about her with more ease. Allowing himself the good memories along with the bad.

"You see me," I realize.

"Always have, Kimeo."

Warmed with the knowledge, I let him lead me from the truck to the lobby of the hospital where I see Kerry already waiting, her hands clasped in front of her. The moment she sees me through the sliding doors she rushes to meet me, her hug so strong it takes my breath away.

"Let's get this bitch's ass kicked," she says, discreetly wiping at her eyes, but in a voice strong with conviction before she tucks my arm in hers and we follow Mal down the hallway.

Mal

"Is she okay?"

Kim blessedly fell asleep about an hour into her treatment and Chrissy, who's been a constant for her, sent Kerry and I to grab a coffee and a bite. We're in the coffee shop in the lobby and Kerry's eyes look troubled.

"She will be. She's been weakened a lot by the aggressive simultaneous protocol but that's just her body—her will is strong. I think what's mostly troubling her now, other than the obvious, is how she'll readjust once she gets back home. She'll probably need something to put her teeth into—she doesn't strike me as someone who does well sitting still."

Kerry tilts her head to the side as she regards me, her eyes every so often trailing over my now hairless head. "You love her."

I look at her, lifting an eyebrow. "You're her friend and were witness to my less than stellar start with her, which is why I won't tell you it's none of your business, but yes, I do. "

The small smile tugging at her mouth gives me another indication of her feistiness. Not that I doubted that, after she about took my head off the first time we met. "So are you gonna do something about it?" she challenges.

"You're pushing, Kerry, but I'll give you this one too because I know you're only looking out for her. I'm planning to let her get settled into her life, to let her get her feet back under her and then when the time is right, yes, I will 'do something about it.' "

"You're an idiot, Malachi Whitetail." She totally surprises me with that and it must show, because she starts laughing when she sees my expression. "Well, you are. I've been with the two of you for a little over an hour now and I can see from the wistful, longing glances she sends you that she doesn't want to do any settling unless it has you in it. The girl is as eager as she is anxious about the prospect of 'getting her life back.' I'm thinking she doesn't want it unless it has you permanently cemented in it."

I lean back in my chair, considering her words. Is that true? Is the anxiety I've felt coming off her these last few days about us? That would constitute a change of plans—a welcome one if you ask me.

Kerry gets up from the table. "Just hitting the ladies' before we head back." She leans down as she passes me, surprising me with a kiss on my head. "You did that for her. You are officially and completely forgiven for being a douche in the beginning." Without looking at me, she struts off, tossing her hair over her shoulder and leaving me chuckling in my coffee. Feisty all right.

"Did you bring the bucket?" Kim wants to know when we get back to the room, just as Chrissy is putting a wet washcloth against Kim's forehead and with a small smile, carries off the evidence of Kim's miserable state. Leaving Kerry to sit with her, I follow Chrissy down the hall.

"Should I be worried about that? I mean, she's been sick quite a lot, and from what I understand it doesn't happen to everyone the way it used to."

"Nah, it may not be the standard anymore, but it's still quite common. She just seems to have a particularly queasy stomach. We've given her something for the nausea every time, it just doesn't seem to help her as much as we'd like it to," she says with a smile. "I'm gonna miss her."

"I'm sure she'll miss you too." I give her shoulder a squeeze, grateful for the great care she's given Kim and return to the room.

Turning the truck in the direction of Cortez, I glance over at Kim. She's looking out the window with a big smile on her face, despite the bucket wedged between her knees. "How are you doing?"

"Great," she declares, "and if it weren't for the miserable state of my body, I'd say perfect. But my headspace is fabulous, despite what my intermittent puking may suggest."

"Good," I approve as I quickly run the backs of my fingers over her cheek before turning my attention back on the road. "I bet a 'fabulous headspace' will outlast an upset stomach any day."

Deciding to test the good mood she's in, I broach the topic of Kerry and my conversation earlier. No time like the present. "So I asked you this morning what you were thinking about so hard, but I never did get an answer—what's on your mind?" I feel her eyes assessing me as her hands fiddle with the handle of the bucket.

"Just...you know? Stuff. I mean, we've been kind of shielded from the outside world this past while and I just don't know where to go from here." Her voice sounds uncertain and although she hasn't specifically said so, I have a pretty good feeling she's referring to us and not just speaking in general terms.

"From here we go home. Your home, if you'll have me, or I'll just kidnap you to my apartment. We'll start each day with a plan. Small ones at first, but bigger ones when you're ready. As long as each day is started with you in my arms, there's nothing we can't accomplish."

The silence beside me is a little disconcerting, so when I spot a wide section of shoulder, I pull the car off the road and face her. "Am I going too fast for you?"

Her snort and chuckle are a relief when she has tears running down her cheeks. "Too fast? No. I just freak out when I find how deep you are able to get into my head." She grabs the tissues I hand her, wipes her face and blows her nose. "I'll have you," she says simply. "And I'd love to make plans with you, every day." She leans in, but before she reached my lips, her body redirects itself over the bucket, heaving helplessly.

Bucket emptied at the side of the road and Kim cleaned up, we're back on the road when she suddenly starts laughing. "That was the height of romance, back there," she says with a hiccup.

"I don't do romance," I tell her. "I just say it like it is."

She tries to put on a straight face, failing miserably.

"Well, honey, if that's the case, then judging from your words and actions, you were born a poet. All that's missing is the poofy-sleeved shirt and the feathered cap."

The growl that visual elicits from me is a trigger for Kim to start chuckling again. And as I turn down the road with Kim's little cottage at the end, and big gangly dog likely waiting impatiently, I feel light and completely happy.

CHAPTER TWENTY-EIGHT

"I have been to the end of the earth,

I have been to the end of the waters,

I have been to the end of the sky,

I have been to the end of the mountains,

I have found none that are not my friends."

~ Navajo

Kim

"What are these?"

I hold up a collection of turbans tied in complicated knots and a stack of cotton beanies in every color of the rainbow. Arlene snorts and Emma throws her a dirty look, but as usual, Arlene is decidedly unimpressed.

"Woman can't sit still," she starts, "so for lack of any grandbabies to traumatize for life with her creations, she's focused her 'crafting' on you."

We've just been back here a day and the first night in my own bed, but this time with Mal beside me was the best night I ever had. Even if all we did was spoon, since I wasn't feeling all that frisky. Yet. Caleb and Katie popped in quickly last night to welcome me home, but stayed only the length of a cup of coffee. Apparently Arlene had intended to sit on the doorstep until she could see us coming around the corner, but Seb put his foot down and threatened to lock her out if she even tried. As usual, Arlene bends to no one, except to Seb. Albeit grudgingly.

This morning Emma, who is a tad more...insightful, called first to see if it was okay for them to pop by. She had something for me I might need. Still feeling a little blech, but I realize there's no time like the present to crawl out of our little 'secure' bubble, so I tell her any time is good for me.

"They're wraps. For your head," Emma adds in explanation. She takes one from my lap and with a few tugs has it firmly on my head. With a smiling Mal and the girls looking on, I head to the mirror on the wall by the front door. It looks good. A little Mediterranean, with the deep red Bougainville flowers sharply outlined against the sky-blue background. It's smooth against my head but with the ends tied in a jaunty tail to the side, trailing over my shoulder.

"What do you think?" I turn to Mal, my hands inadvertently going to touch the ends of the shawl to fiddle.

"You look fantastic," he smiles. "A bit mysterious like those fifties starlets. The colors make your whole face light up."

I smile my appreciation before turning to Arlene, who immediately makes me laugh with her facial expression. "Okay, okay. So I can see she looks good in them," she says more to Emma than to me, "but I still think to get our girl here back in fighting shape, she would've been better served with one of your peach pies."

I barely hear Emma's shocked "Arlene!" as I dart past—still half laughing—to get to the bathroom.

"Sorry," Arlene says sheepishly when I walk back in, cleaned up and proudly donning my new shawl to Emma's obvious delight.

I first walk over to Arlene, hug her and whisper in her ear, "Thanks for a good healthy laugh." Then I turn to Emma, sit down next to her on the couch, put my arm around her and my head on her shoulder. "And thank you for making me feel pretty, even while hanging over the toilet."

They stayed long enough to have me try on every shawl, each a little different then the next, and the cute little sporty beanies.

When they're gone, Mal walks me to the bedroom for a nap. I pull open the bottom drawer of my dresser where I keep odds and ends to put the turbans in when my hand encounters something. When I pull what feels like a book out, I see it's actually a sketchpad.

"What's this?" I ask Mal, when he reaches for it.

"Just some scribbles." He looks a bit unsure when he sees me flipping it open.

"You mind?" I don't want to be presumptuous, but curiosity has me looking at the drawings before he even responds.

"Go right ahead," he says with a smirk.

The first drawing is one of a beautiful baby. If I'm not mistaken, it's his nephew Mattias. The next are sketches of animal life. Beautiful drawings of mountain lions and eagles. Detailed and focused on the heads, with the bodies fading away. It isn't until I get to the second half that I recognize Boo in some of his drawings. Suddenly I'm staring into my own eyes. My hair still long and luscious, my eyes clear and healthy.

It's so beautiful, it brings tears to my eyes. Turning to look at him, I see he is studying me intently.

"When did you do these?"

He shrugs his shoulders. "That first one there I sketched after the first time I showed up here with Drew."

I look at him incredulously. The drawing was done with such feeling, it takes me aback. "But—"

"I know, crazy right?" he smiles. "I think part of me recognized you would be important in my life even then." Bending down to pick me up under my arms, he turns with me to the bed and tucks me in.

I reach out to pull him down and place a hand on his jaw. "I want to hang them up," I tell him.

He is silent for a moment, looking me in the eyes. "Okay."

He leans in and kisses me softly. "Love you, Kimeo."

"Me too, so much," I tell him.

Mal

While Kim was in the bathroom earlier, I had a chance to talk to Arlene about giving notice for the apartment above the diner and she smiled big.

"Neil started packing your shit up as soon as he came back last week. He's just waiting for your okay so he can move it out and move his stuff in. No notice needed."

Well I'll be damned. I'm still considering whether to be angry for the kid's cocky actions or slap him on the back for his foresight, when Kim walks back in. Good to see that despite her almost pallid complexion, her eyes are sparkling today.

A few hours later, with Kim having a nap in the bedroom, I open the door to Neil, whom I called a while ago, letting him in. He's wearing a knit beanie pulled down over his ears and looks like he's dressed for winter.

"What's with the hat, man? It's eighty-five degrees outside—hardly cold enough to wear that thing."

"Shut up. You guys could've warned me my ears stick out. I look like Dumbo. This is the only way I can hide them until my hair grows in again," he grumbles.

"Are you shitting me? You walked around like that for two weeks and you never complained, what brought this on?"

"I don't make it a habit to stare in the mirror if I can help it first of all, and secondly, damn Arlene decided to point it out last week when I walked into the diner. Fucking Kendra was there and she thought it was funny. She told me she always thought Dumbo was cute. Fucking hell. I went straight into the bathroom to have a good look. Man, they're out to there!" He waves his hands about an arm length away from his head in overly dramatic fashion.

I shake my head. "You're an idiot, kid—you should star in a daytime soap with all the drama. If a girl says she thinks the animal you were just compared to is cute, she's basically saying you're cute. Dimwit. And why does this conversation remind me of elementary school?"

"Cute is the absolute last thing I want that particular woman to think when she thinks of me," he bellyaches, confirming my prior suspicions. "And would you quit calling me kid? You're barely ten years older than I am. It's not helping." He stomps off outside to grab the first of the boxes he hauled over from his truck. I rush after him to open the garage door to stick them in there for the time being. At least until I have a chance to let Kim know I'm officially moving in. As of right now.

"So shouldn't we be getting your apartment empty so Neil can move in?"

It's been four days since we got back from Durango and we're on our way to the clinic in Cedar Tree for an appointment with Naomi, who's agreed to take on the day-to-day management of Kim's medical conditions. Already a follow up appointment has been scheduled with the endocrinologist who saw Kim in Mercy Hospital in Durango and started her on Synthroid©, a thyroid hormone replacement she'll have to take for the rest of her life. Naomi is doing some blood work today to keep an eye on her levels and to see whether the dosage needs adjustment.

"Actually—he's already in," I tell her.

"Where did he leave your stuff?"

"In your garage."

In my peripheral vision I see her head whip around. "When?" she half-shouts.

"Day after we got back. But he'd already packed everything a week before, when he got back to Cedar Tree. He did that on his own." I don't know what I expect. Maybe for her to get mad, but she surprises me by laughing heartily.

"What's funny?"

"You," she responds deadpan. "You think you're fooling people with your stoic poker face, but it turns out you're as transparent as the rest of us. Neil was obviously a step ahead of you."

"Bullshit," I say, but it's true. There was a time not so long ago that people never knew what I was thinking. I'd become very adept at hiding any emotion or reaction. It seems those days are over as is evident from the softly snickering woman beside me.

"Look at you!" Naomi enthusiastically greets Kim, admiring the turban-like contraption she's wearing on her head today. "Is that one of Emma's?"

I leave the girls chattering about shawls and make my way over to Kendra, who is sitting at the reception desk looking on.

"Hey you," she smiles as I approach. "Never thought I'd see the day, but you actually look happy. Never seen you smile so much. The hair though? You've gotta grow it back."

I chuckle, running my hand over the stubble on my head. "It's nice and cool though. Light too."

"Yeah, but it's killing your mysterious vibe, ya know? Although I guess you don't need that anymore. I'm glad for you, my friend. She's perfect for you." There is no regret in her voice, just genuine warmth and I smile back at her easily.

"You know, it took a while for me to see it, but once I opened my eyes it was a no brainer. You should try it sometime," I suggest carefully.

"Try what?" she asks, her face scrunched up.

"Try to look at things—at people—with an open mind. Your perfect might be closer than you think."

Before she has a chance to respond, Naomi calls out.

"You coming in, Mal?"

With a wink at a stunned Kendra, I follow Naomi into her office.

Kim

"So when do we get results?" Mal asks as he walks into the kitchen with the last of the groceries we picked up.

"She said she'd call as soon as she hears from the lab. Probably a couple of days. If they need to do an adjustment on the dosage, she'll check with the endocrinologist first and then call the pharmacy with the new script."

He nods his understanding before changing the subject. "What do you feel like for dinner?"

I still get bouts of nausea but today for the first time I'm feeling truly hungry. I eye the steaks Mal is about to pop in the freezer. "Those," I tell him before he puts them away. "I feel like a good grilled steak, a baked potato and maybe a salad, but only a little one." Mal smiles at my response and slaps the meat down on the counter before pulling me into his arms.

"A woman after my own heart. A bloody piece of meat with a side of decked out, starchy carbohydrates and easy on the greens. That's so fucking hot."

I mock-punch him on the shoulder, but can't quite stop grinning. "You just haven't gotten laid in a while—you think anything is sexy," I tease him.

"Damn right. I'm thinking anything and everything about you is sexy," he growls in my neck as he wraps me tight. "Can you feel that?"

Fuck yes, I can feel that. His hard length is pressing in my belly and for the first time in a while, my body seems to happily respond with a tingle. "I don't wanna let that go to waste," I whisper, pulling his face closer to kiss him with all the passion I have in me. The vibrations of his responding groan, as he slants his head to deepen the kiss, raises goosebumps on my skin. With his tongue strong and dominant in my mouth, I give myself over to his control and I easily let him pick me up and sit me on the counter, our contact never broken. When he pulls back, a pathetic little whimper escapes my lips.

"I want to do this properly," he explains, eyeing the plastic wrapped steaks on the counter beside me. "Wrap your legs around me." I comply immediately, grabbing on to his shoulders when he starts walking me to the bedroom, and cling to him like a monkey. He tosses me rather unceremoniously onto the bed, and before I can react, his body looms large over me. Not threatening. Never threatening, but secure and protecting. Straddling me he takes off his shirt tossing it aside, before divesting me of mine, which is sent the same general direction. I barely even notice my bra disappearing, so intent on the heat and need in his eyes. Obsidian. Dark, complex and breathtakingly beautiful—as the man. In seconds he has us both naked, his touch making me feel more beautiful than I deserve to feel. When his fingers slide between my folds I'm already slick and ready for him. He electrifies me when his fingertip lightly strokes over the little ball of nerves, gently rubbing the hood out of the way. The friction of his fingerprint is enough to have me shiver in anticipation. The moment his lips close over my taut nipple I let out a deep groan. I'm close— so close to shattering, but I want to feel him inside me. Need to be full...fulfilled...complete.

"Please Malachi. I need you."

Lifting his eyes he slowly releases my nipple from between his lips with a pop. "You have me," he says simply, before shifting his body so his hips are wedged between my thighs and I can feel the thick head of his cock probing for entrance. Agonizingly slow, he enters me, stopping suddenly only halfway inside. "Fuck. Condom," he says carefully retreating, but I wrap my legs around him and grab the tight cheeks of his ass.

"Don't stop," I plead, wanting the unobstructed feel of him inside me. I don't care about whether this is the right time or way too early to take risks. I don't even care that the likelihood of me getting pregnant—ever—is questionable anyway. All I care about, right now, is to feel alive with the possibility—just the possibility of creating something amazingly beautiful with this man.

His eyes search my face for an answer, and what he finds is calm resolve. All concern bleeding from his own face, he looks utterly peaceful as he pushes back inside me completely.

Bliss.

Two hours and three orgasms later, I'm sitting on the deck in the late afternoon sun, watching Mal expertly flip the steaks on the grill. Baked potatoes in foil are staying warm on the top rack and in lieu of greens, we've sliced some tomatoes, topped them with fresh basil and feta and drizzled them with

Balsamic. Mal approved, saying that only a salad with a healthy dose of protein is a salad worth eating. Spoken like a real man.

"So when are you bringing your furniture in?"

"Don't have any," he answers, shrugging his shoulders. "Only a bunch of boxes with stuff and my clothes."

"No furniture? No bed or couch or anything?" I'm shocked. A man in his early forties surely has accumulated some stuff?

"Nope. Never really settled down anywhere long enough to get any and when I moved in above the diner, it was fully furnished. Never cared much about what I was lying in or sitting on as long as it was functional. I still don't care, as long as it has you on it or in it."

I get up and shove Boo aside, who's been drooling next to the BBQ, waiting for something to fall. Sidling up behind Mal I ease my arms around his waist. "We should look at some new furniture together. I want you to love our home as much as I do."

He covers my hands at his waist with one of his, tilts his face back over his shoulder and looks at me. "I couldn't love my home anymore than I do, *Nizhóní.*" Turning in my arms to face me, he bends down and kisses the tip of my nose before trailing his fingers down from my forehead. A little smile tugs at his lips and with his next words he gives me everything.

"You are *my* home."

EPILOGUE

Four months later

Mal

Turning into the driveway, I'm impatient to feel Kim's body in my arms—her lips under mine. My week in Grand Junction, working a surveillance detail, had been long and tedious, and the hours spent alone in my truck gave me a lot of time to think. Enough time to bring me to what should've been a foregone conclusion. One that had me make an unscheduled stop before I started my long drive back home this afternoon.

I know she's probably already eaten dinner, and given that I hadn't called beforehand because I wanted to surprise her, I don't expect a meal. Although my stomach is telling me it needs feeding. A sandwich will have to do—after.

I know the house is empty the moment I walk in. No Boo trying to knock me over, something he continues to do no matter how hard I try to break him of that habit—and no Kim fiddling in the kitchen or curling up on the couch with her Kindle. She probably took Boo for an after dinner walk on the mesa.

I quickly slap some bread together and with a sandwich in each hand, make my way outside into the chill of a beautiful fall evening. I know what route she usually takes and start walking it in reverse, hoping to bump into her somewhere. I've just brushed off the last bite when I see Boo bounding toward me, with Kim running after him, hollering at him to stop. I automatically brace for impact, first from the dog that I barely manage to push off before Kim hits me full force, almost knocking me on my ass anyway.

"Whoa! Easy, babe, or we'll be horizontal a little sooner than I'd planned." I barely get the words out before Kim has her fingers twisted in the still growing strands of my hair, pulling my head down and plastering her lips to mine.

The kiss is intense and by the time I lift my head to look into her sparkling eyes, we're both a bit breathless.

"I'm so glad you're home. I missed you something fierce," she says, her smile cracking and her face wide open.

"Missed you too, Kimeo. Didn't Kerry keep you busy enough?"

Kim started working with Kerry in the bookstore. The first few weeks part time, but then she threw herself all in. The two of them have just launched a website as well. An online bookstore if you will, where they list their entire inventory of mostly second hand books and will ship throughout the US mainland. Already they've had some great response from people able to find specific books no longer in production or the odd obscure novel. It's fast becoming busy enough to take on an additional part-timer to help deal with the volume of orders.

"I'm never too busy to miss you," she reiterates. "You've been forefront on my mind since my appointment today, but I was waiting to call until after Boo's walk."

Shit. I'd completely forgotten about her appointments at Mercy in Durango today. She was supposed to go with Naomi. I'd been so wrapped up in what I was planning, it totally slipped my mind. Quickly recovering I ask, "Tell me. How are your levels?"

She hooks her arm in mine and we slowly start walking back. "Blood counts are great. Hormone levels are steady and all other tests came back clean. And guess what? I found—"

I stop her and turn her toward me. She's fine, doing great—there is no better time. Before she has a chance to say anything, I slip the little box that has been burning a hole in my pocket all the way from Grand Junction home, into my hand and drop down on a knee. I hold one of her hands tightly in mine and her other one slowly makes its way to cover her open mouth.

"Kimeo." I stop and swallow hard, suddenly left with a blank spot where all the words to my proposal had been safely stored. Nothing. I try again, "Kimeo, I never expected you. My entire life before you I would not have been able to conjure you even in my imagination. You humble me every day with your strength and light and I'm so, so grateful you gave me a clear path out of the solitude I thought I craved. Marry me?"

I mangled the words I had planned, but I'm pretty sure the message still got through okay when she drops down on her knees before me and with her arms wrapped around my neck, her forehead against mine and her eyes wet with tears, whispers, "I would be honored."

I slip the wide band, with a single diamond braced between two teardrop-shaped turquoise stones, on her finger.

"It's perfect," she says in awe as she takes my hand and lets me pull her to her feet. "I have something of my own to add," she says as she looks up at me from under her lashes, brushing her newly grown curls off her forehead. Taking my hand, she places it on her stomach without speaking looking at me expectantly.

It takes me a second, before I throw back my head and let out a howl, which Boo takes as a sign to let out his own. By the time I look back at Kim, she's bent over laughing, with tears streaming down her face.

"Silly boys," she says teasingly.

"My beautiful babies," I tell her smiling eyes.

THE END

ABOUT THE AUTHOR

Freya Barker inspires with her stories about 'real' people, perhaps less than perfect, each struggling to find their own slice of happy, but just as deserving of romance, thrills and chills, and some hot, sizzling sex in their lives.

Recipient of the RomCon "Reader's Choice" Award for best first book, "Slim To None," Freya has hit the ground running. She loves nothing more than to meet and mingle with her readers, whether it be online or in person at one of the signings she attends.

Freya spins story after story with an endless supply of bruised and dented characters, vying for attention!

Freya

https://www.freyabarker.com

http://bit.ly/FreyaAmazon

https://www.goodreads.com/FreyaBarker

https://www.facebook.com/FreyaBarkerWrites

https://tsu.co/FreyaB

https://twitter.com/freya_barker

or mailto:freyabarker.writes@gmail.com

ACKNOWLEDGEMENTS:

I need to thank first and foremost, a woman I am lucky to call a friend and my editor, Vanessa Leret Bridges. It's not just her professional attitude, exceptional understanding of the story or her brilliant suggestions—it's the fact that she continuously challenges me to be better. At every opportunity, Vanessa teaches me more about writing and the English language. She never fails to insert positive comments with sections I miraculously nailed, right alongside her suggested changes. There isn't a moment I doubt she has my, and my book's, best interests at heart. I love you hard.

As always a HUGE thanks to my beta-readers; Kim, Chris, Sam, Deb, Debbie, Pam, Nancy, and Catherine, friends who take time out of their busy schedules and help me make sure I have my 'I's' dotted and my 'T's' crossed before it is sent off to the editor. You girls cannot be replaced. I love you!

I have to specially thank Karen Hrdlicka, who was the first to receive a raw first draft of the manuscript and with infectious enthusiasm helped me make it better. Woman, you have my heart and you know it!

Of course I thank my family because they are behind me with every step. Here at home my man makes sure all is running smoothly, even when I'm not. My children, siblings and parents never hesitate to tell me they are proud of me. I am amazingly blessed to be surrounded by so much love.

I want to thank some of my closest friends, who continue to inspire the strong friendships I try to illustrate in my novels: Linda Funk, Dana Hook, Aimee Shannon and Barb Poretti. Love you girls!!

The two women who are my eyes, ears and voice when I am swamped and who work tirelessly at promoting my work. My phenomenal personal assistants, Francessca Webster and Leanne Hawkes. I don't know what I would do without them. I love you!

And finally, I would be nowhere without the support of the Indie community. The readers, the bloggers and reviewers and my fellow authors and friends. It may not always seem that way, but everyone who takes this book world seriously is professional, helpful, gracious and kind, and I feel it every day. Thank you so much for embracing me!

ALSO BY FREYA BARKER

CEDAR TREE SERIES:

SLIM TO NONE

HUNDRED TO ONE

AGAINST ME

CLEAN LINES

UPPER HAND

LIKE ARROWS

HEAD START

PORTLAND, ME, NOVELS:

FROM DUST

CRUEL WATER

THROUGH FIRE

STILL AIR

NORTHERN LIGHTS COLLECTION:

A CHANGE OF TIDE

A CHANGE OF VIEW

A CHANGE OF PACE

(Coming soon!)

ROCK POINT SERIES:

KEEPING 6

CABIN 12

(Coming soon!)

SNAPSHOT SERIES:

SHUTTER SPEED

FREEZE FRAME

IDEAL IMAGE

PICTURE PERFECT

(coming soon!)

9 781988 733210